OUR FINAL
LOVE SONG

N.S. PERKINS

To all the girls wondering if they deserve better.
Damn right you do.

OUR FINAL
LOVE SONG

PROLOGUE

Emma

I AM THE LUCKIEST PERSON ON THE PLANET.

It's a bold statement to make, I know, and it's not something I've always believed. But at this moment, with the soft summer wind ruffling my hair, it is the absolute truth for the sole reason that I have *him*.

"Just a few more steps," Jamie's voice calls from behind me, goosebumps running down my skin at the feel of his soft breath against my bare shoulder.

The muscles in my cheeks are strained from how long I've been smiling. "I'm done waiting." To prove my point, I try to pull Jamie's hands away from my eyes, but my weak attempt doesn't lead anywhere.

He laughs as his thumb brushes the side of my face. "No, you're not, you dirty snoop. And we're almost there."

He came to get me at my place a half hour ago, making me cover my eyes with a bandana that smelled just like him. When we arrived at our surprise destination, he allowed me to remove the piece of fabric, only for his hands to come over my eyes.

The ground is soft under my feet as I continue making slow steps, my ears attuned to every sound, trying to familiarize myself with where we are. It's not a city, that's for sure. It smells like pinewood and bonfire, and there is practically no noise, save for the song of lonely cicadas.

A few years back, I never would've believed one day I'd be trusting someone to walk me blindly into an unknown place, but that was because I didn't know someone like Jamie Montpellier could exist. Someone who wouldn't care who my parents were. Someone who wouldn't mind the place piano takes in my life because it would take the same place in theirs. Someone who wouldn't dare break my trust, instead encouraging me to finally be honest with someone other than myself. Yet here I am, with the love of my life, walking blindfolded toward the surprise he got me for our one-year anniversary and not even thinking about being scared, because it's him. My Jamie.

"And," he says, the smile evident in his voice, "now you can open your eyes."

He pulls his hands back at the same time I look around me, and the breath instantaneously leaves my body.

"You told me you'd never gone to a drive-in theater, so I thought I'd bring the theater to you," he says.

The first thing I notice are the tall trees, and then my gaze drifts to the ground. A bundle of pillows and fluffy blankets sit on top of a giant air mattress, surrounded by candy, soda, and movie-theater-style boxes of popcorn, the buttery smell finally reaching me. The makeshift sitting area faces a giant white screen with a machine projecting a movie on it, paused for the moment.

My jaw hangs open as I take a few steps toward the setting, which I now realize is situated in the middle of Jamie's backyard, the old Adirondacks and rusty, lit fireplace a dead giveaway.

"Everyone's out for the night, so we have the next few hours all to ourselves here."

Now close enough, I lean forward to touch the dozens of pillows creating a cozy, inviting nook. He must have spent a lot of time preparing all of this.

My throat is tight as I turn to him. I have no words.

Jamie scratches his neck as he looks around. "I know it's nothing big, and I wish I could afford to take your somewhere nicer, but—"

He doesn't have the time to finish his sentence before I jump into his arms, his long arms immediately catching my legs as I wrap them around his narrow hips. "This is the best thing I've ever seen. I love it. So much." I whisper it all against his neck for fear of traitorous emotion blurring my voice.

He pulls his head back so I have no choice but to look him in the eye. "Yeah?" A shy smile reappears on his lips.

I nod vigorously, then land a kiss on his lips. A year of that, and I still can't get enough. We might only be seventeen, but I have a feeling we could be ninety and it would still be just as magical to be in his presence, to feel his touch on me and to smell the soft scent of laundry detergent on his shirt.

"Thank you," I say as I pull back, squeezing his cheeks just a little too hard because god, I love this man. "It's perfect."

He gives my lips one last peck before letting me down to the ground. He opens the top blanket for me. "After you," he says, and I laugh as I get in. While we're leaving for Camp Allegro, our summer musicians' retreat, in just a few days, and the school year just ended, it's still chilly out. The mountain of blankets makes for the perfect place to cuddle in.

"This all feels very romantic, Montpellier," I say, head propped up. "You trying to charm me?" I move forward and bring my hand to his stomach, nails scratching his skin.

He gulps. I love the effect I have on him. Almost as bad as the one he has on me. Every occasion we get to explore each other's bodies feels so new, so scary and wonderful and complex and brilliant. I can't get enough of it.

"I don't know. Is it working?"

I pretend I need time to think before I move my hand away and say, "I guess you'll have to see."

His dark gaze burns through me. "You are the devil, Emma St. Francis," he croaks before jumping on me and tickling me until I'm kicking and screaming.

"Please!" I shout when I can't take it anymore. "White flag!"

"That's what I thought," he says, smirking. He's still over me, breaths coming in and out in pants, his parted lips lighting me on fire. I can't look away from them. He can't seem to look away either. Before I can stop myself, I sit up and kiss him, and the world—the entire universe—disappears.

Sometimes it feels like the love I have for him will overwhelm me. Like no person could hold that much emotion inside of them. I'll surely burst with it one day.

"I love you," I say when our lips part.

"I love you more."

I smile, then lay back and wait for him to start the movie. When he does, he comes as close to me as humanly possible, and we spend the movie joking around and touching each other. And through it all, I find myself thinking, *I will marry this man one day.*

Like I said: luckiest person on the planet.

CHAPTER 1

Emma
Four years later

THIS HURTS.

This hurts very, very much.

The ostentatious red velvet cake is a fifty-pound weight in my hands. I don't know why I'm still holding it. I could put it down—two hours in, and my wrists are howling in pain, the left more than the right, as usual—but letting go of it feels like letting go of the idea that he might remember tonight is our anniversary.

I'm pathetic. Waiting for a man who clearly could not care less about me, and still hoping the tables will turn. The amount of times this exact situation has happened makes it even more pathetic. Or is the word *stupid* at this point? Isn't that what they say about people who expect others to change? Although, I have to say, this is the first time he's missed something so important. Sure, Jamie has forgotten about our date nights plenty of times, apologizing as he arrived just in time for dessert, having missed the dinner reservation by a mile or simply not showing up at my place for a movie we'd planned on watching together, but our anniversary is a first. Last year, he cooked for me in my apartment kitchen, making all of my favorite recipes at once. It was comical—pork tenderloin cooked in red wine and blueberry sauce, rows of sushi made with extravagant fish and bright colors, roasted vegetables sprinkled with butter and spices, huge casseroles of butter chicken paired with freshly cooked naan, all enough to feed an army. It was so extra. I loved it.

For the past year, though, the feeling of loneliness has grown as he's forgotten about me time and time again. I can't recall the number of times I've lain in bed with my phone in my hands, hoping for a goodnight text or a "thinking of you" phone call, only to fall asleep alone.

Again, pathetic.

A tear burns a track down my face before falling onto the cake, the salt leaving a bitter taste on my lips. Another one escapes, followed by two more. I squeeze my eyes shut for a moment, as tight as I can, then exhale slowly.

Calm down.

The tears have smudged a part of the icing design. One of the stars now looks like a smudge of snot. Not that the cake was that nice looking in the first place.

It's always been a running gag between us, how bad I am at art. I cannot draw a flower to save my life, but Jamie has always had a soft spot for my doodles. He used to keep every single drawing I made, no matter how ugly. *I can see the effort you made, and that makes it so much more valuable,* he said to me one night after keeping the portrait I'd made of him while eating burgers at a local joint. The image looked like an eight-year-old's drawing, but he made it to be something special. To make him smile today, I painted onto the cake an image of our first anniversary together, stars illuminating him and me lying in front of the large movie screen set up in his parents' backyard. I spent hours on it, and while it wasn't great, I knew he'd like it.

Or would've liked it, if he'd have deigned to show up.

I sniffle, finally dropping the cake onto the countertop.

This needs to stop. If this were my friend, I would've told her to leave a long time ago. No one should feel like they need to beg for attention and love in a relationship. But how do you make that decision when you still hold so much love for the other person? How do you finally choose yourself over that all-consuming emotion?

A sob racks my chest. I put a hand on my mouth, trying to keep it all in. To swallow it down and bury it deep inside. I never thought

I'd see the day where the final nail would be put in the coffin, but I think this might be it.

I can't break up with him now, though. Not when we're leaving for Allegro tomorrow morning. We'll be spending the next eight weeks stuck together at a retreat for musicians, just like we have for the past several years. Camp Allegro is small; we'd constantly be running into each other, and I don't think I'd be able to tolerate it if that happened while we were broken up. It would hurt too much. Plus, I wouldn't do that to Jamie. Not when I know what this summer means to him.

But once the summer's over…

Another traitorous tear falls, and I wipe it, this time violently.

Enough. I will not cry over this man any longer.

Under the harsh kitchen light, I grab my wine glass and gulp down the rest of my Chardonnay. Once it's empty, I fill it once more and chug the entire thing. Then I pick up the cake I poured all my love into and dump it into the trash.

There. All done.

Finishing up the rest of the wine, I walk to the living room and sit on the couch, grabbing my fluffy pink pillow and hugging it tightly. With my other hand, I turn on the television and settle for a rerun of a rom-com. At least, I think it's a rom-com. Even a few minutes in, I haven't assimilated a single thing that's been said.

I stare like a zombie at the television screen for what could be minutes or hours, until the sound of my front door being opened drags me out of my daze. Still, I don't bother looking back.

"Hey," Jamie says, his voice calm, smooth. His shoes thump on the ground as he says, "I think I finally got it," probably referring to yet another piece he was trying to master.

"Great," I say, my tone flat, my gaze stuck on the two characters kissing in the rain after getting into a fight. What BS.

"What are you up to?"

I don't have time to prepare. In an instant, he appears in front of me, and by the time I realize what he's doing, his face is dangerously close to mine. Reflexively, I give him my cheek, but he must've been aiming for my lips because his kiss lands at the very awkward spot on the corner of my mouth. I don't even have the energy to look embarrassed.

This is going to be a long summer.

"Just watching this," I answer.

"Is it any good?" He's smiling like he and I are in on a little secret. That confirms it: he finally aced his piece. He probably didn't notice how awkward the almost-kiss just was. That's how lost Jamie can get in his own world.

"Yup."

He frowns as he looks at me. "You okay?"

"Yup," I repeat.

His stare remains on me for a moment, but I keep mine on the television, and eventually, he moves to the kitchen. While we don't officially live together—Jamie never agreed to, preferring to stay with his parents for the duration of college—he's here with me a few nights a week. I hear the refrigerator door open as he asks me if there's anything to eat for dinner. I don't mention the Fiorentina steak I was planning on cooking for him, instead saying there's chicken in the freezer. He thanks me and continues roaming around the kitchen, making a cacophony with the pots and pans, until suddenly, nothing.

The entire apartment is silent, save for the soft voices of the characters on TV.

"Emma."

Slowly, I stretch my neck toward the kitchen, finding Jamie standing in front of the trash can.

"Fuck," he says softly, then puts the lid back on and runs my way. "Fuck, Emma, I'm so sorry. It totally slipped my mind."

My throat is tight, but I still manage an "It's fine."

"No, it's not. I'm so fucking sorry."

At first, I believed his apologies. I don't remember the exact moment I realized they didn't mean much.

Jamie drops to his knees in front of me, his cold hands on my thighs. "Happy anniversary." A squeeze of his hands. "I knew it was today, but then I got to the music hall, and then I got into—"

"Jamie, I said it's fine." My tone must be stern enough because he falls silent, his body frozen. I can't continue talking about this. If I do, I'll start crying for real, and then I'll never be able to stop.

Jamie knows as well as I do this is not fine, but for the next eight weeks, we need to pretend everything is okay.

"I..." He stammers a few unintelligible words, then gets up and heads back to the kitchen. I remain in front of my movie as he cooks his chicken and eats. He doesn't take long, probably inhaling the whole thing, and once he's done, he comes back to the living room, taking a seat distant enough from me.

"Are you...okay?" he asks.

I hum in answer, not making eye contact. I can't. It's too hard.

"All right," he says, not at all convinced. "Well, you want to come to bed now?"

I shake my head. "I think I'll just stay here to finish the movie." I can't stomach being in bed with him right now. I need space. I feel like I'm a balloon about to burst. Sad. Humiliated. Disgusting.

"Okay." He hesitates, then leans forward to press a kiss to my cheek. I guess he learned his lesson earlier and took the hint not to aim for my lips. "Good night, then."

"Night."

I listen for the sound of his footsteps, and once I hear the closing of the door and the click of the bedside lamp, I turn the television off. I lay on my side, squeezing my decorative pillow as tight as I can. I wait for the tears to come now that I'm alone, but they don't. I'm all dried up.

This is the end.

CHAPTER 2

Emma

"Y<small>OU OKAY?</small>"
"Yeah, all good." I don't think I've ever told such a blatant lie.

Jamie turns to me with a doubtful look, then returns his gaze to the road. He's holding the steering wheel with one hand while leaning his head on the other. Jamie has always been a casual driver, nothing ever stressing him out, and today is no exception. It makes sense; we're going to his favorite place on earth. What used to be my favorite place too.

When I woke up on the couch this morning, the hell that was last night came back to me, and I fought the urge to bury my head under the covers and spend the day there. Sadly, that was not an option. I need to get through the summer so I can perform in the end-of-year showcase, which means Allegro was inevitable.

The moment the bedroom door opened and I heard Jamie's footsteps in the hallway, I started stretching and pretended I'd fallen asleep on the couch by mistake. He seemed to buy it.

I then spent half an hour in the bathroom doing my hair and makeup. The first day at Allegro always feels like a homecoming somehow. It might be nothing more than a slightly glamorized campground, but it's the people there that make all the difference. I've spent so many of my summers with these people, and even though we don't necessarily talk during the year, our summers belong together.

By the time I got out, Jamie was waiting for me, ready for the short road trip. He didn't bring up yesterday, and I didn't either. Instead, we both faked smiles and got into the car.

Jamie's short, clean nails tap the steering wheel as he puts his blinker on and asks, "You excited about this year's roster of teachers?"

Tchaikovsky plays softly in the background, one of Jamie's favorite pieces. I can almost feel him mindlessly playing the thunderous strokes of the keys against my hand as we watched a movie on our first date. It had made goosebumps raise all over my skin, and he never even noticed he was doing it.

I look at him, lips pressed tight. The right arm of his black glasses is bent at an awkward angle and held together by a piece of tape, something I've seen more times than I could think possible.

Something sharp twists inside my belly at the thought that after this summer, I might never see it again. That I will not hear once more how he stepped on them after getting out of bed and forgetting he'd dropped them to the floor, or sat over them while too focused on one of his new scores, or fell asleep while wearing them.

I breathe in and out. This is not the time to break down.

"Emma?"

"Hm?" I say, blinking. I don't remember ever getting lost in my thoughts as much as I have this past year.

"I asked you if you were excited?"

"Oh. Yeah, sorry, um…" I rack my brain to find the answer to a question I haven't even asked myself once. In the past years, I would plan which pieces I'd want to work on with all the different professors, both old and new, but this year, the excitement is nowhere to be found. I miss it, but I can't seem to get it back. "Yeah, I am," I lie. "Dr. Podimow's going to be there again, so that's great." Teachers usually want us to call them by their first names, but Dr. Podimow has a PhD in music theory, and she scares me more than I care to admit, so I've always referred to her that way. "She might be able to help me with my hand." I stretch my stiff fingers as I say it, looking out the window at the pine trees illuminated by the bright early-day light.

Jamie looks quickly at my hand as he remains silent for a second. Then another.

"Right." He clears his throat, eyes never leaving the road before he says, "I'm excited to work with Jillian most, I think."

It makes sense. She's the most successful of the piano teachers at Allegro, having played concerts in all the great music halls throughout her career.

"Hm."

A few minutes pass, the classical music enveloping the car in a sound that's both comforting and stressful to me. I miss the times when I wasn't nervous about music. When I only lived and breathed for it, and it provided me with such a deep sense of happiness.

Initially, I think the silence between us is only uncomfortable for me, but when I see the looks Jamie repeatedly throws my way, I change my mind.

He scratches his messy hair before saying, "I might actually go talk to her tonight while everyone's at the welcome bonfire. You know, to discuss showcase prep and stuff."

Of course, he will. What else would he want to do on his first night? Certainly not spend time with the girlfriend he forgot about on their anniversary. I let out a burst of air that sounds half like a huff, half like a snort.

It comes out of me so unexpectedly, my eyes widen as the sound resonates through my head.

"What?" Jamie asks.

Crap.

"Huh?"

"You made a sound. Why?"

A fissure runs down the thin eggshell I built around us, naively hoping it would last all summer.

"No, I..." I shake my head. I've made it this long pretending everything was fine. I can continue. "It's nothing."

Jamie turns toward me for a whole second, and it feels like a lifetime. Gone is the pretense that everything is fine, both in his expression and in mine. His eyes are narrowed, a muscle ticking in his tight jaw. A jaw I used to kiss when he made me laugh so much I couldn't breathe, and lips I used to dream of having all over my body. Eyes that made me blush as they roamed over me.

"Emma, please. You're mad."

"I'm fine."

"No, you're not. You're still mad about yesterday." His lips are pursed.

I want to deny it, to push this down once again, but with the way he's looking at me, like he's daring me to deny it, I can't. The words are stuck.

"And clearly," he adds, "you have something to say, so say it."

I lick my lips, knee bouncing. Are we really doing this here? Now? While we're in a car, on our way to spend an entire summer in a relatively small campground where we won't be able to avoid each other?

I guess we are.

"I just think it's funny that you want to spend the first night at camp with a teacher instead of with me and our friends."

"Why wouldn't I?" he says after a moment of silence. "Isn't that the reason why we go to Allegro? To become better musicians?"

"Never mind," I say, looking outside the window. The sky is a blue so bright it's almost white, the beautiful June day not in tune with the way I'm feeling. The wind should be howling; there should be snow in the summer; *something* should show how wrong the world is.

"No, don't do that. Finish what you were saying."

I force my jaw to unclench before I say in a calm voice, "It's not surprising is all."

His dark brows furrow, as the long fingers he has wrapped around the steering wheel tighten. "What does that mean?"

I face him dead on. "What do you think it means?"

"I don't know, Emma. That's why I'm asking."

He doesn't know. He truly doesn't. That probably makes it even worse. He hasn't even noticed how terrible he's made me feel.

"It's not just about Allegro, and you know it," I say. "This has been our lives for a year now."

His brows furrow. "You're not making any sense."

From the corner of my eye, I spot a sign that says, *CAMP ALLEGRO, 20*. Then, under it, in smaller script, *WHERE DREAMS ARE HONED*.

More like where dreams are killed.

Shifting in my seat, I turn to Jamie and say, "Do you remember the last time we had fun together?"

"Oh, come on—"

"Don't 'come on' me. Just answer."

"I…"

"Right," I say, "You don't. Because we haven't had fun in forever. And do you know why that is?"

Silence answers me.

"Because the piano is the only thing you think about." It hurts to say out loud what's been festering in my head for months. I would expect my voice to be loud, but instead, it's soft and cracked. It brings all the feelings I tried to bury back up to the surface. How he's made me feel so alone, so unloved, for months. How even my mother saw how much weight I'd lost from making myself sick to my stomach with worry and sadness. How being ditched time and time again brought me straight back to all the times my parents were not present for my birthdays, leaving me alone at home while they were traveling the world together. Brought me back to a time when I felt like no one would ever truly care for me.

Jamie's throat bobs before he shakes his head, brown strands flying left and right. "No, it's not."

"Yes, it is. It's piano, and then it's the Academy, and then lessons, and then school, and then some more piano, and then I'm there, at the bottom of the list." My thigh jumps up and down. "I don't need to be first or second or even third, but you don't even put me in your top ten, Jamie."

"That's not true," he says, barely keeping his attention on the road.

"You literally forgot about our anniversary even though I've been telling you about it for weeks, all because you were practicing. That's the truth."

His Adam's apple works.

I've tried for so long to keep everything inside, waiting for things to get better but now that I've started, I can't seem to stop. "When was the last time we were intimate, not because of obligation but because we wanted to?" I lick my lips, then release a dry laugh. "I don't think I even remember the last time you told me I looked pretty." This may sound petty, but shouldn't my partner make me feel beautiful? Loved?

"Emma…" His voice is soft too now. Like we both know what's coming, and we're trying to stop ourselves from waking the monster.

Except it's inevitable.

Without looking at him, I say, "We need to face the truth, Jamie."

Breaking the relationship that's been the most important part of my life for years is one of the most difficult things I've ever had to do, yet it only takes seven words.

"We don't make each other happy anymore."

Jamie's sharp inhale makes me realize what I've just said.

I did it. Plunged the knife into the roaring beast. And while I've been thinking about it for a while, it still makes me want to open the window and hurl my breakfast.

He swings my way. "You can't mean that."

I blink back my tears.

"It's…" he starts. "You can't just spring this on me."

"The fact that you haven't seen anything and think I'm 'springing this on you' is part of the problem. You don't *see* me, Jamie."

His jaw shifts. "Fine. Then we'll work on it. We can't..." He shakes his head like he's convincing himself. "We can't be over."

Voice thick with loss, I say, "I think it's already too late."

Just as the last part comes out of my mouth, the car swerves to the right with a loud screech. I let out a small yelp while holding on to the grab handle like I've seen my mother do countless times when I was learning how to drive. The bags that were sitting in the backseat fly through the air. Just as I close my eyes, thinking this is the last moment of my life, Jamie pulls the car back to the left so we're back on the right track.

"Jesus Christ," he mutters, panting.

"What was that?" I say, the panic clear in my voice. "Did we hit something?"

"I don't know. It's like something pulled the car to the side. I wasn't in control. I couldn't even see anything for a second."

What the heck?

My hands are shaking in my lap as I try to catch my breath, and from the silence emanating from Jamie, I'd say he's doing the same. The sound of the engine lowers as Jamie slows the car, Debussy barely audible over the pounding in my ears. I feel like I've crossed paths with death but somehow made it out alive.

Jamie never stops the car, but his hands are now tighter on the wheel, shoulders straight. His focused position reminds me of what we were talking about before the car swerve happened.

I might've semi broken up with the person I thought was the love of my life.

I don't know what else there is to say, and Jamie doesn't seem to either. My left hand twitches repeatedly, something it does when I'm stressed, at least since it got injured.

Five minutes later, Jamie pulls onto the exit leading to Allegro, then slows to the stop sign.

"Emma."

I turn to find Jamie's eyes on me, soft and hot-cocoa brown. "Don't do this to us," he says.

A knot forms in my throat. Even if I wanted to, I can't speak. I don't trust myself. The temptation to tell him to forget everything and to take me in his arms is a tsunami in my head. I know if I look at him longer, I'll break.

Biting on my lower lip hard enough to draw blood, I move my head left and right, then stare out front. Jamie gets the hint and resumes the drive. Less than a mile later, the old, rusty sign spelling CAMP ALLEGRO welcomes us, and the pressure inside the car somehow increases even more as we pass its threshold.

Jamie is silent, although his body language is anything but. The veins in his neck are pumping, his jaw so tight it forms an angle that could probably cut diamonds. His eyes never stray from the dirt road.

We follow the path surrounded by coniferous trees so tall they seem to shield us from the outside world until we finally reach the gravel parking lot, surrounded by dozens of tiny rustic cabins. Behind them, I know, sits the outside center stage where our weekly performances take place, as well as the large cafeteria and main ground where the bonfires occur. It should make me feel good to finally be back after a year.

Good is the last thing I am, though. In fact, the nausea that was churning through my gut before is worse than ever.

When Jamie brings the car to a stop, we spend a moment motionless. Getting out of the car means facing what has been said. It means taking our first step in this camp as something other than a couple entirely besotted with each other. I'm not ready.

When I move to open the door, Jamie says, "Wait."

I freeze.

"Are we not going to talk about this?"

"I'm not sure what there is to talk about," I say. What options do we have other than breaking up?

He jerks back. "What do you mean, 'nothing to talk about'? You'll end a five-year relationship just like that? Without even fighting about it?"

My shoulders slump. Everything about this makes me feel defeated. I hate that he's suffering, and I hate that I'm suffering, and I just hate this.

Again, I open my mouth to explain everything that's inside, but nothing comes out. It's too much.

"I can't," I end up saying. "I need space. I can't..." I swallow. "I can't think." He's right. We do need to have a longer conversation about this, but I don't trust myself to have it now. If I do, I'll probably just give in and accept continuing on the path we've been following for a year now, and I'd remain just as pathetic as before.

Jamie's lips are pinched together as his gaze alternates between both my eyes. I realize he's blinking fast, and I don't want to start thinking about what this means.

The silence is thick in the car before he says in a softer voice, "I really hurt you that bad?"

My lips wobble, and I shut my eyes.

His swallow is audible. After inhaling deeply, he nods repeatedly while toying with the broken arm of his glasses, then says, "All right. We'll talk about this later." With that, he turns and exits the car.

I take a second to breathe through everything. Once I'm fairly certain I'll be okay, I follow Jamie outside, and we both pick up our bags in silence. Without me asking, he still lifts the heaviest ones for me, and it only adds another chip to my broken heart. He's such a good man, which only makes this harder.

We make our way to cabin fourteen, the one I've shared with Jesy ever since we first came to Allegro as scrawny teens. Thankfully, we don't cross paths with anyone on the way there, and as soon as we reach the front steps, Jamie drops the bags he carried for me and leaves in the direction of his cabin, his long legs striding faster than I've ever seen them.

The moment he's out of view, I let out the biggest sigh. How did the day turn so wrong?

"EMMA!"

I don't have time to prepare myself before Jesy comes out of the cabin and pushes her wheelchair so fast that when she hugs my torso, I topple over and land straight on my butt on the freshly cut emerald grass. The scent of summer overwhelms me.

I grunt, then laugh for the first time today. "You really need to work on your welcoming technique." She did the same thing last year, and I had a large bruise on my left butt cheek for a week.

"I can't help it. I've missed you too much." A huge grin brightens her face.

"I missed you too," I say, pushing myself up. Jesy offers me a hand, her excitement visible. I swear I've never seen this girl in a bad mood, and with her, you have no choice but to feel better.

"You cut your hair?" I ask as she helps me to my feet. "I thought you didn't like it last year." I've always thought the short black bob looked gorgeous on her, but she spent the whole summer complaining about it.

"Huh?" She closes an eye. "I've never cut it before. But you're right, I hate it."

"Yeah, you did. Don't you remember? You threatened to shave your head a few times during our day at the beach because you couldn't tie it up."

Jesy looks at me with a weird expression before saying, "Did you smoke something before coming here?"

I roll my eyes. That's probably the last thing I could possibly have done, and she knows it.

She gives me another side glance, then drops the subject and pushes my hip toward the main ground. "Come on, let's go say hi to people."

I resist, standing my ground. Usually, I'd be all for socializing right away, but today that might mean crossing paths with Jamie, and after the car ride we just had, I need a breather.

"Actually, I think I—"

I'm interrupted by a voice shouting, "Hello, ladies!" And while the voice is familiar, the blood in my veins freezes. I shouldn't be hearing it. Not this year.

Slowly, I twist my neck in the direction of the voice, and what I see almost makes me fall to my knees.

Irène Sancerre, co-founder of Camp Allegro and ex-world-renowned ballerina, is standing ten feet away from us, waving. Her short white hair is pulled back neatly, her smile wide and honest. She looks good.

Which would all be fine and dandy, if not for the fact that she passed away last August.

CHAPTER 3

Emma

I MUST BE DREAMING.

Or maybe Jesy's right and I've been drugged somehow.

My mouth is hanging half open as I stare at the spot Irène—or whoever it was who was here just now—just vacated.

"Emma? You okay?"

I hear Jesy's voice, but I can't seem to make myself answer. If this is some kind of joke, it's not funny. At all.

Irène has always been a permanent fixture of Camp Allegro, and while we weren't close per se in my years here, she knew of me, and I definitely knew of her. She and her husband were the faces of the camp, after all, on top of being two of the most awarded and acclaimed ballet dancers of their lifetime. You couldn't not admire her, even from afar. When she died last August, the whole camp was shaken. She was old, sure, but she was like a pillar, strong and unmovable. In our minds, she was immortal. No one could believe what had happened, least of all me. While I'd never had long conversations with her, I'd been a fan all my life.

And now here I am, feeling like I've just seen a ghost. Because I have.

"Em? You're scaring me now."

I lift a hand to my lips, realizing I'm trembling from top to bottom.

"Who did we just speak to?" I croak.

"What?" Jesy frowns, watching me with the careful consideration you would a sleeping lion. "Emma, what's going on? Are you sure you're all right?"

"Just—" I swallow, my throat dry. "Who was that?"

Still wary, Jesy says, "That was Irène? I don't understand…"

She continues talking, but my brain silences her. This can't be right. Birds are still singing around us, and the sound feels even more wrong than this morning.

"She died," I whisper, more to myself than to her.

"What was that?"

Louder, I repeat, "But she died. She's…dead." My head shakes from left to right. How is she not freaking out?

"What do you mean?" No trace of humor is left on her freckled face. "Do you want to sit down? You look a little pale."

Ignoring her, I say, "Irène Sancerre died in August of last year. The whole camp was shaken. No one played music for a whole week while we were grieving her."

Jesy's smile appears again, but this time, the laughter is nervous and not amused. "Em, you should really sit down. I think something's not right with you." She puts a hand on mine. "Want me to go get the nurse?"

I take a step back.

What the heck is going on? Did I actually hit my head?

Jesy looks behind her before she returns to me and says, "Irène is very much alive. In fact, she wasn't even here last August. She went with Alessandro for an interview tour in Europe. Remember?"

My head shakes left and right. That's not possible.

Irène and Alessandro went on their summer tour two years ago. Not last year.

Jesy's teeth sink into her bottom lip as her green eyes search mine. I wish I could offer her reassurance that I'm good, but I can't. A thousand questions swarm my head, starting with what happened to me and whether I need to be hospitalized. In the end, though, I only come up with one.

"Jesy, how old are you?"

She furrows her brow and shakes her head. "What kind of question is that? You know how old I am. We're the same age, Emma."

"I know," I say slowly. It *is* a weird question. Jesy turned twenty-one last month. Pictures of her doing shots at a bar for the first time were all over social media. "But just humor me."

With one lift of her brow, she proceeds to make my world crumble. "I turned twenty a month ago. You even sent me a happy birthday text. Do you not remember that?"

No. This can't be. How could we be one year back? As far as I know, scientists haven't been able to crack time travel yet.

Yet when I take a good look around me, some things start to make sense. Jesy's short hair. The cabins that are still a pale brown, when a painting crew came and varnished them all on the day we left camp last summer. Two dead trees standing to the right of our cabin, when I could bet my right hand they were cut down last year after Jesy and I complained that we were scared of them falling on our heads overnight. And of course, Irène.

The fact that I think time travel is the most logical explanation for what is currently happening makes me think there's a very high chance I do need hospitalization.

"Are you going to tell me what's going on now?" Jesy asks, bringing her wheelchair closer to me. She is still looking over her shoulder every few seconds, probably looking for help for me.

I don't take long to think of my answer. "Nothing. I just, um, forgot." I even force a laugh that is definitely not my best one, but if I *am* having some kind of mental episode, I'd rather Jesy not know about it. No matter how much I like her, I don't know that she wouldn't tell someone else, and this can't get out to the rest of the camp. I'll figure it out by myself.

"You forgot how old we are?"

I shrug and pray she doesn't call me out on my BS. "Rough night. I'm still half asleep." Nudging her shoulder, I say, "Come on, didn't you want to go say hi to people?" Wandering around might help me come up with some logical explanation. I'm not sure I believe that, but it's not like I have any other solution at the moment, so I'll just have to roll with it.

Jesy eyes me suspiciously for a moment before saying, "Sure. Come on."

I follow her, pasting on yet another smile and hoping for the best.

* * *

Today has been the weirdest day of my entire life.

I've walked around camp, hugging old-time summer friends and trying to catch up by listening to stories I'd already heard. I mostly stood there smiling and trying not to break down into panicked screams while people talked about basic things as if a whole year hadn't just occurred. No one seemed to realize something was wrong, so I didn't say or do anything to attract anyone's attention. When people asked how my school year went, I simply nodded and said, "Great!" It would've been hard to explain that my junior year was horrifying when they still thought I'd just completed my sophomore year.

The one silver lining in this is that it kept my thoughts away from the whole Jamie situation. Maybe this was my mind's way of coping with our semi-breakup, and I'm still in Jamie's car, sleeping against the passenger door. I so wish that were the case.

Even after wandering around camp for the afternoon and for dinner, I haven't seen him. Granted, when we're here, I barely see Jamie, period. Even though crossing paths with him is inevitable at some point, usually, while I hang out with friends and try to socialize as much as I can, Jamie is practicing and practicing and practicing some more. He was always intense, even though it became worse this year. He's probably in a booth right now, running scales and getting ready for a long night of perfecting his craft.

Dusk has fallen over the camp, pinks and purples coloring the sky as we walk toward the welcome bonfire. While not everyone participates in the weekly bonfires, most join the first one. It's a no-pressure moment where we sing songs—which get worse the tipsier people get—some joining us with instruments, some dancing by the fire, and some just chatting with people they haven't seen for a year. It's always one of my favorite moments of summer.

But this year, I feel queasy and am thinking there's a fifty-percent chance I'll barf or pass out. I probably shouldn't go. Even if I've tried my best to appear normal, I've probably been acting weird, and people will start wondering what's going on with me. Might be better to disappear for the night.

Sparks dance on the horizon from the gigantic bonfire as dozens of young adults with beers in their hands and sunburns on their cheeks sing a Coldplay song, harmonies sharp and perfect. This is what you get from going to a camp for talented artists. When Jamie and I first registered as teens, it was easier to secure a spot, but nowadays, kids need to undergo a small audition to be able to attend. The camp has gained in popularity in the past years after so many of our alumni were admitted to prestigious schools or featured in Hollywood productions and Las Vegas residencies. Even without having the pretense of being a competition, there definitely is pressure to perform well—at least *I* feel pressure.

Jesy's laughing at something Julia, her girlfriend, has said when I tap her shoulder. She turns to me, her face so happy and free. It doesn't matter that she's one of the most talented musicians here, maybe tied with Jamie, and that people have expectations for her; she always looks relaxed and carefree. It's always driven me crazy, not with anger, but with envy. I wish I could be her when I grow up.

"Hey, I think I might actually—"

My sentence drifts off as I catch sight of something I never would've expected.

Jamie is sitting cross-legged next to the bonfire, alone in a crowd. We're still far from the throng of people, but I would recognize that shape anywhere. Lanky limbs and a tall frame that always appears smaller than he is because he always curls up around himself, as if wanting to take up less space. Even from here, I can see that the shirt he's changed into is buttoned unevenly.

God, I already miss him.

What is he doing here? Wasn't he supposed to go speak with that teacher tonight? Or was that only in the real universe?

As if sensing me watching him, his eyes shoot straight at me, and the moment they meet, I realize something's wrong.

"What's that?" Jesy says. She then follows my line of sight and adds, "Oh, there's your man!"

My man. Right. Because last year, when we arrived here, we were happier than ever together.

Something twists in my stomach at the thought of how far we've fallen, and instead of answering, I simply smile and nod. Seems to be my motto of the day.

The closer we get to the bonfire, the more I see the panic in Jamie's eyes. In fact, it probably mirrors mine.

Could it mean…?

"I'll be right back," I tell Jesy before trudging toward the man who's occupied my mind for half a decade.

Just act natural.

"Hey, what's—"

"Can we talk?" Jamie interrupts. "Like, now?" There's an emotion in his eyes that wasn't there this morning, which means he probably doesn't want to talk about us.

"Uh, sure." The welcome word's about to start, but I think this year, it's by far the least important thing going on.

Once he's up, Jamie leans forward to grab my hand but stops himself mid-movement. Even though he doesn't touch me, it feels like he's hit me in the chest.

This was what you wanted. I can't blame him for respecting my wishes.

He starts walking away from the crowd, toward a narrow and rocky pathway that crosses the forest bordering the plot. We've used this trail so many times before, so I know it leads to a private lakeside spot we often hang out in.

The second we're out of earshot from everyone, Jamie turns

to me and, without wasting a second, says, "Have you noticed anything different around camp?"

I blink. "W-what do you mean?"

"I don't know, anything? The color of the cabins? The booths in the music building?" He's speaking fast, gaze wide.

I swallow, then nod.

"And does that seem strange to you?"

Once again, I just nod. My heart drums in my chest as I wait for him to say it.

His lips twist to one side. "Emma, did we go back in time?"

I inhale sharply, both in relief and in distress. On the one hand, Jamie just proved I'm not going insane and I'm not in this alone. On the other hand, the only other person who seems to be in this messed-up situation appears to be the man I'm infinitely confused about.

"I think we did," I confirm, my left hand once again starting to shake.

Jamie drags his long, thin fingers through his brown strands, seeming on the verge of a nervous breakdown. I can understand the feeling.

"I don't get it," I say, resuming my trek toward the lake. He follows. "You and I seem to be the only ones who've noticed something's wrong."

"I know. It's fucked up."

Feeling heavy all of a sudden, I let myself fall down on a large rock and lean my elbows on my knees, gaze lost on the shimmering lake that's come into view. The moon is now out, creating a hazy glow over the water.

"There must be a reason for this," I say. "Why else would it only be us?"

Jamie doesn't answer. Instead, he slumps down next to me, body forming a comma on the neighboring rock.

"If there's a reason, then we must figure it out," he ends up saying. "The junior showcase is happening this year, but in the present time. We can't miss it."

Another punch to the stomach.

At the end of summer, every student of the camp offers a performance at the Allegro showcase, hopefully showing all they've worked on throughout the lessons of the past eight weeks. This showcase is especially important for juniors, since each year, recruiters from the National Academy of Musical Arts, or NAMA, attend and have the power to offer up admission spots into post-graduate programs to the students who impress them. It's a huge privilege because those students don't even need to audition during their senior year of college. They just get in.

There's nothing Jamie desires more. Nothing I should desire more either.

My hands curl into fists. "Right. That's *definitely* the most important part." Not the fact that we've literally traveled through time or that we might be stuck here forever, in a land of mosquitoes and cedar-scented cabins, awkward run-ins with our exes a daily occurrence.

In a sense, this is good. It's a reminder that music is and will always be his priority, and that's okay. I just can't remain by his side for it.

"We both worked for this all year. Don't tell me it's not important," he says, eyes narrowed behind his glasses.

"You're right." I look away. "We lost ourselves for this. Might as well find a way to get back and at least make it count."

"Emma…" His sentence ends on a sigh, and I'm too tired to try and figure out what it means.

"I'm sorry." I plaster a smile. "It's okay. I get it." He has every right to choose different priorities than me, and my goal isn't to make him feel bad about himself, although maybe I have without even realizing it. It's not because I want more for myself out of a relationship that it makes him a bad guy. Quite the opposite. He's one of the best.

Plus, he's not wrong. We *have* worked all year for this. If we go back in time, I'll be able to get through the audition, and even though there's almost no chance I'll be picked, at least it will be done. My parents will stop asking me about it. A weight will be taken off my shoulders. The sooner it's done, the better.

I get up from my rock, and just as I go to take a step away, a hand lands on my wrist, so soft and warm, I repress a shiver.

"Don't let this be the end of us," Jamie's soft voice says behind me. "Please."

I close my eyes. Why does he have to make this even harder?

Without turning around, I say, "It's never going to be the end, Jamie. You're always going to be my friend, no matter what we decide."

"Your friend," he repeats. Something that sounds shockingly close to heartbreak tints his words.

I'm still not ready to have that conversation. In the car, when I finally decided to expose the truth, I thought it'd be simple. I'd tell him how I felt, he'd agree, and we'd decide that splitting was for the best. I didn't expect the fight he's putting up. I'm not sure how to respond to it. Not yet.

Putting on my steel armor, I turn to him and give him a firm nod. Then, closing that chapter, I say, "Come on. Let's find a way to get back to the future."

CHAPTER 4

Jamie

I STILL REMEMBER THE FIRST TIME I SAW EMMA ST. FRANCIS. It was a cold February day. My family had just moved to Portland, Maine, from Massachusetts to be closer to our grandparents, and because there was no other choice, I'd had to transfer to a new school in the middle of the year. My social situation was already bad at my old school, but at least I'd had a few people I could eat lunch with. In Portland, I knew no one. While I didn't mind eating alone, I did mind people looking at me like I was an alien invading their school. Nothing like the judgmental eyes of a hundred teenagers to make you question your worth.

That first day, the minute my fourth period ended, I rushed out of class to the music hall. That was the one thing I'd looked up online prior to transferring: whether I could practice. And thank god, I could.

It didn't matter that I'd almost ran to get there first, though. A group of girls was already sitting in one of the soundproofed rooms, their lunchboxes balancing on top of a glossy black piano. Even though the last thing I wanted was to attract attention, I stood still for a second, as if something was pulling my attention in that direction.

And that's when I saw her.

She was sitting in the middle of the group of girls, her dark hair tied in a long braid, her pink lips forming an entrancing smile. Everyone in the room seemed to be watching her, and like them, I couldn't stop looking.

The first thing I thought was that she was the most beautiful girl I had ever seen.

The second was that she reminded me of an aurora borealis. Something people can't look away from; something that even makes *you* feel magical just by looking at it. I'd been obsessed with those ever since I'd picked up my first nerdy science picture book as a kid, and this was the closest I'd ever come to seeing one.

I'd told her exactly that a few years ago, while we were lying in her dorm bed after making love. She didn't believe me at first, and when I finally convinced her, she laughed for five minutes straight. I loved how it made me feel. Making Emma laugh wholeheartedly, with her mouth open and a snort sneaking out here and there, completely carefree, always felt like a triumph. There was no better feeling. There *is* no better feeling.

It might have been another two years before we actually started dating, but the moment fourteen-year-old Emma's eyes met mine and she smiled at me, I knew I was a goner.

And now, in the blink of an eye, I've lost her.

How did I fuck up so bad?

Once again, I feel my heart rate picking up and my breathing getting erratic, and I have to push those thoughts down. A panic attack is the last thing I need right now, although with the day I'm having, it's almost inevitable.

I'm walking behind her as we escape the forest and dodge the crowd currently belting out Céline Dion's "It's All Coming Back to Me Now" around the campfire. Emma said it would be better if no one saw us, because if they did, they might ask questions about what we're up to. I don't see how that would be such a bad thing—maybe we're not the only ones in this predicament, and someone else around camp is freaking out at the idea of having been brought a year back in time—but I'm not saying a thing. Not when I'm in such a fragile situation with her.

"This way," she whispers over her shoulder before trudging a path between the cabins surrounding the bonfire circle. I continue following her in silence, and soon the singing starts getting smothered by our labored breathing and the sounds of leaves cracking and pebbles rolling under our feet.

"So what's the plan?" I ask once we're finally far enough that I'm sure no one could hear us. Emma always has a plan, and today, I'm really fucking thankful for that. If I can keep myself busy with something, then it might keep the panic at bay.

"Well, first," Emma starts, never stopping her power walk, "I think we should establish how this time travel thing works."

"Pretty sure neither one of us will be able to understand the science behind time travel in a single summer," I quip.

She throws me a stink eye over a shoulder, then turns back around. Is it me, or is she walking even faster? "I mean the parameters of *our* time travel. Is it limited to a certain place? Are we the only ones to know? Is there something we can do to go back? Et cetera." She grunts as she hikes over a boulder. It doesn't matter that my legs are about two times the length of hers. I'm probably more breathless than she is. Why did we have to cross another forest again? "I know this morning, we were in real time. I watched the news, and everything made sense, meaning something happened between the moment you came to pick me up, and the moment I saw Jesy and Irène in front of my cabin."

"Wait. You saw Irène?"

That makes her slow down, and after a soft nod, she says, "Yes."

I hadn't thought about it, but now that she says it, it makes sense. Our camp director hadn't yet passed away last June. It didn't even occur to me that through this messed-up experience, we might see literal ghosts from our past.

"What about you?" Emma asks.

"Huh?"

"What made you understand we were in the past?"

I hesitate to answer. The truth is that Jeremiah asked me if I'd finally mastered Rimsky-Korsakov's "Flight of the Bumblebee," which I finally did in July of last year. He and I had popped a bottle of champagne that night, so I knew there was no way he could've forgotten it. However, piano seems to be a big no-no with Emma at the moment. Bringing back the memory of the hundreds of hours I spent practicing that piece would probably only prove her point.

God, how did I never realize she felt that way until it was too late?

Earlier in the car, when she said we were not happy anymore, I was at a loss for words, because never in all the years I've spent by her side have I considered myself unhappy. And the fact that I didn't see *she* was makes me want to punch myself in the face. Repeatedly.

"I just realized that everything Jeremiah was saying in the cabin didn't make sense," I end up answering.

Emma's indigo eyes study me for a second before she returns to her semi-hike. I'd never realized how leveled the camp was until this moment.

"So you think it's the camp?" I ask.

"I'm not—" Her sentence is cut when she trips over a hidden root. My heart skips a beat as I watch her arms pinwheeling, and before she can fall, my instinct takes over and I grab her hips. Her body bounces off mine, but at least she doesn't hit the ground. Her soft vanilla perfume envelops me, smelling better than ever before.

"You okay?" I ask, my heart pounding in my ears. Her hair is in my face, and I have to fight the urge to bury my nose in it. Before, I would've done it in a heartbeat, but it wouldn't be fair to her. Not if she doesn't want me anymore.

"Yeah. Uh…" She clears her throat, then slowly moves away from me. "Thank you."

My fingers fall to my side, cool at the loss of her warmth.

We continue walking, and finally I see where she was leading us.

"You want to leave?" I ask her. This is worse than I thought. Is my mere presence pushing her away?

"Not permanently, but yes. We need to see if the whole world is back in the past, or just here."

I exhale. That makes sense. She was always the smarter of the two of us.

"Do we take my car?" I say.

"We'd probably be better off just walking. Will attract less attention."

I don't think people really care that much about what she and I do, but I won't argue. Instead, I trail next to her, my fingers itching to touch hers again. They don't.

We walk in silence on the gravel path until we near the insignia of the camp, and just as we do, I feel something's not right. Like we shouldn't be doing this. I don't voice my worry, and soon, I realize this was a mistake.

The moment our feet touch the ground under the large *CAMP ALLEGRO* letters, something buzzes through my entire body, like some kind of electrical current. And when we take that last step, we hit a wall. Not something we can see, but something we can feel, as if we've just run straight into a glass door. But more than that, the wall itself pushes us away. Emma and I take a hit as we're propelled back, a whooshing sound filling my ears. We don't have the time to shout before we fall on our backs, the shock reverberating down to my shins.

We both grunt. I blink fast, the back of my head pounding.

"What the fuck was that?" I say through gritted teeth, rolling to my side to make sure she's okay.

Emma doesn't move from her position, her gaze lost in the stars above us. With the pain still echoing through my body, I decide to imitate her. We're both on our backs on the gravel, which shouldn't be comfortable, but somehow isn't so bad. The sky has darkened in the past hours, and the barely there moon shines a sliver of light that illuminates Emma's profile.

"I guess that means this thing *is* related to the camp," Emma says, her voice silky soft.

A sigh bubbles out of my throat. If someone had told me yesterday there was such a thing as going back in time, I would've laughed in their faces, and now here I am. Trapped in a summer camp, with no way of going back to the one thing I've worked for my entire life, all the while seeing the person I love slipping through my fingers.

Today fucking sucks.

Again, I feel the claws of anxiety grip at my throat, but I try to focus on the here and now, on the sharpness of the rocks beneath my back and the smell of pine and vanilla surrounding me, all the while taking in deep breaths. I'll have the time to worry later. I don't need to give Emma another reason to see me as not worth fighting for.

Hands resting on my stomach, I croak, "So what do we do now?" She doesn't have any reason to know more about this than I do, but that's always how it's been when I'm in a situation with too much panic and too few known variables: I turn to her.

"I guess we go back and try to figure out why this is happening. If we do, maybe we'll find a way to reverse it." She scratches her cheek. "In the meantime, we should just keep practicing for the showcase as if we were in real time. We have eight weeks to figure out how to go back. Should be fine."

"Piece of cake, really."

She huffs a laugh at that.

We stay on the ground in silence, watching the stars, for another long moment. While thinking about the fact that we're stuck in this camp—literally—is making me feel claustrophobic, looking at something as infinite as the sky gives me some comfort.

With a groan, Emma lifts herself to a sitting position, then back to her feet. I imitate her, and when she extends a hand to help me up, I take it.

"Another thing," she says.

This doesn't sound good.

"For the moment, we should probably act as if everything is… normal, in front of people."

"Normal?" I ask, and when she doesn't reply, I add, "You mean, with this whole time-travel thing? Or…" I swallow. "Between you and I?"

She doesn't quite meet my eye as she says, "Both."

It feels like she's just slapped me in the face.

"So you want the image of being with me, but you don't actually want *me*. Got it." I shouldn't be surprised, but somehow, this hurts almost as much as hearing her say she's not happy.

"It's just…" She drags a hand through her hair. "Word will spread, and people will start asking questions, and I don't even know what I'd say."

I should've expected that. Having to expose her private life like this to everyone at camp would be incredibly difficult for her, and the last thing I want is to cause her more trouble. Plus, to be honest, I'm not ready to tell people either. I don't even think I could say the words to someone else. *Not together. Broke up.* If we have broken up, that is. I'm not sure what we are exactly, and I don't want to risk asking. I'd rather live in the dark than to officially have lost her.

"Plus," she continues, "if we're last year, then it means Molly is coming to camp later this summer. Don't you think it would be easier for her if she didn't have to deal with…that?"

"Shit," I say. I hadn't thought about that. My littlest sister is coming to Camp Allegro for the second—or I guess, *first*—time, and last year, she had a hard time. The camp offers short stays for younger artists, and while Molly was over the moon to practice the cello with great teachers, being away from home for so long was hard on her. She'd never been away from our parents and all our siblings before, and while she's not as anxious as I am, she was still worried. The one thing that got her through it was Emma. She's pretty much her idol, and also like a big sister to her.

Oh fuck. This is so bad. Rationally, I understood the meaning of what Emma told me this morning in the car, but I don't think I'd realized the extent of what it truly meant until now. It feels like the sky I was just observing has fallen on my shoulders, and I can barely stay upright.

My lungs fill with a deep breath. "Yeah, okay."

"Thanks."

I nod.

A soft wind ruffles the leaves of the trees surrounding the parking lot, the only sound around us.

Emma sits up. "Okay, well, I guess we should probably go to sleep. Maybe tomorrow will bring some new ideas."

"Sure."

Her lips twist to one side as she looks my way before she says, "Good night."

"Good night."

I watch her as she turns to leave, her hips swaying with each movement.

My aurora.

I don't know who I am without her, and frankly, I don't *want* to know. She's the best part of me. Always has been, and if it were up to me, always would be.

So one thing's for sure. I'm not letting this relationship go down without a fight.

CHAPTER 5

Emma

T HE MOMENT BEFORE I OPEN MY EYES THE NEXT MORN-
ing, I have a second of intense panic. What if this is some
kind of Groundhog Day and I'm back to yesterday morning, the car ride and breakup and weird déjà vu feelings coming
again and again?

But when I look around me, I see I'm in the small wooden
cabin I share with Jesy. I'm in the top bunk, the space around me
clean and empty. Meanwhile, without even needing to look, I
know the whole wall around Jesy's lower bunk is covered in pictures of people close to her and random mementos she's kept over
the years.

Okay, so at least I won't be reliving the same day over and
over. But what if I have to relive this year, or even this same summer, repeatedly? A shiver runs down my spine. It's just been one
day, and I think it's already the worst one of my life.

I jerk up in bed, careful not to make too much noise as I
climb down the ladder and put on my loafers. Once I've gone
to the bathroom and made sure I looked presentable, I leave the
cabin. Jesy is still snoring loudly as I close the door behind me.

I've worried enough for one day. Time to take action. Jamie
and I have a whole summer to figure out how to go back, and I
hope to god it will be enough. As much as I resent the space piano
has created between us, I know what this showcase means to him.
And to me.

Until recently, that showcase was my dream too. I couldn't
wait to get on that stage and show everyone that I was good too.

That my parents hadn't lied about me. The two of them would be there and feel proud that I represented them like this. I would've kept the legacy going. And most importantly, I would've been happy because I loved it. The piano was a safe place for me.

But somewhere along the way, that passion waned to a point where it became barely present. I can't say exactly when it happened, but it did. At some point during the past year, I started looking at the piano with fear and hurt instead of love in my eyes. Started focusing on everything that was at stake instead of simply the music. And while no one seems to have realized it, it's been eating me up from the inside for months on end.

The air outside is brisk but fresh, nothing like the garbage-and-exhaust scent close to college. A few inhales is enough to clear my head, at least a little. The camp is silent, most people still sleeping at that hour, so I get to walk around without meeting anyone. Eventually, I get to one of the benches facing the infinite-looking Moosehead Lake, and I take a seat, getting lost in the view. Maybe staring at something beautiful and calm will make me see what I'm missing, and the answer to our question will pop into my head.

A girl can hope.

The water laps at the shore in small waves, lulling my eyes to a close, when my phone rings, making me jump upright.

MOM is written in bold letters on my screen. It's like I've summoned her with my traitorous thoughts about the piano, even this early in the day.

I consider letting it go to voicemail, but that thought doesn't last long. This is the perfect way to know if the whole world has stayed in the past, or if it's just this camp.

With a clear of my throat, I press *ACCEPT* and say, "Hi, Mom."

"Emmaline." Her voice is calm but direct. That's how I know Dad must be around. "How are you doing?"

39

"Great." The lie rolls easily off my tongue. "You? How's the tour?"

I hold my breath. Last year, they weren't on tour. If I remember correctly, they were recording the soundtrack for this small-budget indie movie, which ended up being a huge success at the Toronto International Film Festival. If they are back in time too, I'll just say I was confused and mixed up their schedule.

"It's going amazing," she answers, sounding pleased.

A gush of air escapes my chest. So the rest of the world *is* still in normal time. I'm not sure whether to be relieved or even more worried.

"Actually, that's kind of what I was calling you about," Mom continues. "Yesterday in Paris, Huguette Beloeil came to meet me and your father backstage. You remember her, right? She's on the board at NAMA."

A fist wraps around my heart, clenching and tightening until I feel lightheaded.

"Uh-huh," I say in a squeaky voice.

"She told us she loved the show, and then she asked about you. We told her you'd be in the Allegro showcase this year, and she promised to place a good word in for you with the recruiters. Isn't that great?" She actually sounds excited about it, which is so different from the neutral, polite tone she uses for most conversations, even with her own daughter.

"Yeah, amazing," I say, no conviction in my words.

To an outsider, being the only daughter of two of the most recognized pianists of our time should be a blessing. The opportunities! The industry contacts!

The bone-crushing expectations!

Vivienne and Franklin St. Francis met at NAMA in the eighties and fell in love at first sight, at least according to the myth they've become. In their freshman year, they won multiple awards each, and right after graduating, they were hired to compose the score for one of the biggest movie franchises to ever exist. Their careers boomed after that, and they've been composing, playing shows, and being the perfect musician couple ever since.

And then there's me. The daughter who's good, but never great. Even less so since the accident that messed up her hand last year.

"Have you been having a good time? I heard the roster of teachers is great this year," Mom says.

"Well, I just got here yesterday, but sure, yeah." I don't mention that I will never meet that particular roster since I'm stuck in the past.

"Oh, really? I thought you left last week. Must've mixed things up." She hums. "Well, I'll let you get to it, then. The showcase will come faster than you think."

"Right." As if I wasn't acutely aware of that.

In the back of the call, I hear someone calling her name. She doesn't acknowledge it. "Want me to give Sebastian Lee a call? I know he's—"

"Please don't," I interrupt, too fast. "I'll be okay."

"Vivi!" I finally recognize my father's voice. "We have an interview in fifteen. Did you forget?"

Saved by the bell.

Mom answers something faintly, then comes back to me and says, "Honey—"

"It's okay, Mom, I actually have to go," I lie.

"Are you sure?"

"Absolutely. Say hi to Dad for me. Bye!"

I don't wait for her answer before I press the *END CALL* button. Even then, the tightness in my shoulders remains. I hate how her calls are always so professional. Even worse when it's my father. Sometimes it feels like they see me as a student. Like without the piano, I wouldn't even exist.

"Hey."

I yelp before spinning around, a hand clutching my heart.

41

"Jesus, Jamie. You want to give me a heart attack?" It's like he's appeared out of thin air.

He gives me a half grin, but it looks a little sad. His hair is mussed, flatter on the left than on the right. His glasses have fingerprint smudges, and I fight the urge to clean them.

"You were talking with someone?" he asks, hands in the front pockets of his dark jeans.

"Yeah. My mom called."

His brows furrow.

"They're still in the present—well, future," I add.

Jamie takes a seat next to me, scratching his stubble-covered jaw. "And she was able to call you?"

"Apparently."

"That's weird," he says. "Why did the call come to you and not Future You?"

"Future Me?"

"Well, yeah. We must have current selves in the future, or else people would have wondered whether we've disappeared, right?"

I didn't even think about that. The actual-time Jesy would have noticed if I hadn't shown up yesterday. Same for Jeremiah with Jamie.

"Maybe there's a missing people mission going on as we speak." I lift a shoulder. "My parents might just not have heard of it." When they're on tour, they're always out of it. They can forget to call for weeks sometimes. I've long since stopped hoping they would remember important things happening in my life.

"My parents would definitely have sounded the alarm."

I chuckle. "That's true. Probably would've asked for an Amber Alert."

"No such thing as having adult kids. Still just a babe." He offers me a tentative smile.

I feel my lips start to curl, then clear my throat. Looking back at the water, I say, "Anyway, if there are Future You and Me, I have no clue why the call came to me. Still haven't figured out all the rules of time travel."

"Sure am wishing I'd taken that physics class last year."

"I'm sure the teacher would've covered the subject in the first class of the year," I say.

"Don't see why not."

I repress a snicker just as the sound of my belly grumbling takes the entire space.

"Jeez, did a whale crash somewhere?"

"You know," I say, "that joke hasn't gotten funnier the two hundred times you've used it."

"You sure about that?" Again with the almost shy grin. "Come on, let's go feed you."

"Sure." I look down at my flannel pajamas. "Uh, just let me go change."

I hurry back to the cabin, still careful not to wake Jesy the Grizzly—seriously, how can someone so small snore so loud?—and dress in a skirt and a long-sleeved T-shirt, put on mascara, brush my hair, then walk back outside. When I turn toward Jamie, I feel, rather than see, his gaze roam over my body. I ignore it.

"Ready?" he asks.

Maybe this was a bad idea. Eating breakfast together feels intimate somehow. But I really am hungry, and he's here, and we have things to do, so I'll just have to ignore this feeling in my chest.

I nod, then walk with him toward the cafeteria. We stay silent through the trek, which I'm thankful for. Every time he speaks, I'm afraid he'll bring up the topic of us, and I'm still not sure what I'd say. We haven't broken up officially, and right now, as we're the only two people on earth who seem to know we're stuck in the past, I don't think it's time to broach the subject again. He seems to agree.

"It's so weird to know there's probably a double of us living our future lives at the same time," I say as we cross a small bridge overlying a rushing river that empties into Moosehead Lake. The sky is cloudy today, but it's still warm. It might rain later, which means we'll get the perfect practice temperature. I used to love locking myself in a soundproof room and playing the piano as rain trickled on the roof over my head, feeling like me and my music were alone in the world. Today, though, I think I'll focus on finding out why we're here.

"What do you think our current selves are doing?" Jamie asks.

"I don't know. Practicing, probably."

Silence falls. I guess that's a taboo subject now.

There's also the fact that in the current world, we've had no reason to hang out together after the discussion of ending things, so we're likely not even talking. Based on how tight his jaw is, it's clear Jamie came to the same realization once the question left his lips.

I clasp my hands in front of me. *Way to kill the casual vibes of the morning, Emma.*

We enter the cafeteria, a larger building made of the same material as our honey-colored cabins. The smell of eggs, bacon, and toast fills my nostrils, and I hum. Breakfast has always been my favorite meal at camp. It's nothing fancy, but it tastes so much better than the healthy things I buy at home.

Jamie and I get in line, which is short considering it's barely 7:00 a.m., then fill our plates and head to a table in the back of the room. This has always been our spot, where Jamie would be able to eat without having to socialize with anyone but me if he didn't feel like it.

"Hey, lovebirds!" Carl, one of the older theater kids, shouts at us when we pass him on our way to the table. The rest of his gang wolf-whistles. I smile tightly and keep walking, hoping my reddening neck and cheeks don't betray me. I sneak a glance at Jamie, who's not smiling one bit. While last year he might've cracked an embarrassed grin and continued on his merry way, now he can't even pretend he doesn't hate the attention. At least he hasn't said anything that would've destroyed our cover. If he had, I have no doubt this would get back to my parents in less than a day, and I'm not ready to receive a call—from my parents in the past, present, or future, who knows at this point—about why I'm ruining such a good thing. My parents couldn't dream of a better son-in-law than Jamie, mostly because he's one of the only pianists who can play the way they do. I'll need to tell them the truth at some point, but right now, my heart is already broken, and I can't have their remarks piling on top of it.

Once we sit down, I dig through my eggs. Meanwhile, Jamie plays with his food, but doesn't eat anything. No wonder he's this thin. Half the time he gets lost in his world and forgets to eat, and the other half, he has a whole plate of greasy food in front of him but doesn't take anything in.

The silence between us brings me back to the heavy car drive from yesterday, which was almost as uncomfortable as this. I really messed up by bringing up the piano this morning.

After taking a gulp of coffee, I say, "So. Game plan for the day."

Jamie lifts his gaze from his eggs, and I'd swear I see some relief in his eyes.

"The rest of the world is in normal time, meaning that there's something with this camp we need to figure out."

"Like what?" Jamie asks.

"Not sure yet." I take a bite. "In movies where something like this happens, there's often a reason behind it, like preventing an apocalyptic event or saving a house from burning down. So maybe we need to figure out a way to save the camp?"

Jamie's lips purse. "Are we actually basing our game plan on shitty nineties movies?"

"You got a better idea?"

Jamie lifts his hands in the air and shakes his head, though I can see the smirk he's trying to hide.

"Besides, some of these movies are masterpieces."

"Masterpieces?" He snorts. "I think Michelangelo just rolled in his grave."

I narrow my eyes. "Jamie, you think every rodent movie is peak cinema. Be for real."

He snorts. "Rodent movie?"

"The rat who controls a cook in a kitchen? The rat who gets flushed away down a toilet?" I lift my brows. "You eat it all up."

"Okay, that sounds way worse than it is."

"Does it?"

Jamie pauses before saying, "At least my grandmother never thirsted over my rodents."

The memory hits me in the face. Christmas five years ago, Jamie by my side while the awkward family dinner went on at my parents' manor, Nana Anne telling the entire table how she found Bill Murray to be a "nice piece of man." She then proceeded to slurp down her soup, some of it dribbling down her chin, as Jamie started choking on his canapé. I had to fight my laughter as I tapped his back.

I have to fight the same amusement as I purse my lips. He does the same, his eyes dancing.

I'm not sure I like what's happening here. Swallowing, I look away.

"You're right, though," Jamie says after a bite. "I don't have a better plan, so let's try this one first. Maybe Bill Murray was the answer all along."

My chest loosens, glad for the transition opportunity. "I can try to speak to Irène and Alessandro. You could try to see if anyone else seems to be in the same boat as us?" I ask. If we're here because the camp needs to be saved (still not sure what that would have to do with us, but that's a problem for another time), the best people to ask are the owners of the place. "We should probably do that before our private lessons begin."

"Sure."

I finish my last bite, then get up. "Good luck," I tell Jamie. Just as I grab my plate, I spot Jesy entering the cafeteria and waving at me. A few other people are looking at us. Since Jamie won performance of the year at the showcase two summers ago—which he'll win again in a few weeks, if history repeats itself—he's become kind of an art camp superstar, especially with the younger kids.

I never would have left him this abruptly before, with a simple goodbye. It's not believable one bit. So, willing my heart not to get overwhelmed, I lean down and press a soft kiss to Jamie's cheek, the stubble rough under my lips. I force myself not to inhale. The smell of his detergent and woodsy soap would only make me overwhelmed.

I feel him stiffen under me, the short moment of contact lasting a lifetime.

When I pull away, he still doesn't move. I feel everyone's eyes on us, and I hate it. I hate everything about it.

Eventually, he glances my way, and the tightness in his expression makes my hand start to shake.

I turn away and leave before anything can be said about what just happened.

CHAPTER 6

Emma

I'VE NEVER BEEN TO THE CAMP'S MAIN OFFICE TO SEE IRÈNE
or Alessandro.

Sure, throughout my summers here, I've seen the two directors countless times. They were almost always there during the weekly bonfires or volleyball tournaments. They also gave a few lessons on stage presence and art in general. I know the dancers in the camp have had more lessons with them, but as a pianist, I always had to deal more with individual teachers or Ms. Yancey, the director of the music program. Even without being a personal student to Irène, though, everyone was sure to have been impacted by her. She was a calming presence during showcases. An encouraging voice at the halfway mark of summer, when everyone's solo performances felt impossible to perfect in less than a month. And most of all, an example of what it is to be in love.

I can't remember a single instance when I saw the two of them looking anything less than head over heels in love. More than once, I've rounded the corner of the administration building to find them walking hand-in-hand or laughing at something the other had said or twirling softly under the moonlight with no music on. It's something I'd rarely seen. While my parents have been together for decades, they've never looked at each other that way, or at least not in front of me.

I wrap my arms around my middle as I make my way to the offices, trying to steel myself to not react when I see someone who's been dead for a year, at least in my head. The early morning air is cool, but it doesn't stop people from bustling around. To my left, two dancers are practicing what looks like a difficult lift, dressed in yoga pants and tight tank tops, sweat drenching their foreheads. Even from here, I recognize the song they're dancing to: the theme from *The Trust Fall*, my parents' big music break. I look away and hurry toward my destination.

Once I reach the front door of the administration building, I stop, staring at my reflection in the windows.

Irène never died. You're just having a regular conversation.

I've got this.

Shoulders straight, I step inside.

The offices form a large square, each room surrounded by large windows facing either the camp or the forest behind. The middle of the space is occupied by musical instruments and a small stage. I've never practiced here, but I know some people do, when the music rooms are occupied or when they want to practice on a smaller stage before the end-of-summer showcase.

Easily recognizing the directors' office, I head over and knock on the door.

No answer.

I lift my index finger to my mouth and start chewing on the skin bordering my nail, only realizing a moment later what I'm doing and forcing my hand down. My old etiquette tutor would be ashamed.

I wait a minute in front of the door, but when no one answers after a second

knock, I turn to leave. Maybe they're not awake yet.

I cross back through the center space, the whole room filled with the soft hum of the AC. It's rare to find a spot so quiet at Allegro. There's always someone playing the guitar or singing or choreographing a group number to an ABBA classic.

My footsteps resonate all the way to the cathedral ceilings, and just as I'm about to exit the room, I come face-to-face with a piano. It's nothing like the five grand pianos we have in the music rooms, but is instead an old Yamaha, the brown wood chipped in some places. Something about it pulls me forward, maybe its flaws in a scene of perfection. I run a hand over its cherry top, then drag fingers across the keys to play a simple scale. It's been tuned up, that is clear.

My watch indicates it's not even eight. Our lessons won't start before nine.

"Hello?" I call out loud, looking left and right. When silence answers me, I take a seat on the creaky bench while I stretch my left hand. Ever since the accident, it's been stiff in the morning.

I run a few scales, the motions coming to me as reflexively as walking. Ever since I was a kid, I practiced scales and arpeggios for hours every single day, sometimes on my turned-off electric piano while watching TV or studying. Even so, my muscle memory is a little hindered by the fact that I haven't been the most assiduous with my technical practice, especially in the last two weeks. I hadn't been on campus since the semester ended, so I didn't have the music room calling to me every evening after classes.

My hand doesn't feel that bad this morning. There's barely any pain when I play. And before my first performance lesson, I should probably run through my showcase piece at least once.

My father picked it for me. He said it's the perfect composition to show the wide range of a pianist's skills. Mom agreed, so I did too. Mozart's Sonata no. 18 is far from an easy piece, but if they said that was the one, then that was the one. They know better.

Sitting up straighter, I let my shoulder relax, crack my neck left and right, then start playing.

In less than a minute, I know exactly what the outcome of this practice will be. Okay. Nothing better than that.

I hear the disappointment in my piece. It's like every single note is dripping with *bleh*. And I don't even know why I'm surprised; I haven't had a great performance in a long time. Since last summer, maybe. After the accident and the surgery, I had to take some time off to let my hand recover, and when it was time to start again, everything in my life felt like it had fallen off the rails. Jamie wasn't there anymore, locked in his practice room. My parents were calling every day, asking me how my playing was going and telling me I just needed to put my mind to it. At some point, I realized I couldn't remember what I'd ever loved about playing. I think I might've forgotten even before the accident.

The farther I get into the piece, the more embarrassed I become. It's a small blessing that no one's here to witness it. Being "okay" in a world expecting excellence is the worst kind of failure.

It's something I know Jamie has never once experienced. Every time he plays, he's entrancing. Almost perfect. And he will give everything he has to reach that *perfect* title. He'll get it. I might have a career only playing weddings and receptions, but he'll fill concert halls one day. I know it.

Stop thinking about this.

I move into the adagio—the second part of the piece—and mistakes accumulate. I can almost imagine my father standing behind me, saying that my staccato isn't sharp enough or that my two hands seem disconnected from one another. I know both those things are true, but I can't correct them. Every slip makes me see how I don't have a chance at one of the two NAMA early admission spots. Before my accident, I might have had a shot at second place, if the universe was smiling at me on that day. But now? Now it seems like the Titanic crew shooting their flare gun in the middle of the night while they have less than an hour before most of the passengers drown or freeze to death. A shot in the dark.

The muscles in my arms tense with each new wrong finger movement, and the more I progress in the song, the worse I get. My eyes are wide open, staring blindly at the damaged wood as I think of the shame I will bring my family when I ultimately fail.

If I don't succeed at the showcase, I could always go through the traditional admission process for NAMA, or even apply to other great music schools in the country, but I'm not even sure I'd be good enough to make it through. I'm not being a pessimist, just a realist. I can hear how my music sounds. Plus, the simple thought of practicing for another year like I have the past year with the hope of making it through an audition... I'm not sure I would survive it.

I've already lost too much sleep over this year's showcase. Hopefully, in less than two months, it'll all be over.

By some miracle, I make it through the piece, my shoulders slumping over the keyboard the second the last note evaporates. My teeth are clenched tight.

I jump when clapping comes from behind me, and after turning, I find Irène standing there, a warm smile on her face. Even at her age, she reminds me of my first piano teacher, Suzanne, with her twinkling eyes and encouraging words. She was the queen of tough love, telling me when I sucked, plain and simple, but also telling me I had the potential not to suck anymore. Even though I don't know Irène that well, I'd bet that's how she is as a teacher too.

"Superb," Irène says with her elegant French accent. It still feels strange to hear her voice again, but at least I'm not gawking at her with deer-in-the-headlights eyes like I probably did yesterday.

"Thank you," I answer as I get up and push the seat back under the piano. She probably doesn't believe what she's saying, but I love her for pretending.

"How are you doing, *ma chérie*?" she asks, leaning her hip against the piano.

"Oh, perfect. You?"

She nods, not answering the question. Maybe she knows I'm lying.

"I, uh, I was actually coming to speak with you."

"Sure," she says, not missing a beat as she turns to her office and gestures at me to follow, as if we've done this plenty of times. She unlocks the office before we step inside. It's large and airy but still filled with stuff, from countless trophies to picture frames and trinkets from around the world. A masquerade mask, probably found in Venice; tickets for a show at the Paris Opera; a photograph of a young Alessandro holding a golden puppy, smiling brightly. The place is not messy per se, more like lived-in. It smells like lavender and coffee, a blend I never would've thought could work, but somehow, it does.

"Please, sit," she says. I expect her to have a seat behind her desk, like a school principal, but instead, she grabs a bouncy ball and sits on it in front of me. "What can I do for you?"

"I…" My fingers tap my corduroy-clad thighs rhythmically. "This might seem strange, but I was wondering how the camp was doing."

"Pardon?" Irène says, putting down the cup of coffee she'd just lifted from the small table to her left.

"I mean…" My nostrils flare. Why didn't I think this through? Of course, she'd think this is more than strange. I lick my lips. "You know how much I love this camp. At least I hope you do."

Irène's lips curl up, like a proud mother hearing that her toddler is the only kid who hasn't put a piece of plastic in one of their facial orifices that day.

"And I just wanted to make sure that it would stay in business for the years to come."

Better. At least, I think.

"Huh," she says, still grinning. "Well, I thank you for your concern, but I can assure you that the camp is more successful than it has ever been."

"Oh?" I add a smile when I realize I sounded a little too surprised.

She nods enthusiastically. "We are getting more applications than ever before, and we have been granted more funding from private and public sources so that we will be able to offer more scholarships to students who cannot afford to attend in the future."

"That's fantastic," I say, meaning it wholeheartedly. Jamie has always had to work all year on top of his studies to be able to come here each summer. I can't imagine what a scholarship could have meant for him. For us.

"So you're not closing down anytime soon?" I ask again, just to make sure I'm not missing anything.

"*Non, madame.*" She winks. "And even if we did have problems,

I can assure you that neither I nor Alessandro would give up on this place in any lifetime. It is our baby."

"That's good to hear." I offer her a polite smile as I get to my feet. I'm not sure whether to be relieved or discouraged. On the one hand, this camp I do love deep down is not struggling, which is great news. On the other hand, there goes my plan to go back to our time.

"Emma," she says, which surprises me. I knew she'd recognize my face, but I didn't think she'd remember my name. When I signed up at sixteen, it wasn't by using my parents' names. I did it myself, for myself. It was probably foolish of me not to expect her to hear about it somehow. "Are you sure everything is good?"

Her deep green eyes make something in me stutter. I'm not sure why. How many times have I been asked that exact question and had to lie my way through it? But maybe it's the way she asked it, like she knew what the answer was.

Not trusting my voice, I nod.

One of her eyes narrows, and she doesn't say anything for a moment. I'm under her scrutiny, and I don't like it. If someone watches you too closely, eventually, they'll see everything that's wrong, which is the last thing I need.

"All right," she ends up saying, "But if ever there is something you would like to talk about, my door is open. Okay?"

I nod again, then say, "Thank you for your time."

"Of course, *chérie*."

Fighting the urge to tell her that actually, everything in my life is going to hell, that I have no idea what I'm doing, and that my heart is in shambles, I turn around and exit the room. In passing, I throw a dirty look at the piano that proved just this morning how much of a failure I am, then make my way outside.

I have to find Jamie. We need to figure out a new plan, and soon.

CHAPTER 7

Jamie

THIS FEELS LIKE LOOKING FOR A NEEDLE IN A HAYSTACK.
No one around us appears confused or lost like Emma
and I are, and as far as I know, nothing seems amiss in the
camp.

I leave the dance building feeling even shittier than before.
Apparently, starting the day with your girlfriend giving you a kiss
only for the sake of pretending in front of people is not a good omen.

Hands in my pockets, I kick a large rock in the gravel pathway,
but it doesn't budge, instead sending pain straight through my toes
and leg. I hiss a "fuck."

I pissed off someone up there. I truly must have.

A curly haired guy sitting with his back leaned against a pine
tree looks up from his sketching pad, brows high. I look away and
walk faster to my cabin. Drizzle makes my shirt cling to my chest,
warm yet still raising goosebumps down my arms.

I'm dreaming of undressing from these wet clothes and going
to bed in the hope of waking up and realizing this was just a bad
dream when my phone vibrates in my back pocket.

> **Mom: Just received your USM tuition bill for your fall
> semester. Will leave it on your bed.**
>
> **Mom: Hope you're having a good time at camp! Love
> you xx**

So Emma isn't the only one who can be contacted by the outside world. I'm still not sure why the messages aren't directed to

our current selves, but I'll take it. Although with that kind of text, I might be better off having the messages transferred to another me.

Just thinking about all the student debt I've accumulated over the last three years makes me break out into cold sweat. If I had to start again, I'm not sure I'd do an undergrad before applying to music school. At the time, fresh out of high school and bright-eyed in regard to our future, Emma and I thought we might benefit from having more time before getting down to business. Have time for Thursday night outings and extracurriculars. Have time to be a young couple in love, all the while getting a good basic music education. We both applied to the music undergraduate program and went in thinking we'd have a great time before real life started, which we did. However, my bank account would beg to differ.

Mom and Dad never had the means to send all five kids to college. They've been the best parents I could imagine, and I've never needed for anything while growing up, but we've always been warned that if we wanted to conduct higher studies, we'd need to fund them ourselves. With my work money going toward music camp, I'm filled to the brim with tuition debt. It's not like they ever expected us to go to college anyway. I grew up knowing there would be a place for me at the diner if I wanted it, and it would be greatly appreciated if I did take it.

I never did, sadly. Not after I fell in love with the piano in my second-grade music class, and certainly not after I was laughed at in school time and time again because my parents were "burger flippers" who couldn't afford all the things other parents did. It was like that in Boston, and it remained that way when we moved and opened the new diner in Portland. I was never ashamed of my parents, far from that. They're the greatest people in the world, hard-working and kind, but that didn't matter to all those shitty kids, and that got to me. I hated my secondhand clothes and my hand-me-down sneakers. I hated feeling less than. I still do. And piano has always been my escape from that. With it, I could become someone great. Someone people would respect. Someone Emma could be proud of being seen with.

Me: Thanks. Love you too.

I go to ask her if Molly's excited to come to camp, but just then remember Molly only came to Allegro last year, so Present Mom wouldn't understand since Molly isn't returning this year. She hadn't enjoyed it enough for Mom and Dad to think it was worth all the money.

I'll probably put my foot in my mouth if I continue texting someone living in a different time than me, so I put the phone back in my pocket.

"Jamie, wait up!"

I turn to find Emma speed-walking toward me, her hair braided tightly behind her head. Simply seeing her feels like getting punched in the stomach repeatedly.

"Hey," I say, slowing down. "Find anything good?"

She shakes her head. "It was a dead end. Apparently, the camp's doing better than ever."

Shit. That means we're not going back. Which means I'll never actually audition for NAMA, which means all my decisions leading to this will have been for nothing, which means I'll have disappointed my family, and to Mr. and Mrs. St. Francis, I'll look like—

"Hey, it's going to be okay," Emma says, her cold fingers grazing my wrist. The touch sends electricity through my hand, making me flex it.

I force myself to breathe steadily as I nod.

Emma has helped me through enough panic attacks to know what I look like when I'm not feeling well. Still, I nod, hoping she'll let this go. I want to be there for her for once rather than her being there for me. She's done that enough, and apparently, I haven't returned the favor. How did I not see she needed it? How was I so fucking blind?

"It's all going to be fine," Emma says. "We'll find another way back."

"Yeah, I know," I say, as if I wasn't thinking the total opposite a second ago.

Show her you can be her pillar too.

"In the meantime," she says as she crosses her arms over her chest and walks under a large tree that mostly shelters her from the drizzle, "let's just continue preparing for the showcase."

My steps halt. I didn't think she'd bring it up with me. Not when my constant worrying about it made her think she wasn't the most important thing in my life.

But if she talked about it…

"How's your prep going?" I ask tentatively, joining her under the tree.

"Fine," she says, even adding one of her unnatural smiles for the record. She can't hide from me, though. At least not like she does from everyone else. I see the way she instinctively grabs her left hand and massages the palm with her right thumb.

The sight of it only makes me feel guiltier.

If it wasn't for me, she'd be playing as well as she always has. The notes would be flowing from her fingers. Music is in her blood, sure, but it's also in her spirit. She's one of the hardest-working musicians I know. People might think it comes naturally to her, but I've seen how much she's worked to get to where she is now.

When I suggested we go on an overnight camping trip last summer—take one of the camp's canoes and head out to one of the campgrounds around the lake, to relieve some of the pressure we were both feeling about the upcoming showcase—I never thought I'd be condemning her, which also meant condemning us. It was such a stupid fucking mistake anyway. I carefully lifted the canoe out of the water with her, I swear, but the terrain was a lot rockier than I'd expected, and when we started walking with the boat over our heads, I tripped over a large root. One stupid root. That was all it took for my weight to shift and for the canoe to fall over her, sending her down and having her hand crack against a boulder. I still remember the scream she let out as her fingers broke. It's a sound I still hear in my nightmares sometimes. It was all my fault, but while I didn't get a single scratch, Emma's hand was shattered.

I'll never forgive myself for it.

"If you ever need help with some of your pieces, you can ask me, you know," I say, the same way I have a hundred times before. She always declines, but it's the least I can do. She lost her music because of me. I still would've offered either way. In all honesty, I can't think of a single request she could have that I wouldn't agree to. Climb Everest with her? Done. Bury a body? Just let me grab my shovel.

And yet, I've let her down in all the ways that count.

"I'm fine," she repeats, dropping her hand as if I hadn't seen her already. "Just tweaking a thing or two." She rubs her lips. I want to kiss them.

"Can't wait to hear it." Hopefully, she'll let me soon. Listening to her play is something I can't get enough of. She looks like a queen when she does. Strong, powerful. A force that could rattle the world. Seeing her like that, in her element, makes me want to drop to my knees and worship every single inch of her body.

And if everything goes the way she's planned, at the end of the summer, we'll perform, and then never see each other again.

I can't even think about it. Not if I don't want to start panicking again. Because while not getting into NAMA would break my heart, losing her would be devastating. Besides, what good would it do to be seen as worthy if she doesn't want me anymore?

A cold sweat threatens to cover my forehead. She can't leave. I can't lose her. I simply can't. There's no me without her. I need her sunshine when I'm a dark cloud in a crowd. I need her reassurance when I'm a mess. I need her love, just like I need to give her my love.

Emma looks down at her watch, shifting her weight. "Okay, well, I have to go, but I'll let you know if I find anything new."

"W-where do you have to go?" I feel like a kid holding on to their comfort toy, but every time she leaves, I'm afraid it will be the last time. She's sand slipping through my fingers no matter how hard I grip it.

"This trivia thing Jesy organized for lunch."

"Can I come?"

There's wariness in her gaze as she says, "You want to come for a trivia game?"

"Yeah?" I clear my throat. "Why not?"

"Just…You've never participated before."

"So?"

"So nothing." She shrugs.

I pause for a second before I tilt my head and say, "You know, maybe us being here isn't such a bad thing."

She frowns. "I'm sorry?"

"Maybe we should see this as a…" I search for the right words, my breath fogging up my glasses. "An opportunity to rediscover ourselves. A second chance."

"An opportunity to rediscover ourselves?" she repeats slowly. For a second, I'm sure I see something like hope in her eyes, but as fast as it appeared, it's gone.

"Yes," I say, even more convinced than before. I don't know how I didn't see this right away.

She looks away, blinking fast. "I don't know, Jamie." A breath leaves her lungs. "I don't think I can go through that again."

"Go through what? Loving me?"

"No, not loving you." She picks at the skin around her thumbnail, and without looking up, she says, "Convincing myself to end this."

"Then don't. Don't end it."

Her eyes close, lips pressed tight. She's shutting me out again.

"It's not fair, Emma. You dropped this on me all of a sudden and then expected me to be okay with you calling it quits without any warning? Well, I'm not. You're still my girl." My throat is tight, and I'm fighting as hard as I can to keep the pressure behind my eyes under control.

Emma turns so that her back is to me. "Don't make this harder than it already is." Her voice is raw, and I so wish she would turn around so I could see what she's actually feeling.

Ignoring her plea, I say, "I'm not giving up on us. I can't. I'll…" I throw my arms in the air. "I'll woo you again."

A soft snort comes out of her, spontaneous, which gives me hope. "Woo me?"

"Yes, woo you." There's confidence in my tone. "I did it once. I'll do it again." While I'm still not sure how someone like her could have fallen for someone like me when we were sixteen, it happened, which means it can happen again. I just need to prove to her what she means to me, which is the entire universe. "We're not over," I add, shaking my head. "I refuse to believe that."

She doesn't say anything in response, which is better than a flat-out refusal.

"You'll see. I'll make you love me again."

She sighs, the sound as soft as an August wind, but even though it's not a convincing yes, it's better than an outright rejection. It's everything, really. The only indication I need that there's still a chance.

This moment feels huge. My axis has been turned, and now I know where I'm headed.

This feels like the moment in a movie when everything seems lost. We're brought to the edge of our seats. We don't know if the hero will defeat the villain. The fighting couple is at its breaking point. The score has reached its peak, the final love song about to play. Things could go either way.

This is our final love song. My one last chance.

And if there's one thing for sure, it's that I'll hold on to that inkling of possibility with the weight of all my dreams and hopes. I'm not letting go. Never again.

CHAPTER 8

Emma

"I S EVERYONE CLOTHED IN THERE?" I SHOUT AS I KNOCK at my cabin door.

"Yes," two voices grunt from inside, only one laughing afterward.

"I told you it would never happen again," Jesy says once I come in. She's seated at the small vanity we usually use for hair and makeup, except now a large piece of bright lime-green cloth covers it. Julia, her girlfriend, is sitting on Jesy's bed, her shaved head bent as she works on another bright piece of textile. While I can't see her face, she's definitely snickering. Probably remembering what happened two days ago when I came back inside unannounced to pick up a book I'd forgotten. That was a clear change from last year's summer—otherwise I obviously would've thought to knock before.

"Sure." I grin, bumping her shoulder with my hip as I walk past her.

She snorts.

"What are you working on?" I ask as I climb the ladder toward my bunk. I'd forgotten my sweater before going out for dinner, and while eating inside was fine, it's pretty cold out, and I'm not sure I'll survive tonight's outdoor practice with bare arms. I could always go inside, but there's something liberating about playing in the wild.

"Costumes," Julia answers, not looking up from her embroidering.

"Are you performing soon?"

"Yes," she says, her voice flat.

All right, then. I glance at Jesy, who offers me a small smile, as if apologizing.

Julia and Jesy have been together for two years—or I guess a single year in this world—and I can't remember a time when Julia didn't seem bothered by my presence. It's like I did something to her at some point, but I can't remember what it might be. Or maybe she just doesn't like me. The logical part of me knows that not everybody can like you, but the bigger part of me feels disappointed and a little hurt every time I see the way she looks at me.

"These look great," I tell them both as I climb down the ladder, my cardigan in hand. "I'm excited to see them live."

Now that I think of it, I'm pretty sure I remember seeing them during one of last year's Sunday Jams, where people showcase what they've been working on. I don't remember them being made in my cabin, though. Maybe because this time last year, I was spending most of my time with Jamie.

After a second of silence, Jesy says in an overly joyful voice, "Thanks!" With her usual flair, she wraps around her shoulders the piece of fabric she's bedazzling—who knew all this time there was a bedazzler in our cabin?—and says, "Maybe I should keep one for my showcase performance next year." She lifts her chin, smirking. "I'm sure the recruiters would love this."

"As if you'll need any help convincing anyone to take you on," I say with a squeeze of her shoulder. If I had to bet who would get that second spot beside Jamie, I'd have to go for Jesy. No one plays the violin like her, and I'm sure she's even better in current time. From what I've gathered, she's always been a natural like Jamie, but the string scars on her finger pads show how much she's worked for this too.

She shrugs while returning to her bedazzler. "Nothing's certain. And anyway, I'm not even sure I'll want a spot."

"What?" I sit down cross-legged next to her chair, ignoring Julia's weird stare. "Since when?" This doesn't make any sense. I've lived this summer before, yet I have no recollection of her ever mentioning something like that.

"I don't know. I like the violin, but I like other stuff too, you know? Can't say for sure if it's what I want to do for the rest of my life when there's so much out there I might like even more." She says it in a careless way, like regardless of her decision, everything will be fine. "Anyway, I still have more than a year to think about it."

My mouth opens, but no words come out. I stare in shock—or is it envy? She's expressed so simply what I've been feeling inside for years, but more than that, it sounds easy to her. And in a sense, maybe it is. She has the privilege of making decisions for no one other than herself.

If I chose another career for myself, this wouldn't only impact me. It would impact my parents and the narrative they have worked so hard to create. Multiple articles have already been written about how the St. Francis piano legacy would be continued with my arrival in the music scene. I never asked for those articles to be written, but my parents had spoken with people before I could even agree to it. Stepping back now would mean crossing a large, crimson X on what they've led the world to believe, and that would mean tainting the reputation they are so careful with. The one thing worth protecting at all costs.

I'll never forget the months of canceled tour dates a few years back when Mom could not get out of bed. Her eyes were bloodshot and empty, and I could hear her stomach growling from the other side of the door, yet she couldn't make herself get up to walk to the kitchen and get something to eat. Later I learned she'd been diagnosed with a major depressive episode, but back then, I couldn't figure out what was happening to her. In the newspaper Dad kept in the living room, I would see articles mentioning how the St. Francis family had decided to take a sudden break from touring to record a new album in New Zealand while spending time with family. Meanwhile, Mom was lying in bed with the same clothes for days, and I had to be homeschooled for weeks on end by teachers who'd had to sign

NDAs. I wasn't even allowed to share the truth with Jamie, and by that point, he was my best friend. I did tell him, but only years later, when we'd been together for a while. My parents were perfect musicians who formed the perfect couple and eventually got to create the perfect daughter who'd maintain the perfect legacy. It didn't matter whether that was the truth or not.

As I stare at her, her face free of tension as she threads a needle through fabric, I fight the urge to tell her, *Me too!* To shout about how I'd love to continue studying, to get the chance to do things that are unrelated to music. *I'm not the person you think I am*, I want to add.

The words remain inside.

When I was in fifth grade, I made the mistake of telling my best friend Kailie that my parents had gotten into a big fight the night before and when I'd tried to stop it, my father had called me something mean. The next day, a reporter called our house asking about a potential divorce. The rumor never made its way officially into the media, thank god, and I stopped talking to Kailie right away, but the experience taught me a lesson. No one can share your secrets if they don't know them.

I wish I still had the careless trust I granted everyone when I was a kid. Back then, to me, everyone was good until proven otherwise. It would be so freeing to tell Jesy everything I'm experiencing. About Jamie, and the piano, and the time travel. But it doesn't matter that I've liked this girl ever since that first summer at camp when she welcomed me with a Hershey's Kiss on my pillow, or that she and I have shared so many good moments over the years. I can't get myself to do it.

"I'm happy for you," I end up saying, pushing past the knot in my throat. "That you're figuring things out for yourself, I mean."

"Yeah," Jesy answers. "We'll see. I still have time to decide."

Lucky her.

She returns to her work, and just as I move to get up, Julia says,

"I need more of this velvet. Be back in a minute." Bending forward, she drops a kiss on Jesy's head before striding away.

My friend watches her with stars in her eyes. When she turns back to me, her cheeks are pink, lips curled. "God, I love that girl. Like, really love her."

That makes me smile, even though her words are bittersweet to hear. "I'm happy for you," I repeat.

Letting her head drop back, she looks at the ceiling and sighs. "After my parents got divorced, I started thinking love was bullshit, but now..." She turns to me. "Do you believe in true love, Emma? Like, soulmate type of stuff?"

The bittersweet turns to sour in my mouth.

"I..."

Again, with the urge to blurt out everything.

"Dumb question, of course, you do," Jesy adds, a jab to the face she doesn't even realize she's thrown. "But apart from you and Jamie, do you? Believe in it?"

I swallow, then paste on a smile I've practiced so many times before, it's become second nature. "Sure."

And that's the truth. I do believe in love when it comes to them. Maybe I'm not meant to have this full, ever-lasting love, but she is.

"Ugh," Jesy says, "It's scary. I don't ever want things to change between us."

Something builds in my chest at that, and for a moment, I don't know if I'm going to laugh or cry. I never wanted things to change between Jamie and me either. And yet.

The inkling of hope that brewed in me at Jamie's words this morning was stupid. Realistically, we both know we don't work, at least not anymore. We tried, and we ruined that beautiful love we had. And that's not all on Jamie. I let it morph into something full of dread. Something that reminded me how hard it is for someone to love me fully.

Julia comes back inside with her hands full of material at the same time Jesy asks me, "You okay?"

I blink fast, then say, "Mm-hmm."

"Of course she is," I'm pretty sure I hear Julia mumble.

Not as subtly as she thinks, Jesy shoves Julia's thigh with the back of her hand before throwing me an overly happy look.

I hold back a sigh, return Jesy's smile, then get to my feet and say, "Okay, well..." My gaze strays toward the door as dread fills me. I don't want to go to my practice. I know it won't be good, and I can't even blame it on my injured hand. The other one isn't doing a much better job these days. Plus, practice means being locked in a room with my thoughts, and those are far from helpful.

"Actually," I say, looking at the both of them, "Do you need an extra hand with that?" Maybe while I'm here, I could try doing something different than last year. Make at least one good thing out of this return to the past.

Julia only eyes me even more warily than before, but Jesy rolls her wheelchair to me and hands me the green fabric with a "yes, please."

I look over to Julia, who just shrugs and dips her head toward the space I just vacated.

Grabbing the fabric, I nod to them and set to work.

CHAPTER 9

Emma

I NEED A TIMEOUT.

My thoughts cannot seem to quiet down. Even when I try to be fully there and enjoy the moments I'm spending with friends, I'm all over the place. Too many things have happened in a single week, and I can't get my mind to focus. I've tried meditating, practicing, socializing, but nothing has worked. I keep getting pulled back to the "What's going to happen to us?" and "Did I make the biggest mistake of my life with Jamie?" So I'm trying one last thing.

Walking with my beach bag hanging from my shoulder, I avoid the cluster of people playing with Frisbees and rackets or simply soaking up the sun by the lakeside. Even Irène and Alessandro are there, sitting on camping chairs apart from the crowd, sharing a single cone of ice cream. Alessandro is holding it, so I wonder if Irène used my go-to move and said she didn't want any, only to eat half of his share.

Instead of passing through everyone, I take a detour through my quiet path in the woods. Some people see me, and I wave subtly, but I try my best not to make eye contact so no one follows me. My towel is wrapped tightly around my body even though I'm wearing a modest one-piece underneath. No need for people to notice my protruding hipbones or loose-skinned thighs. Plus, I couldn't wear makeup if I wanted to go in the water, and I'd rather others not see my acne stress-breakout. The people who said acne was just something you experienced in your teens were liars.

When I finally cut through the sparse forest and find the small, hidden piece of land that can act as a beach, I drop my towel to the ground and rifle through my bag. Here, I'm far enough from the rest of the campers that I can put on some music without people hearing, so I get my portable speaker out and put on my favorite Thomas Rhett album. Then I stretch my shoulders and head into the water. Its coldness bites my skin, but it's a good kind of pain. One that grounds me to the moment. I need that right now. Something to keep me from drowning in my own thoughts.

Pushing through until I'm soaked to my shoulders, I inhale deeply and put my head under. A gasp comes out of me when I reemerge, my toes and hands already going numb. It's so different from the heated pool I love to lounge in when I visit my parents, but somehow, this feels much better.

Even with my teeth chattering, I take another lungful, then start swimming.

I aim for the middle of the lake, not caring how far I make it. I just need to move. My legs kick and kick, never stopping as I clear my head. Every time a new thought comes through, my thundering heart pushes it away. I don't think about being stuck in time. I don't think about my ruined relationship. I don't think about the sweet but strong lady that will soon disappear. I don't think about the years to come, or the career I need to make for myself. Breathing becomes the only thing I can focus on. That, and not drowning.

Once I make it far enough that I feel I won't be able to make it back if I continue, I stop, then let myself float on my back while I catch my breath. This feels good. I'm not a good swimmer, far from it, but there's nothing quite like it when you need to spend some energy.

Somewhat rested, I make the swim back to the shore, following Thomas Rhett's deep singing voice to guide me. When I can finally touch down, I stop abruptly, chest heaving and throat burning. I don't feel cold anymore. I focus on the melodies around me as I catch my breath, then let myself float on my back again, the midday sun shining on my skin, its heat contrasting with the crispness of the water.

"What are you doing?"

I jump, water splattering around me as I try to take a stand on the muddy ground. My heart goes back to being thunderous, and it only calms a little when I spot Jamie standing on one of the boulders bordering the lake, barefoot, his jeans frayed and washed-out.

"Jesus, you almost gave me a heart attack," I say, hand on my chest. "What are *you* doing here?"

"Was looking for you. Figured I'd follow the sound of that old country twang and would find you there."

"Happy you were right?"

"Very. Although I do think you need to broaden your musical horizons." He wrinkles his nose, hands on his hips. "You know, there's no shame in admitting you finally came to your senses about this."

I narrow my eyes, plunging my body back to my shoulders. "You're just a snob. And you need a specific kind of musical intelligence to appreciate country music."

"Guess I'm really fucking dumb then."

That gets my lips to quirk up, which in turn makes him beam.

Carefully, he slides off the boulder and rolls up his jeans so he can stand in the shallow water. "Seriously, though, what are you doing?"

"Oh, you know, just figuring out the theory behind black holes." I look around me. "What does it look like I'm doing?"

"Trying to prove to someone you're the new female Michael Phelps?"

I narrow my eyes, which only makes him get closer to me.

"I needed to burn off some steam."

"Can I join?"

I roll my lips behind my teeth, looking around me again, but this time only to notice we're alone in this part of the lake. We can barely hear everyone else enjoying the water yards away.

"Um, sure."

He doesn't need extra confirmation before he's stripping off his pants and shirt, then wading through the water only in his black boxer briefs.

"Jeez, didn't know I'd agreed to a strip show."

He snorts. "Nothing new, yeah?"

Right. I clear my throat as he makes his final steps my way, then dives headfirst. When he comes out, his dark hair is plastered to his face, droplets falling over his long nose and dark pink lips, and I feel my mouth dry. Clearing my throat again, I force myself to look away, then return to my position floating on my back. I wouldn't if we were in front of everyone, but this is just Jamie. He's seen all the parts I'd rather hide.

Ripples come from my left, and a second later, I spot Jamie floating next to me, eyes closed and head angled toward the sun.

"You had the right idea," he says after a while, voice low.

"Right?" As I feel the water flowing around me, the muffled music coming from the shore and the warmth of summer on my body, I think to myself this is probably the first moment of the past week I've enjoyed thoroughly.

Beside me, I see Jamie's hand moving softly, and while at first I think he's doing it to feel himself float, I see he's actually playing something over the surface. I wonder what he's playing. Before, I would've asked. Now, I'll leave it to him.

Focus back on the moment.

And I do. I don't know how much time passes where we just float and breathe.

"You think it's just as nice in real time?" Jamie asks.

"I don't know."

"Hopefully not."

I turn to him, snorting. "Why?"

"Would be nice if we had something on those fuckers."

That makes me laugh out loud. "Is that what you call the future us now?"

"Yup."

"Not sure Future You would like it."

"Future Me can go to hell."

I snicker again, but when my laughter dies down, I start frowning. "You really think things are much better in real time?"

Jamie takes a moment before he says, "I don't know, but at least they don't risk having to repeat an entire year of their lives."

My lips twist to the side. I know Jamie sees the possibility of an extra year as a nightmare, but when I think about it, it doesn't sound so bad. In some ways, I might even be thankful for parts of it. Sure, I want the showcase to be over with, but I also wouldn't mind having an extra year of college.

"Won't you miss it?" I ask. "School, I mean."

He shrugs, still looking at the cyan sky. "Not really, no. I mean, NAMA is still school anyway. Plus, if we go back, we'll still have senior year to go through."

"It won't be the same," I say, referring to his first point. "It'll be about becoming a better performer and musician. Not about learning new stuff about the world."

"And that's supposed to be better?"

I don't bother answering that yes, I think it's so much better. I love my art history classes, my essay writing sessions and class discussions. I love coming back from my day and falling asleep with my head full of new knowledge. I used to feel that way about learning new skills, but now, every time I master a piece, I just have to move on to a new one. It feels like checking off items on a list that doesn't mean much. Meanwhile, knowledge feels exponential. Like I'll never have enough, but I still want to try and get as much as I can.

"Well, it's useless to think about all that now anyway," he says, shifting so he's now standing in the water, droplets sluicing down his sharp collarbones and pectorals. I look away. "Maybe the current world sucks."

"Yeah. Maybe we were sent here for a reason back there, actually."

"Maybe a comet fell on NYC and NAMA closed its doors and

I would've been stuck working at the restaurant instead of getting out of there."

"Would that be so bad?" It doesn't seem so to me. Having a simple life, far from people's judgmental eyes. An honest job working with some of the best people I know.

"Yeah, it really would."

I wait for him to expand on this, but he doesn't. Still, I see something's going on in his head by the way his lips move to one side and his brows shift. That something is dark, dimming his natural light. I don't like it.

"Maybe in real time, they've asked Shania Twain to record a new national anthem and the universe wanted to spare you of that," I blurt out, wanting that look to go away.

He bursts out in laughter at that, letting the sun shine through once again.

"Thank you, then, universe," he shouts at the sky, white teeth glinting over the water. "I'm eternally grateful." He looks down at me then and smiles so openly, it takes my breath away.

I've always liked this side of Jamie. The one people don't see because of his shy exterior. The side he keeps for his close ones, although even with his family, it's tamed. He often tends to fade away when all his siblings take over the conversation. Seeing him like this, totally open, has always felt like a gift.

"And why were you also brought here, then?" he asks, moving closer to me. "Sounds like your idea of a dream."

"Who knows? Maybe there was a different reason altogether for me."

Jamie's eyes stay on me for a long moment, as if he's deciding on what to answer. In the end, when he opens his mouth, it's to say, "You know what I'm thinking about right now?"

"Hm?"

He stares at me with this incredibly serious face before he says, "How three years ago, this is the exact spot where I got a leech stuck between my toes."

73

"Oh, Jesus effing Christ," I sputter, jumping upright and running out of the water, splashing Jamie with my heavy leg movements as I hurry back. I remember that moment now. Vividly. And if it happens to me, I just might die.

Jamie's roar of laughter is sharp behind me. "It wasn't that bad!"

"I had to peel it off your foot with tweezers, Jamie," I deadpan, not turning back. "I'm *not* reliving that scene, ever."

"Fair point," he says, still laughing.

When I finally reach the shore, I sit on the boulder Jamie was on earlier and examine my legs. Nothing. I get back up, then turn my back to Jamie while lifting my hair and ask, "Anything?"

He takes a moment to answer, and when he does, his voice is rough. "Nothing."

"Thanks."

I go to grab my towel and wrap it around me, but when Jamie comes out, I remember he doesn't have anything for himself. He starts shivering the moment he gets out, looking at his jeans as if he'll use them to dry off.

"Come here," I say.

He obeys, and when he's close enough, I remove my towel and start patting his chest dry, then his arms. Jamie is stiff as I do so, and I force my breathing to remain normal. This is just a favor I'm doing for him. I wasn't about to let him freeze.

Once I'm done with his upper half, I realize I can't do this with his legs. That would be way too much. Instead, I tell him, "Lean down." He obeys once again, and I use my now-wet towel to dry his hair as best I can, mussing it up while doing so.

His Adam's apple bobs as he straightens himself, forcing my gaze to stray to his naked chest. While I can't see his eyes, the warmth I feel tells me he's probably doing the same.

I blink, then force myself to look at something else. Anything will do. I turn toward the forest, and as I do, I spot two people walking through the trees, their line of view right on us. I squint, then recognize Jeremiah and his dance partner.

I'm taken aback. I don't know why—it's not like we're some-where completely remote, but somehow I'd forgotten people could potentially see us here. My mind slows as I try to imagine what we look like from an outsider's point of view. Do we look in love? Or more like two people faking our way?

Reflexes take over, and the moment Jamie's roommate's eyes land on us, I lean forward and grab one of Jamie's hands between the two of mine.

His head spins my way at the touch, cheeks pink. His lips part as he blinks once, twice, then follows to where my gaze is aimed. He exhales deeply.

Jamie waves at Jeremiah, who waves back. His body is stiff be-side mine, and when the second the duo leaves our view, Jamie lets go of my hand like it's made of hot coal. "All clear," he says.

"Oh, yeah. Okay."

Jamie takes the towel from my hands and finishes drying him-self. Meanwhile, my hand drifts to my mouth, where I start chew-ing at the skin of my thumbnail. Even with the warm day, I start shivering.

After rubbing his head with the towel, he gives the piece of cloth back to me and starts dressing in a hurry, almost tripping as he puts on his jeans.

"You're leaving?" I ask—stupidly, mind you, because clearly he is, but I'm still reeling. From the heated gaze, or the hand-holding, or the rapid hand-dropping, I'm not sure.

"Yeah. I have somewhere to be."

"Oh," I repeat. "All right."

He finishes tying up his shoes, then stands straight. He gives me a quick flick of his brows, then turns.

"Hey," I say before he can stride away. "Everything okay?" He seems to be reeling too. Everything was okay before, or at least I thought so, and now it's like I'm contagious.

"Sure." He tips his head toward the forest, giving me a small smile. "I'll see you later."

"Okay." I wave, but he's already gone, walking like he's being propelled by an engine. I watch him until he disappears from view.

Lips tight, I return to my boulder, shoulders hunched as I stare at the lake. I'm not sure what just happened, and I'm even less sure how I feel about it. His reaction might have been normal, but somehow the buzzing I felt in my chest as I watched him leave tells me there was something there.

I spend the rest of the afternoon trying to convince myself I'm wrong.

CHAPTER 10

Emma

I T'S BEEN MORE THAN A WEEK, AND I STILL HAVE NO CLUE HOW to bring us back.

Everywhere I look, it's like there's a clue I'm missing, but I can't for the life of me figure out what is going on. I've come to the conclusion that maybe we're just part of a universe glitch and Jamie and I were the two unlucky people who got stuck in it.

As I walk toward the music building, the camp feels truly alive. It's one of the first days since I got here where it really feels like a pure Allegro day. To my left, a troupe of contemporary dancers is practicing their choreography on the outside stage, the sun blazing on their sweaty skin. The acoustic rendition of some metal song is clashing with the concerto the string quartet to my right is practicing at the same time. I hurry inside the music building to escape the cacophony.

"Emma! Hi!" a male voice I don't recognize exclaims as soon as the heavy door closes behind me.

Clutching my music binder closer to me, I look up to find a guy who's probably in his young thirties approaching, an overly-eager smile on his lips. His pale blond hair is combed to the sides, pale blue eyes stark in the illuminated room. Once he's close enough, I vaguely recognize his face, but I'm not sure from where.

"Hello?" I say, sounding more questioning than affirming. I still paste on a close-lipped smile.

"I'm Cole Preston. I'm replacing Dr. Podimow for your performance lessons this week.

"Oh, right, Cole," I say, the name finally ringing a bell. Dr.

Podimow went on vacation last year—the only one I ever remember her taking—and I spent one or two lessons with this man instead. If I remember correctly, he was nice. A little cocky, but nice. "Sorry about that. It's nice to see you again," I add.

He pulls back with a curious expression. "Have we met before?"

Crap.

"Sorry, I'm so silly." I chuckle while digging my nails into my palms, his scrutiny overwhelming. "I meant it's nice to *meet* you. Dr. Podimow has spoken very highly of you."

"Ah, great to hear," he says, gesturing for me to follow him into one of the booths. Once we sit, me at the piano and him on the small sofa next to it, Cole chuckles and says, "Yeah, I'm pretty sure I would've remembered meeting you."

I blink, cheek twitching. "What do you mean?"

"Well, let's just say I was quite ecstatic when I saw your name on the student roster."

I blink once more.

"You know, I hope it's not indiscreet to say, but *The Last Letter* soundtrack is the reason I started playing the piano."

I give him a small smile, then bring my focus to my hands resting on the piano. The man already knows of me, and my parents are part of his music origin story. This is just fantastic.

"I'm not my parents, though," I say, letting out a laugh I hope only sounds fake to my ears. "Wouldn't want you to get your expectations too high."

"Humble, I see," he says, leaning back in his chair. I cringe at the word. If only he knew.

With his index finger, he points to my binder. I give it to him, a drip of sweat running down my back as he browses my music sheets. Meanwhile, I cannot calm my thoughts.

I don't remember having this conversation with him in the past. Maybe I did, but it didn't affect me as much because I didn't feel as much pressure last year. I wasn't the best in the class, but I could still play well, and I felt confident in my skills. Or maybe we never had this exact conversation, which is why I don't remember. That's something I've noticed this summer: while everything started the same, I'm seeing some changes, probably because I'm not the same person I was, and that affects the way I initiate or respond in conversations, which can then veer in altogether different directions.

Maybe last year he recognized my family name and I was flattered. Now I'm wondering if I'll even be able to play the piece he picks, with my crappy hand and my even crappier morale.

"This one," he finally says, selecting a Bach concerto I've been playing for years. I let out a small breath. This I can do.

Cole's glacier eyes climb to me, almost animalistic. "Show me what you got."

* * *

"There you are."

I spin around to find Jamie sauntering my way, his dark hair all over the place, so familiar in its messiness. The white T-shirt on his back is one I recognize, considering I gave it to him two Christmases ago. It sports a quote from one of his favorite books, an underdog story about some young girl who came from nothing and ended up on top of the world with her magic powers. During our second or third date, when he was still too shy to talk much, he suggested we read it side by side, cozy in my living room, my parents away for the night. To be honest, I don't remember much of it. I was too busy thinking about how good it felt to have him next to me, and wishing he'd turn and kiss me, to focus.

"I've been looking everywhere for you," he says.

I look around, at the camp's small library, a sunlit room full of books old and new. "I've been here for a while," I say. After my lesson, I was still reeling from my nerves and felt the need to busy my head with anything other than the piano, so I came here. While I'd never used the library before, I thought it'd be a quiet place, perfect to help my mind go blank. Case in point: I've been able to forget about the hour I spent next to my teacher who expected to find Michelangelo, only to find a carnival caricaturist instead. Sure, his words were complimentary, and he actually gave me some great corrections, but I was still able to see the hint of disappointment in his eyes. Not the prodigy after all.

"And what are you doing here exactly?" Jamie asks as he takes a seat in front of me, his elbows dropping to the table as soon as he sits.

"Looking for answers." A small cloud of dust fills the space between the two of us as I close the book I was reading.

Jamie picks it up and lifts it to his eyes. "*Music and the Soul*," he reads aloud before looking at me with a confused expression. "Why, exactly, are you reading this?"

"Oh, you know, just a newfound passion for spirituality." I take the book back from him as he snickers. "*Obviously*, I'm trying to find answers on how to go back."

"And you're hoping to find answers on time traveling in this tiny-ass art library?"

"Oh, because you got a better idea, Einstein?"

His lips twist to the side, but there's a glimmer of humor on his face.

This feels good, to be back to some light conversation without feeling the need to bring up our possible breakup, just like yesterday at the lake. I like this easiness between us. It's been a while since I've felt it. In fact, it reminds me of our high school days, when we'd spend our free time in the library or the music booths, arguing over what event started the First World War or which composer, Mozart and Beethoven, should be considered the best of all time. We'd often bet kisses over who could come up with the most convincing argument, and even if we lost, we won.

"Come on," he says, getting up from the chair he just sat on.

I look at him, brows high, not moving from my seat.

Hand extended, he makes a *come here* movement with his fingers. "You need to clear your head for a minute."

"Who are you and what have you done with my—" I bite the

inside of my cheek. "With the Jamie I know?" This is usually my job. I'm the one who has to remind him to stop playing for a second so he can sleep or eat or drink.

"You look tired," he says, "and this 'research' doesn't seem to be going anywhere."

"You're just full of encouraging words today, huh?"

He grins. "Come on." He moves toward me and puts his hands under my arms. I squeal, jumping to my feet. He knows how ticklish I am.

With a smug face like he knows exactly what he's done, he says, "I'll come back and help you here afterward." One of his hands lifts in front of him. "Scout's honor."

His mood is definitely different from the way he left off yesterday. Whatever bug bit him then, it's gone, and I'm not about to bring it up.

"And where do you want to take me, slacker?"

"Sunday Jam," he says.

I frown. "You don't even like going to those." Every time I have offered for the whole time we've come here, he's complained that a concert that has no theme and is all over the place shouldn't have the right to be performed. And every time, I told him that it isn't a concert, just people playing and singing and dancing for fun, but he wouldn't have it.

"I know," he says, grabbing my wrist to lead me outside the library. "But you do."

* * *

I hate to admit that Jamie has a point, but Jamie has a point. This *is* all over the place.

On the stage, five actors are competing in an improvisation tournament. To their left, on the ground, two tall guys with dreadlocks are playing the steel drums while a pink-haired girl is humming a melody on top of it. On the dock where people usually go for tanning sessions, one of our most renowned ballet duos, dressed in baggy jeans and sweaters, is dancing to the music that is so unlike their usual, it's almost comical.

It's probably the most fun I've had in a while.

Everyone is sitting on whatever surface they could find, from camping chairs to tree stumps to beach towels on the sandy ground. The scent of wood and ashes from yesterday's bonfire has permeated the air. Behind the stage where the actors are playing, an older couple is slow dancing, as if separated from the outside world, their own song playing in their heads.

Of course Irène and Alessandro have to be this cute during the one summer when I'm questioning everything I thought I knew about love.

Around me, people start applauding, and I join them even though I'm not sure who we're clapping for.

"The theater kids are done," Jamie whispers in my ear while nudging my knee, as if he knew I was confused. A shiver runs down my spine at the feel of his breath on my skin. He's sitting so close to me, I can smell the clean scent of his shampoo, and for a second, I can imagine letting go and leaning my head on his shoulder. It would be warm, and I'd feel safe and understood, despite it all.

That's one of the first things I realized when we started hanging out in high school. Jamie made me feel like I could be myself, and he wouldn't want me to change. I didn't have to spill my heart to him. It was like he saw through me right away. Keeping secrets was useless because he knew everything, always, and I somehow never worried about whether or not to trust him. It was instinctual.

"Duet! Duet! Duet!"

Jamie nudges my shoulder with his, bringing me out of my thoughts.

I look around, alert. "What did I miss?"

"Where did you go?" he asks, amused, not bothering to answer my question.

I shake my head, face hot. "You're the one who's supposed to be lost in space, not me."

"Those rules have been overused, don't you think?" He smirks. "Time I take care of you for once."

I don't know how to answer that, so I just stare.

While we haven't talked again about his intentions to flirt with me, or whatever the word he used was, I see how his plan could work, and that's scaring the living heck out of me. I can be his friend—I *want* to be his friend—but more would be stupid. We've done this before. It did not end well. I can't put myself through it again. While we're in a gray zone, after the summer is over, we'll need to officially end this. What I feel about him is inconsequential.

The thought makes my stomach drop.

"So?" he asks, dipping his head toward the stage and once again bringing me out of my thoughts.

"So what?"

Behind us, people continue shouting, "Duet!"

"You want to do this or not?"

It's at this moment I realize people's faces are turned toward us. They want *us* to duet.

Oh crap.

While Jamie has never liked coming to these things, I've always found ways to bring him once or twice every summer. And most times, I'd drag him onstage to play a duet with me. Last year, we were both so busy practicing, I think we forgot to attend even one Sunday Jam.

But once again, this repeat summer is different, and because Jamie decided he wanted to be social and dragged me here, we accidentally put ourselves at risk of this happening. My left hand is twitching uncontrollably from an accident that has technically not happened yet, and after my lesson this morning, I feel less competent than ever before.

In summary, things are peachy.

"Do we have any other choice?" I ask him in a low voice.

"We always have a choice." He shrugs with those narrow shoulders I used to daydream about. "I can tell them to fuck off if it'd make you feel better."

"I would rather die than have you do that."

He grins, knowing I'm telling the truth, which is probably the precise reason why he's said it. He would probably rather die too than have to say anything in front of a crowd this big.

Not seeing any other choice, I say, "I guess that's what usual Jamie and Emma would do."

"Right," he says behind me as I get to my feet. A second later, I feel his tall body hide the setting sun from behind me. At least I'm not alone.

On the stage sits the usual black Yamaha piano that's brought outside every Sunday, but as if out of nowhere, someone brings a second keyboard, this one electric.

My heart starts beating faster as I look around at the crowd that's gotten quieter in the past minute, focused on the two of us. I turn to Jamie, and as he alternates between both of my eyes, he must see the panic in there. Touching my elbow, he leans down and says, "Wanna do it like before?"

I could probably melt in relief just then.

The vigorous nod I give him makes him smile, like we're in on a secret no one else is. In a way, I guess we are.

"Come on," he whispers, tipping his head toward the one piano we'll share, just like we did during the first years we partnered together. We take our seats, the outer side of our thighs touching so we can both fit on the narrow wooden seat. The feeling both makes me want to ask for another seat and get even closer.

"Relax," he whispers in my ear. "I got you."

The roles are reversed when we're at the piano. That's where he becomes comfortable, like it's exactly where he's supposed to be.

I look up, and for a moment, the crowd disappears, and there's only the early autumn color of his eyes, like leaves turning to a light amber. In them, I see he knows I'm struggling, which makes no sense, considering I've never given him an inkling things weren't going well with our beloved instrument. However, there's no denying it. It's all there in the cautious but encouraging way he's looking at me. I shouldn't be surprised. He's always been able to see right through me. Well, almost always.

"What do we play?" I ask softly.

"'Bohemian Rhapsody'?" he says, and despite my heart beating fast, I break out into a smile. The first contemporary song I mastered, loving the feel of playing a popular song that's so at odds with my classical training.

I nod, and without even needing a word, we both start playing at the same time. I would bet even our breathing pattern matches. It's always been like this when we play together. Like we become one entity.

My hands aren't as steady as I would like them to be, but the music still comes out nice, emotional but also fun, and even though my fingers slip from time to time, my shoulders loosen. Another plus of playing a song everyone knows and loves is that without a doubt, people will start singing, and your mistakes will go incognito. Maybe another reason why Jamie chose this song. I wouldn't put it past his smart brain.

And with him by my side...I don't know. It's like the piano isn't as scary anymore. In my periphery, I see people starting to move around, some slow dancing as couples, others dancing with their friends as if they were in a club. Behind us, some people accompany us to sing the harmonies, making the melody fuller, stronger. Some eventually join to scream the opera parts, making everyone laugh, myself included. After that, I realize most of the dread is gone and has been replaced by fun. I play the staccato with a smile on my face, and I see Jamie doing the same.

The sun is slowly starting to set, the sky now a pale lilac reflected on the shiny top of the piano. I can see it coloring Jamie's hair too, as if shining a spotlight on him. With the way he's picking up on my mistakes and making me appear like I'm flawless, he deserves it.

The whole song happens the same way it started. With Jamie and me as a single player. He doesn't need to tell me which parts he wants to play or when I should shift on the seat to give him enough space to climb up a key. It's so natural to play with him.

When we get to the end of the song, where there can only be one player, Jamie looks at me and gives me a small nod, letting me finish it. It's a simple sequence that I could do with my eyes closed but that holds everyone listening in anticipation as they sing the slow lyrics.

The second my foot lets the pedal go after the final note, my fingers loose as I lift my arms off the keyboard, the crowd erupts in cheers, and I'm pretty sure I hear Jesy's "Fuck yes!" somewhere in there. I laugh, looking around and giving a cheesy fake bow.

When I turn to Jamie, I find his gaze on me, warm and bright. Maybe even proud.

"Thank you," I whisper, truly meaning it.

He smiles in return, and I'm pretty sure the way my heart flip-flops isn't a good sign. Not a good sign at all.

CHAPTER 11

Jamie

T HE MUSIC IS FLOWING WELL TODAY.
Ever since we got here, it hasn't been its best, but for
some reason, things are going okay now. I'm not sure how
long I've been in this small booth, but I should probably look at the
time. That's part of what fucked Emma's view of me, after all.

The truth is, I both did and didn't realize I'd been spending
more time practicing this year than ever before. I wasn't stupid;
when I'd get out of the practice rooms and it was already dark out,
and I'd look at my phone and see it was already too late for date
night or even a phone call, I'd realize I'd been there a long time. But
then again, I didn't think I was overdoing it since my pieces weren't
perfect. Every time I heard a mistake, I knew I needed to practice
more, no matter how tired I felt. I didn't think to look at the clock. I
just played until it was perfect, until I felt like what I was doing was
good enough. It never had anything to do with Emma. Or at least, it
didn't entirely have to do with her. My main reasons for playing are
for me, but I do want to be a musician that's worthy of her. I don't
want to grow old together only for her to one day regret not going
for one of the smart, handsome, successful men her parents introduce her to all the time. I can't even count the number of events I've
accompanied Emma to where every guy was even more impressive
than the previous one. She's never made me feel like I was subpar,
but I have eyes. I don't need her to tell me. And while I'll never be
as good-looking or as smart or nice as she is, I can at least hope to be
successful enough that it doesn't matter. It's the one thing I have. Or

at least the one thing I thought I had. Now I see my greatest strength was my pitfall, and what does that leave me with then?

My foot slips from the pedal, my last note cut short, and I let both hands drop to the keys.

Grabbing my phone from my back pocket, I turn it on. I probably shouldn't turn it off anymore, but it's a reflex that's hard to get rid of. I don't want to be distracted when I'm in the zone. When everything is going well and it feels as if the music is literally coming out of me, there's no greater feeling. Or *almost* no greater feeling. I'd take a hug from Emma over this any day.

Still, I can't hide that it is one of my favorite things. When I'm having a good performance day, I could play for hours and never get weary, not only because I want to be the best, but also because playing makes me feel good. Here, with this instrument, I can be whoever I want. Not the boy whose parents own the diner on the wrong side of town, or the awkward guy no one wants to play with at recess, or the lanky, boring guy Emma St. Francis has linked herself with for some unknown reason. I can be me. I can be the person who has a shot at becoming something.

I sigh in relief when I see I've only been here for two hours. Shouldn't have missed anything major. The one thing I did miss was a Facetime call from Mom. I dial her back.

"Jamie!" she squeaks as she answers after only one ring. She's standing in the kitchen of KD's, their restaurant, a pen spiked through her messy dark bun, while Dad is chopping what looks like onions in the back, the T-shirt on his back stamped with the restaurant's logo. His bald head shines from the neons above him. "We miss you, baby," Mom adds.

"Miss you too," I say, thankful there's no one in here to hear my mother call my adult self "baby." Just in case, though, I grab my things and exit the building so we can talk in peace. "How's everything going back home?" *In the present time,* I want to add.

"Oh, it's fine. You know summer's the slow season," she says with a shrug. I try to look for the hint of concern in her voice, but I can't say for sure what she's thinking.

I've never understood why people on vacation stop buying junk food, but the same thing happens every year. During the school period, no one can resist Dad's Quebec poutine recipe, but July and August are slower months.

"Will you be okay, though?" I ask.

"Don't worry, son," Dad shouts from the back as Mom gives me her reassuring smile, which is the dead giveaway there *is* something to worry about.

"We'll be fine," she says. "We let Sammy and Mike go so we could give most of the hours to your brothers and make sure we don't lose too much money, so everything will be good." Sammy and Mike were two of the diner's part-time cooks. As if to prove this, she turns the camera so I see Jonah and Mason in the back of the kitchen, one flipping patties on the grill, the other washing dishes in the large metal sink, both with the same dark, messy hair as my own. The image is weirdly angled, telling me Mom probably spun the phone to film with the front camera instead.

"Simon's at the cash register," she tells me before shouting, "Boys, say hi to Jamie!"

Mason gives me a big wave—he's only fifteen, young enough to still see me as his big-brother-hero—while Jonah, my older brother by two years, only lifts his eyes at the camera. I guess I'll call Simon, my second older brother, another time.

"Enough of this boring talk anyway," Mom says, overly happy as she flips the phone back to her. "How's everything at camp?"

"Uh, it's...full of surprises," I say, the only way I can avoid lying to my mother while keeping everything that's actually going on secret from her.

"Exciting!" she says, not picking up on my weird tone. "And how's Emma?"

I swallow, hoping my face hasn't paled. I haven't told any of them what's going on between us—not that I even know myself—and

I'm not planning on doing it now. If everything goes according to plan, by the end of the summer, we'll be back in the present time, and Emma will be in love with me again. I can't imagine an alternative without feeling like a part of my chest is being ripped away from me, so I'm not even entertaining another option. I'll just have to do whatever I can to make it happen.

"She's good. Working hard."

"I'm sure she is," Mom answers. "You both need to be careful not to overwork yourselves."

"Yeah, Jay, don't overwork yourself playing your little piano," Jonah grumbles in the back.

"Jonah," Mom warns in the tone that used to make me scramble away in fear.

"What? Can't I at least say that it's bullshit that I'm stuck working here while he's out there playing rock star?"

"Hey, language," Dad's heavy voice says.

Mom lets the phone drop on what I assume is the counter while they talk, probably forgetting that I can still hear everything.

"You'll change your attitude right now, boy," Mom hisses.

"It's not fair. He always thinks he's so much better than this place, and you guys act like he's the freaking Messiah."

The next words are muffled, and I'm thankful. Nausea churns in my gut. I play with the tape around the arm of my glasses, all the while wishing I'd never called Mom back.

Finally, the phone gets picked up, and Mom's face reappears. I can't spot anyone else in the room. Her skin is blotched with red.

"Jamie, do you mind if we call you back?"

"No, it's fine. I was about to go practice anyway," I say, the lie coming easily to my lips.

"All right. Well, have fun, baby." Her eyes are duller than before, and this time, I know I'm not imagining the fake smile.

"Thanks. Love you."

I hang up, then let my forehead bang against the outer wall of the music building. This is exactly what I was saying before. When

I'm playing, I don't have to worry about any of this. About whether Jonah's right and what I'm doing is a waste of time. I don't have to *think*. The piano isn't a ball and chain. It's freedom.

I wish I could put in words how I don't think I'm better than any of them, but I also cannot stomach staying at the diner all my life. It's not a question of superiority, it's a question of doing what feels right to me.

"Everything all right?"

I lift my head to find Irène and Alessandro walking in my direction, their hands linked between them. I didn't even hear them approach.

"Just some stuff at home," I say, another lie easily rolling off my tongue. "I'm okay, though. Thanks."

Just then, the door from the music building I exited a minute ago opens, and out comes Emma and some handsome blond guy. She's smiling at something he said, never once spotting me. They talk for a second, too far away for me to hear what they're saying, then she waves goodbye and walks away from him. He continues watching her for a long, long time.

My vision is pure crimson.

I force my fists to relax as I look at this fucker's smug face. I don't remember ever seeing him before. He looks a bit old to be a camp member, but it's possible. Or maybe he's just a visitor.

Knowing Emma doesn't love me anymore is one thing. Seeing her with another man… My chest starts rising and falling fast, too fast, a throbbing sound in my ears as I try but fail to calm myself down. They looked good together. I'm sure this guy wouldn't forget his fucking anniversary because he was stuck on a bar of his stupid music sheet. He probably has a color-coded planner to remember everything and has the means to sweep her off her feet and bring her to fancy places in his fancy car with his fancy clothes. I bet this guy wouldn't feel worried about getting her parents' approval. He'd just instinctively know he could make her proud.

The one thing that allows me to calm down, if only a little, is the thought that this guy could never love her the way I do. He might be better than me in every way, but he'll never win on that part. And I might not have much to give, but it's hers, all of it.

"Should I repeat my question now?" Irène says, reminding me of their presence by my side. "Still all right?" Alessandro shoots her a look like she'd have been better off minding her own business, but he says nothing.

I feel the furthest thing from all right, so I only lift a corner of my lips and stay silent.

"I would not be too worried if I were you," she says.

"Agreed," Alessandro adds, his bushy brows climbing on his forehead. His dark skin wears age spots all over, while short, frizzy gray hair covers his head.

"What are you saying?" I ask, alternating between the two of them.

"We are saying that girl is in love with you, son," Alessandro says, his accent thicker than Irène's, and not the same either. Italian instead of French.

I can't keep the huff from getting out. If only they knew I'm on this impossible quest to make her love me.

"*Il ne s'en rend même pas compte*," Irène tells Alessandro in rapid French.

"English, please?" I say, hating myself for sounding irritated, but I can't help it. Seeing Emma with this man, and then having these two tell me something I wish was true but isn't...it's a little too much.

"We are simply saying not to give up. There is hope," she says.

My jaw falls to the ground. "How—"

"How do we know there is trouble in paradise?" she says as Alessandro chuckles. "Oh, *mon chéri*, we are old, but not *that* old."

"That's not what I was saying, but—"

"We know what it is like to struggle when you have been to-gether for what feels like forever," Alessandro says. "But a little ad-vice? Do not give up. The other side of this is worth it." He dips his head at his wife, and the look they exchange makes me wish I wasn't there. It's too intimate.

But at the same time, it gives me hope. If two people like them, who look so in love it hurts, could have survived hardships, then maybe it's possible for us too.

"Thank you," I tell them both. "I think I needed to hear that."

Irène winks at me, and then the two of them turn and walk away, his arm now wrapped around her waist. He's much taller than she is, but he bends to the side to hold her properly. I'm sure his back hurts, but it's probably worth it to him. I know exactly how that feels.

Folding my legs, I let myself crouch into a seated position against the side of the building as I continue watching them. Even from here, I can hear when he says something that makes her laugh out loud.

They look so perfect together. I've chatted with the two of them individually a couple of times in the past years, and they weren't that much alike. She's fiery while he's all soft words and quiet stares. But when you see them together, you notice how their differences make them an even better fit. Like two pieces of a puzzle.

And soon, one of those two pieces will leave forever.

It doesn't make sense. She's right. They're old, but not *that* old. It doesn't make sense that she would die so suddenly. Something must've happened. Maybe even something avoidable.

My mind blanks, vision clearing.

Wait.

I sit straighter as I repeat that sentence in my head.

Oh.

Oh.

CHAPTER 12

Emma

"I CAN'T BELIEVE I DIDN'T THINK ABOUT IT FIRST," I SAY AS I pace around my cabin, barefoot on the dark linoleum floor. Meanwhile, Jamie's sitting cross-legged, his weight resting on the arms extended behind his back. He came in while I was cleaning the place—Jesy is incredibly messy, and she doesn't mind when I tidy things up—so I don't feel disgusted for him. When I want to avoid doing things I need to be doing, I clean.

"I don't know," he says with a smug grin. "Must be all that country music you're listening to that's getting to your brain."

I narrow my eyes. "Right. Because all those superhero movies you watch are so intellectual."

"I'm just saying, maybe you should consider improving your tastes. Broaden your horizons, you know."

Crossing my arms, I say, "If you and Shania Twain were in a fight, I know who I'd put my money on."

"Yikes. I'll try not to take it personally."

"Whatever helps you sleep at night," I say, fighting the twitch in my cheek.

He shakes his head, laughing. "The level of love you have for that woman is irrational."

"Oh, and you're the picture of rationality?"

He gives one solemn nod.

I tilt my head. "Need I remind you about the rodent movies?"

He laughs, not even bothering to answer. Instead, he says, "You're something else, Emma St. Francis, you know that?"

Something flutters in my stomach. I don't know if it's the sound of my name coming out of his mouth, the flirty and callous tone he used, or the look he sends my way, like he's seen too much. Either way, it needs to be toned down, and fast.

I clap my hands. "Okay, back on track, Montpellier. Irène's death."

"Right," he says, his humor dissipating quickly.

As I said a minute ago, I can't believe I didn't think about it before. Why else would we have been brought back to a time so close to the date she passed away? This has to be it. We need to prevent something that hasn't happened yet. It makes so much sense now that I see it.

"Let's go over what we know about her death," I say, grabbing a notebook and a gel pen from the vanity before I take a seat on the floor in front of Jamie.

"Which is a whole lot of nothing," he says.

"Jamie, this is serious."

"I know it is, but it's the truth."

And when he says it, I realize it's true. We were never told how Irène died, just that she did, and that the family, aka Alessandro, needed privacy in their time of grief. Sure, there'd been rumors floating around, but nothing concrete that we could base ourselves on.

"Do you remember what you were doing when you got the news?" I ask him, putting my notebook down on my lap.

"I was practicing," he says softly. "You came into the booth and told me."

"Right." I remember that moment, feeling my heart break over a woman I barely knew, but felt a deep sense of attachment to somehow. "And I'd learned the news from Dr. Podimow, who came over to the bonfire to tell us that Irène had died but that the camp would continue to run normally." I dig through my memories to find more information we'd acquired at some point in time, but can't find anything. "I can't think of anyone telling us exactly what had happened to her."

"It must've been sudden," Jamie says. "Like a car accident or a fall."

"Why?"

"Well, if she'd been sick, we would've heard about it before, no?"

"Yeah, that's true." I shrug. "That means we need to stop a mysterious event we don't know about from happening sometime in mid-August. Easy peasy."

"Your optimism astounds me."

Despite the messed-up situation, Jamie pulls a grin out of me, which in response makes him smile wider.

Outside the cabin, something creaks loudly, making Jamie and I jump to our feet.

"You think the perfect couple's in there already?" a feminine voice says.

Jamie's eyes flick to mine, full of questions and surprise. My neck warms.

"Let's find out," another voice says. Jesy.

Before they can step inside, I react instinctively and grab Jamie's hand in mine. He throws me a questioning look, but I act as if I haven't noticed. The last thing I need right now is Jesy starting to question how my relationship is going, and before last summer, when everything started going to crap, he and I were inseparable. A part of my body was always meeting one of his, and vice versa. It was like we were two magnets and couldn't stand being separated, even by mere inches. There was something so comforting about his touch, like with him by my side, I'd never have to face anything alone.

And then there was the accident with my hand, and Jamie won performance of the year again at the sophomore showcase, and then we came back home, and I became the last thing on his mind, as if I was nothing more than a second thought.

Ignoring the knot in my throat, I prepare to face Jesy, who says the moment she enters with Julia, "Hey! Didn't know you guys would be in here."

"We were just leaving," I say, and Jamie only nods, silent. His hand twitches in mine as we stand in front of the two girls. I don't let it go, but I wish I could. I don't like touching him like that. Not when it's fake.

"Oh, okay," Jesy says, a new pile of fabric on her knees as Julia pushes her wheelchair inside.

"But let me know if I can help you with any of that when I come back," I tell them, pointing at the material.

"Sure thing, Cinderella," Julia tells me with a smile so fake it actually pains me. It won't help matters if I stay here with them, though, so instead, I wave, then drag Jamie outside, closing the door behind us. The moment we're out of view, he lets go of my hand. Just like he did at the lake, when it felt like my touch had burned him. I try not to let it sting, especially since I'm the one who's suggested we end our relationship, but I can't always explain my feelings. Most of the time, they rule over me.

"Why did she call you Cinderella?" Jamie asks, turning my way.

I force my shoulders back up, then say, "I don't know. She doesn't like me." I scratch my arm. "Must be some kind of jab."

Without speaking it out loud, we both head right, in the direction of the water. The lakeside has always been our spot. I guess some things never change.

"Why don't you say anything?" he asks, gravel crunching under his feet.

I lift a shoulder. "It's whatever, and Jesy's happy with her. I wouldn't want to create trouble for no reason."

Jamie is silent for a while before he says, "I don't like it."

I turn his way.

"She shouldn't speak to you that way. You deserve better."

My gaze drifts to my feet, walking carefully over the pebbles cluttered with twigs and roots. Dusk has fallen, closer to night than day, and in this trail, light barely passes through the thick foliage.

"You do deserve the best. You know that?"

His words feel like a thread yanking me back in time, to that night with the cake in my kitchen two weeks ago, and to all those other moments of loneliness, and it hurts. God, it hurts. I want to let them go, to move on, but I can't. They're buried inside me.

As if reading my thoughts, he adds, "I'm sorry I didn't give you the best."

When I finally look up, I find his dark eyes full of so many emotions, I can't begin to make sense of them.

"Thank you," I say with all the honesty I have. He didn't have to say it. Didn't have to be graceful about it. But what did I expect? This is Jamie—the best person I know.

We continue walking until we get to our small clearing in the forest where a small wooden bench rests, offering a glorious view of Moosehead Lake reflecting the newly there moon, almost full. We both sit down, quietly enjoying the view for a minute.

"This is the weirdest summer I've ever had," I say after a beat.

"Tell me about it."

I don't feel equipped to figure out what I want to do with my life, let alone save a life. At least Jamie has his own life under control.

Something vibrates in my pocket. I pull out my phone, and when I see the name on there, my eyes widen. My dad rarely texts or calls. Something like hope starts simmering in my chest, but when I read the message, the feeling disappears in a blink, and I have to hold in my groan.

> **Dad: I spoke to Dr. Podimow today. Remember, we went to NAMA together? And she told me your rehearsals weren't going as well as planned. What's going on?**

Even though he's being subtle about it, I know Jamie's read the text message alongside me. It's not like I could hide it forever anyway.

"Apparently, even my current self sucks," I say with an awkward laugh. It's kind of terrifying to know there are two of me out in the world, living and breathing concurrently, only in different times. And what's worse is, neither one of us is able to be a good version of Emma. There doesn't exist a universe, whether in the present or in the past, where I'm not a disappointment.

"Do you think your hand's the problem?" Jamie asks, his voice so low it stays confined within our small corner of the world. "Because if it is, when we get back, I could help you. Maybe we could—"

"Jamie, can we not?" I push the meat of my palms into my eyes, wanting all of this to disappear for now. "Can we not think about the piano for now? Just give me five minutes."

Instantly, I feel bad for snapping at him. It's not his fault my playing's been getting worse, and it's not his fault I'm tired of thinking about it. He's offered to help. Has been offering for a year, actually.

"I'm sorry," I say softly, putting my phone back in my pocket without an answer to my father. "This isn't on you."

He still doesn't say anything, but he scoots closer on the bench. Not close enough that we're touching, but still near enough that I feel his body heat, and it's reassuring. Once again, he's here, and poof, I don't feel so lonely.

I don't remember the first time I saw Jamie, but I have a clear picture in my head of the moment I decided I wanted to know him, this guy who was always by himself but somehow never looked alone. There was something so intriguing about him, when he locked himself in the windowed booth for the whole break period. Maybe it was the way he played, or maybe it was the way he did not seem to care one bit that he was alone. He had his piano, and he didn't need anything else. The obvious passion he had for it was enough. And suddenly, as my friends were talking over sandwiches and crunching celery, I looked at him and thought, *I want him to be this passionate about me.* I craved having someone who would treat me with the reverence he gave his piano. Someone who would love me without limit, and who I could love without limit in return. So during that lunch break, I left our soundproof room without a word and made my way to Jamie's. I remember watching him for five, maybe ten, minutes, entranced, before I knocked and walked inside.

At first, he watched me with wide eyes. I thought maybe he hadn't seen me before and was wondering who the heck I was. I must've looked creepy, but I pushed through my discomfort.

"Hey. I'm Emma," I said.

"J-Jamie," he answered.

Without asking, I took a seat next to him on his piano bench and looked at the piece he was playing. One of my favorite of Bach's Sonatas. I'd been practicing it over the summer. It made me smile.

"You mind if I stay here?" I asked.

He shook his head, still wide-eyed, and once that hour-long break was over, I knew I'd found my new best friend, who then became my first boyfriend, who then became my everything.

And now here he is, seven years later, about three feet taller and with a sharper jaw and a better haircut, but still the same passionate kid I met at fourteen.

Jamie's head tilts toward me, still facing the water. Seagulls screech from the beach to our left, where kids are probably making a fire as we speak. The water laps the shore in soft strokes. Otherwise, we're in complete silence.

Until from one moment to the next, we're not.

A soft violin melody envelops us, coming from god knows where. Probably a student practicing for their next Sunday Jam performance. And as if fate is playing a weird trick on us, the piece they're playing is none other than that sonata I watched Jamie play that first day in the booth we shared.

I snort internally. Good one, universe.

I'm not sure whether Jamie realizes it, but all of a sudden, he's on his feet, a hand extended my way, his torso bent so he can reach me.

"What?" I ask.

"Come on." He curls his fingers once, twice. "Let's dance."

"To that music?" I ask, pointing behind me.

He shrugs. "There has to be some advantage to living in a semi-constant flash mob for two months, no?"

I eye him for another second, and this time, a smirk pulls one side of his mouth up, as if he knows I'm starting to mess with him with my silence.

"Please, Emmaline, will you do me the honor of dancing with me?"

I start grinning too. I can't remember the last time we danced together. Maybe I should be worried about what this means for us, but for now, I can only feel my increasing heart rate and the urge to get closer to Jamie's warmth. I want it. Too much to think about the consequences.

"Well, when you ask like that…" I say, then grab his hand.

A current runs from the tips of my fingers to the lower end of my body. It's nothing like how I grabbed his hand in the cabin earlier today. This feels real—maybe a little too much so.

Slowly, he lifts my left hand so it rests on his shoulder, then takes my right one in his. Meanwhile, his other hand rests on my hip, fingers dangerously close to my panty line. I'm hot all over.

And then we start dancing.

At first, our bodies are separated by a wide space, neither one of us willing to take that last step, but the more we sway to the melody of the talented violinist, the smaller that gap seems to get. Maybe it's the hand on my hip, or maybe it's the inner magnets I was mentioning, but before I know it, my cheek is resting on his chest, so warm it makes me close my eyes. Under my ear, his heartbeat thunders. I'm glad to know I'm not alone.

Crickets chirp in the moonlight and fireflies twinkle through the darkness, the moment almost ethereal. Here, we don't feel like the Jamie and Emma who've been struggling, the ones who don't remember how to be together, no matter how much love there is between us. It's simple, in this alternate world of touches and stolen glances.

Eventually, the musician stops playing, but our dancing continues still. Jamie's chin is now leaning on the top of my head, the soft scent of his shampoo and laundry detergent wrapping me up.

I never want to move away.

My feelings are so contradictory, which is probably what makes them so hard to express. I might know that we don't work, but when I think that, after this summer, a moment like this one might never happen again, I want to weep.

There is nothing fake about this. Not the way his arm is now wrapped around my lower back, long fingers splayed wide over me, not the hum he sometimes lets out when I shift against him, and not the absolute comfort I'm feeling.

I breathe in and try to stay grounded to the here and now. I focus on the rustle of the leaves in the wind and the lapping of the water against the shore. I think of the humidity of the air clinging to my skin and the softness of Jamie's T-shirt under my cheek.

And despite it all, I can't help my mind from wandering.

"Jamie?" My voice is soft, but it still feels loud in contrast with the silence we've been basking in.

"Yes?"

"I'm scared."

He doesn't question what I mean by that, maybe because even he knows I'm not sure what the answer would be. Maybe he knows I'm thinking about what this summer means, and how we're stuck in the past, and how I don't know what we'll do about Irène's mysterious death. Maybe he knows I wish we could stay in this moment forever, but I don't know how to make us work, and I'm not sure if there even *is* an us anymore.

There is so much to be scared about, and he understands all of it without my saying a word.

No question leaves his mouth. Instead, he only squeezes me harder.

As if he knows it's all I need.

CHAPTER 13

Emma

I WANT TO GAUGE MY EYES OUT.

Closing my computer, I press my palms against my forehead. How can someone's death remain such a mystery after an entire year?

I haven't been able to find a single piece of information online about the circumstances surrounding Irène's death. Not one. I was lucky enough that the internet on my phone was still in present time to be able to see everything that's been posted in the past year, but still, nothing has come up. The only articles I found mentioned the death of Irène Sancerre, ballerina extraordinaire in the 1960s and owner of the prestigious Allegro Camp for Gifted Artists. If we were back in the present, I could ask people like Jesy or Julia if they'd heard anything else, but as it is, they don't even know she's dead.

I need Jamie. Maybe he'll have been luckier than me in his research, or maybe he'll even have found a better solution. Grabbing my umbrella, I step outside the cabin.

After our…*moment* two days ago, we split up to find more information about what led to Irène's death, and I've waited as long as I could before getting back to him. Plus, I appreciated the excuse it gave me. I needed space. What occurred at the lakeside shouldn't happen. If it did, it would mean falling back into his arms without any certainty that things would change in the future, and I can't. No matter how much I wish I could stay with him forever, a life like last year wouldn't be healthy, and by that, I mean for the both of us. I see how, because of the disappointment and sadness

I felt, I was probably a terrible girlfriend when we *were* together, and I care about him too much to not wish something different for him. It doesn't matter that thinking about him with someone else one day makes me want to curl up in a ball and slowly wither away. He deserves the best, even if I'm not the one giving it to him.

So distance was key.

I step into the music building after a brisk walk through camp, faint sounds of violins, cellos, and drums reaching me as soon as the door closes behind me. The AC is turned on to the max, and the difference from the thick humidity outside makes goosebumps appear all over my arms.

Most of the individual booths are occupied, which makes sense. Tuesday afternoons are always free time so we can do whatever we want that isn't music related, but as you would expect at an art camp, people cannot stay far from their instruments for too long.

Case in point: Jamie practicing in the windowed room to the far right.

I step closer to him, unable to stay away even if I wanted to. It's almost as if light shines out of him as he plays. Day-to-day Jamie is attractive as it is, but piano-playing Jamie? That's as close to a supernova as I'll ever come.

I near the door as much as is physically possible, and even then, he doesn't notice me. It's always been that way. When it's him and his piano, the world could be on fire and he wouldn't have a clue.

This close, I can hear the soft notes of his piece, even through the insulated door. I recognize it immediately. Chopin's *Op. 10, No. 1 in C Major*. One of my favorites to see Jamie play. The *étude* is also called *Waterfall*. When you listen to it, it makes sense. The notes come out as smoothly as if falling from a cliff and into a wide basin of water, as long as the pianist knows how to play it. And boy does Jamie know.

Watching Jamie play is maybe my favorite thing to do on

earth, which probably makes me sound like a walking contradiction, but I can't help it. Standing here, watching the notes slip out of his fingers like running water, I can almost forgive how he prioritized this over everything else. Because, in some way, when you play that well, you shouldn't be doing anything else. I love the way my mother and father play, but in my mind, they don't even come close to Jamie.

He's so beautiful when he's like this. His tall and slim upper body is bent all over the keyboard, as if he wants to get as close to the instrument as he can, almost wishing he could live inside of it and be a part of its being. His eyes are closed, long lashes fanning across his sharp cheekbones, and I know without talking to him that he's feeling the music from within. His fingers move effortlessly, the tell of a good pianist. This is a hard piece to play, but he doesn't show it. His technique and passion do all the hard work.

The way his hands move is so entrancing, I find myself getting lost in space. I just stare and stare, thinking back to a time when those hands were on me, finding the exact spot that made me moan or gasp. I know how the tips of those fingers feel, how those parted lips taste, how that long neck stretches back when he climaxes.

I shake my head. I can't be thinking about that now.

My focus returns to his playing, and I try to keep all the dirty thoughts away. It works...mostly.

Jamie reaches the end of the song, so much love and reverence poured through the bars.

I can't help it. The moment the last note resonates through the booth, I clap for him.

Jamie's eyes snap open, and when they land on me, they widen. Color rises to his cheeks, something I rarely see. In a jerky motion, he gets up, making the seat fall backward. He almost trips over his feet as he gets to the door and opens it.

"Did I miss something?" he asks.

"Oh, no. No, sorry," I mumble, blinking. "I just wanted to talk. No rush."

"I'm done," he says with a fast shake of his head. He returns to pick up his music sheets, which I know for a fact he doesn't need, and in his hurry, drops them all to the floor. I grin, then bend down and help him pick them up.

And of course, when Jamie bends down, he doesn't realize the huge proportions of his body and his head knocks straight into mine, the way it has one too many times.

"Ow!" we both shout at the same time, but while he remains upright, I fall on my butt from my crouched position.

"Oh my god, I'm so sorry. You okay?" he asks, scurrying my way.

"Yep." I run a hand over my forehead, where I know a bump will arise later today. I snort. "You really *are* hardheaded."

His lips twitch. "I could say the same about you." His fingers dig through his brown strands, rubbing at a spot on his temple. "Dare I say, even more?"

"I need some armor to protect myself from you."

"Won't keep me away, trust me."

My grin stays in place even though we seem to be getting awfully close to the flirting territory, which is a no-go.

He's still rubbing his head, so I lean closer, climbing on my tiptoes to inspect him. "Are you really okay, though?" Without thinking, I let my hand make its way to his scalp, fingers teasing his hair before touching the small bump there, probably a mirror image of mine.

"Y-yeah," Jamie says, statue still.

I part his hair around the spot, but when I don't find any blood or wound, I step down.

"You'll survive," I determine as I remove my hand. While doing so, I realize how long his hair has gotten, some of the silky curls now forming true curlicues. Grabbing one between my thumb and index finger, I say, "We should probably cut this before your sister gets here. It was much shorter last year."

"Uh." He gulps audibly. "Yeah, you're probably right."

"Probably?" I say, an eyebrow up.

"I'm sorry, *definitely* right."

Molly is arriving in three days and will stay for a few weeks. She's probably the sibling of Jamie's we're both the closest to, and while lying to her about our current relationship will be challenging, I'm excited to see someone from our external world again. It's only been two weeks, and I already feel homesick. Molly has always treated me like a big sister, and I know how much she loves Jamie and me together. I'll need to up my acting game with her around, though, because she knows us much better than the rest of the campers, and she's smart enough to tell when something isn't right.

"Want me to cut it?" I ask, taking a step back and letting go of the strand.

"Uh..." He messes with his hair. "Yeah, sure." I don't know if that's a hint of self-consciousness I hear in his voice, but I have to admit it's cute.

"All right, come on."

* * *

"You should probably take off your shirt."

"I'm sorry?" Jamie asks, lifting his eyes from the hair salon chair I made up for him, which is basically his vanity seat covered with a plastic bag.

"Your shirt." I scratch my neck. "You know, because I don't have a cape."

"Oh. Right."

He doesn't move.

"You don't have to," I say in a hurry. "Whatever's best. I just didn't want you to be itchy with all the hair and—"

"No, no, you're right," he interrupts, and why in the world are we being so awkward?

Jamie starts removing his T-shirt, and suddenly, the stain on the ceiling above the bunks becomes fascinating. Once he's done and has taken his seat, I look down, but focus on his hair and not on the stretch of skin on full display in front of me—and certainly not on the kind of thoughts I had while watching him play.

I drag my fingers through his hair, which has been humidified by the rain outside. "You trust me?"

"As long as you promise not to make me look like that actor you like in the period movie you always watch, then yes."

I gasp. "Sir George Knightley has a great 'do for his period, thank you very much."

"Sure, if you have a kink for sideburns."

"What makes you think I don't?"

"I thought I knew all your kinks by now," he says, and it takes all the strength I own not to react. It's not like what he's saying isn't the truth anyway. Jamie and I have learned about sex together. I know what he likes, and he knows what I like, because we discovered it all at the same time.

"I'm full of surprises," I whisper as I pick up the pair of scissors I found in the painting and sculpture building. I know I'm again walking into the flirting zone, but it's like I can't help myself. I'm Alice in Wonderland, and that familiar closeness is the delicious-looking magic cake.

My belly is flush with his naked shoulders as I grab a strand and start cutting.

It's not the first time we've done this. In the past years, Jamie would often forget to get his hair cut because he'd be too busy with school, work, and piano, so I would end up doing it for him, sometimes *while* he was playing. My parents offered multiple times to grant him a loan for his studies and for camp so he wouldn't have to work at the restaurant during the year, but he wouldn't have it, and I can't blame him. He wants to make his own way. It's admirable. Plus, his parents needed the help.

The cabin is silent as I cut, the snips of the scissors loud in the space between us. Jamie's breaths are deep and long, and I really, really need to stop my gaze from dropping down his chest.

"So," I say after clearing my throat, "where's Jeremiah today?" His cabin is noticeably empty, just the two of us in this space that is usually quite vast but which feels incredibly tiny at the moment.

"He went home for the day. See his parents, I think."

"Oh." I cut another strand, which falls over his shoulders. "Are you envious?"

"Yeah," he says, looking my way through the mirror in front of us. "I wish I could go help for the day. See them."

"I'm sure they're happy you're taking the time for yourself."

"That's if Future Me is also spending the summer at camp."

"Right," I say, confusing myself with the timelines again. "That lucky prick, eh?"

"Yup." Jamie smirks before he adds, "Although I don't think he should do it."

"Do what?"

"Stay. Not go and help."

"Why?"

I cut a strand a little too short, letting out an "oops." Jamie's gaze flies to mine, but I ignore it. A professional through and through. When he gives up and puts his guard down, he explains, "Jonah thinks I'm an asshole for being here."

My face pulls into a frown despite myself. "No he doesn't."

"Yeah, he does. He practically said so on the phone yesterday."

Heat floods my chest, and not the good kind. Jaw tight, I say, "He's the asshole for saying that. Plus, I haven't forgotten that time I found him naked on the couch after he got blackout drunk." I look up in the mirror, finding his gaze. "I'd be happy to become the asshole and remind him if need be."

"Did you actually say the word 'asshole'? Twice?"

"So what if I did?"

His lips curl into a grin before he shakes his head.

"I stand by what I said," I say.

"Oh, I know you do."

I smile quickly, rubbing his head to make sure I haven't forgotten any part on his right. "It might be hard for them to realize why you're here, but it doesn't matter. You know. That's what matters."

"Yeah, I guess," he says, slumping in his chair. I pull him by the underarms so he's sitting straighter. "Sorry," he says.

"If I mess up and give you a cheap Halloween wig haircut because you can't sit up straight, I can't be held liable."

"Wait, what?" he says, looking in the mirror, alarmed.

"Calm down. It was a warning."

"Mm-hmm." He eyes me suspiciously before he visibly relaxes and asks, "What about you? Envious you can't go back home?"

"Nope," I say, and leave it at that. I don't want to think about my father's pressuring texts—which I ended up regretting answering—or my mother's inquiries over the phone. I certainly don't want to think about how empty their house always feels, even when they're there. Visiting them, even if I could and they weren't on tour, would make me feel more alone than staying here, even in an alternate timeline.

Satisfied with the side of his head I've completed, I move to the next, dragging my finger in the strands to evaluate the length before I resume my cutting. With this angle, I have to move closer to him to get it right. My face is close enough to his upper body that I can notice when his neck muscles strain.

Jamie inhales sharply. "Anyway. Did you find anything interesting?"

"About what?" I ask, standing straighter.

"Irène?"

Oh, right. The reason why I went to see him. I don't know how it slipped my mind. I clear my throat. "Nothing at all. You?"

"Jack shit."

And there goes my hope of him having found a miracle solution.

I get lost in my thoughts as I continue cutting, trying to find the missing piece of the puzzle without any success. Once I'm done with the top strands, I brush the cut hair off Jamie's neck and shoulders. The second my skin comes into contact with his, he jumps.

"Sorry," I say, removing my hands. "My hands are cold, I know." I rub them together.

He pauses before he says, "Right." His tongue darts out to wet his lips before he says, "But go ahead."

"Sure?"

He nods.

Without meeting his eyes, I bring my hands back up, then wipe the strands off his skin. It's so soft. It's been a while since I've touched him just for the sake of it. My fingers linger there as I drag my pink-painted nails across his back, ever so slowly. My chest fills with air as I repeat the movement, but when I spot the shivers across his skin, I realize what I'm doing and remove my hands.

What am I even doing?

"All done," I say in a low voice.

"T-thanks."

I return to my cutting, focused once more on not staring at him. After a minute of silence, Jamie says, "There's probably only one thing left to do."

I look up.

"About Irène, I mean."

"Oh," I say, pulling a long strand between my index and middle finger. "What's that?"

As I let go of the cut hair and grab the next part, I notice Jamie's fingers strumming against his thigh, and a pang of longing hits me square in the chest at the sight. Jamie has always practiced his pieces on any surface he could find, and oftentimes in the past, that surface was me. We would be lying in bed after making love or while watching a movie and he'd play on my belly, on my thighs. Sometimes I'd correct him when I noticed a mistake, and sometimes I'd just enjoy the feel of his fingers on my skin. It felt like being an artist's canvas.

I can't remember the last time he did it.

"We'll need to talk to Irène directly," he says, bringing me out of my reverie.

"And how do you suggest doing that? 'Hey, Irène, we're from the future, and you're going to die, so please don't'?"

"Yes, Emma, exactly that." He gives me a comical applause.

"Careful, Montpellier. Remember who holds the scissors here."

"Sorry, ma'am."

I snicker.

"Maybe she does have a condition we never knew about, and if there's something we could do to prevent it from killing her, then we need to know about it," Jamie says.

Moving on to the front of his head, I have to lean over Jamie because of the way he's seated, which I'm starting to see is not ideal. Once I'm settled, I get to work on the last section of hair and only realize I've basically pressed my chest to his face when he gulps air as if he hasn't breathed for an entire minute and mutters under his breath something like, "*Jesus,*" before he says louder, "I'm really trying to have a PG conversation here, Emma, but you're making it very fucking difficult."

"Oh," I say, taking two steps back. "I'm sorry."

"I wasn't complaining," he says, Adam's apple bobbing. "Just explaining so you don't think I'm some kind of pervert."

I don't get what he's saying until I flick my eyes down and see he's straining against the zipper of his jeans.

It's my turn to swallow forcefully.

Without a word, I return to my cutting, this time forcing as much space as I can between our two bodies. I don't know what he's thinking, and I'd rather not. Jamie doesn't say another word after that, but the tension between us is thicker than ice. Is he thinking about my body? About how it felt to be pressed together, his pelvis against mine, his mouth on my breasts, his tongue on my skin? Is he remembering all the times we brought each other to places I didn't even know existed?

My god, it's hot in here. And I *really* need to stop my mind from going there.

I hurry through the last of the haircut, realizing only once it's done that it's not exactly symmetrical, and it's for sure the worst one I've ever given him, but it's done! As if I've just deactivated a bomb, I step back another three steps and say with too much force, "You're good to go!"

He eyes me warily, but I see something other than doubt in his eyes. Something really close to lust. His pupils are dilated, undiscernible from the dark irises. I break the contact first.

After a long moment, in all his long-limbed sexiness, Jamie gets up to look at himself better in the mirror, and after a millisecond-long glance, he turns to me and says, "Best haircut of my life."

CHAPTER 14

Emma

M Y FIST IS UNSTEADY AS I KNOCK ON THE MAIN OFFICE'S
door.

After talking about it last night, Jamie and I
weren't able to come up with any good ideas on how to approach
Irène about the subject of her nearing death, so I decided I'd
wing it this morning. But now that we *are* this morning, I feel like
jumping back to yesterday to tell myself to stop being stupid and
prepare. Maybe I could've avoided this whole nausea-and-stom-
ach-cramps thing.

Too late. Before I can steel myself for what's to come, the office door opens, showing a radiant Irène dressed in a soft linen
blouse and black cigarette pants. Again, I have to remind myself
that she's in her eighties and not late sixties, with her stylish long
bob and straight posture.

"Emma, *chérie*, come in!" she says, not seeming startled at
all to see me here. We've seen each other more this summer than
ever before, yet she's not fazed by it, or at least she doesn't show
it. Maybe she's like that with all campers, acting like they were expected when she has no idea who they are. This camp has become
popular for a reason, and she's a big part of it.

"I'm sorry to bother you again," I say as she indicates for me
to sit in the chair I used the last time.

"Oh, nonsense. It is always nice to see fresh faces in the office." She makes her way to the back of the office, facing away from
me. "Can I offer you anything? Coffee? Tea?"

"Tea would be great, thank you."

She boils water and proceeds to pour it into two cups, then brings one to me before she takes a seat facing mine, still on her bouncing ball.

"So," I say after taking a burning sip of Earl Grey. "I wanted to discuss something with you, but it will sound weird, and I apologize in advance for it."

"Weirder than asking about the camp's success?"

I wince internally. "Yes, even weirder than that."

She grins. "You go right ahead."

All right. Moment of truth.

I can't believe I'm doing this. What would people think if they heard? I'd pass for a psycho, probably.

"Again, this might sound strange, but is there a possibility that you might have any... health issues?" God, it sounds even worse out loud.

Her face blanches, and while she didn't expect my question about the state of Allegro, I know this is much different. She puts her cup of tea down before intertwining her fingers together. "I am not sure I understand what you mean." Her French accent is thicker than usual.

"I..." The air feels hot in the office, and I can feel sweat forming under my arms. Repositioning myself on my chair, I begin again. "There's no way I can explain this without sounding out of my mind, but ever since the beginning of the summer, I've had a... *feeling* that something might happen to the camp, or you."

"This is..." Irène starts, but stops midsentence, mouth twitching to the side.

"Crazy, I know. But I can't shake this feeling, and I wanted to make sure everything was okay."

Her head sluggishly bobs up and down. "And because I told you the camp was doing great, you assumed that 'feeling,'" she says with finger quotes, "was about me."

"Precisely."

We both remain silent for at least a minute, and while I study her as best I can, I can't figure out what she's thinking. If someone had come to me to tell me they had a feeling something bad would happen to me, I'd call them mad, then be frightened that what they'd said was true.

And now here I am, telling all of this to an elderly woman. In great shape, but elderly nonetheless.

I'm a horrible person.

I bring my thumbnail to my mouth, but realize what I'm doing just in time and put my hand back in my lap.

After what feels like an eternity, Irène leans forward, her lips curling into a meager smile. "There is nothing about me you need to worry about, *ma chérie.*"

I narrow my eyes slightly. "I'm not sure whether that is an actual answer or not."

"For you, child, it is."

Another cryptic answer.

Despite her words of reassurance, I feel even warier than before. There's something I'm missing, that much is clear. Why else would she answer that way?

"Irène—can I call you Irène?"

She snickers. "It *is* my name."

"Right." I smile. "Irène, I'm not coming to you in need of being reassured. This feeling, it's very strong, and if there's anything I could do to avoid something happening, I'd rather know it."

"You can rest easy. I will be all right."

I'm not sure that's much better.

In a swift movement that is unlike her, Irène climbs to her feet and turns her back to me, shuffling through papers on her desk. "Is there anything else I can help you with?"

"No, th-that's it," I answer softly.

"Great." Looking over her shoulder, she throws me a smile. "Have a good day, dear."

A dismissal if I've ever heard one.

"You too," I say as I leave the office, the warmth I felt a few minutes before replaced by a cold draft, making me shiver. I've lived through a lot of strange moments this summer, but that one was near the top of the list.

I need Jamie's opinion on this. Maybe he'll know just what to do. A girl can hope.

I make my way through the administration building, but once I'm halfway through the airy hall, a deep but faint voice calls behind me, "Ms. St. Francis."

I turn to find Alessandro standing behind a door that seems to lead to a…closet?

"Hi," I say to him once I'm close enough. "And please, call me Emma."

"Emma." He smiles, although it seems strained. "Would you have a minute to talk?"

I glance behind him. "In there?"

He nods.

I don't know why I keep getting surprised about the turns this summer is taking. Last year, I would've been weirded out, but now, I barely flinch as I walk inside the closet with an eighty-something man with whom I've barely spoken in my life. I'm not sure whether I should laugh or cry about what my life has become.

The door closes behind me, and in the musky darkness, I say, "Hm. Cozy."

To my right comes the sound of rustling, and then a light bulb is turned on. I look around, spotting cleaning supplies and rolls of toilet paper. If I'd had to guess who I'd one day get into a closet with, I would've bet on Jamie before Alessandro.

Irène's husband is dressed in khakis and a black vest over a dress shirt, the collar ironed and sharp. His thin hair is combed to one side, and the scent of his spicy cologne fills the room.

"I'm sorry to bring you here," he says with his thick European accent, "but I needed to speak with you in private."

"All right," I say, only half wary.

He clamps his hands together to stop his fingers from fidgeting. "I heard you talking to Irène."

I suck air through my teeth.

"She would be very angry if she knew I was doing this, so please, if you do not mind, keep this for yourself."

I nod, staying silent. I don't want to make him second-guess what he's doing here, and somehow, I know this will be important.

He swallows, the sound loud in the cramped space.

"Irène is…not well."

When he doesn't continue, I say, "'Not well' how?"

"She has had health issues for a while, but it has sadly been getting worse recently. She is more tired than usual, but she does not want to rest and take it easy this summer."

I ball my hands into fists in order not to bring my nails to my teeth.

"How serious are we talking about here?"

His lips quiver for a moment, and he needs to take in a deep breath before saying, "It is quite serious, but it is also very variable and unpredictable."

So she *did* have something. She still might have died from something else, but this is the best lead we've received since getting here, so we need to look into it as much as we can.

Even though it's not good news, I can't wait to tell Jamie. I had a similar feeling in eleventh grade when we were working on a science project—building a projectile, or something like that—and I'd just found the missing piece to get to the right result. I'd had this bubbly feeling in my chest at finally getting my answer, and the first thing I felt like doing was grabbing my phone and dialing him. His excitement had matched mine, just like I know it will now.

Here, in this world, Irène is not dead yet, and there might be a way for us to help her. To avoid it, even.

Alessandro's hands are still clamped together, but they're

visibly shaking. I give them a light touch and say, "I'm really sorry to hear that."

"Thank you."

When he doesn't speak, I shift on my feet. "I'm still a little unclear about why you wanted to tell me this, though." Not that I'm complaining, far from it, but why me? Why now?

"Because I was hoping you could help me."

"In what way?"

"She needs to slow down. Her doctor has said it, and I have been telling her every single day, but she is stubborn as a mule and will not listen to me."

"And you think she will listen to me?" I release an awkward chuckle. "I'm sorry if you got the wrong impression, but we're not that close. I don't think she would want to hear it from me any more than she would from you."

For the first time today, he grins. "She is right. You two are alike."

"Alike?"

"Yes. Irène sees her younger self in you, and I have to admit, I see it now."

"I don't..." I shake my head. Irène is a force of nature. She became the first ballerina over five foot five to make it into the Paris Ballet Academy in the sixties, traveled the world to give conferences to young dancers, and opened what has become the largest artistic retreat for young adults in America. She is what every artist aspires to become. An inspiration for everyone. There is nothing similar between us. Even if I somehow overcame all my difficulties with the piano, I could never be a fraction of the icon she has become.

"It's quite a compliment," he says, as if I didn't know that. "She's the best woman I know."

"Oh, I know, and I can believe that."

Alessandro's expression falls, and for a second, I can see myself being in his shoes, my love struggling while I can't do a thing about it. In this vision, the other person is Jamie, and while we're not really together anymore, the thought is deeply, crushingly painful. I, too, would do whatever I could. More than that.

"So? You will help me then?" he asks.

"I wish I could, but I'm not sure I'll be able to."

"Just try? Please?" he says, and there's so much hope in his voice, I know there's no way I could say no even if I wanted to.

With a hand on the paper-thin skin of his forearm, I say, "I'll do my best."

CHAPTER 15

Emma

WHERE IN THE WORLD IS HE?
She's going to be here any minute, and as it is, I'll be the only person here to welcome her. The one she doesn't really want.

Molly loves to appear brave—something I admire about her, because I definitely wasn't as strong as her when I was twelve years old—but I know she found it hard being here last summer. She's used to waking up and having at least four people in the house to wish her a good morning and ask her how she slept. Here, sure, she's surrounded by people at all times, but there's no mom or dad to comfort her if she's having a bad day. This is an artist's retreat, not a regular summer camp, and even the shorter stays for young kids are heavily learning oriented. Last year, every time I would see her, her eyes would be red rimmed and she would look lost. I want this repeat summer to be different so she can keep better memories of this place, just like the ones Jamie and I have after all our years here, but for that, it would be good to have actual family with her more often throughout her stay.

I look down at my phone again. Twenty minutes late.

Just as I put my phone back in my pocket, a yellow bus appears down the gravel road, and all my hope of Jamie being there for Molly's arrival goes down the drain.

The second the bus comes to a halt before me, I force a confident, and hopefully warm, smile on my lips. Kids start coming down the short stairs, and eventually, a tall girl with red hair and wary eyes is there. Her hands are gripped tightly around her backpack's straps as she looks left and right, and when her gaze lands on me, I spot the drop of her shoulders and the relief on her face.

"Emma!" she says before jogging to my open arms.

"Hey, Mol." I hug her tight like I wished my mom would have when I was her age. "I'm so happy to see you. How was the drive?"

"Long," she says. I try to step away, but she holds on, so I hug her a little longer.

When she finally moves away, she goes back to looking left, right, then over my shoulder. "Is Jamie here?" she asks.

My heart breaks in half. How many times was I that little girl, looking for my parents during my debate competitions or school talent shows? More often than not, I'd be searching for nothing. They were mostly only there when it was piano related, and even then, they were often absent due to some concert or interview outside of the country. When I graduated salutatorian of my class in high school, I was called forward during the ceremony, and while there were thousands of people in the room clapping for me, the only thing I could focus on was finding their faces, only to not see them anywhere. Mr. and Mrs. Montpellier cheered extra loud for me, which eased the pain, but only a little. I later learned they'd been kept up during a photo shoot for some big magazine and couldn't leave. Mom felt terrible about it, and I told her it was fine, but deep down, it hurt me more than I cared to admit.

"He's..." What am I even supposed to say? That he forgot his sister? Tucking a red strand of hair back in her ponytail, I say, "He's been held back in some group lesson that's running a little longer than usual, but he told me to tell you he'd find you as soon as he can." The lie rolls easily off my tongue, and I don't even feel bad about it. If I can avoid breaking her heart, it's worth it.

"Oh," she says. "Okay."

Behind her, the bus leaves, and the group of kids who just hopped off form a circle around a young singer I've seen around camp a few times. She seems to be telling them where they need to go next.

"Come on," I tell Molly as I squeeze her shoulder. "Go with the group. We'll find you later, 'kay?"

She nods, then gives me one last quick hug before joining the other kids. Once I see she's okay, I turn and head toward the one place I know I'll find him.

* * *

"What do you think you're doing?"

Jamie's head jerks up, false notes ruining the song he was playing a second ago. His dark hair is all over the place, as if he's run his hands through it innumerable times. At least it's shorter now. His glasses have been tucked in his back pocket, a new piece of tape around them.

"What—" he starts.

"Your sister arriving at Allegro today?" I say, fuming so much I'm surprised no fire is coming out of my nostrils. "How many times did I tell you it was this morning?" The last time was just last night, after I told him what I'd learned from my discussion with Alessandro.

"Yeah, I know that, but..." He lifts his left hand to take a look at his watch. "Fuck."

"Fuck is right."

He drags two hands down his face. "Emma, I'm sorry, I got lost in my practice and—"

"I don't want your apologies. Save them for your little sister, who was expecting her big brother to welcome her to a new camp."

"Shit," he says, getting up from the bench. Meanwhile, I stand in the corner of the booth, arms crossed. I'd like to think the main emotion I'm feeling is anger, but it's not.

What it is is disappointment.

No matter how much I tried not to, I'd started to get my hopes up in the past weeks. The man I'd started to see was so different from the one who was by my side all year long. I saw the way he'd started prioritizing things other than music. Spending time with me again, and not only out of obligation. Having lunch with Jeremiah in the cafeteria sometimes, laughing and caring about what his friend had to say. Joining activities with other campers. I didn't want to become hopeful again, but it happened, whether I wanted it to or not. Maybe, just maybe, he and I could work again one day. Maybe breaking up wasn't the solution, because he had understood what I'd meant when I said I couldn't stand coming in last anymore.

But today just proved I was right to be wary. Music will always be his first, second, and third priority. If practicing for the showcase made him forget his own sister, what will it be like when we return to the real world and he starts studying at NAMA? I'll be back where I was, waiting for him at a restaurant, only to end up ordering alone because my long-time boyfriend forgot and was a no-show. Maybe even worse. And I'll have to live through that hurt again.

I can't. I just can't. I never needed to be his moon and stars, but I needed something. I needed him to remember I existed, even just from time to time.

And while feeling abandoned by Jamie was one thing, it was nothing compared to how it felt to be forgotten by my own family.

"She was looking for you, you know. Because you'd promised to be there."

"I lost track of time," he says as if that's an excuse.

"Well, you should've found a way not to." Everything in me is tight, a bowstring ready to be released. I hate this feeling. I turn to leave, but before I can touch the doorknob, I spin around and say, "Do you know how humiliating it is to wait for someone who clearly forgot about what he promised you? How belittling?"

He swallows. "We're not talking about my sister anymore, are we?"

"If the shoe fits."

He apologizes again. "I'll do better next time."

I let out a humorless laugh. "How many times do you think I've tried convincing myself of that exact same thing?" My voice has gotten louder. I clear my throat. It's not worth getting emotional about it anymore. Enough. I shake my head. "It doesn't matter anyway. We're not together, so that won't be a problem again. Just don't do the same to your sister, okay? Please?"

"Oh no, you don't get to do that," he says, walking toward me.

"Do what?"

"Act as if this is over when it clearly isn't."

I cross my arms in front of my body. "It is. We already talked about it."

"No, we haven't," Jamie says. "You told me you wanted us to be over, and then you never allowed us to talk it through. You haven't even given us the chance to fight about this!"

Tension has filled the tiny room, enough that I feel we're about to burst.

And you know what? Maybe it's time we do.

"You want to fight? Fine. Let's fight." I let all the emotions I've pushed down bubble out of me, and for the first time in a long while, I don't care what I look like doing so. Tears burn my eyes as I say, "You hurt me, Jamie. You hurt me in the past, and you've kept hurting me every time you made me feel worth less than everyone and everything in your life. Some nights, I would be so worried about what it meant that you hadn't answered my texts for days that I wouldn't be able to eat." His eyes widen, but I don't stop. Not when my face is already twisted by all the emotions I'm feeling. "I would question all the things I'd said and the moves I'd made, wondering if I had made you angry with me or if your love for me was gone. I looked physically sick, and you didn't even notice. I made you come first, and you always put me last."

I'm breathing fast, not truly believing that I said it all. That the words are out. I can't take them back.

I expect him to burst out too. To tell me all the things I did wrong too and why I'm as responsible for this failed relationship as he is. Instead, what I get is a soft shake of his head and an "I'm sorry, Emma. I'm sorry. I'm so, so sorry." It's so low and raw, it takes me by surprise. Didn't he ask for a fight?

I swallow, waiting for his next words. Only, they don't come.

Steeling myself for the storm that doesn't seem to be coming, I say, "That's it? You're not going to try to justify yourself?"

Another shake of his head. "I can't. There's nothing I can say to explain this. I sucked, plain and simple, and I didn't realize it was that bad, and I hurt you, and…and…" He inhales, but the way his lungs expands is shallow. His throat bobs as he tries gasping in more air, but it doesn't help.

"I'm sorry," he repeats, eyes lined with silver. "I'm so sorry. I fucked up. I fucked up. I—"

"Hey, hey," I tell him, but it's no use. Not when he's in that state.

His hands are buried in his fingers as he starts walking in circles around the cramped room, breathing too fast. He's whispering words I can't understand from the strain in his voice.

All the frustration leaves my body, my focus now on him and him alone. I've seen him have panic attacks many times before, but I can tell this is going to be a bad one. Every time it happens, I wish I could take that distress from him and bear it myself. And it being because of something I said? There's nothing worse.

"Jamie," I say, putting my hands on his shoulders and trying to catch his eyes. "You're okay. Just breathe, please. Breathe."

"I—" Tears line his cheeks as he continues trying to gulp air, his skin pale.

"Look at me." I increase the strength of my grip on his shoulders, trying to bring him back. "Jamie, look at me."

"I can't, I can't…." He gives a violent rub of the back of his hand against his cheek, sniffling. "Please go, I—"

"Jamie, look. At. Me." I take his wet cheeks between my hands and force his gaze up. And when it meets mine, I feel like falling to my knees.

Doing what I know works for him, I take a step forward and wrap my arms tightly around him, the pressure enough to crush him against me.

"You're okay," I say against his chest, rubbing a hand down his back. "You're okay. I'm right here. Just breathe."

His body is shaking against me, but already, I feel his breathing calm down.

"Shh. It'll pass. Just focus on your breathing."

He does, or at least tries to. I can hear the pounding of his heart as I continue squeezing him.

"I'm…I'm sorry. I don't want you…want you helping me."

I ignore him, only rubbing his back harder.

"J-just give me a minute. I don't w-want you to think I'm—" He inhales a saccadic breath. "—I'm doing this to manipulate you, or—"

I pull back, just enough to meet his gaze again. "Jamie, stop this. You know I'd never think that. Stop. Just breathe."

The soft and citrusy scent of detergent envelops me as he continues trying to calm himself down. I never let him go, even when another wave of panicky breaths hits him.

"I'm right here with you. Just breathe."

"I'm s-sorry," he says again.

"Stop apologizing. I don't mind one bit. I'm not going anywhere."

This time, he squeezes me back before he says, "I hate that I-I'm like this."

"Stop it. You're okay," I say, even when his words hit me like a truck. "Just focus on me. Focus on my touch, on my voice."

And by some miracle, he does. I continue giving him reassuring words, and minutes pass before his breathing and heart rate come back to something close to normal. Even when he seems better, neither one of us moves. We're protected here. In a world of our own, where only love reigns and outside problems don't exist. Slow dancing while the world around us is on fire.

When he finally pulls back, he wipes his eyes without looking away before he says, "God, I'm sorry."

I open my mouth, but he interrupts with a firm. "No. It's my turn to speak now."

I link my hands together, nodding.

Jamie exhales loudly before he says, "I'm so sorry for hurting you, Emma. S-so fucking sorry. And I don't know if I even deserve for you to forgive me, but it won't stop me from trying to show you that I can be better. For you." He takes a step forward and brushes a strand of hair away from my face, a move that makes me feel cherished and cared for, all at once. "But if I can say one thing, it's that my carelessness had nothing to do with you. I've been terrible at time management and at making you feel loved, but you've always been number one in my heart, and I'm sorry my actions didn't show that."

I stand frozen. What do you answer to that? To what I didn't even know I needed to hear until now?

Jamie rubs his thumbs against my cheeks as we both stare at each other, into each other. Maybe no words exist when everything has already been said.

Softly, Jamie presses a long kiss to my forehead, and when he pulls back, there is a lightness in his eyes, even with the tears still staining his cheeks. "I guess one good thing came out of that shit show, at least."

"What's that?"

"You got mad."

"Huh?"

"You," he says with a little squeeze of my cheek, "got mad."

"You're happy that I got mad."

"That's what I said, isn't it?" His cheek ticks in the smallest semblance of a smile.

"But why?"

"Because getting mad means you still care." He licks his lips, and I'm fairly certain he's stolen a glance at mine. "It's the first time this summer that you've shown you still care, and if I have to take any bit of hope I can find, then I'll take it."

I still struggle with what to answer when he pulls back and gives me a firm nod.

"Now if you'll excuse me," he says, "I have to go welcome my baby sister." Then he leaves, and I stand there for minute after minute, wondering what in the world just happened.

CHAPTER 16

Jamie

I'M FUCKING EVERYTHING UP.

I thought winning Emma over would be relatively easy. We'd spend time together, and she'd realize how good we are together. Because we *are* good. She makes every moment better, and without wanting to sound conceited, I think I can make her happy too. Make her lose some of that seriousness and feel lighter, at least at times. I never doubted we were good. What I hadn't realized was how deep her worries about this relationship ran, and our conversation three days ago forced me to come face-to-face with it. I thought she'd meant she simply wanted us to spend more time together, but that wasn't it at all. She wanted to feel loved, which I thought she did, but clearly I was wrong. It had never occurred to me that she might feel that way because, in my heart, she's always been at the center of everything. She's never not in my mind. Life takes form around the shape of her. I can't wrap my head around the fact that I was enough of a dumbass that she felt unloved.

And to top it all off, I went ahead and had a fucking panic attack in front of her. Deep down, I know she'd never judge me for it, but it was the worst possible timing for it. I wanted to prove to Emma that I could listen to her and grow from it, but instead, I started panicking at the thought of everything I'd done wrong and got in a headspace that I couldn't come back from. I was mortified. She wasn't mad. More than that, she was there for me. When she needed me, I ended up needing her more. Way to show her that I can be the man she needs.

And yet, I'm not giving up. Just like I told her five days ago, I'm hopeful. If she'd given me no emotion, I'd have thought maybe it was the true end, but she still cares. I'll take that as a win, because that's the only option I have. The alternative is accepting moving on to other things, and I won't. I've been in love with this woman since I was a scrawny fourteen-year-old, and that's never going to change. I'll do better. Put timers on when I play, no matter how annoying they are. Make her see she's not a secondary thought, but the first thing I think of when I open my eyes in the morning.

The wind is sharp today as I walk around camp, light gray clouds covering the entire sky, no hint of sun present. I bury my left hand in my hoodie as I make my way toward Emma's cabin, a brown lunch bag containing a ham sandwich hanging from my other one. I didn't see Emma in the cafeteria over lunch, not that I was looking for her (of course I was). I'm not sure if she got caught up in practice, but I can't count the number of times Emma has brought me food in the past when I'd forgotten to eat, so it's more than time for me to return the favor. Take care of her, for once. Ever since the beginning of summer, I've tried to time myself so we could share at least one meal every day. I don't know if she likes it, but it's what I got. Anything to make her hold on to me a little longer. And while we haven't talked more about anything serious, things have been good. At least I like to think so.

Sounds of laughter come from inside as I knock on the ochre-tinted wooden door. Not just any laughter, but Emma's. I would recognize it anywhere.

"Yes?" Emma says as she opens the door, a little winded. Her smile falls a little when she sees me. "Oh," she says.

"What a warm welcome," I say.

"I'm sorry. I was just expecting someone else."

"I'll try not to be insulted."

She does a quick eye roll before nudging me inside. Behind her, Jesy is lying on her back on top of her sunshine-colored bedspread, a book held up over her eyes. She throws a wink my way.

"You're fine," Emma says. "Just a surprise is all."

"A good surprise, I hope."

With a smirk, she says, "An okay one."

"I'll take it."

She laughs, then goes to her vanity and starts tying her hair in a ponytail, not a strand out of place. "So, can I help you with something?"

"Just wanted to bring you lunch, in case you hadn't had any." I lift the brown bag in proof.

She blinks at me before color rises to her cheeks. "Thank you, really, but I already ate." She tightens her ponytail. "There's the volleyball tournament this afternoon, remember?"

The second she says it, I notice the yellow jersey she's wearing, which makes the golden shade of her skin glow even more.

I rack my brain to find the memory of her telling me she'd signed up, but I come up empty-handed. Did I miss that too?

"I didn't know you'd signed up."

"It was a last-minute thing. They were missing a team, and I decided to go for it. Asked Jeremiah if he wanted to be my partner, and he said yes."

"You asked Jeremiah?" I cross my arms after dropping the bag on the vanity. "Okay, now I'm really trying not to get offended, but you're making it hard."

She cocks an eyebrow in the mirror. "Why? It's not like you would've wanted to anyway."

"Why not?"

In the back, I spot Jesy sitting up and lifting herself to her wheelchair before she mumbles something and exits the cabin.

"Because you don't have an athletic bone in your body."

"And you do?" I say.

She snickers. "Maybe not, but I still thought it could be fun, and I know that's not the type of thing you like." She turns to grab her sunscreen and Camp Allegro hat, but I block her way.

"Fuck Jeremiah. I'll be your partner."

"Oh, don't be jealous now." She gives my chest two soft taps. "I'm bad enough on my own, and I'd like a fighting chance."

"I can be your fighting chance," I deadpan. "I'm tall. Isn't that what half of being a good volleyball player is?"

"Sure thing, honey," she says with another tap before trying to move around me. I don't let her.

"Come on. We make a great team together. You know it. I'm sure we can win this."

She mirrors me by crossing her arms in front of her chest, and I try my damnedest not to look at her breasts being pushed up. A massive fail.

"Didn't know my eyes had moved down there," she says.

Fuck.

I look up in a heartbeat, finding her grinning.

"It's Wednesday. Don't you have those private lessons with Frankie anyway?"

"I'll cancel," I deadpan.

She gives me a doubtful expression.

"Can't you at least give me the benefit of the doubt that I'm trying to do better?" I say.

She looks taken aback, eyes round. "Sure. I'm sorry." She lifts a shoulder. "But that doesn't change the fact that you and me playing sports together is a losing recipe."

"I'll bet you we can win the game."

She laughs as if I'm joking. "And what would you like to bet, Mr. Sports Are My Life All of a Sudden?"

"A kiss."

Her face drops.

I take a step forward, her vanilla smell *everywhere*. "And not just some shitty kiss-on-the-cheek-just-for-show. An actual kiss."

She purses her lips before saying, "Fine. But if I win, you need to listen to Luke Combs's entire discography and admit it's good."

"So you're going for torture, I see."

"Shut up. Do we have a deal?" She extends a hand my way.

I shake it firmly. "Damn right we do."

Finally, I let her move past me, and she almost runs outside the cabin.

"Hey! But you can't suck on purpose!" I shout behind her.

She laughs out loud. "Don't worry, I won't need to try to be terrible."

* * *

In hindsight, that was a very bad thing to bet on.

I can recognize my strengths. I'm good at a few things, but sports? Never been my thing.

"Jamie!" Emma shrieks as she hits the ball, apparently looking to give me a pass. Except I can't gauge where it is going, and while her aim is absolute shit, mine is probably even worse. I land with my face in the sand every. Single. Time.

The crowd boos us, and I mutter, "You do better, assholes." Thank god this isn't a piano recital because my attitude toward the audience would've had me canceled in a minute.

"It's okay, babe," Emma says, and I hold back a cringe at the sound of the pet name. Even when we were the most in love, we never called each other "babe." I turn to her, and she's giving me a cat-like grin. The vixen.

"I know, *babe*. We'll do better next time."

But next time comes, and we, unfortunately, do not do better. Emma gives it her all, just like she does with everything, but it's not leading to much. Sweat drips down her brow, which she wipes with the back of her arm. Her chest is rising up and down as she studies the net as if she'll be able to understand its magic and make us win all of a sudden. At this point, losing is an inevitability. We've lost point after point. I try not to let my ego get wounded, but easier said than done.

"Come on, Em!" Jesy shouts from the sidelines, her hands cupped around her mouth. "Put that pretty ass to work!"

Emma's face immediately becomes fire red, and the glare she sends Jesy in return is worth all the money in the world.

I laugh out loud but stop when I become the recipient of that glare.

"She's right, you know," I whisper. "*Very* pretty."

Her eyes narrow. "A little less talking and a little more winning, maybe?"

"Sure thing. Same for you, though, right?"

I can only see slits of her eyes when she says with a teasing, pointed tone, "Right."

Someone blows a whistle to my right, and we get into position, our gazes trained on the ball. Just like before, I try to give it my all, but even as I make every effort to send the ball to the other court, it hits the net dead on. Then, because I have zero coordination anywhere other than in my fingers, I land badly and fall to the ground, eating sand for the thousandth time today.

Fuck. Me.

I stay there for a moment as I try to catch my breath when a shadow ends up looming over me. Emma extends a hand my way, pinching her lips not to laugh.

"You sure you aren't regretting not letting Jeremiah be my partner?" she says.

I take her hand and get to my feet, but before letting go, I say, "Not for a second, sweetheart." With a drag of my thumb over her thundering pulse, I add, "You?"

She acts as if she's thinking for a moment before she shakes her head, her nose scrunched in that way that brings me to my knees.

I'd eat sand a million times more if it meant I got to see it again.

"Nineteen-two," the ref shouts, as if wanting to dig the knife deeper. The two points we made were because of the opposite team's failed serves.

Emma flinches but brings a smile to her lips just as fast. Losing in front of everyone is probably torture for her.

Enough. This is where it ends. I don't want her to be humiliated any more than she already is, and I really, really want that kiss. *Need* it.

When the giant facing me serves like a fucking NVA player, I don't bother trying to make a pass, which Emma and I suck at anyway. Instead, I use my height to my advantage and jump, blocking the ball the moment it crosses the net and hitting it to the ground. The two opposite players throw themselves down, but it's too late. The ball has already touched the sand.

"We made a point," I whisper, awestruck as I look at the other team's disappointed faces. I repeat it louder, the words sounding weird even coming from my mouth.

To my right, I hear a high-pitched scream a second before Emma throws herself at me, wrapping her legs and arms around my body like a baby koala. I laugh, hugging her tight.

God, what I would give for all these people to disappear so I could hug my girl privately? Even so, I don't think it's for show, and that makes the embrace infinitely better.

"WE MADE A POINT BY OURSELVES!" she shouts, almost piercing my eardrums.

"Damn right we did."

Emma is smiling wide in my arms, but at some point, she seems to realize she just threw herself at me, and her smile dims a little. She clears her throat and unwraps her legs from around my waist so she can fall back to her feet. When I don't have any other choice, I let go of her. I instantly miss the heat of her body.

"Another one like that, 'kay?" she tells me as she walks back to her spot. I nod.

Unfortunately, my single point must've been beginner's luck because it doesn't happen again, and two points later, the other team wins. Honestly, it's not like it wasn't deserved. I overestimated the power of my wishful thinking.

Emma goes to shake hands with our adversaries, smiling politely at them like only she can at people who just beat us. I follow her, but my face is not nearly as pleasant. These two fuckers just stole my kiss away from me. Couldn't they have been just a little worse than me? If I give them a handshake that's tighter than necessary, it's not my fault.

Once we're done with our congratulations, I move to my water bottle, gulping it all. Sweat has gathered on my forehead and nose even without any trace of sun. I probably should start exercising when we get back to the real world.

"Good game, partner," Emma says as she sidles up next to me and grabs her own bottle. After drinking, she gives me a look that could be described as nothing other than pure evil. Then, knowing exactly what she's doing, she leans forward and gives my cheek a heavy kiss for show, the smack of her lips audible by everyone. Bringing her pink lips to my ear, she whispers, "A very valiant effort." Then she gets up, starts walking backward, and from an angle only I can see, she winks.

"Luke Combs," she mouths silently over her shoulder.

I shake my head. How did I fall so hard for the biggest tease I know? Unclear. But one thing is for sure: it was inevitable. If I had it to do again, I know I couldn't help it.

CHAPTER 17

Emma

A S SOON AS I WALK OUT OF MY LESSON WITH DR.
Podimow, who's been tougher than ever since she came
back from vacation, I try but fail not to replay the entire
last hour in my head. My hands are wrapped tightly around my
binder as I try to put space between me and that booth.

A few other musicians are practicing or getting lessons in the
music building as I cross it. I even pause for a moment to watch
Molly play her cello, her red hair tied in a ponytail as she listens to
her teacher's corrections, then applies them perfectly. From the little I can hear, she's doing great. She's had dinner with Jamie and I a
few times since she arrived at camp, and she was saying that things
were going "okay," but clearly, they're going better than okay. I'm
happy for her. She deserves her success.

Not wanting her to spot me and break her focus, I walk away
from her booth, and that's when I look up and see Irène, who's
sweeping the floor of the outdoor stage, her back bent as she moves
fast along the wood slats. She's working a form-fitting dress covered
with a silk blouse, something I could see my mother wearing on a
talk show.

"Hi!' I shout to get her attention. I haven't had a chance to talk
to her since I spoke with Alessandro more than a week ago, but I
don't have anything scheduled for the rest of the day, and after the
practice I just had, it seems like a good distraction. My left hand
kept cramping, and Dr. Podimow even stopped me one time and
told me it'd probably be better if I started over again. It was humiliating. Hopefully, it will stay between the two of us, although

I know she's not above reporting back to my parents. She does in the future, after all.

Irène stops sweeping when she sees me, the strange way she behaved after our last conversation nowhere to be seen.

"Emma! How are you, *chérie*?" she says as she gets down from the stage. Her shiny Dr. Martens squeak against the floor, almost covering up the cough she lets out before she says, "Had a good practice?"

The lie brushing off the failure that was today's practice clings to the walls of my throat. We're well into July, and things haven't improved. If it continues like this, even if we get back to our normal time, the showcase will be an embarrassment. What's worse, parents usually come, so mine will see my humiliation in real time. Panic has become a permanent fixture in my life.

I shouldn't talk about it. I think back to my mother lying in bed with empty eyes and an emptier heart, all the while the media thought she was doing better than ever. Fake it till you make it. They told me later that the lies had allowed them to continue having a successful career. But keeping all of this pressure to myself is becoming hard, especially with each day where my playing doesn't improve.

Irène tilts her head.

I shouldn't. I really shouldn't.

"It wasn't so great," I say, overstepping all the protection mechanisms I've been taught because Irène looks comforting and motherly and I can't hold it in when she offers to listen like that.

"Oh, it happens," she says like it really does happen. After looking me up and down, she says, "Care for a walk?"

I nod.

Once we're out of the building, the hot summer air smelling of pine trees and sunscreen, she says, "During an entire summer in Paris," she says, the sound of the city coming out of her mouth, nothing like how a born-and-raised American would say it, "I could not get a single pirouette right. You should ask Alessandro. I was close to giving up."

"And how did you get over it?" I ask, fighting the urge to pull at the skin around my thumbnails.

"I practiced a lot, and eventually it unlocked, although they were never my strong element."

"And what if you'd kept practicing and it still didn't work?"

Her lips form a thin line. "Then I would say to maybe take a step back to try and understand what exactly is not working."

But what if I do take a step away, only to realize that it's made me worse? Or that I am the problem, and there's nothing I can do about it?

"I'm not sure I have that kind of leisure," I say.

"If I remember correctly," she says, twigs crunching under her boots as we approach the lake, "you still have more than a year before your junior showcase. Correct?"

I hum in agreement, even though the truth is that I have less than a month left. If we find a way to get back, that is.

"That means you still have a lot of time to improve for your audition." Her steps slow down as she turns to face me. "Or to even decide if you want to pursue piano as a career."

I trip on a branch, only barely catching my balance before falling face first into the rocks.

"Oh my," Irène exclaims. "Are you all right?"

"Fine," I mutter in response, still running over her previous question.

This is the first time in my life anyone has ever suggested I think about whether I want to be a pianist when I grow up. It's always been sort of assumed, from the moment I was born to two music geniuses, and even more when people saw I was quite good at it.

"Why would you say that?" I ask tentatively. "About the piano, I mean." Above us, the leaves in the taller trees are ruffling in the wind. A storm is probably coming.

"Oh, no reason."

I stare at her with what I assume is a disbelieving look.

She chuckles. "I just want all students to know that coming to

Camp Allegro does not mean they have to practice their art professionally in the future. It is possible to enjoy something greatly without wanting to do it as a job." She gives me a side look. "Especially if one does not seem to be having a good time while practicing."

I have no idea how she's seen all this side of me when no one has before, and we've barely spent any time together.

"Are you a seer?" I ask, only half joking.

"I wish. But no, I only have a good eye for my students."

She continues walking, and I follow. Birds are chirping in the trees, and the water is lapping against the shore in soft waves. I look at the lake, where the sunset is reflecting on the water's surface, and notice how beautiful this place is. I've been so stressed this summer, I almost forgot. This will be my last time here. After these next few weeks, this is it. Unless Jamie and I have to spend eternity here, replaying this Groundhog Summer over and over again, but that's a problem for another time.

"You know, my parents were farmers."

"Really?" I say.

Irène reaches the water and keeps on walking around, not caring that the ground has become uneven, full of boulders and branches. I guess it's easier with her sturdy boots. Quickly, I remove my sneakers and put my feet in the cold water, sand snaking through my toes as she stays on the bank.

"Yes. Lavender. Quite the thing in the south of France."

"Must've been nice," I say.

"It was all right. A fun hobby. Not what I wanted to do with my life."

I give the water a small kick, splashes landing on my jeans. "Did your parents expect you to take over after they retired?"

"More than expect. Demanded." A gush of wind ripples over us, blowing our hair to the right. Irène wraps her shawl tighter around her thin shoulders. "But I had to follow my heart, and one day, I decided to take a chance and told them I wanted to pursue dancing. And you know what happened?"

A shake of my head.

"Nothing at all. They were disappointed for a day or two, but when they realized I was serious about this and would be unhappy staying in Provence, they came to me and asked me what they could do to help me achieve my goals."

Pressure builds in my throat, behind my eyes, though I'm not sure why. This is a nice story.

"I never had children, Emma, but from what I've gathered in my long life, the most important thing for a parent is to see their child happy. Yes?"

I nod, even though I don't really know. Irène has never met Franklin St. Francis. Has never seen his analytic eyes and expecting tone. Never experienced what it was like to be scolded at twelve years old after my performance on one of America's famous talk shows, after I'd messed up some notes from the stress of appearing on live television. She doesn't know that my father has no clue whether I'm happy or not. If he cared, wouldn't he have asked how I'm doing this summer? Or even tried to get to know me better while I was growing up?

"Sometimes, making those kinds of decisions only requires *un peu de courage.*"

"Something I wish I could have more of," I say.

"Oh, you are courageous all right. I have been watching, remember?"

"You know, when you say it like that, it's kind of creepy."

Irène laughs. "Don't worry, *chérie.* I am too tired to creep anyone out."

As she says it, my attention shifts to her, and for the first time, I notice it: the way she's breathing, fast and shallow.

"Are you all right?" I ask her, just like she asked me before, extending an arm toward her. Is it me, or does she look unsteady all of a sudden?

"Yes, I'm fine," she answers in a voice that is airy and not at all like the one I've been listening to for the past ten minutes. I wait in silence as she catches her breath.

When she looks better, I go sit on a large rock a few yards away, and Irène follows, releasing a soft groan as her knees crack.

Looking forward at the water, I say, "You know, I've spoken with Alessandro."

Her head snaps up, no traces of her previous good mood left. *All right, Emma. You made a promise.*

"He mentioned I wasn't wrong to be worried about you," I say.

"I will strangle that man," she deadpans, getting back up.

"Please," I say, holding on to her hand. "Could we just talk about this? We *did* just go over my life challenges."

She considers this before sitting back down. "I don't like talking about my health, Emma."

"And you think I like talking about how much my parents' expectations affect me?" It did feel good to talk about it with someone I have come to trust, but she doesn't need to know that.

She purses her lips.

"Don't worry," I add, "he didn't tell me what's...*bothering* you exactly. But I would be happy to offer a nonjudgmental ear if ever you want to talk about it."

"I guess it is too late to hide anything, thanks to that old fart," she says, making me burst out laughing. Her low giggles join mine before she sighs. "I have what is called aortic stenosis." Her lips are turned downward now. "One of my heart valves is closing up more and more, which makes it harder to pump blood to the rest of my body."

"That sounds serious."

She blows a raspberry. "It is, but I have also had it for a long time. Some days are harder than others." Leaning back, she gazes out at the group of friends on the horizon, canoeing across the lake. "And I know I do not have long."

My breath catches.

"W-why do you say that?"

143

She gives me a smile, which sounds counterintuitive because she's the one who just said she doesn't have long. "I am a ballerina. I know my body quite well, and I know when it is tired. And it is getting more and more tired."

My nose tickles. *Don't cry.* This is not the place nor the time.

"And is there—" I clear my scratchy throat. "Is there nothing doctors can do about it?"

Her boot moves up and down as she wiggles her foot over her knee. "I have other health conditions that make the operation for this condition very tricky, and frankly, I am glad. I would not want to die on an operating table. I would much rather live the life I have been given for as long as I can, and when my time comes, I will be at peace with it."

I only realize a tear has escaped my eye when she says, "*Oh, ma chérie, ne pleure pas.*"

"I'm sorry," I say, wiping my face. "I shouldn't—"

"It is quite normal to feel emotions, Emma. You should not hide from them."

"Look at you, comforting me. This is ridiculous," I say with a wet laugh.

"I have seen much worse," she answers.

Once my tears have gotten under control, I say, "So is there a way I can convince you to slow down?" I cringe as I think back to the way she was sweeping the floor earlier, as if she doesn't have a whole cleaning crew dedicated to keeping Allegro clean.

"Not a single chance. I am living my life, not cowering away in bed."

I chew on the inside of my lip. I wish she would listen to me, but deep down, I know she's doing the right thing. It's brave of her, to face life as it comes when she knows it could make her lifetime shorter, but at the same time, I understand what she means. What's life's worth if there's no life in it?

"Alessandro won't be happy."

She laughs, dropping her head to my shoulder, her legs kicking like a little girl's. "Too bad for him. He will forgive me."

This conversation has objectively not led to anything good. Irène's heart isn't working well, and there's no way we can make it better. She won't slow down, even if she's aware it could kill her. And in all likelihood, it will. In less than a month. It also means this isn't our way back to our time.

And yet, I'm feeling a heavy sense of peace. Like whatever happens, we'll face it, and things will be okay.

If Irène can believe it, then so can I.

CHAPTER 18

Emma

THE THREE KNOCKS OF MY FIST AGAINST JAMIE'S DOOR pierce the peaceful midmorning silence around the cabin. I wait for a second, smoothing my skirt, but no one comes.

"Jamie?" I call out.

No answer.

I turn around to go look for him elsewhere but the sound of the door opening makes me look back. A hint of disappointment pinches me when I see it's Jeremiah and not Jamie. His braids are pulled up in a bun on top of his head, a loose tank top covering his chest.

"Hey, Emma. What's up?"

"Oh, hey. Is Jamie around?"

"No," he says, "but he should be back soon. I think he said he went for a swim." Still in the doorframe, he looks behind his shoulder. "You can come in to wait for him though."

"Oh, sure, thanks."

I follow him inside, where he leans down to grab his backpack and ballet slippers. "I have to go, but feel free to chill here in the meantime."

"Thank you," I repeat.

"See ya," he says before he closes the door behind him, leaving me alone.

All the campground's cabins look the same, but even with my eyes closed, I could tell this is Jamie's. He has the bottom bunk, and the space smells just like him. Lemon and a hint of mint. His half of the room is messy, with sheet music thrown haphazardly and clothes strung all over the place. The bed is unmade, the gray bedspread thrown out as if he got up and immediately left for practice. The one thing he loves almost as much as his piano is his sleep.

I have to admit, it's all very cozy. I've been taught from the time I was a little girl to keep my things clean and tidy, especially if someone was coming over, and my apartment shows that. There is a specific place for everything, and nothing is amiss. It used to drive Jamie crazy, and while I like to tease him about how I'd rather be kempt than the opposite, there's something refreshing about visiting his place and seeing it lived in. When I'd go to his parent's place and see the unmade bed in his room, I'd have the urge to get in and steal some of its warmth, like it was a black hole sucking me in. As if the fact that it showed it was slept in made it more inviting.

I have the same feeling now. If I close my eyes, I can pretend I'm back in his room. I just got to his place, and while Jamie isn't back from practice yet, Karen, his mother, has made me chamomile tea and told me to sneak some cookies into Jamie's room for a midnight snack. She kisses my cheek before wishing me a good night, and then I disappear into Jamie's room, where I'm waiting for him in this space that's impregnated with his spirit. Nothing is wrong between us. Our love is stronger than everything, and I can't think of a single thing that could tear us apart.

Making my way to his bed now, I sit on the edge and rub my hands down my thighs. After a minute of looking at the nostalgia-inducing messy space, I can't help myself. I have to busy myself tidying things up. Some people could find it insulting, but I know Jamie. He loves when I clean his space. He used to tell me he could never organize things the way I did and he felt sharper when his things were tidy.

There must be a hundred loose sheets on this bed. His binder is on the ground, so I grab it and start stacking his papers inside in the right order. I imagine nothing could be worse for him than to start playing a piece, only to realize his music sheets are all over the place. I put the concertos together, then the sonatas, then the suites, then—

My fingers freeze on a piece of paper I've never seen before. It's caught my attention because it's so different from the others; the sheet is thinner, not made of the same paper, and the notes have been hand-drawn. Brows furrowed, I read a few lines.

It's only when I see the handwriting in the margins that I realize it's Jamie's. He's composed this.

I gape with my shoulders hunched for a long, long time.

How did I not know my boyfriend is composing music? It seems like something he would've boasted about, and I would've been more than proud of him for it. It's something he did mention he'd like to try one day, but he never said anything about having started already.

I pick up a few other sheets, all seemingly part of the same piece.

This feels like intruding. For some people, music is irrelevant, but for a musician, and especially for a composer, a composition can feel like a journal. So much can be expressed through music. Anger. Euphoria. Sorrow.

And here I am, with his thoughts translated through notes. A peek into his mind.

Just like the urge to clean, I can't help it. I gaze back at the door to make sure there's still no sign of him, then get up and look for the electric keyboard he always brings with him. Once I find it—under one of his pillows—I read the first few lines, and before I can stop myself, I start playing.

The second I hear the notes, I'm hit with so much emotion, I have to steel myself to continue playing. The chords he used, the mix of major and minor keys, the soft melody… It's a love song. There's no doubt about it.

And it's so freaking beautiful.

I blaze through the second page, amazed that my…that Jamie wrote this. It's something I could imagine hearing in a romantic movie, when the leads are returning to each other after years apart. It's majestic, grandiose even, but also intimate. There's nothing overly complicated about it. The technique necessary to play it is readily available to most pianists, yet it doesn't make it feel anything less than what it truly is.

A masterpiece.

When I finish playing through the sheets I have, my heart is beating fast. I know there must be more to it because it doesn't feel complete, or maybe he hasn't finished writing it all, but I'm still in awe. How did he do this? Translate so much emotion with a combination of eighty-eight notes?

I feel like crying for some reason, which is stupid. I have no reason to be this emotional over this.

Exhaling sharply, I add the sheets to the binder, then continue sorting through the ones still lying on the bed. I won't ask him about this. I'll wait for him to tell me, if he ever does. Already I feel bad for intruding.

I organize a few more classical pieces I've heard Jamie play countless times, until I land on another of Jamie's handwritten sheets, this time the first page of the piece.

And when I see the title of the song, my heart doesn't just speed. It stops entirely.

"My Aurora."

I don't even need to think about what an aurora means to him. To us. It's all there, in a supercut of us from years before.

Suddenly, I can't hold my tears back anymore. They fall in thick splotches onto my hands, each one so incredibly heavy.

After the incident with Molly, I told myself I'd stop putting hope into this relationship, but how can I move on when he's all I dreamed about for so long? And now this? This beautiful song I can't get out of my head? I don't know how I'm supposed to keep my resolve and protect my heart when he makes it so freaking hard.

I try to remember why I decided to end things. Eyes closed, I enumerate reasons in my head, but the words blur rapidly, replaced by every single thing I feel for him.

This feels like a failure somehow. In all my life, I've never stood up for myself. Not when my parents told me I couldn't have people over in case they were trying to use me to get to them. Not when I had to go on live television for an interview even though I feel like throwing up during public speaking. Not when I had to get braces at an age younger than most because my teeth were too crooked and my parents wanted to make sure they were perfect by the time I started playing seriously. Telling Jamie I wasn't happy was the first time I did, and now I can't even hold steady with resolve. What does that say about me? That I have no backbone? Or that I'm so emotionally jaded that I can't even understand what I truly need?

I'm drying my tears when I hear someone outside the cabin. In a swift movement, I get up, abandoning the binder behind me and rubbing my sleeves over the remnants of my breakdown.

"Oh, hey," Jamie says as he walks inside the cabin, his hair wind-blown and paler from all the sunlight he's had in the past month. "What are you doing here?"

"I, uh…" What *am* I doing here again? I get lost in my thoughts as I stare at him, at his sharp jaw and long neck, at his old high school sweatershirt and ripped jeans. I blink, overwhelmed by the feeling. This isn't just nostalgia. It's something stronger than memories, something I don't want to let go of.

He raises an eyebrow, and I clear my throat. "Sorry, um, I needed to talk to you about what Irène told me last night." Thank god my voice doesn't sound thick with tears.

"Is it bad news?" A notch forms between his thick brows. "You don't look so good."

"Always just the right words, huh?" I laugh, but it's not convincing.

He rolls his eyes. "You know that's not what I mean. You always look great."

The second he says it, it's like we're brought back to our car ride to Allegro, when I told him I couldn't remember the last time he'd told me I looked nice. The last thing I need to talk about after playing his composition is this.

"No, it's not great news," I say, bringing us back to the important matter.

Jamie takes a seat on the bed I just vacated, thankfully not commenting on the fact that his music sheets have been tidied up, then says, "I'm ready. Hit me with it."

I go over everything Irène told me yesterday, minus a few personal details we discussed. Jamie listens intently, chin resting on his fists.

"So she's not the solution," he says matter-of-factly once I'm done.

I shake my head, lips thin.

Silence, then a muttered, "Fuck." He presses his thumb and index fingers to his eye sockets. "We're running out of time."

"I know," I say. "I'm sorry."

"No, there's nothing for you to be sorry about." A sigh leaves his lips, his shoulders dropping at the same time. "We'll figure something out."

"Since when are you an optimist?"

"Since I realized I didn't have a choice but to hope the universe doesn't hate us."

I snicker.

"Plus, I have our high school salutatorian with us. We'll be fine." He grins.

I try to answer with a smile of my own, but I have trouble forcing it on. I feel lost, in all spheres of my life. This is the first time I'm at such a loss for answers, and seeing that Jamie still has hope I'll find a solution only makes me feel even more incompetent.

Jamie's eyes narrow in on me before he says, "Come on. We're going." He even steps forward to grab my hand.

"Going where?"

"Karaoke."

"Karaoke," I repeat. "Are you serious?" What has this guy done to Jamie?

"Why not?" he says. "These things are supposed to be fun."

"Sure, if you like public humiliation."

"Or if you like letting go for an evening." He shrugs. "Plus, you should like it. It's your kind of place."

"What does that mean?"

"You know. Playing all that corny music you love so much. I'm sure you'll fit right in."

"You actually think you're funny, don't you?"

"You're the one who said it."

I poke him in the stomach. "You admitted last week that Luke Combs's music is good."

Jamie looks down at me, his glasses even more crooked than usual. Then, he leans down, his lips almost touching my ear as he whispers, "I lied."

"You little bastard."

With a wink, he lets go of my hand and exits the cabin. His legs are way too long for me to have a chance of catching up with him. I run after him anyway, my giggles probably heard by the entire camp.

* * *

"This was horrifying."

"A true massacre of the great work that is 'Lady Marmalade,'" Jamie says, tutting.

"How is it possible to be in a camp full of artists and not a single person we heard tonight sang on key?"

"One of the world's greatest mysteries. When a karaoke machine comes out, everyone forgets how to sing."

I nudge him with my shoulder. "It was kind of fun, though."

"Yeah?" He grins.

"Yeah." I tilt my head. "Even though my ears will probably never heal."

With a lift of his shoulders, he says, "Hearing is an overrated sense anyway."

The sky is a dark blue, a million stars lighting the way. Another thing I love about this place: the way the stars seem so much brighter. There's no light pollution in this remote part of Maine, making the view above the lake an absolute work of art.

I must've slowed down because Jamie stops next to me, looking up as well. We remain here in silence, staring at the universe above our heads until I notice Jamie dropping down to lie on his back, arms behind his head.

"What are you doing?" I ask, laughing. The ground is wet with the rain that we got this week, droplets tickling my toes through my sandals.

"Lying down," he says with a grin, like that's the most natural thing in the world. "View's nice." He nudges me down, and I must be kind of strange too because I follow. It is indeed wet, but the air is warm, the ground smells like freshly mowed grass and fresh earth, and it *is* nice.

"So, is this your new kink? Lying on the ground in random places?" I ask, remembering the day we tried to exit the camp and were propelled back. I shift closer to him so I can move away from the rock digging into my back.

"Nah." His head turns my way. "And if it was, it would still be better than questionable haircuts."

I knew he wouldn't let go of that sideburn thing. Eyebrow raised, I quip, "*You* have a questionable haircut."

"You gave it to me." As if in reflex, he drags one of his hands through his hair, only accentuating the strands I cut too short. It's not that bad, but it still makes me want to laugh.

"Mistake number one: trusting me with scissors." I shrug. "You dug your own grave, Montpellier."

His lips twist before he grins wickedly. "It was more than worth it."

I laugh, shaking my head before I return to my stargazing. It doesn't take long before I find myself gasping. "Look, a shooting star!"

"Make a wish." I feel Jamie's gaze on me, and it doesn't matter how strong I try to be. Those freaking magnets still work their magic and force me to look his way. Or maybe *he* is the magnet, a siren calling me to the deep. His eyes are dark as espresso shots, lined with the fainted trace of gold.

My wish should be to find a way to go back home or to get my piano playing back on track. But for some reason, all my thoughts stick to the person gazing at me.

Unfortunately, I don't have time to make my wish because the second I close my eyes, someone says, "Emma."

Alessandro is standing behind us, smiling at us like he's busted two teenagers making out in the bushes.

Jamie and I jump to our feet, wiping the dirt off our butts. "Alessandro, hi," I say. I shouldn't be this flustered. We weren't doing anything.

So why does my core feel on fire?

"I have been meaning to talk to you," Alessandro says, hands clasped in front of him. His head is covered with a vintage fedora, something I usually hate but looks adorable on him.

"Yes, I need to speak to you too." I glance at Jamie. "Well, *we* do."

Alessandro waits, an unreadable look in his eyes. When I shake my head softly, his smile slumps.

"There was nothing to do," I say, hating myself for being the cause of the heartbreak on his face. I would give him all the good news in the world if I could. I put a hand on his forearm, just like I did in the closet. "She's aware of everything, and she wants to continue to live the way she always has."

"I was afraid that was what it would come to."

I lick my lips, feeling cold for the first time tonight. "It's hard, and easier said than done, but I think at this point, we need to support her in her decision."

"I know." He coughs a little, his hands unsteady. "It is foolish of me to want more than what we already had, isn't it?" He offers us a smile, but it's wobbly. "Sixty years, but I would still ask for sixty more."

I feel Jamie's gaze on me once again, but I resist him, this time. I'll break down if I meet his eyes. I know I will.

"I'm sorry I couldn't do more," I say, gasping softly when Jamie's warm hand lands on the small of my back.

"You did enough," he says. "Now we can only hope."

My mouth twists to the side. It feels unfair, to let him believe she might still have years when Jamie and I know she doesn't have a month. When I finally find the courage to look up at Jamie, his expression tells me he's thinking the same.

I hesitate to say anything, but when Jamie gives me a soft nod, I say, "Alessandro, it might not be so long now." I don't elaborate, and I don't even know if it's a good thing to tell him, but if I was in his shoes, I'd want to know.

He doesn't ask me how I know that. Instead, he offers me the saddest smile I've ever seen and says, "I know. I have a feeling too." He exhales shakily, then turns and leaves.

My heart breaks with each of his slow steps away.

CHAPTER 19

Emma

THE MOMENT MY INDEX FINGER SLIPS ON THE WRONG NOTE for the tenth time today, I let my palms drop flat against the keyboard, creating a loud, shriek-like sound that makes the people outside of the booth turn my way. Crap. I force a smile and wave at the two trumpeters who are looking at me weirdly.

What I'm doing now is pretty much the opposite of what Irène suggested, but we're three weeks away from the showcase—not that we're in any way closer to getting back to the showcase *year*—and I can't afford not to practice. The thing is, the more weeks pass, the readier I need to be, but the less effort I feel like making. Ever since I had that conversation with Irène, everything in me seems to have gotten worse. Every morning, I wake up with a tighter knot in my belly at the thought of needing to practice again.

I crack my neck left and right, then my fingers. Time to get back to it.

I barely get through the first page of the sonata before my phone starts vibrating in my pocket repeatedly. A phone call.

"Hello?" I answer after accepting the call without looking at the caller, not caring that I was interrupted—the first sign that things are wrong.

"Emmaline." My dad's voice is sharp and dry. "Nice of you to finally answer."

I must have missed his previous calls, too focused on trying to get through the piece. "Sorry. I, uh…" I scratch my throat. "How are you? How are things at home?" I hope my voice doesn't show how surprised I am that he's the one who called.

"Oh, you know."

No, I don't.

"We might be going back home for a few weeks before hopping back on tour. I thought you should hear it from me if anyone asks you at camp," he says.

"Why? Is something wrong?" My jaw tightens. Stopping in the middle of a tour is never good news. "Is Mom okay?"

"She's fine. Just a little tired."

My entire body is strung tight. "Isn't that what you said when she had her last episode?"

"Emmaline, don't be impertinent," he says. "Are you alone, at least?"

"Yes, I'm alone." It's irritating this is what he's concerned about. Almost as irritating as him downplaying what's going on. "Can I talk to her?"

"She's resting."

"How bad is it?" I ask.

"It's fine. But if anyone asks, tell them we're renewing our vows in a quiet ceremony abroad."

This time, I can't stop the tension from breaking free. "Are you serious right now?" It's always been like this, but somehow, today, it gets to me. Bad. I can't believe my mother is suffering, and the only thing on his mind is finding a way to cover it up. I can't imagine Jamie doing something like that to me.

"We need to do what we can to preserve what we worked our whole lives to build, and you know this," he deadpans, voice emotionless. It's like I'm speaking to a robot, always.

"Of course. Nothing is more important than that, is it?"

"What has gotten into you?" Dad says with a raised voice.

Sighing, I close my eyes and let my forehead drop to rest on the piano. "Nothing. I think I'm just tired of... all this."

"Well, I hope you get it together. Your audition is soon."

My nostrils flare. "Showcase, not audition. And trust me, I couldn't possibly forget." No matter how much I might want to.

"All right, then. Have a good night."

He hangs up before I can say another word. Not even once did he bother to ask how I am doing.

I don't know why I'm surprised. It's nothing new. But while he's the same, maybe my perspective has started to change with everything that's been going on in the past weeks. I wouldn't have been as hurt by this conversation in the past, but now... I know he loves me, but I don't think he *likes* me, and that's just as painful, if not worse. In a way, maybe he doesn't know me well enough to like me. I'm not a flesh-and-bones person to him. I'm the legacy.

I try to get back to my practice, but it's clear after a few minutes that it's pointless. Nothing works, so I decide to pack my stuff and leave. I'll get up earlier tomorrow instead.

As I walk across camp toward my cabin, I cross paths with Jesy and Julia—who still hasn't smiled at me once—but no matter how much I try to muster enthusiasm for what Jesy says, it must sound fake. Eventually, I fake a headache and slip away.

I try to focus on the song of the cicadas and the view of artists carving a piece of clay on a picnic table next to the administration building, but thoughts of the phone call keep returning to my mind like a boomerang. He wasn't even mean to me—in fact, this is probably his way of showing he cares, at least a little—but it still made me feel empty.

Above the lake, the sun is barely setting. Two large seagulls soar on the horizon, blending with the peach-colored clouds, the moon a soft ball of butter slowly taking its position. I take it all in, trying once again to let my thoughts go with the wind, but what remains is a stomachache and a feeling of helplessness.

Yeah, going to bed early to ruminate is probably a bad idea. Maybe when I arrived at Allegro, it would've been the only option in my mind, but now, I see I can do something else. The one thing I know could make me feel better.

I don't feel like running from him anymore.

With a sudden change of heart, I shift on my feet and head

closer to the camp's entrance, where Jamie's cabin sits. I might not be able to put into words what's going on with me, but at least he'll be able to take my thoughts somewhere else, one of his many talents. There's always the strong possibility he won't be there, but I'm willing to risk the disappointment.

Stupid? Definitely. But that seems to be my curse with him, and here I am, asking for more.

When I'm close enough to Jamie's cabin, I hear his voice, and something loosens in my chest. He's here. The sound is a soothing balm. Whatever happened this past year doesn't change anything. This specific voice will always make me feel safe. Home.

Except as I approach, I hear another voice. Lower. Jeremiah's.

Once my feet reach the front steps, I lift a fist to knock, but before I can connect with the door, I hear my name, and I freeze.

"—was your idea?" Jeremiah's muffled voice says.

"No, hers." Jamie sounds off. Sad.

"Bro, I'm sorry. That sucks."

A pause, then, "Better that than not being with her at all."

Is he...? No, he can't be.

I get even closer, my ear pressed to the door like a stalker. If this were in any other circumstance, I'd feel terrible about eavesdropping, but if he's doing what I think he is, then I have a right to know. At least that's what I tell myself.

"You're good actors," Jeremiah says with a chuckle. "I never would've been able to tell it was fake."

The nice feeling that was starting to fill my body is gone, replaced by a sense of betrayal so deep, it forces the air out of my lungs. Jamie has never shared things I didn't want him to before. Never. It didn't matter that he could've sold me out more times than I can count. He's always been the one person I felt comfortable enough to share things with. For a while after my friend Kailie betrayed me, I thought I would remain lonely for my whole life. Always friendly, never the real friend. And then I met him, the one person I felt I could trust.

My throat is tight as I knock on the door, louder than I probably should. I can't hear any more of this. Footsteps come from the other side, and a second later, Jeremiah opens the door.

"Hey," I say, not even able to fake a smile. "Can I see Jamie for a sec?"

"Sure thing," Jeremiah says, and I could swear he's eyeing me differently now. As he should. He knows I'm a liar. Maybe he's even known about some of it for a while and has been judging me since the beginning of summer. He turns around to call Jamie's name, but before he can, the person who just stabbed me in the back is there, looking unfairly cute in a black cable-knit sweater and washed-out jeans.

"Hi," he says with a genuine grin, but he must see in my face something is wrong because it falls almost instantaneously.

"Care for a walk?" I ask.

He eyes me warily but still nods. On his way out, Jeremiah whispers something in his ear, and the thought that they might be sharing secrets about my private life, which I worked so freaking hard to keep private, makes me want to crawl out of my skin.

When the door closes behind Jamie, I grab his wrist and lead him away to the parking lot, where I know we won't be bothered, and if I walk faster than usual, he doesn't question it.

"What's going on?" he finally says when we've reached a quiet, mostly hidden corner of the lot.

Focusing on his chin instead of his eyes, I say, "Why did you tell Jeremiah what we'd agreed to keep quiet?"

His whole body stiffens. "How... You heard us."

"I did."

He winces, and I'm not sure if it's because he regrets doing it, or if he simply regrets being caught.

"I'm sorry. It kind of came up, and—"

"Our faking a relationship came up? Really?" The words come out louder than I intended. I'm not one to blow up, but if there's one thing this summer has proved, it's that whatever I thought I knew about myself was wrong. I feel like a boiling teapot of emotions right now, and I can't seem to control any of them. I hate it.

"*Your* faking, Emma. I'm not faking a damn thing here, in case you forgot."

I shuffle back a step. Meanwhile, Jamie throws his hands in the air before burying them in the roots of his hair. Above us, the sky cracks, and I notice for the first time how gray it's gotten in the past ten minutes.

"You can't expect me to have no feelings about it," he says. "Knowing that you act all lovey-dovey in public while you hate me in secret? It's fucking excruciating. But I do it because I said I would." He inhales deeply, and all the while I can't get a single ounce of air in my chest. "So yeah, I had to talk to someone about it because it's driving me nuts."

A drop falls on my forehead, then one on my nose.

"I'm sorry," I say, and I mean it. This is the first time he's mentioned feeling that way, but I should've seen it. Expected it. Some part of me probably did, even though I didn't want to acknowledge it. "I thought you were on board with the idea, but if you don't want to, we can stop."

He drags his hands down his face, which has started to get wet from the rain, before he fully explodes.

"That's not the fucking point! The point is I want you, and you don't want me, and that hurts like a bitch," he yells.

And that's when it starts to pour. Like in a movie. All of a sudden, we're both drenched, and the rain falls so loudly around us, I can barely hear him. It's so theatrical, I feel like the universe is once again playing games with us.

"Well, at least now you know how it feels," I shout back, letting all my feelings out. The pain, the frustration, the love, it all comes out in those nine words.

His eyes land on mine, so fierce they could light a fire in this storm. I'm breathing fast, the rain freezing me to the bone, but somehow, I'm numb to it. It's all secondary. The only thing I can feel is him.

His chest is rising and falling fast too as he stares at me.

"I never meant to hurt you," he says sharply.

"And you think I did?" I thought we were both okay with it. I didn't think I was forcing him to do anything he didn't want to do. He wanted to keep Molly unaware. It never crossed my mind that this would be painful for him, or else I wouldn't have suggested it.

"I don't know, Emma, and that's the thing." He shakes his head, drops of water falling down his glasses, over his nose, across his lips. His steps bring him closer to me, the torrent heightening around us. "You have so many facades, sometimes, it's like I don't even know you."

I clutch the sleeves of my shirt with both fists as his words land like a blow to the jaw. It hurts even more because I feel like I *am* vulnerable with him. I was just thinking about how I've let him in more than I ever have anyone. Flashes come of those nights in my apartment, when we'd lie in bed and talk for hours. Sometimes it would be three in the morning, and we'd both be falling asleep, but we couldn't stop ourselves from talking. His fingers would be tracing shapes on my hips and back, and I'd be muttering senseless stuff without him even correcting me. I can't count the number of sleepless nights we spent simply talking to each other. I recall the time I broke down in his arms and told him how scared I was that my mother was struggling again and how powerless I felt, and the day I shared how growing up under the eyes of what felt like the entire music world often felt like a curse. I'm reminded of the nights I let him discover my body, offering the most intimates parts of me to him, wanting him to see it all. To love it all.

Yet here he is, telling me he doesn't know me.

I don't try to hide the emotions in my wet eyes. "And sometimes," I say softly, which comes out as barely a whisper over the rain, "it feels like you're the only one who does."

Something in his face changes. His eyebrows knot. His jaw

clenches. His gaze softens before turning fiery again, but this time, not in anger.

No, when those eyes dip to my lips, there's only one emotion in them, and it lights a fire in my core.

The smell of petrichor fills my nostrils as my own gaze falls to those plump lips, parted and dripping.

What happens next isn't expected. I don't think about it. It's instinctual. The moment he takes that last step between him and me, I climb to my tiptoes, wrap my arms around his neck, and slam my mouth to his.

The sound Jamie makes when we touch is enough to make my toes curl in my shoes. It's a *finally* and a *please don't stop* and a *more* all at once.

His hands land on my upper thighs, and like I have a thousand times before, I jump so he can carry me in his arms as his kiss fills me from everywhere.

Water sluices over our faces as his tongue shatters through my mouth, making me gasp. I can't remember the last time we kissed that way. It's not soft or romantic. It's raw, electric, passionate. All things we haven't been in a while, but god, it feels good. Too good.

My nails scratch at his scalp as he kisses me harder, deeper. I moan, rubbing my pelvis against his, and now he groans. I can't even find it in me to care about whether someone sees or not—that's how good it feels, to be connected to him again.

Jamie seems to want to keep this moment private, though, because while his lips never move away from mine, he starts walking toward the tree line, as if I weigh nothing.

Thunder claps above us, and lightning may or may not have struck, but I can't open my eyes to look. I'm too lost in the lemon scent of his hair, in the taste of mint on his tongue from the gum he was chewing, and in the sense that finally, I'm back where I've been wanting to be for months.

"God, Emma," he groans. While continuing to walk, his lips move away from mine, only to land on my jaw, then on my neck.

Eyes closed, I tilt my head back. His tongue darts out to lick water droplets from the line of my neck, and I'm burning. My blood is boiling inside of me.

My pulse is thrumming in my head, my thighs tightening around him as I let him taste my skin.

"This feels..." I mutter, not able to find the appropriate words. Instead, I pull him back to me, and as I bite his lower lip, I rock against him, feeling the delicious length of him under me.

Jamie lets out another deep sound as I take his mouth, wanting so much more than this. He kisses me with everything he has, and I match his desire, the pent-up emotions let loose. His tongue teases mine in the way he knows drives me insane. I pull at the roots of his hair, wanting him closer, closer—

Jamie groans again, but this time it's different somehow. I feel his grip around me tighten, and he mutters, "Oh shit."

I never realized what it would feel like to be as tall as Jamie. But now, as I see the world tumbling to the side, I get an idea. I have the time to shriek and hold tight to him, bracing for the upcoming impact. It feels like ages pass as trees tilt at strange angles, and finally, I feel the slap of the ground against me.

"Fuck," Jamie grunts, "are you okay?"

My neck hurts, and I think I hit my forehead against his chin at the same spot I already had a bruise on, but despite it all, I can't help but laugh.

"You broke my fall," I say when I realize we both landed on Jamie's back.

He moans in response, this time from pain instead of pleasure. "I might never walk again."

"Drama queen."

"You think catching your whole ass body isn't hard?"

"If I remember correctly, we fell because you tripped," I deadpan. "You and that new lying down kink."

He groans. "It was slippery, and I was busy thinking about other things."

A grin climbs up my lips. I can't start thinking about what it all means. I can at least give myself another minute to enjoy the feeling before I start to freak out.

Jamie stays on his back, but I roll myself off, then dust my pants off. We fell into a pile of wet leaves, and while my clothes were already a mess from the rain, now they're thoroughly dirty.

Wait.

We fell in leaves. Not in gravel, like in the parking lot.

I jump to my feet and start spinning in a circle as I look around.

"Why are you imitating my childhood dog chasing after his tail?"

"Because," I say, pointing around us. "Look where we are."

Jamie lifts himself to a seated position with a groan, then starts looking.

I see the moment when he realizes. His eyes widen, mouth opening. "Did we just..."

"Yes, we did." I laugh, arms spread wide, spinning again. "We crossed the camp's borders."

CHAPTER 20

Jamie

"WHAT DOES IT MEAN?"

I don't know, and to be honest, I don't really care. I'm still stuck on the part where we kissed after what feels like a lifetime, and I have a raging hard-on, and fuck, do I love this girl.

"Jamie?" Emma asks. The rain has calmed down, and now that we're not in the heart of a storm, I can see how rumpled she looks. Hair wild, lips swollen, eyes wide.

"I mean," I say as I get to my feet and wipe my jeans, "something changed when we crossed the camp's border together." Her cheeks blush as if the mention of what just happened is too much for her. "So I guess it means this time-travel thing really is related to one of us and not to the camp itself."

"Right," she says, taming her hair, her eyes on the ground. "That would make sense." Her lips twist to the side. "Actually, give me one second." Then, she's off, jogging toward the camp. I remain in place and wait for her to come back a minute later, a disappointed look on her face.

"What was that?" I ask.

"Thought for a second we might've been brought back to real time," she says, breathless.

I give her a sad smile, then look behind my shoulder at the road that leads out of the camp. "Should we see how far away we can get?"

"I mean, we could, but as long as we stay in the past, there's not much use to it."

I cross my arms. "Right. So not that cool of a discovery when you think about it."

"Not true," she says. "It's still a clue as to why we're here and how we can get back."

"Something about us."

"Yes." She takes my arm in her hands to inspect it. I realize I'm bleeding from where a loose branch cut into my skin. "Does it hurt a lot?"

When you're touching me, Emma, I could be on fire and I wouldn't realize it.

"I'm okay," I say.

"All right." Without another word, she lets go of me and starts walking back toward the cabins, her gaze straight ahead. I recognize my Emma then. Hyper-focusing on a task to avoid talking about what just transpired between us.

Gravel crunches under our feet, the air still humid, everything damp. I could probably wring a liter of water out of my clothes. Still, I'm not cold. I'm not over what happened, and I desperately need to know what it means. Can I do it again?

"I can't think of something about either one of us that would warrant a return in time to change," she says, more to herself than to me.

And that's when it clicks.

"The accident," I say.

She stops in her steps.

Jesus, it's so clear now. How did I not see it before? Because of me, she's been struggling with her piano. If we hadn't been on that camping trip last year, or if I hadn't slipped while carrying the canoe, then her hand would still be perfect, and she wouldn't have any trouble playing. I know she resents me for it, but maybe it runs even deeper than what I'd assumed. Maybe this is the universe telling me to correct this shit so she can be as good as she used to be, and then she can forgive me for it. Maybe that's our chance to work once more.

"What do you mean?" Emma asks, although it's unnecessary. It's clear she knows what I'm talking about by the way she just gripped her hand.

"If we go back to the trip we took last summer, then we can avoid having the accident, and your hand might become as good as new."

"But that's not possible. We're already back in time, and my hand is still messed up," she says.

I look up as I process the timeline of things, then say, "Right, because you're still the you of the future. But if we change what happened in the past, then the you from the future might change. We might reverse everything."

She blinks. Blinks again.

"I'm not sure I'm smart enough for all this," she says softly, making me grin.

"Me neither, but I think this might be our solution."

Tugging the sleeves of her shirt so they cover her hands, she says, "I don't know..."

"It will work," I say, convinced now. This is the way to go. It will help us. "Let's do it. Let's go back and change the future."

She scratches her neck, then says, "You really think this might be it?"

I nod. Why isn't she more excited? She'll be back to her best self. She won't have those cramps that annoy her anymore.

And maybe, just maybe, that'll get her to love me again.

She licks her lips. I can't look away. It takes me right back to that kiss, and fuck, I'm straining against my zipper again. I try to adjust myself as subtly as I can, but based on the look Emma throws my way, I fail terribly.

"Fine," she ends up saying. "Let's do it."

I can't help the smile that overtakes my face. One night, two days, alone with Emma, correcting everything. This is the perfect plan.

"Okay," I say like an idiot because that seems to be the only thing I'm able to be around her.

She gives me a small grin before turning back toward the camp.

"Oh, and—" she starts, again not meeting my eyes. "About what just happened."

Something stutters in my chest.

"We probably shouldn't repeat that." She scratches her arm. "At least not until we've both figured out exactly what it is we want."

As if I don't already know what I want. Still, I nod. When she kisses me, I want her to mean it, and she can deny it all she wants, but that kiss? It did mean something.

"Great," she says, nodding a few times. "And no need to fake anything in public anymore. Let's just be ourselves. 'Kay?"

Lightness fills me. I should've known that she wouldn't ask me to continue doing something that made me feel bad. It's not like her to be mean. She was raised in a world of sharks and still grew up to become a dove. A miracle. I dip my head and say, "Sounds good."

* * *

"What the hell are you watching?"

I look up from my computer to find Jeremiah's head hanging upside down from his top bunk, his eyes riveted on my screen.

Which is showing a superhero movie that technically hasn't come out yet.

Fuck.

"Oh, just a fan-made trailer," I improvise.

"Damn," he says, still analyzing it. "Those losers are getting good."

I try not to laugh when I think that I'm one of those losers, considering the pathetic amount of time I spent as a twelve- and thirteen-year-old making fan-made trailers of future movies based on the comics I'd read as a kid.

Noticing Jeremiah still scrutinizing my screen, I close the computer and say, "It kind of sucks."

He looks a little suspicious, but thankfully, he doesn't ask more questions and goes back to lying on his bunk. Jeremiah minds his own business, and I didn't have time to tell Emma that earlier, but I trust him. If you tell him to keep something quiet, he'll bring it to his grave. I know if I wanted to, I could tell him all about our stint in the past, and I did consider it, but only for a second. It's between Emma and me, and I like that we have this little secret. It feels like it's her and me against the world, literally.

Just as I go to open a book—which was published more than a year ago, thank god—a knock comes from the door. I jump, my pulse skyrocketing at the thought it might be Emma. It doesn't take a second before I'm at the door, and while I can admit there's a tiny bit of disappointment when I see it's not the person I was expecting, I smile at my little sister.

"Hey, what's up?" We've hung out much more this summer than last, which I have Emma to thank for. Now that I've done it, I see how stressed Molly was about Allegro, and I'm happy that in the future, there's a chance the memories she'll keep will be the ones from this repeat summer, instead of the shitty ones from last time.

"Nothing," she says, but the frown on her lips tells me the opposite.

"Mol. Come on."

She remains silent, although I notice the way she eyes Jeremiah behind me.

"Gimme one sec," I say before I put my sneakers on and come outside with her, closing the door behind me. Her arms are crossed over her Taylor Swift Reputation Stadium Tour T-shirt. I fight the urge to smile as I remember the night we got it together. My sister has been a fan through all of the artist's eras, and when I heard she would be coming to Foxborough, I started saving up from my shifts at the restaurant to buy tickets. Molly was still little at the time, and the stars I saw in her eyes when she opened the gift were worth all the money in the world. The show itself was great, but my sister's happiness was even better. Molly is often reserved and lonely— which probably explains why she's the sibling I'm closest with— but that night, she was uninhibited, belting out the lyrics to every song. I know I always tease Emma about her love of country music, but even I wasn't able to resist the good ol' "Love Story" guitar riff.

The way she looks right now is the total opposite of that night, though. There is no trace of a smile as she looks at me expectantly, as if I can help her when I don't know what's wrong.

"Did something happen?" I ask her as I sit on the steps leading up to the cabin.

She shrugs.

"You're starting to worry me." She's never come to my cabin before, even when I offered, which means something must've happened. "Are you having problems with your cello? Do you need me to call Mom?"

That gets her to shake her head vigorously. "Please don't."

"Okay, then tell me what's going on."

"It's nothing." She sighs, shrugging her fiery-red hair behind her shoulders. "Just some girls that were mean."

Shit. "Do you want me to go get Emma?" She would know what to do about girl problems.

"No, please don't. I don't want her to think I'm a loser," she says in a low voice.

"Come on, you know she wouldn't think that." As I say the words, I realize I'm being incredibly hypocritical. I'm the first person who needs reassurance that Emma won't judge me, but when I look at it from an outsider's perspective, it's clear it's not something she would do. Still, if Molly doesn't want me to tell her, I won't.

"Do you want me to go kick their asses, then?" I ask her, which finally brings a smile to her lips.

She snickers. "God, no."

"All right," I say, "but the offer remains if you need it." I'm not the confrontational type, but for my little sister, I'd stand up to anyone.

"Thanks."

Molly doesn't say more, but she doesn't leave either. Maybe she just didn't want to be alone in her cabin. I get the feeling.

A breeze coming from the lake tousles our hair, and coupled with the chilly night air, it makes me repress a shiver. I put an arm around Molly's shoulders and rub up and down her arm. If we were home, she'd never let me—she hates looking weak in front of her four older brothers—but here, she doesn't seem to mind the comfort.

"You know," I say, "I had some bad experiences with bullies in the past too."

Her brows are furrowed. "No, you didn't."

I huff. "Oh yes, I did. That bastard Tom Jenkins kept making fun of me at school. Don't tell Mom I said that."

She gives me a lopsided grin.

"He'd make me trip in the hallway and tell me I was a sissy for playing the piano instead of playing sports like a real guy. Real BS." I skip over the part where he would make people in class notice how I'd been wearing the same pairs of jeans for three years straight and how they were becoming too short for me.

"So what did you do?"

"Nothing."

She frowns.

"I told myself I'd become the best damn pianist I could and he'd regret laughing at me when I became a successful artist and he remained the kind of loser who would get trapped into some MLM and whose idea of fun would be to go drifting in Wal-Mart parking lots with his dropped Honda Civic during winter time."

Her eyes are narrowed, maybe in confusion, and yeah, maybe I went a little too far. I squeeze her upper arm. "What I mean is, the best revenge you can offer is to be above whatever it is they're saying about you, to focus on yourself, and to become better than them." I can't remember the number of times I repeated that same thing to myself. That's actually what led me to write my first composition. I felt like a pile of crap after that asshole Tom had spotted me getting out of my dad's beat-up minivan and proceeded to tell everyone that I probably lived in a dump. It was such a cheap shot, and it was far from the truth, but the humiliation I felt on that day threatened to drown me. And instead of letting it, I pushed all of those feelings into music. That first song might have been crappy, but it got me hooked. Ever since that day, I've used my music sheets as a journal. Easier to write down arrangements than thoughts and feelings.

As I composed that first song, with tears streaming down my cheeks and my shoulders becoming less and less heavy, I thought maybe *this* would be the best revenge. Using all the negative feelings these people had instilled in me and transforming them into something people could listen to. Something people could be moved by, just like I've been touched by so many artists and songs in my life.

"Yeah, I guess," Molly says. She leans her cheek against my shoulder.

"Want to tell me what happened now?" I ask her.

"Nah. But thanks for trying anyway."

I grin, then hug her. "I love you, Mol. Always there for you if you need it."

"Thanks." She claps my back twice. "You're an okay brother, I guess."

I burst out laughing. "And you're terrible, you know that?" I pull at her ponytail, which makes her shriek, then laugh.

"Come on. I'll walk you back to your cabin."

CHAPTER 21

Emma

"DO WE HAVE EVERYTHING?"

I look back to the approximately eight hundred bags we have packed in the canoe. Whoever said camping was a fun and easy way to travel was a liar.

"I don't think we have any more space inside anyway, so I'll go with yes," I answer Jamie.

The sun is blazing, the air already stupidly hot despite the early hour. At least we're not getting rain. I remember last year, we had the same temperature, which makes sense, considering it *is* the same day.

I wonder what today looks like in real time. Is there sunlight filling my mother's bedroom as she lies in bed? I hope so. She doesn't need more gloominess.

"You ready for this?" Jamie asks. He's near me now, hands on my shoulders. His usual glasses have been replaced by sunglasses, and a simple black baseball cap covers his head. We'll need it with that heat.

"Ready," I say, not ready at all. If it was only up to me, we'd be staying here, where we have actual beds and food that we don't need to rehydrate. But when Jamie suggested we do this, I couldn't tell him no. He looked so excited about the idea, and after I'd learned I hurt him, even unintentionally, I would've done anything to make things better. Hopefully, this will. Although by the way he kissed me two days ago after he told me the truth, I'd say he's not holding a grudge.

Plus, this trip might lead us somewhere with our time-travel issue, and although I'm not convinced it is the solution, I'm not about to turn my back on the only lead we have at the moment.

"Come on," I tell him as I hop (or, more like, carefully but unsteadily step) into the front of the canoe, and the boat shifts with Jamie's weight when he joins me. By the loud thump his body makes as it drops onto the small wooden bench, I'd say his entrance lacked grace, just like mine, although he does have the excuse of being a thousand feet tall.

"Have a nice trip, lovebirds!" someone shouts behind us.

Laughing, I turn and wave at Jesy. I didn't know she was there, but I'd recognize her high-pitched voice anywhere. When she turns her chair around to leave, I drop my hand, and my gaze lands on Jamie, who was already staring my way.

"What?" I ask, still smiling.

He shakes his head. "Nothing."

"Really, what?" I say with a chuckle. The way he's watching me isn't how he's been looking at me all summer. A worriless gaze meets mine.

"Nothing, really. You just looked happy."

Heat rises to my cheeks, the redness I'm sure obvious to him. Without answering, I turn and tell him, "Let's go, then, Captain."

A moment passes before he says, "At your service."

This is it.

We start moving our bodies in awkward humps to make the canoe move forward, and when we're deep enough into the water, we push ourselves with our paddles to finally leave the shore.

"Do you know where we're headed?" I ask him once we've started paddling, soft gurgles of water filling the serene silence.

"Absolutely not."

I spin on my seat, eyes wide.

"Kidding. Of course, I know."

"Wouldn't have been the first time," I mumble as I return to my paddling. A blissful breeze cools the surface of the lake, contrasting with the torridity of the air. The red paint of the canoe is chipped, and the bolts are rusty, but other than a creaking noise when I shift my weight, it seems to be doing the job.

"Oh, come on," Jamie says, snickering. "That was one time."

"One time too many! It took us five hours of paddling for a trip that should've taken one last year," I tease.

"But this is our second chance summer. It's all going to be fine."

"And I'm supposed to trust you?"

"Damn right you are. I have a good inner compass."

"Said every man ever. And yet…"

"If I remember correctly, you're the one who constantly plays copilot princess in my car, and yet we somehow always find a way to miss our exits because you forget to look at the map."

I shrug, then throw him a smirk over my shoulder. "Oh, absolutely, but I've never pretended otherwise. You, on the other hand—"

"I know where we're going," Jamie repeats in a serious tone.

My lips stretch in such an insincere smile, it makes Jamie roll his eyes. "Sure thing."

* * *

On second thought, I should never, ever have trusted him.

It's something I should know by now about him. Jamie hates pulled-pork sandwiches, his favorite book is the first of the Percy Jackson series, which he fell in love with at twelve years old and has read about fifty times since, and his sense of direction is absolute crap. I teased him about it, but in the end, I let him lead us blindly.

And here we are, six hours later—yes, actually six—completely, unmistakably lost.

"Did you bring a paper map with you?" I ask as we paddle around the small bay we've found ourselves trapped in for the fifth time.

"Sorry, forgot to time travel to the nineties to grab one."

I spin in my seat and glare.

"Too soon?" he says.

"Yeah, too soon."

I let my gaze travel around, not recognizing a single element of our surroundings. "How did we even get here?" I say. Last year, we got lost in the main part of Moosehead Lake and simply couldn't find our campground, but this time, it's even worse. It's like we're in an alcove of the main lake, but we've been looking for a while now and still haven't been able to find how to get back to the main part.

"I thought we were supposed to find the canal that gets us to the other part of the lake here." His voice is low, the same way it is when he's had a bad practice session.

"Jamie, you know I'm joking, right? It's fine," I tell him over my shoulder. "If we don't find our way, we'll just camp somewhere random." It's not like we didn't do the same thing last year, but I won't say that. "It'll be an adventure."

"No, it's not fine," he says, the faint trace of humor that was there a minute ago vanished. "We were supposed to do things differently this year." Without looking at him, I know he must have removed his hat to drag a hand through his hair, and maybe even pull at the roots. His mouth must be twisted to one side as he bites the inside of his cheek.

"And we have!" With a lift of my tired arms, I bring the paddle back inside the canoe before doing a one-eighty to face Jamie. "I've never seen this place, which means last year we got lost in a totally different place."

"Not funny."

I grin, then make a small space between my thumb and index finger. "Maybe a little?"

"Not even that."

"Oh, come on, you Debbie Downer. We're in the sunshine, it's not too hot, and we have food, water, and two tents. The worst-case scenario here is not that bad at all."

"I know, but we were supposed to find the actual campground this time."

"You're the one who didn't want to bring an old-school map," I mutter under my breath.

"Not funny."

I lift my hands, only grinning a little. "Fine. I'm done." Extending my leg, I kick his shin softly to take him out of his crappy mood. "Honestly, though, it won't matter if we're in an actual campground or some random place in the woods. I can't remember precisely how I hurt my hand last year, but I'm sure it had nothing to do with the campground."

His eyes narrow. "Is this supposed to be a joke?"

"What? Why?"

He looks at me like I just grew a second head. "Because we both know how you hurt yourself. It was my fault."

"Oh, come on, Jamie, it wasn't. The canoe fell."

"Yes, it fell because I tripped and my grip slipped."

"I can't say I remember that," I say. The permanent notch between his brows tells me he doesn't believe me, but so what? It's the truth. My memories of that day are a blur, and I have no clear recollection of how I hurt my hand. The only thing I remember vividly is the pain, so sharp it felt like my arm was being torn in two. And then Jamie was there, soothing me, helping me somewhere safe, then jumping back in that miserable boat to go get help. Then there was the motorboat that came to get me, and then the hospital, and the surgery, and the physical therapy, and all of the school year that followed. I didn't come back to Allegro to finish the summer, and Jamie only came for the showcase, which earned him his award. That's all I remember. Nothing about the event itself.

"And anyway," I add, "if that's what you're worried about, I'll let you carry the whole canoe by yourself like the caveman you're acting like, and there won't be any risks to my hand."

That gets him to crack a smile. Bingo.

Before, it wasn't so bad, but now that I've stopped paddling for a minute, I realize how tired my arms are. I'm sore in my shoulders and my neck, and I don't know how long I'll be able to continue doing this before I can't handle it anymore.

I *really* need to start exercising more.

"How about this," I say. "We stop here for today, maybe even go for a swim. We set up our tents, make sure you don't randomly drop a canoe on my hand, and tomorrow we turn around and make our way back, hopefully back to our time."

His lips twist to the side.

"It's okay, Jamie. Really." My hand lands on his, warm and a little sunburnt. "This is going to be great."

He hesitates, clearly not happy about his failed plan, but he must see how this will lead to the same thing. We won't have a bigger chance of magically messing with fate if we're anywhere else, and at this rate, the only thing that will actually hurt me is an extra hour of paddling.

"All right," he says.

We head toward a spot on the shore where trees are sparse, hopefully enough that we'll be able to set up our two tents. I didn't want to make things even more ambiguous by having us sleep in the same space, and Jamie seemed to agree with me, so we each packed our own.

A loud scratching sound echoes as the tip of our canoe skims the muddy ground of the lake. I get up, only grabbing one bag with me because I'll need to pull on the nose of the canoe to bring it safely to shore.

"Don't worry," Jamie says behind me, also on his feet. "I'll do it."

"No, no, I'm good."

Those words must trigger the universe. It must be that. Because one second, I'm standing upright in the wobbly canoe, and the next, I'm falling to my side, the entire boat tipping.

What is it with this summer and the crappy falls?

I don't have time to scream, it all happens too fast. In a breath, water clouds everything. I feel it drench my shirt, my hair, my face, my lungs. The world becomes soundless, as if everything turns to slow-motion. I can almost see it from a bird's-eye view: my body going under, breath caught in my throat as I fight against gravity pulling me down. We're in the shallow part of the lake, but it doesn't matter. When I finally bring my head out of the water to gasp and inhale a lungful of air, I spot the dozens of bags we'd packed now floating around the upside-down canoe, our tents, clothes, and food probably ruined. Jamie is lying on his side in the murky waters, groaning.

And my hand—my *freaking* hand—is stuck between two rocks.

CHAPTER 22

Emma

OUCH.

"Jesus Christ, Emma, are you okay?" Water splashes from my left as I assume Jamie runs my way.

"Great," I grunt out. Crap, this hurts. I try moving my stuck hand, but it only sends shocks of bright white pain through my arm and even to my neck. I don't know if there's blood, and I'd rather not look. I've never been good around the sight of it.

"Fuck, how did this happen?" Jamie blurts as he reaches me and throws himself to his knees, water dripping from his hair to his nose and cheeks. "Did I do something?"

"Not your fault," I grunt out.

I don't know how we're surprised I hurt myself. Didn't we see each other at the volleyball game? Did we need more proof of what crappy athletes we are? Who did we think we were, going around acting like we can change the future with our outstanding outdoorsy skills?

Jamie grunts as he shifts forward in the shallow water to help me sit up. Only when he sees I'm not at imminent risk of drowning does his gaze stray to my hand. By the face he makes, I know I don't want to look.

"I guess the universe doesn't want my hand to go back to normal."

Jamie's jaw ticks once, twice, before he turns and whisper-shouts, "Fuck!"

I stay silent as he pushes his hair back, and when he returns to me, I say, "I'm sorry." I don't know what state my hand is in, but from the feel of it, I doubt it will be good enough that we would be sent back to the future.

"No, sweetheart, no, it's not your fault," Jamie says as he pushes some of the wet locks away from my forehead.

I try to ignore the tightening in my belly at the sound of the term of endearment and instead focus on how I can un-trap myself.

"Okay, I think if I lift this rock, you'll be able to slip your hand out," Jamie says.

"Does it look bad?" I ask, semi-ignoring what he's said.

"Not sure. It's not bleeding, but I can't say what the hand looks like."

Amazing.

"How bad does it hurt?" he asks softly.

"Not too bad."

"Liar." He brushes my forehead again, then says, "You want me to try this?" he asks.

I nod. The sooner we know, the better.

"I'm so sorry." Jamie counts to three, then uses his entire body weight to pull the rock away from my hand.

"Shit!" I cry out as I bring my damaged hand to my chest. Somehow, this hurts even more than being crushed in the first place.

"I'm sorry, I'm sorry." After dropping the rock, Jamie returns as close to me as physically possible so he can look at the hand I'm holding close to me. "Does anything feel broken to you? Can you move your fingers?"

I try to wiggle them, and while it hurts so much my breath catches in my throat, they do move. "I don't think anything's irreparably messed up."

"Okay, that's good."

I don't bring to light that while I might not need surgery again, it doesn't mean I'll play better with this left hand than the one that was operated on. Jamie looks shocked enough by the turn of events as it is.

"Let me go get the first aid kit I packed in my bag. Be right back."

It's at that precise moment that we both seem to realize our bags are currently floating away from us. Jamie crouches so he can be in a prone position in the foot-high water, then swims away to grab our wet bags. He collects the two that strayed the farthest, then picks up the ones that stayed close to the upside-down canoe and brings them all back to shore. Still gripping my wrist as if it'll help in any way, I get up and carefully walk to him. While it feels good not to be sitting in cold water anymore, my clothes are soaked through, and now that the sun is hidden behind the heavy branches of the trees above us, the wind is less comfortable than it was before.

"Thankfully for us," Jamie says as he scavenges through the bag he'd packed, "my parents enrolled me in junior scouts when I was eleven."

"Is that supposed to make me feel better?"

He throws me a glare. "Yes. We learned how to make bandages, and I think I remember how to do it."

"I'm sure it'll be just as good as a surgeon's," I say. Jamie turns again to give me a dirty look, but when he sees I'm grinning, his face softens.

When he finally finds the elastic wrap in the first aid kit, Jamie makes his way to me, then sits on a rock close to mine, our knees grazing. He looks hyper-focused as he carefully takes my hand in both of his and places it on his thigh. With the same meticulousness he would use to perform difficult runs, he unwinds the band and wraps it around my hand. The pressure feels both great and terrible at the same time.

"I'm sorry," he says when I hiss. His face is so close to mine, I can feel his breath on my cheek, droplets of water falling from his curls to my legs and feet. I'm pretty sure Jamie hasn't even noticed that his sunglasses are tilted unnaturally on his face from the fall, his attention only on my hand. Without thinking about it, I lift my good fingers and straighten them.

"It's fine," I say. "I'm sure Papa Scout would be proud of you."

"Damn right he would."

Jamie brings the elastic wrap all the way to my elbow, then hooks it with a metal pin. I fear it might be a little too tight, but I'll die before saying a word. He's looking at it with a proud smile, and I'd rather lose my arm from lack of blood flow than steal that satisfaction away from him. It's better than what I would've been able to do by myself anyway.

"All done," he says.

I look up, finding his coffee eyes on mine. It's difficult to get a breath in, and I'm not sure it's due to the fall. "Thank you."

"Anytime." His lips tick up. "Although I'd prefer you not almost die on me another time."

"Oh, please. It was just a small fall."

"A small fall that took years off my life."

"You didn't even hurt yourself," I argue.

He burns me with his stare as he says, "I'm not talking about me."

I swallow. When he doesn't look away and it feels a little too intimate, I get to my feet and roll my shoulders. Meanwhile, Jamie settles into his rock with a loud exhale.

"So what do we do now?" I ask.

"I don't know." He doesn't open his lids. Even though we've only been here for a few minutes, I can see the toll this has taken on him. He really thought this camping thing would be the solution to all our issues.

"I don't think I can paddle back to camp with only one hand."

"You definitely can't."

"We could call for help? I'm sure someone from camp could borrow a motorboat to come get us."

Jamie scratches his head, not quite meeting my eye. A dead giveaway he's hiding something from me. "I might not have packed the satellite phone."

"What? Why?" I try to sound calm, but the only thing that comes out is a nervous laugh. I really, really don't wish to be stuck in this lost wood for weeks.

"Didn't think we'd need it."

"Really?" I say, eyebrows high. "Because we have such a good track record of not getting lost or hurt?"

"We were only supposed to go to a campsite an hour away!"

"My point exactly."

He rolls his eyes but doesn't say anything because he knows I have a point. This is the reason why he had to make the trek back to Allegro last year after I injured myself. We didn't have a phone, and because there's no reception around the lake, we hadn't brought our cellphones with us. He must have been so convinced this year would be good, he didn't even consider something else could happen to us.

"It's fine," Jamie says. "I'll just paddle back to camp and come get you with a boat."

"No. You're not leaving me alone here." I don't even know where we are. There could be all sorts of things in the woods, and while Jamie couldn't save me from a wild animal, I'd rather not face it alone.

"I did last year," he states.

"Last year was different." I couldn't have waited a few hours or days to feel better. I needed immediate medical help, and that was more important than my fear of being alone.

I wring water out of my hair, then go back to sit on the rock next to his. "We can stay here for a day or two until my hand gets better, and then we can try to paddle back."

"You'd really prefer that?" he asks.

I nod.

"All right, then," Jamie says, but even if he's agreeing, something doesn't seem right.

"Hey, look, it's fine. We're all in one piece. This is just our weird adventure being prolonged a bit."

He doesn't answer.

Lightly, I tip his chin so he's facing me. "Jamie, it's okay."

That gets him to wince.

"What?" I ask. "What's wrong?"

"We might have another tiny problem."

"Tell me."

"The little food we'd packed is probably wet and inedible now."

My eyes close by themselves, and the biggest sigh escapes my lips. I hadn't even thought about that. We'd brought bread, cheese, and dry cereal. No way they're still good.

We're stuck in some random woods a year in the past with only three usable hands and no food.

"Then I guess you'll go and find us things to eat for the next few days?" I say with a large smile, sounding like a question.

"Who do I look like, Bear Grylls?"

"I don't know, you're the one who boasted about being a teen scout!"

"Yeah, but I only lasted one summer," he says as he scratches his neck. "Only got to the first aid and knot-tying part, not to the cooking meals in the wild."

"Great." I give his thigh two taps. "Well, at least I can rest assured that if we magically find a boat to sail back to camp, your knots will come in to save the day."

He taps me back. "I wasn't the one responsible for making the program," he defends himself.

"Sure, buddy." I grin at him again. "It's fine. I'm sure finding things to eat isn't that complicated."

* * *

In hindsight, saying finding food in the wild is an easy thing probably jinxed it.

We found a whole lot of nothing while scavenging the makeshift campground we made, and after each eating four red berries we weren't convinced were not poisonous, we decided to call it a day and pretend we weren't that hungry anyway.

I slap my arm where I feel a mosquito trying to bite me.

"They're everywhere," I mutter. I must've done this dance three thousand times in the past hours.

"No, they're not. I'm fine." Jamie grins. "I feel like you're hallucinating them at this point."

"Am not." I shrug. "Guess my blood is just a delicacy to them."

"And mine's what, then, a pile of shit?"

"You said it, not me."

A pause, then, "Is it weird I find it kind of hot that your blood is bug fine cuisine?"

Laughter explodes out of me. "Yes, it is."

He gives me a careless shrug, the smile on his lips illuminating his entire self. I'm so happy he doesn't have his somber expression anymore. I'll get bitten three thousand more times and make more crappy mosquito jokes if it means he can remain this way.

"I think you're getting tired," I tell him with a nudge of his shoulder.

"Yeah, let's blame it on fatigue."

I look down at my watch—still working despite the water, thankfully—and while it's only 8:00 p.m., I'm drained. "Wanna call it a day?"

"Sure," he says.

I walk away to grab the heavy bag containing my tent, wincing as I try to lift it from the ground.

I hadn't noticed how close he was until Jamie's low voice is right there, saying, "Let me."

No, it doesn't send shivers down my spine.

"It's fine," I say without turning. "I can do it, but thanks."

"Don't be stubborn. You only have one hand."

"So?"

"Emma."

"Fine," I say, because if he's serious about wanting to help and doesn't see it as a burden, then he can be my guest. It would be arduous to do it on my own.

Jamie moves swiftly as he builds the tent, and I help him as much as I can.

"Sit," he says.

I stay right there, handing him the pieces he needs before he asks for them.

"It's wet, you know," he says once he's done building it.

I touch the outer material of the tent, and sure, it's a little damp, but it'll probably dry fast with the outdoor air.

"It's fine."

"Take mine," he says, pointing at the bag that took in way less water than mine, thanks to the dry bag he'd put it in while I'd forgotten to use one.

"No." He shouldn't pay for my mistakes.

"Emma."

"Jamie."

"I'm serious."

"Me too. I'm fine. I swear. And I won't budge, so better get to your own tent. It's getting dark."

He glares, but I stand my ground with my arms crossed in front of me, even though the fact that he's arguing for my sake is sending my belly aflutter.

"Fine."

Jamie gets to work, and a few minutes later, his tent is erected next to mine.

I yawn. "All right, time for sleep."

He stands in front of his door, his gaze moving from my tent to his, a muscle in his jaw ticking. Without looking at me, he says, "Okay. Good night."

"Good night."

Half of his body is inside his tent when I say, "Jamie?"

He freezes.

"Thank you. For everything."

His throat bobs before he nods once, and then he's gone.

A cold gush of wind stops my staring trance and forces me

inside my own tent. Except, as soon as I zip myself in and feel the thick, frigid humidity, I realize maybe I should have accepted Jamie's heroic offer, after all.

I'm fine. This is fine.

Wrapping myself in my damp sleeping bag, I lay on the freezing ground, forcing myself to imagine I'm in some warm, cozy place. Maybe lying on a Caribbean beach, or reading by the fire at home.

It only takes five minutes for my daydreams to burst and for my teeth to start chattering so violently that the sound resonates in my skull.

It's fine, Emma. Death by hypothermia isn't such a bad way to go.

I bring my legs to my chest and close my eyes. I figure I need to spend as little energy as possible, so I stay immobile and wait to fall asleep, which unfortunately doesn't happen, no matter how much time passes. All the tiredness I had earlier disappeared when I became a living icicle. I try to meditate, to sing a song, to go through a score in my head, but in the end—more precisely, when I think I'm going to lose one or two toes—I give up.

Body shivering so much it probably looks like I'm dancing, I stand up and escape my tent. Outside, the air is even colder, something that shouldn't be happening in August in Maine, but it's like this little zone of forest has its own microclimate. It's damp and dark and probably barely fifty degrees.

I walk the two steps to Jamie's tent. Since I can't knock, I unzip a corner of it, which takes me a long amount of time considering the way my hands are shaking.

"Jamie?" I whisper.

"Yeah?" he answers right away. I unzip the door a little more to find him sitting up in his sleeping bag. "Is something wrong?"

His hair is all over the place, eyes small and red from sleep. At least one of us was able to get some shut-eye. A pillow crease lines his cheek, and when he puts on his crooked glasses to see me better, I almost melt.

"Sorry to wake you, but—"

"Who cares? What's going on?"

"I'm just…" This feels wrong. I'm the one who asked him to bring two tents so we wouldn't confuse our feelings, and now I'm walking to his tent in the middle of the night to share it with him. It's embarrassing, but I guess it would be even more embarrassing if I died of frost because I was too proud to ask him for help. "I'm really, really cold in my tent, and I was wondering if—"

I don't have time to finish my sentence before Jamie has opened his comfy-looking sleeping bag, holding it up for me.

"Come on," he says. "Hop in."

"Oh, but I can sleep in another sleeping bag, I just need less humidity."

"Emma, you're shaking like a leaf, and your lips are almost blue. You need warmth."

I twist my lips to the side. "Are you sure?"

"Of course I'm sure." He lifts the corner of his sleeping bag even higher. "Come in."

I only hesitate a second longer before giving up and doing as he asks. It would be stupid not to. Besides, how many times have we slept together like this? Hundreds? It doesn't mean anything. It's for life-saving purposes.

It's what I tell myself when I lie next to Jamie and almost moan at the feel of his hot body against mine. He's careful not to touch me too much, but in a single-person sleeping bag, it's almost impossible to avoid.

Jamie clears his throat. "Do we need to get naked or…"

"You keep your clothes on, Montpellier."

He chuckles, the sound reverberating all through my body. His breath is warm on the back of my neck, making goosebumps rise on my skin.

We shift so we can settle into some spooning position, the way we used to sleep in the twin bed he had in high school. It's nostalgic, but also new.

"Are you sure this is okay?" I ask, facing the side of the tent.

"Emma, you're fine." As if to prove this, he drapes a loose arm over my hip. Some of his skin makes contact with where my shirt has ridden up, and the feeling is heavenly. I can't remember the last time we touched for the sake of sharing our bodies.

Crickets chirp outside as we pretend this is nothing new and important, the lake creating a lulling sound with each lap of the water against the rocks.

Once I can finally feel my toes again, I say, "I feel like Bella in *Eclipse*, when she needs to cuddle with Jacob to preserve her warmth."

"I have no idea what you're talking about."

I look over my shoulder and find his dark gaze already on mine, as alive and warm as his body. "No. You can't pretend you don't know what this basic piece of pop fiction is."

"I really don't."

I open my mouth in protest. "This is blasphemous." Shaking my head, I add, "All those freaking rat movies and no *Twilight*?"

"It was two movies! Two!"

Ignoring him, I say, "When we get back, we'll watch all the movies."

He lifts a brow, his lips twitching. "Together?"

I return to my previous position facing away. "If you want," I say, barely audible.

"Fine, then. I'll watch them with you."

"Five movies of pure perfection. You won't regret it."

"Trust me, I know I won't."

Despite all the weird stuff that's happened today, a soft smile covers my lips. This isn't so bad after all. My eyelids are heavier now that I'm not freezing my butt off, and the sounds of nature are calming me down. It's peaceful, when we forget that we're lost.

"Thanks for sharing your body heat with me."

The arm he has on my waist tightens. "Anytime. Seriously."

I settle onto his inflatable pillow with him, and while he

probably has my hair in his face and a numb arm, he doesn't complain about any of it.

"Good night, Jamie."

"Good night, Emma."

I might be already dreaming when I feel the soft press of his lips on the crown of my head.

CHAPTER 23

Jamie

T HE FIRST THING I NOTICE WHEN I WAKE UP, EVEN BEFORE I open my eyes, is the scent.

Emma's scent. Vanilla and something floral. Lilies, maybe? It doesn't matter that she's fallen into shady water yesterday and didn't get to shower. She smells like herself. It's not fair, truly. I missed this smell so much that I can't help but inhale deeply again.

The second thing I notice is that we're somehow even closer than we were when we fell asleep, which almost seems impossible considering I already felt like there wasn't any room for either of us to move in the sleeping bag, yet here we are. My arm is draped over her body, her nose buried in the crook of my neck, soft bursts of air warming my skin every time she exhales. Her dark hair is spread across my pillow, and when she shifts, it sends shivers all over my body.

I still can't believe she came to me last night. When I opened my eyes and saw her there, it almost felt like a fever dream. It couldn't be her. Emma's ego can be pretty big, so for her to come to me for help... She must've been close to hypothermia. I don't mind, though. Not at all. In a way, I'm thankful her tent got wet. If it hadn't, maybe we wouldn't have had this night, and I don't know how many else we'll get. If I don't succeed in winning her back and tonight's temperature isn't as bad, it might be the very last one spent by her side, her body against mine. My grip around her tightens. If I could do something to imprint myself on her and never let go, I would. It might sound pathetic, but I don't care. No one has ever loved me like she did, or seen me as she has. No one has been able to understand me from a single glance or to make me feel safe enough to break down, knowing they'll be there to catch me. I don't remember what the world is like without her by my side, and I don't want to know. Yet if she doesn't want me anymore, I'll have no choice but to let her go.

But yesterday was a step in the right direction. A step that's made me fall asleep with a smile on my face and wake up the same way.

A soft sound escapes her as her body wakes up, the hands she had brought to my sternum clenching, then relaxing.

"Morning," I say, my voice gruff.

While she was rousing before, this seems to have woken her up real and true. Her eyes jerk open as she pulls back—as much as the sleeping bag allows. Something in her gaze clears when she looks at me, as if remembering what happened last night. Right. She wouldn't have voluntarily gotten that tangled up with me if she'd realized it was happening.

"Good morning," she says, immobile.

"Sleep well?" I add a smirk. She doesn't need to know how much the sight of her pulling away breaks my heart.

Being in love with someone who's fallen out of love with you is its own kind of torture. Every time I try to get the spark back and I'm met with dull eyes, I die a little inside. I can't believe that's how Emma felt—how she thought *I* felt about her. I've been such an asshole.

She nods. "Thank you for this. I'm sorry again I—"

"Hey," I say, nudging her chin with my finger. "Nothing to be sorry for. I was glad for it."

That seems to settle her down, her body relaxing against me as she shifts around the sleeping bag. I would've expected her to jump out and away from me the first chance she got, but apparently, she wants to enjoy this warmth a minute longer. I can understand.

"Jamie?"

"Hm?" Eyelids heavy, I settle back on the pillow.

"Is that a flashlight in your pocket or…"

My eyes burst open, and I have to cough to hide my laughter. "Want the real answer or—"

"Oh my god," she groans as she opens the sleeping bag and rolls herself away from me. Even though I already miss the feel of her, I laugh out loud.

Mouth agape, she says, "I can't believe this life-or-death situation of ours is making you horny." She throws me a look. "Is *that* your new kink I didn't know about?"

"I'm not horny. This is a reactionary boner."

"Reactionary or not, it's rude," she says, smirk barely contained.

"It's not like I'm in control here, am I?" I shrug. "Plus, this really isn't my kink. I only have one."

"Which is?" she asks.

"You."

She stays silent for a second before she lets out what seems to be a "what-the-fuck-even-is-my-life" bout of laughter, and I join her.

"You waited a long time to get that one out, did you?" she says between giggles.

"Spur of the moment, I swear."

Once we calm down, I spot the way her eyes roam from the tent we had to share to the makeshift bandage on her arm, and then to me, lying on my back and probably with mud streaked on my face. She shakes her head. "This is all a little ridiculous, isn't it?"

"Won't argue with you on this."

She sighs, then gets up to exit the tent. Meanwhile, I avoid looking at her any more than I need to and wait for my flashlight to go away, my stomach rumbling. We'll need to find food today, unless we want to starve to death in the next few days. When I'm sure I'm good, I get up and join her outside.

"So," she says the second the tent has been zipped back up, "I was thinking we should go on a little scouting trip. Figure out what we've got around, you know."

The perfect word to describe Emma this morning is *restless*.

She's all over the place, opening one of our food bags and picking up pieces of wood (one-handed, mind you), all the while never quite looking at me.

"Sure," I say hesitantly. My feet drag me closer to her, but still, she doesn't stop. "Hey, you okay? Is it your hand?" Lightly, I touch her bandage, the skin around it red, but not completely discolored, so I take it as a win.

Emma inhales sharply when I touch her, and after swallowing, she says, "No, it's fine." She wiggles her fingers but immediately winces. "Okay, maybe not *fine* fine, but it will be."

That gets me to grit my teeth. I can't believe it had to happen to her again. She couldn't catch a break? I would've given everything for her to be able to play without any limitations, the way she used to. I stole that away from her, and now that she had a chance at it, we blew it.

"Jamie?"

"Huh?" I look up to find Emma looking at me with creases on her forehead. I must've missed what she was saying.

"It's going to be okay. We'll find a way back."

I don't know which *back* she's talking about, but it doesn't matter. At the moment, both seem far, far away.

"Right," I say with a scratch of my neck. "You want to go now?"

"Unless you've got a magic protein bar for us to eat, we probably should go soon if we don't want my stomach to auto-digest itself."

I nod, and once I've tied my running shoes and then hers, we're off.

At first, we're silent, the only sounds between us the rustling of the leaves and the faint flow of a river nearby. The ground is mostly flat, which is helpful considering my poor cardio and Emma's precarious situation. I wouldn't want her to climb onto something, only to fall and hurt her hand even more. With our luck, it would be likely.

Once we've been walking for what must be close to thirty minutes, Emma once again slapping herself for "mosquitoes" every five seconds, we find a small clearing next to the river, where a few bushes producing what looks like blackberries are resting. Emma and I seem to spot it at the same time, and we both rush to it, dropping to our knees before filling our mouths like animals.

"Oh my god, these taste like heaven," I say.

"Better than heaven. Like…better than Olive Garden's breadsticks."

"Better than that extra fry you find at the bottom of your McDonald's bag."

"Better than those little peanuts on top of Drumstick cones."

"Better than a perfect, crunchy grape when you've eaten a whole bag of mushy ones."

"Yeah, don't push it."

I snicker when I see her mischievous grin.

Once the ache of hunger in my belly has calmed down, I turn to Emma, who's still filling her mouth with five berries at a time. Laughing softly, I lift a hand and wipe some of the juice that's dripped from her lips to her chin.

Sheepish, she snickers and says, "Again, I can't believe this is our life now."

"Do you think our current selves are doing any better?"

She shrugs.

"What do you think we're doing?" I ask.

"I don't know. Hopefully stuffing our faces."

"Is there a chance we're making out, you think?" I say with a waggle of my brows.

She laughs, then pushes my shoulder. "I don't think so. We're both probably working on our pieces for the showcase." With a look I don't recognize, she says, "Maybe we're even working on some other stuff."

I don't know why, but the way she says it makes my shoulders tense. "Like what?"

Her lips twist from one side to the other. Finally, she sighs and says, "Jamie, I found your composition. Or at least one of them."

Something acidic burns my throat. "What?"

"I didn't mean to, but I was clearing things in your cabin, and I just stumbled on them, and I'm so, so sorry, I—"

"Did you play it?" after swallowing harshly.

I don't even know why I'm asking. If she's being this fidgety, it means she has.

Her voice is soft as she says, "Yes."

My mind blanks. I should feel angry, or worried, or embarrassed, but somehow, the only emotion that fills me is neither of those; it's relief. I've never had a way with words. Most of the time, I trip over the important things I need to say. Music, though, has always been my outlet. I've poured my heart and soul into this composition for the past months. Emma's a brilliant musician and an even more brilliant person, so I know she understood this, and with that title? There could be no confusion in her mind. She had a clear view into my thoughts.

The only thing I come up with to say is, "Then at least you now have an idea of the way I feel about you."

Emma blinks fast, and I get up and turn to look for more berries before I can let her say anything else. I'm not ready for her to let me down gently. I want to hold on to all the hope I can. She must get it because she doesn't say anything, and eventually, she joins me to look for more food. I don't feel like I'm dying of hunger any longer, but if we're going to stay here longer, we'll need more than a few handfuls of blackberries.

As we move out of the clearing and back into the forest, I hear something I haven't heard in a long, long time. Emma is humming in a low voice, as she looks from left to right, her ponytail swishing over her shoulders. She used to do this when she was in a really good mood, like when she'd come back from getting her nails done or when she'd be studying on a spring day, the temperature finally warm enough to go outside without a coat on for the first time of the year. I hadn't realized she'd stopped doing it until now, and fuck, that hurts. How long was she unhappy? Months? Years?

And why start singing again now, when we're stuck in the

middle of nowhere? As she bends to steal a glance into a bush, she looks as breezy as can be, nothing like the stiff girl I left for camp with at the beginning of summer.

Once she realizes the bush is empty, she straightens and resumes her search. Her steps are fast and carefree, and even though the terrain is almost risk free, she finds the one root in the path, and of course, she trips over it. My heart skips a beat. I don't think, only jump forward to catch her mid-fall. Her eyes are wide when she turns back and looks at where I grabbed the back of her shirt to keep her on her feet. She exhales, then laughs softly. "Thank god for you."

Once she's straightened, she wipes her hands over her thighs and gets back to her trek, as if nothing happened. As if she didn't almost fall on her hand again. Meanwhile, I'm still trying to convince my nervous system that nothing happened, pulse erratic.

This makes no sense. She just came close to possibly ruining things even more, and she barely reacted. She's not even holding her injured hand to make sure it's protected. She should be right there with me, freaking out, but instead, it's as if this is a day like any other.

"How are you so okay right now?" I blurt out. The words come out unexpectedly, but I couldn't hold them in. I need to know. There has to be a logic behind it, and I'm not seeing it.

"What?" she asks, head tilted.

"How are you not more bothered by this?" I point at her hand.

She shrugs. Actually *shrugs*. "It's not the end of the world. I'd figured it wouldn't be our way back anyway."

I ignore the fact that she didn't tell me this before we left, and instead focus on the first part. "What do you mean? This has been hindering your playing this entire year."

"Again, not the end of the world."

"But…but it's ruined everything," I babble, a sour taste filling my mouth. How can she be so calm about this? The more she explains, the less sense it makes.

"What do you mean?"

I pace around the narrow path through the trees. "I fucked up with the canoe, and then your hand was messed up, and then you started having the cramps while playing, and you've hated me for it, and—"

"Whoa, whoa, whoa, don't put words in my mouth. I never hated you for that." She chuckles. "I didn't even remember it was you who'd dropped the canoe!"

"But things have been bad since then," I say slowly. I realize this now. It wasn't clear to me when we got to Allegro, but now that I think back on it, I can see how things were different between us. We weren't good anymore, and for some reason, I didn't notice it. Or maybe I did notice it, but I decided to bury my head in the sand.

"Maybe I've been distant since, but that's not because of the accident itself," she says, looking at me like I'm missing the big picture.

"I don't get it," I say.

"Jamie, I didn't care about the hand. What I cared about was *you* caring so much about the hand."

"What?" I say, taking a step back.

Emma shakes her head. "Never mind." She even has the nerve to give me a plastic smile I've seen on her lips a thousand times before, when she talked to teachers or when she had to speak in public.

"No, don't give me that," I say.

"It's okay, Jamie." She returns to her scavenging and leans over a bush, spreading the branches to look through.

"Stop being Emmaline right now."

That gets her to stop in her tracks.

"Don't give me a bullshit façade. That's an Emmaline thing to do, and Emmaline might as well be in that other dimension, for all I care," I say, arm thrown to the side. "I want to know what *Emma* thinks."

I got her. I can see it in the way her shoulders have dropped. I only have to wait another second before she deflates like a balloon, then turns and says, "All right. Imagine this." Her cheeks are pink, as if I've riled her up. I'll take that over blankness anytime. "I hurt my hand. I was in pain. I didn't know what would happen. And every time I saw you and tried to talk to you about it, you would tell me to get back to it and start practicing again." She drags a hand down her ponytail. "I wanted a boyfriend, not a freaking colleague. I wanted you to tell me that it would be okay if I didn't play as well as before, not to tell me to get back to it." Her throat bobs. "*That's* the truth."

My mouth hangs open as I replay her words. Then I say, "And you've never thought to question why I was doing it?"

"Why were you doing it, Jamie?" she says, voice too calm.

"Isn't it obvious?"

She lifts her brows.

"Because I was plagued with guilt," I say, hands gripped behind my neck. "I thought I'd fucked up your hand, and the only way I could live with that guilt was if you could play again. I fucking hated myself." The guy from the shitty side of town who broke the hand of the two piano prodigies' daughter? How could she not come to realize how out of my league she was after that?

Her face transforms into a deep scowl. "But I never resented you for it. It was an accident. Things weren't that good before for me anyway. I wouldn't have cared." Looking at me deeply, she repeats, "It was an *accident*."

"It doesn't matter. I thought you'd hate me forever for it."

"I wouldn't have," she says. Then, her lower lip wobbles, which is something I've rarely seen on her. It twists me up inside. "But how did you think it would make me feel when you only cared about my hand? And then when we got back from camp, you started to practice more than ever and you would go days without thinking about me."

"I always think about you, Emma," I say honestly, my voice croaky. I barely recognize it.

"But you didn't show it," she says, gulping. "It looked like you'd given up on me."

"And I didn't want you to give up on me," I whisper before I close my eyes, feeling heavy. So heavy. *How did we make such a mess of things?*

"I don't know," she says, making me realize I've asked the question out loud.

When I reopen my eyes, my vision is blurry. "I wish I'd been by your side. I'm sorry."

She nods, but things don't change with a single sorry. I know that. We have more bridges to cross before we can even dream of the possibility of a future. I can see in her eyes she's still wary of me. Words don't mean a thing when you don't prove their worth.

"And I'm sorry I didn't make you happy," I add, my voice cracking once again. *Get it together, Jamie.* "But if it makes any difference, you never made me unhappy. Not a single second." I push against the knot in my throat and step closer so she can see the truth in my eyes when I say, "You've always been my happy place."

She blinks once, twice, then nods and picks up my hand so she can give it a squeeze.

A touch has never felt so good.

CHAPTER 24

Emma

"HOME SWEET HOME," JAMIE SAYS ONCE OUR CAMP-ground comes into view.

It's stupid, how relieved I feel to see it. It's not like our two small tents by the water are a castle, but after walking around the woods for hours on end, they bring me some sense of comfort.

"Your hand holding up fine?" Jamie asks over his shoulder.

"Mm-hmm." I stretch and flex my fingers to show him.

"Good."

This easiness between us, even after one of the most intense conversations we've had in our relationship, is strange but also isn't. This is Jamie. I might not always bother him with my problems, but deep down, I know if ever I need someone to talk to, I'll go straight to him. He gets me. I don't know how I ever forgot about that.

"How long do you think we can survive off this?" Jamie asks, looking down. In the makeshift pocket we created with the folded hem of Jamie's T-shirt sits a few handfuls of berries.

"Don't forget this," I say as I lift our other finding.

"Oh, I'm not eating that."

"Why not? It's perfectly good rhubarb."

"Rhubarb does not simply grow in the middle of untouched forest. I refuse to believe that."

I huff, walking faster so I can keep up with his ten-meter-long legs. "Of course it does. Where do you think the first person who ate rhubarb found it?"

"I'm guessing not in some random-ass New England forest."
He glances at me and shakes his head, grinning. "But if you want
to take your chances and bite into that stick, then be my guest."

Eyes narrowed, I say, "Snob."

He laughs.

After I hear my stomach grumble for the twentieth time
today, I look back at his pocket of berries and say, "It's better than
nothing, but not sure it's enough."

"I mean," he says as he removes his shirt carefully so he can
place the berries down on the ground. I look away quickly, feeling
myself flush at the sight of that lean body and creamy skin. "We
have fresh water here, so while it's not amazing living, we can definitely *survive* for a while."

"I'm not sure if this is a good thing or a bad thing."

He snickers. "Oh, come on, it's not so bad, is it?"

And when I look at his grin and think of the way we slept last
night, I think, no, it's not so bad at all.

To him, I shrug. "My hand already doesn't hurt as much, so I
think tomorrow we should be good to go."

"We'll take however long you need." His dark brows are high
on his forehead as if he's trying to convince me of this.

Something twists in my gut.

I offer him the tiniest of smiles, then go inside my tent to
get some space. I need to keep myself together, but my wayward
thoughts about Jamie aren't helping. First, he lets me into his
sleeping bag to warm me up, and I feel like I could stay in that position forever. I can barely look at him from how disgustingly into
him I am. And then, he brings up the accident, and once again,
things become tense. But even then, he never lets me off the hook.
Never tells me this is too much for him and it's not worth it. He's
picked up my slack and doesn't seem ready to give up. Maybe
some women would find that annoying, but I don't. It shows
how much he cares. And even though everything is far from resolved, after we finished talking and returned to our food hunt, I

felt lighter somehow. Nothing is clear in my head, but at least our cards are on the table.

Right now, he's only sitting outside this thin tent wall, maybe lying on his back with his eyes closed against the sun, or sitting up and practicing a piece on a wooden stick. I can imagine the working of his throat as he drinks a gulp of water, or the flex of his biceps as he scratches his neck. Even fictional, the image makes me wanton.

I'm pathetic. Truly. If I listened to what my gut said, I would exit this tent and tell him to forget everything I've ever said. I'd say I understand now, and we can go back to the way it was. However, I'm not ready to take that risk. Not yet, at least. If I decide to, it'll be because I've been convinced things will be different when we go back. I know I won't survive it if I let him back into my life, only to be left out again, so I need to be careful.

Like Jamie said: this is such a mess.

I remain an extra minute inside the tent before I resolve I need to get out. The sound of the zipper opening makes him jerk up from where he was lost in thoughts, sitting on a rock. I force myself to not let my gaze drift to his stomach, which I know feels soft and warm and—

"Everything okay?" he asks.

"All good," I say, hoping my thoughts don't show on my face, but when I feel warmth in my cheeks, I know it's game over. The sun rays are burning my skin, sweat dribbling down my back. I lift my good hand to shield my eyes from the sun, and when I drop it back down, Jamie's grinning.

"What?"

"Your whole face is purple now."

Huh? My eyes narrow, but when I look at my hand, I realize what he means. The blackberries. They stained my fingers, and apparently, I have some on my face now too.

"I don't think I've ever seen you so dirty. It's fascinating."

"I can be dirty."

"Oh, I know that," he says with a mischievous smirk, which makes me roll my eyes. "I meant in public. Never a hair out of place or lipstick that's anything but perfect."

He's right, but the way he says it…I'm not sure it's meant to be a compliment.

"You want dirty?" I say. Before he can answer, I run to the lake, pick up a big glob of wet mud, then throw it at his smug face.

It might only land in between his pecs, but the effect is just as amazing.

"Oh, you didn't." Jamie tries to keep his voice serious and deep, but the fun he's having shows on his lips.

I grin.

Just as I lean to grab another handful of mud, he starts running after me, and I know I've made a mistake. Shrieking, I scurry away, but I'm not fast enough. In ten strides, Jamie meets me and plucks me from the ground. I scream again, which only makes him laugh. He's carrying me on his shoulder like a potato sack, still careful not to touch my hand.

"Put me down!" I say in between fits of giggles, pounding against his butt with my good fist.

Surprisingly, he complies. Only, we're right on the edge of the lake now, and before I can run away again, he grabs a huge lump of mud and drops it on my head. I gasp.

And that means war.

In a second, I pull him into a bear hug, rubbing my nasty hair all over him. Laughter fills my ears, both his and mine, and I can't even find it in me to be mad at him. I'm breathless, running around and throwing mud everywhere, feeling some of it drip onto my cheeks, my clothes, my feet. Jamie's glasses are smeared in dirt, and he doesn't care one bit.

"Ow!" Jamie shouts after he falls to the ground, body half sprawled in the water.

"Oh my god, are you okay?" I say, running toward him.

I only realize it's a trap when I'm close enough to see the

smirk on his lips. Too late. He has the advantage and shows it by putting a huge pile of mud inside my shirt.

"You little prick!" I shout before I throw myself onto him.

"Gotcha." He laughs, strong enough to push me off, and then he's running away, mud and pebbles flying with each of his steps. I don't waste a second following him.

Who would've thought it would take me getting lost in the middle of a canoe expedition to feel this free?

We continue fighting until we're drained. Once Jamie throws yet another mud missile that misses my chest by a mile, I lift my hands in the air and say, "Time out." My chest is rising and falling in short pants, and I'm so hot I feel I could drink two gallons of water.

Jamie seems to be happy about my truce because he comes to me and drops to his butt, as breathless as me. I join him, facing the water that looks sapphire blue from here.

"Oh boy," I say once I look down at myself. There's mud everywhere. "That was a bad idea."

The man who confuses me to no end lifts his shoulders in a casual motion. "We needed to shower anyway."

"Shower?" I look behind us. "Excuse me, did I miss the Hilton that popped up in the forest?"

"I mean bathe. Swim. Whatever."

Bathe. Here. Together.

What?

"Oh, I don't know if—"

"Emma, we're nasty," he says, getting back to his feet. "Come on."

I don't take his outstretched hand. This is a bad idea.

"Just g-go ahead, and I'll go later," I say.

He rolls his eyes. "Oh, come on. We're not five years old." He makes a *come here* motion with his fingers. "We can both wash at the same time without it being weird."

I lift an eyebrow.

"I won't look. Scout's honor."

Why am I even considering this? I must have a death wish. Or maybe I'm just incredibly stupid. Still, I take his hand and get to my feet.

"We both know how great of a scout you were," I mumble when he turns around and walks toward the lake.

"Heard that!"

I grin.

When he starts removing his shorts, I spin and squeeze my eyes shut. *Sure, Emma, you want to avoid being confused about Jamie? Why don't you just get naked with him in the lake? It'll definitely help!*

I rub at my dirty chest, then shake my head. At this point, what's the worst that can happen? I'm pretty sure we've hit rock bottom multiple times already. Not overthinking this, I undress in a hurry, then walk into the lake, careful to keep enough space between the two of us. As soon as I reach a deep enough part of the lake, I feel myself relax, which is crazy. Jamie has seen me naked more times than I can count, but this is different, right? It wouldn't mean the same thing when we're in such a precarious place.

Exhaling, I submerge myself in water, scrubbing my scalp as best I can without shampoo in water that's not even clear, all the while forcing myself not to think about the possible fish and other slimy things swimming under my feet.

I don't mean to look when I emerge from the water, but the moment I open my eyes, he's here, in all his glory, water sluicing down his hair and chest, down to the dark trail of hair that leads to—

Oh my god, *I* am being the creep he promised he wouldn't be. Swallowing forcefully, I sink deep into the water and finish scrubbing myself. In two minutes, I'm done, and I return to the shore, not turning around to see if he's watching. I don't know how it would make me feel, to have his eyes on all of me. Probably more lustful than anything else.

Once I've put on the last clean shirt I brought with me and a pair of shorts, I dare to look back, and sure enough, Jamie's still in the water, his dark gaze right on me.

My belly has no right clenching the way it does. No right at all.

* * *

After a few hours of small talk followed by another meager meal of berries (he was right, the rhubarb wasn't rhubarb), the sun has fallen and the chill has settled again. It's better than yesterday, but only a little. The wind coming from the lake is crisp and unforgiving.

"You ready to settle down for the night?" Jamie asks once I've put on my hoodie and sat back down next to the fire he built us— thanks, Boy Scouts!

"It's like seven p.m. I'm sure even Alessandro and Irène would call us elderly."

"Not much to do here," he says, and is it me, or did that sound suggestive?

Definitely me.

"True," I say, wiping the muck from my butt as I get to my feet. "Well, good night, then."

"Where are you going?"

"My tent?"

"Why?"

"Want me to sleep in the woods with all the bears and coyotes?"

He chuckles. "First, there's no bear or coyote here. And second, no, I mean why not in our tent?"

I open my mouth, but no sound comes out.

"It's gonna be cold tonight too. It'd be smarter to stay together."

My hesitation doesn't last long because he has a point. No matter how awkward it might be to wake up tangled up like we did this morning, it would be worse to freeze in my tent by myself.

"Fine," I say, "but only because I don't want the bears to eat me alone tonight."

"You'd rather they eat me too, huh?"

"We go down together or not at all."

He shakes his head and laughs as he watches me walk into *our* tent. Once I'm in, I rush to the sleeping bag. If I'm there first, it won't look like I'm trying to rub myself on him like I did yesterday, but really, there's no safe way to enter a sleeping bag where someone is already lying and look casual.

Jamie notices that a minute later when he removes his shoes and climbs in, apologizing approximately fifty times as he settles into a comfortable position.

"You're fine," I say once he's said his last sorry.

We're both immobile in the sleeping bag, unlike yesterday, when we kind of cuddled for warmth purposes. Now I don't have the excuse of being cold. Plus, we have all that was said today between us, which is creating this safety net. Neither one of us wants to cross a line when we don't even know where the line now lies.

But slowly, sleep comes for me.

It isn't restful. I'm plagued by back-to-back nightmares, one where my mother ends up being stuck in bed forever, never recovering from her depressive episode, and the other where Jamie has a new girlfriend and stares at me as he kisses her, all the while I empty my lungs with a cry of despair.

Fun.

Thankfully, I wake up in the middle of said nausea-inducing kiss. Or rather, I'm woken up. Something rustles outside the tent, the sound making me tense.

"What the heck was that?" I whisper-shout.

Jamie is already awake, his eyes wide as he looks left and right, quiet.

I imitate him, not caring about the way I'm clinging to him. Maybe I already was when I woke up and just didn't notice.

And then, another rustle. Louder this time.

I jerk in the sleeping bag, biting my lips so I don't scream.

"Who was saying there were no bears and coyotes here?" I whisper.

"It's not a bear or a coyote," Jamie says. I don't miss his hand curling over my lower back.

"What is it, then?" I hiss against his chest.

A pause, then, "I don't know."

"There you go. Bear."

"Not the time, Emma," he says, and that does it for me. If he's worried, then I should really, really be worried.

"Oh my god, we're going to die."

"We're not going to die."

"What will happen to our future selves living their best lives when we die? Will they just disappear?"

"They'll stay where they are and continue living their best lives because we're not dying," he says, just before pulling away.

"What are you doing?" I hiss.

"Going to see what's happening."

"Are you insane? What are you going to do? Fight a freaking bear?" I'm sitting up now, my arms moving all over the place. He can't go. He can't.

Another rustling. I close my eyes, trying to find a prayer but remembering I'm not

religious and don't have a god to pray to.

Please, universe, stop messing with us.

"I can't just stay here while you're freaking out," he says, but I recognize the trill in his voice. He's as uncomfortable about this as I am. He unzips the tent.

"Yes you can! Just come back! We'll ignore it!"

Looking over his shoulder, he says, "I'll be right back."

And then, nothing.

I wait for a shout, or a roar, or a zip of the tent to tell me he's back, but the only thing that greets me is silence.

Long, painful silence.

Oh god. Maybe he's dead already. Maybe it was a quiet bear and it was a rapid death.

Minutes pass as I stare at the door, the sleeping bag wrapped tightly around me. This can't be happening.

Something rustles again, and when I finally hear something, it's Jamie shouting, "Fuck!"

I yelp, still trying to keep quiet. I feel tears burning the back of my eyes. What if this is it, and I never see him again? I couldn't. Not knowing the way we left things, so unclear, so—

The tent door opens, and I shout, "Jamie!"

"It's fine, it was only a—"

He doesn't have time to close finish his sentence, because the second he steps inside the tent, I jump on him like a maniac, my arms wrapped so tight around his neck that I fear I'll break him.

"Hey, I'm fine," he says, laughing softly.

"I thought something had happened," I say, sounding embarrassingly like a damsel in distress, but you know what? Screw it. I *was* a damsel in distress, and while Jamie might not be a knight in shining armor, he did go there to make sure we'd be fine.

"It was a small fox. Surprised me is all."

This is the moment when I should let him go. When I should step back and say I'm glad he's okay, then go back to sleep. No bear was involved here. No one was hurt. It was nothing.

Yet I can't stop my arms from shaking, and something protective inside me tells me not to let him go. I want to inhale more of his smell, to feel his breath on the top of my head. I want to envelop my entire body around him, to keep him inside me so nothing can ever get to him.

"Emma," he whispers, squeezing me between his arms. "I'm okay."

We stay like this, kneeling across the floor of the tent like he just came back from war, not talking, just feeling each other. My blood roars in my ears, chest tight. He holds me until after I stop shaking, and then some.

Once I finally feel like I'll be okay, I pull back, bringing my hands into fists. I embrace the new kind of pain in my left hand. It brings my mind away.

"Please..." I lick my lips. "Please don't do something like that again, okay?"

A side of his lips lifts. "I told you, you're not getting rid of me that easily."

He says it as a joke, but it's not a joke to me. I can't imagine losing him definitively. All that's transpired between us doesn't matter when it comes to this. To the thought of not seeing him again.

My breaths come in soft pants as I glance down at his lips, pink and soft looking, and before I realize what I'm doing, I'm kissing him.

He doesn't hesitate to kiss me back. One soft press of his mouth to my top lip, then the bottom one, and then he's there, all over, everywhere, and I'm gone. The only thing on my mind is the feel of his long fingers on my cheeks, of his tongue against mine and his warm chest pressing flush to me. I moan when he bites softly into my bottom lip, as if he's hungry for more.

But just as fast as he's responded to me, he pulls back. Even in the darkness, I notice the blazing fire in his eyes.

"Is this real?" he asks, breathing fast and loud. "Tell me it's real." His eyelashes fan his cheeks. "I can't if it isn't."

I swallow, then nod. "It's real. I don't know what it means, but it's real."

Apparently, he doesn't need more than this. No confirmation about where we stand or what will happen. Just proof that I'm in this moment just as much as he is.

He thunders back on me, and I sigh like I've been away from him for years. I want to taste him, all of him. Jamie's hands roam over my rib cage, the base of my breasts, my nipples, which he rubs in tight circles. I let my head fall back, almost groaning.

"I can't believe you ever thought I didn't think you were the most beautiful thing on this planet," he says before dipping to my neck and kissing me there, then licking a trail from my clavicle to my ear.

"Jamie," I whisper, tension building between my legs. I need more.

He knows. Before I can even ask anything, he's there, his hardness grinding against where I need him, leaving me panting.

This reminds me of when we were sixteen, starting to discover each other's bodies, but also our own. I had my first orgasm with him. Learned what I liked and what I didn't by having him try stuff. This feels like then, when we hadn't gone all the way but wanted to get drunk off each other, wild touches roaming over clothes. Except now, we're adults.

It doesn't matter, though. We still look starved, like we don't want things to go too far, but we're also very much in need of everything, all at once.

Jamie's teeth scratch my ear lobe as his hips move faster against mine, jerkier, creating the most delicious friction against my core. It feels so good. It's nothing like the way we acted with each other when sex felt like a task more than something enjoyable. This? This is pure desire. We don't think about the way we move, or the sounds we make, or the way we kiss. We're just trying to feel as much as we can, and it's working. God, it's working.

"Are you gonna come?" Jamie asks.

"Uh-huh," I moan, pressing kisses to his neck, then to the notch at the tip of his rib cage. I feel wetness gather in my panties the more I grind against Jamie's erection, the pressure so perfect, so raw.

And that's when it happens. I orgasm, panting against the skin of his neck, mouth open, hands gripping at his nape, the sensation so intense it brings tears to my eyes.

A second later, Jamie jerks against me, and soon come the soft sounds I know he makes when he comes.

I feel his body relax on top of mine, and for a beat, we remain in silence, pulse against pulse.

"Wow," he says.

"Yeah, wow."

I should probably move away. The moment is over.

Except it isn't. Because even after we've both orgasmed fully clothed like teenagers sneaking away from their parents, Jamie comes back to me and presses his lips to mine again, this time slow, soft.

These kisses are even better.

CHAPTER 25

Emma

J UST LIKE YESTERDAY, JAMIE IS ALREADY AWAKE BY THE TIME
I open my eyes the next morning. This time, though, I don't
move. I want to enjoy this moment a little longer. I stay immobile as his hand rubs up and down my back, the callouses on his
fingers tickling my skin.

I should be shaken by what happened yesterday, but frankly, I'm
not. It's like all we've been doing this summer has led to this. Like
it was inevitable for us to happen, two comets who had strayed but
would eventually collide again. It doesn't mean we can move on as
if the past year didn't happen, but it does mean I want to consider
trying again. This, what we have? It's strong. Special. It would be
obtuse of me to overlook the possibility of working through this.

"I know you're not sleeping," Jamie's gruff voice says.

"How?" I say, my cover blown.

His hand never stops rubbing me as he says, "You've stopped
snoring."

"I don't snore."

That gets him chuckling. I elbow him in the ribs, which makes
him laugh even more.

"It's cute, though. Like a little bulldog."

"You've got a real way with words, don't you?"

He presses a kiss to my forehead in answer.

Finally, I lift my head to take a good look at him. Creases from
his pillow line his cheek, his eyes are swollen with sleep, and he's
the sexiest man I have ever seen.

"Hey," I say.

"Hey," he answers, grinning. Neither one of us brings up last night, and I'm thankful. I need time to put my thoughts in order and to make a final decision, and he probably knows this.

"My hand feels pretty good this morning, so what do you say we try to head back? I think I'll die if I eat one more berry."

His light dims before he nods and says, "Sure."

I frown. "Why the face?"

"What face?"

"That face," I say, poking his pouting lips. "It's supposed to be good news."

"Yeah, it is. But I mean, it isn't so bad here." And with the way he looks at me, I know he doesn't mean the impromptu camping site.

"No, it's not," I say honestly. "But it doesn't have to be bad when we get back either."

"Yeah?"

Pretending I can't feel my cheeks burning, I say, "Yeah."

That gets his genuine smile to come back on, full force. "All right, then, let's hit the road."

* * *

"What if we're stuck on this lake forever?"

"We won't be," Jamie answers. "We're almost there. I'm sure of it."

"Forgive me for being doubtful of your directional gut feelings."

A slap of his paddle on the water before my entire arm gets splashed. I throw a glare over my shoulder, which is answered with a guilty grin.

After getting up, we packed quickly and got back in the canoe, trying to follow the reverse path we used to get to our campsite. However, it's difficult to know whether we're headed in the right direction or not, considering the fact that the shore is just mile after painful mile of the same pine trees and mountains. There isn't a single big landmark we could base ourselves on, no matter what Jamie says (*yes, I remember that tree!*), so right now, I have an intense feeling we'll be camping on another lakeshore tonight.

That wouldn't be so bad though.

"Your hand still holding up okay?" Jamie asks.

"Yep." I flex it again. It hurts, that's for sure, but it's tolerable. "Won't be any Martha Argerich anytime soon, but I should be able to perform at the showcase anyway."

After a loaded pause, Jamie says, "I promise I don't only care about your hand, but I do want to apologize one last time for everything that happened to it."

I stop paddling and turn to face him. "Jamie, stop it. I'll throw you overboard if I hear you apologize one more time."

"Feisty," he says, but I know the smile he's giving isn't a hundred percent real.

I give him a stare down before putting my good hand on his knee, rubbing my thumb over the inside of it. "Plus, I told you the hand was only part of the problem." I lift a shoulder. "Honestly, it kind of gave me an excuse for not being at my best."

His head tilts to the side. I can see he wants to ask more about this, but thankfully, he doesn't. One day, I'll tell him about how painful it was to plateau at twenty-one, good but never great. That will be for another day, though.

Turning around, we return to our silent paddling, and after what must be another half hour, Jamie says, "Look!"

I squint, not finding what he wants me to look for until my gaze lands on the small plot by the lake filled with golden-brown cabins.

"You did it," I say in awe.

"I told you I knew those trees we passed!"

"You'd said that fifty times before. I thought you were trying to give me hope."

"Nuh-uh. Didn't need it," he says smugly, as if he knew all along where we were when I know for a fact he was as lost as me. I won't throw it in his face though, because we're finally back!

We start paddling faster toward camp, and as we get closer, I see a small crowd of people forming by the lake. Eventually, I'm able to see Jesy in her wheelchair with Julia by her side. Molly. Jeremiah. Alessandro. Irène.

"Emma!" Jesy shouts once we're close enough for me to see the deep lines of concern on her forehead. "Thank god!"

The moment our canoe scratches the bottom of the lake, Jamie and I leap from our seats. This time, Jamie's hand is right there on my lower back as I exit, careful not to tip the canoe over.

Jesy wheels her chair closer to the shore so that as soon as I step onto the camp ground, she opens her arms wide for me to hug her. I run to her and wrap my arms around her shoulders. She squeezes the crap out of me in return.

"Where the hell were you?" she shouts into my ear. "We were all worried sick here!"

After a long moment, she lets me go, and for some reason, a knot inside my chest tightens. She really does look worried about me. Not like someone who's pretending to be my friend, but more like a family member who'd run through scenarios of what could've happened to me when I didn't come back. There's no faking the glaze in her eyes, or at least I don't think so.

Something else fills me then: guilt. I've been keeping so much from her, wanting to keep appearances, but she's not some simple colleague. She's a friend. A good friend.

After blinking repeatedly, I say, "We got lost, and then I hurt my hand, but we're good."

"You should've called!" Jesy says.

Beside us, I see Molly speaking to Jamie, and she looks mad, mouthing intensely at him. She's probably giving him a similar speech.

"We didn't have a satellite phone with us," I say. Now that we're here, though, I'm excited to go find my personal phone and see if I've received updates about my mom. I don't think she'd ever put herself in danger, but when someone is in true despair, it's hard to guess what their brain could make them think and do. I can only hope my father has been there to support her.

"I was so worried," Jesy repeats. "You could've been eaten by a bear or something."

She's speaking loud enough that Jamie hears it—I know he does when I spot the laughter he's fighting to keep in check. When he glances my way, I lift a brow as a, *see?*

"No bear involved," I tell Jesy. "Don't worry."

"Well, thank fuck for that."

I put a hand on her shoulder. "I'm sorry we got you worked up. Won't happen again."

"Better hope not," she says.

"Jes, come on," Julia calls from behind her. "They're fine. We can go eat now."

I see there's one person who didn't miss us during our disappearance.

"Go," I tell Jesy, rubbing her arm up and down. "I'll tell you all about it before bed."

Jesy only hesitates for a second before nodding and making her way to Julia, who dusts a kiss on her cheek before they leave.

"Happy to see you back," someone says to my left. Irène is approaching, and while her skin is pale and dark circles line her eyes, she's smiling. "I told Alessandro you were probably only looking for some intimacy out there." She smirks.

Oh god.

"We would've done the same," she says with a wink.

Aaaaand I didn't need to know that.

"Hey, you hungry?" Jamie asks me, coming close enough to put a hand on the small of my back.

"Starving," I say.

Irène narrows her wrinkle-lined eyes at us, maybe wondering why we look like the two last candidates on *The Amazing Race*, but she doesn't ask.

"Please be safer next time, yes?"

We both nod.

She seems satisfied with our agreement because, without a word, she turns and leaves. I don't miss the way she breathes heavily through her mouth instead of her nose as she walks away.

Jamie interrupts my staring by saying, "I think Molly gave me a bigger speech on accountability and communication than my mom ever has."

"I love that girl."

"She loves you too. They all do."

He's said it often in the past, but every time, I gulp it down because I love his family more than he could imagine. Admire them, really. They work as a team at the restaurant, then come back home and argue and fight and laugh like a real family does. It's beautiful to see. Every time I'm invited for dinner at their place, I have to restrain myself from staring at them in awe. It's such a special dynamic, seeing them all together. Molly arguing with Jonah about the relevance of fantasy novels in school curriculums while Mason stuffs his face and laughs at the way his siblings are shouting over green beans and a pot roast, their parents bellowing to keep it down. Ever since I was a little girl playing with my dolls alone in my room, I've had the dream of having siblings, and while my parents have always been adamant about not wanting more kids, I gained some, if only for a few years.

"Think your family would adopt me when I grow up?" I say as we walk toward the cafeteria. The air smells like garlic and butter the closer we get. I'm surprised Jamie doesn't make his stupid whale joke at the howl my stomach makes.

"Careful what you wish for," he says.

I picture replacing the silent dinners in my apartment or the tense ones at my childhood home with ones surrounded by his family, chaotic and fun. "I think I'd like it."

He snickers. "Sure you would."

"What does that mean?"

He buries his hands in his pockets and glances at me like I'm kidding. "Come on. Stop messing with me."

"I'm not messing with you." I slow my steps. "Why would I be?"

His lips twitch. "I mean, don't get me wrong, I love my family to death, but we're lightyears away from yours."

"Yes," I say, no longer amused. "And that's a *good* thing."

"Debatable."

"No, it's not."

Without looking at me, he continues walking and says, "That's easy to say from your side. Try having a rich girlfriend while your family barely makes ends meet."

I stop him in his steps with a firm hand on his arm. "Jamie, what is this? Since when do I care about your family's money?"

He doesn't answer.

"I don't. It never mattered to me." And I can't believe he ever thought it did. It's almost hurtful. Money is the last thing I would judge a person on, especially after seeing how rich people can be so incredibly poor.

His nostrils flare before he clears his throat. His gaze is lost on a group of girls heading into the cafeteria. "Every time you asked me to move in with you and I had to tell you no because I couldn't afford to, it killed me a little."

The emotion in his eyes makes me feel like tearing up. All this time, I thought he didn't want to live with me. It was hurtful to see him find excuse after excuse, but the truth is so simple.

"Jamie, listen to me," I say, pulling on his arm again so he finally looks at me. "I. Don't. Care. I don't." My hair falls over my forehead as I shake my head. "You and your family are perfect, and I mean it when I say it would be an honor to be a part of it."

The skepticism I see in his eyes kills me softly. Did he truly doubt this all this time? Thought I judged his family in secret?

"They love you, and that's the most precious thing they could give you. I'd much rather have my parents be home and care like yours do than see them being on the cover of magazines or talk shows. I swear." I squeeze his palm in mine. "You should've told me, about the apartment. I would've stopped bugging you about it, and I wouldn't have cared. Money means nothing." I swallow. "All I ever cared about was you."

Jamie still doesn't speak, but with the way he nods, I know my message was clear.

"Let's go eat now."

He smiles, this time soft, real, and oh so beautiful.

CHAPTER 26

Emma

T HE FOLLOWING WEEK GOES BY IN A BLUR.
Jamie and I go back to our regular tight schedule, Jamie acing his performances while I push through the pain and try making the most of what time we have left, but it feels quite useless. We haven't found a way to go back to our time, so as it is, there won't be any showcase for us.

While I can't speak for Jamie, I've started to make my peace with it. My focus has changed. I've spent more time helping Jesy and Julia with the final touches on the costumes, ignoring the semi-nasty looks the latter has thrown my way every time, gone to all the bonfires and random weeknight activities, and obviously, spent time with Jamie. We haven't kissed again like we did while camping, but it doesn't matter. The connection is still there, when he gazes my way because of an inside joke while we're in public, or when he finds a way to touch me even when it's clear he doesn't need to. If I believed him, I'd have had "something on my cheek" approximately a hundred times in a single week. I don't mind it, though. Not when I've pretended there was something in his hair more times than I'm ready to admit.

We don't talk about serious things. We don't question ourselves. We simply hang out like friends who are thinking of becoming something more, and it feels incredible.

This fluffy feeling in my chest is so strong, it makes me wish for absurd things. At some point yesterday, while I was watching Jamie mime a slice of Swiss cheese during a game with Jeremiah and his girlfriend, I found myself hoping we wouldn't find a way back to our time, because if we do, what then? Right now, it feels like nothing is serious. We're in some parallel universe, kind of like when you go on vacation and become problem free for the duration of it. It's easy to pretend everything is fine when you're sipping on piña coladas and toasting on the beach for hours. But when we come back to real time, there's the possibility that our healing, but fragile, relationship will crumble once again. Here, we're safe, and I know that I find myself falling for him with every day that passes, just like I did at sixteen.

"What are you thinking about?"

"Huh?" I turn to Jesy, who's watching me from the opposite side of the picnic table with narrowed eyebrows.

"You looked lost in thought."

"Oh. Yeah, just—" I puff my cheeks and exhale a large gush of air. "I don't want this summer to end."

She pouts dramatically, taking my hand in hers before saying, "There's always next year."

I bite my lip not to make a face because no, there is no next year. If we end up finding a way back, I will never attend Allegro again, and while I hope with all my heart we'll continue seeing each other, I can't say for sure that Jesy and I will keep in contact. Maybe Future Jesy is going to move across the country with Julia, or maybe they'll become part of exclusive artists' circles, which I won't be invited to because I'll have failed to get into any good music school. It would hurt. While we don't talk much during the school year, I know she's only a phone call away, and the same applies to me.

"Yeah," I say, forcing a smile.

Jesy frowns deeper, but just as she's about to speak, she looks over my shoulder and I hear someone call my name.

Alessandro is standing there, waving in that charming way of his.

"Sorry," I tell Jesy, then walk to Alessandro.

"I was about to come looking for you soon," I tell him as a greeting. "I haven't seen Irène for days." That's not unusual per se, but ever since the summer began, I've seen her every now and then at public events, and I haven't since we've come back from our camping trip. I never would have noticed last year, but I wanted to speak to her, so I've been looking this time.

"That is actually why I came looking for you."

My throat tightens at his tone.

"Something wrong?" I ask, voice high-pitched.

Please, no. Not yet. I know in reality her death day is scarily close—not counted in weeks anymore—but I can't face that yet. In my head, Irène was perfectly fine until she died, but when I think hard about it, I can't remember seeing her around a lot before she passed.

"She is too tired to get out of bed," he says softly, eyes red. "But she asked me about you."

Don't you dare cry, Emma.

"Oh?" I croak out.

He nods. "I thought you might want to come see her, yes?"

"You don't think she'd mind?"

He shakes his head, white eyebrows low above his deep-green eyes.

"All right, then," I say, my heart beating faster. I don't know why I'm nervous. It's only a conversation. Maybe it's because Irène is this big, statuesque figure who's unflappable, and the thought of her lying in bed, sick, is hard to come to terms with.

Alessandro makes quiet small talk as he leads me toward the bigger cabin next to the administration building, the one they use as a house during the summer months. Once we arrive, he opens the door and lets me in first.

"Thank you," I say before crossing the threshold. The interior of the cabin is decorated simply, not many knickknacks lying around, unlike their office. I assume most of their things remain at their permanent house and they don't bring much with them for the summer. A small wooden table sits in the middle of a kitchenette, and a top floor only separated by a railing seems to hold a large living room area. A hallway leads to a few closed doors, most likely bedrooms.

"Last one on the right," Alessandro tells me before climbing the stairs, as if he wants to give us time alone. Bracing myself, I walk to where he has directed me, and when I open the door, I try not to let my shock transpire on my face.

I fail.

"I am okay," Irène tells me from her spot on the bed, but even her smile can't convince me. She seems to have lost weight even in the few days since we've seen each other, her chest frail as she breathes faster than someone lying down should. Her skin is almost translucent, the bluish veins stark against it. She points at a small couch next to her bed, which I sit on.

"How is everything?" She lifts her eyebrows. "I never did get the story of what happened during your camping trip."

"That's what you want to talk about when..." I make a vague gesture around her.

"Yes, it is. And if you want to fuss around me like Alessandro does, then I will invite you politely to let yourself out."

I would roll my eyes if I didn't think that'd make her madder. "Fine. Let's talk about random things, then."

"Perfect," Irène says with a more pronounced French accent than usual. "So, camping?"

"It was good. We had fun, even with the mess we created." I lift my hand, which I've left in a brace the infirmary gave me once we came back.

"That must not be good for playing," she says.

"I remove it for practice."

"And how is that going?" she asks with a knowing look, chest rising and falling as if she's just run five miles.

I scrunch my nose. "I'd rather not talk about my playing right now, if that's all right with you." With anyone else, I would've lied and said things were going amazing, but Irène already knows I'm not doing so well, so I can be honest. Plus, if she sets rules about dead topics, then I can too.

"Fine," she says. "Let's talk about your *chéri*, then."

"Always interested in the good stuff, huh?"

She grins.

"We're doing...okay, I guess."

"Better than when you arrived in June?"

I blink.

"Please, Emma. You thought you were being subtle?"

I kinda did, yeah.

She purses her lips. "And I told your boy the same thing. I have eyes everywhere."

So Jamie and Irène talked about us at some point. Interesting.

"Well, then, yes, better than when we got here."

"And what seemed to be the problem, before?"

I snicker, but there's no humor in it. "What wasn't?"

She tuts her tongue, then repositions herself in the bed. It's a struggle, as she barely seems strong enough to lift her hands, so I get up and help her—that is, until she shoos me away like a mouse in a bedroom. "No fuss, I said."

"Fine, fine," I say, hands in the air as I fall back into the fluffy couch.

It takes another minute before she's finally in a comfortable position, less slumped than before, and she can get enough air in to talk in a semi-normal way.

"How long have you been together?" she asks.

"Five years," I say, not believing it myself. It sounds so long, but I can still remember the day we officially met, and that first time I invited him out to eat lunch with me, and the time I told him if he kissed me, he'd make me the happiest person on earth—he'd jumped on me in an instant, as if he'd been dreaming of doing that exact thing for months. Those memories are so fresh in my head, I can't believe they're that old. When I think about Jamie and me, we're still those kids who didn't know anything but wanted to discover everything together, and at the same time, the adults we've become, who aren't sure how to fit together anymore.

"That might sound long to you," Irène says, her hands clasped in her lap, "but to me, that is barely anything."

I can imagine, when she's been with Alessandro for decade upon decade.

"But even I can recognize that after five years, you might have settled into some kind of routine. And you know what?"

I chew on my thumbnail as I wait for her to tell me that routine is bad, that we need to keep things exciting as a couple to survive the long run.

"That is the most wonderful thing you could experience."

My eyes narrow before I lean forward, waiting for her next words like they could mean life or death.

"Everyone always says the best part of the relationship is the beginning, where everything is new and exciting, and you feel sparks everywhere, but I disagree." She turns her head to the left, and eventually, I see she's looking at a picture frame of her and her husband in what looks like a lavender field.

"It is easy to light a big, theatrical fire, watch it blaze, and move to a new one once it runs off. It is *much* harder to keep a small flame burning steadily through storms and gales." Her gaze softens as she continues looking at the picture. "But there is a beauty in having this small fire that is with you through it all, not strong in its size but rather in its steadiness."

I'm not sure if it's her words or the tender way she's looking at the photograph, but something in my chest tightens. She barely knows me, yet she found the one thing I needed to hear. Something I've started to realize with Jamie. Yes, a new lover can bring you the excitement of discovering and being discovered in return, but how can that compare to someone who already knows all of you, the good, the bad, and the ugly, and still decides to stick by your side?

When she turns back to me, she's smiling sadly. "It will never be easy, to keep the flame burning, but it is worth it, *ma chérie*. So worth it."

I dip my head once, the ball in my throat too heavy for me to speak.

"Think about that before making a decision, hm?"

I nod.

Although deep down, with the way my heart feels, I'm not sure there is more than one possible way to go.

CHAPTER 27

Emma

I'M ALMOST OUT OF OPTIONS.

Practicing 24/7 hasn't helped. Taking a step back hasn't changed a thing. Asking for help from teachers has only made me feel worse. So, I'm at the point where I've decided to give up and hope for the best.

With my afternoon now cleared up, I head to the lake to get some time to read one of the books I'd brought with me, something I haven't given myself the opportunity to do even once this summer.

With the lake a few yards away, I cross paths with a small group of teens, and I do a double take when I recognize the redhead of the group.

"Molly, hey!"

She turns and immediately smiles. After saying something inaudible to the group she was with, they continue walking while she stays with me.

"How are you doing?" I ask her after hugging her tightly. If I remember correctly, she only stayed four weeks last year, and since this is Saturday, this should be her last full day here.

"Good. Excited to go home."

"I'm sure your mom will be really happy to see you."

"I think she even made a cake."

I grin because I remember she *did* make a cake, which she'd sent photos of last year to Jamie. I'd been in rehab by then for my post-op recovery, but he'd sent me a text with the forwarded picture, and it had made me smile. She's such a mama hen.

"You're lucky to have her," I say, trying hard not to think of my own mother, who probably hasn't even gotten out of bed today. Even when we talk on the phone, I feel like she doesn't tell me everything, and I can't rely on my father to tell me the ugly truth. He'll always minimize what's happening to her, so long as the pretense holds. It kills me not to be able to help her, more than it ever has during her previous episodes. Maybe because I'm older now and can see how heartbreaking it is that she has to fake happiness when she's in such a dark place.

"Yeah, she's good."

"And I see you've made friends?" I nod toward the group of kids that just left down the path.

"Yeah. Met most of them at the education center. They're nice."

"Education center?"

"The place where teachers give lessons to kids with special needs?" Molly says with a red eyebrow up.

"Oh, right." I'd heard of the place a time or two, but never got the chance to see it. In all the years I've been at Allegro, my priority has been my music and Jamie. I'd barely set foot in buildings that were not piano related before this year. "How'd you end up there?"

Molly's eyes light up as she explains, "During orientation, we visited, and one of the instructors told us they always need students as assistants for the lessons. One lunch hour I was alone—"

"Molly, you should've come to us!" I interrupt.

"It's fine. Didn't want to bother you while you were together."

Oh, the irony.

"Anyway, so I went there, and it ended up being fun. I've gone a few times." She points behind her with her thumb. "Actually, I was on my way there now."

"Oh, go ahead then! Don't let me hold you up," I say, smiling. "It was nice seeing you."

She gives me a corner smile.

"Have a nice trip home tomorrow," I add.

"Thanks." She starts walking away, and just as I turn toward the lake, she says, "You want to come with me?"

I look back.

"To the education center, I mean." She lifts a careless shoulder, but I know her enough to guess when she'd like me to do something.

"For sure," I say, linking my arm through hers, then following her down a path I've rarely used, surrounded by tall lilac trees that permeate the air with their soft floral scent. We eventually end in front of a small building that's more modern than the others, with solar panels on the roof and better accessibility ramps than in the older cabins. As soon as we step over the threshold, I'm hit with a harem of mismatched sounds and squeals.

"Hey, Addy," Molly says to a young woman with curly brown hair and a smattering of freckles who's looking down at a large tablet.

The girl—Addy—looks up at us and gives us this megawatt smile. I like her already.

"Hey, girls," she says, coming our way and briefly hugging Molly. "You here for the afternoon lesson?"

"Yeah," Molly says, and before I can stop her, she leaves me to attend to a group of kids banging on mini drums.

I must have my betrayed face on because Addy laughs and says, "Little sister?"

"Kind of." I steal another glance at Molly. "I wish she was."

"Oh, I get that. I have one—well, a little brother—and he's kind of a hurricane but I wouldn't trade him for anything."

I smile, once again feeling thankful for Jamie's family.

"So, what do you do?" Addy asks as she tucks a curl behind her ear, a sparkling ring full of diamonds on her fourth finger.

"Huh?"

"What can you help with? Lesson wise, I mean."

"Oh. I'm a pianist by training."

"Great! You can join me in the music class then," Addy says, her excitement contagious. I'm not sure how useful I'll be, but looking at her, I feel confident I can create a roomful of mini Mozarts. "Follow me, we were just starting."

The building is an open space, and as she leads the way, I find my eyes drifting to a large room surrounded by windows, where a beautiful blonde who appears to be in her early twenties is standing in front of a canvas, teaching a dozen kids of all ages. Even from here, I can tell her realistic painting is breathtaking.

Before me, Addy snickers at something while looking down at her tablet.

"Look at what my husband just sent me."

She continues walking backward as she faces me with the tablet, which shows the picture of a dark-haired, incredibly handsome man frowning as he wears a tiara and smudged lipstick. Next to him stands a toddler who's trying to fit in the selfie, smiling with all her baby teeth while holding the lipstick in her chubby hand.

The man is clearly different, but for a moment, I'm able to imagine the dark curls belonging to Jamie, the baby a mix of him and me. The mental image sends a pang through my heart.

"Mary-Helen—that's my daughter—she loves playing dress-up, and he cannot resist her, no matter how much he likes to pretend he's not totally smitten."

I smile. "She's beautiful."

"Thanks." She looks down at the image one last time. "He's not so bad either."

"Not bad indeed."

She snickers just as she takes a turn and enters a room full of all kinds of instruments, both plastic and real, with what must be fifteen kids spread around. Half of them look less than ten while the other half are likely preteens and teens. Some play together, others focus on instruments by themselves. The sound only these few kids can make is astounding, but I don't care. They all seem to be having the time of their lives.

"Are they all campers?" I ask Addy.

"Some of them come here for a few weeks, but others only come for the day with their parents." She frowns as she looks at something to my left. "Tobias, careful with the xylophone!" She blows air into her cheeks. "You'll see," she says once she returns her attention to me, "it's not like your regular music classes, but it's still good. Our main goal is for kids to have fun, not to play perfectly."

I nod. I can handle that, I think.

"Okay, buds!" Addy says, clapping her hands to get everyone's attention, and while I never thought she'd succeed with a group of excited kids, she does, at least partially. "We have a guest here today." She turns to me and whispers, "Crap, I forgot to ask you your name! I'm so sorry. Sleepless nights and all."

"It's fine," I say, laughing. "I'm Emma."

To the group, she says, "Who wants to show Ms. Emma what we worked on last week?"

Hands lift in the air, and when Addy claps her hands again, most kids scurry to their instruments. Some stay where they were, either reading a book on the ground or playing with something unrelated to music, but Addy doesn't make a fuss about it. *Fun before all.*

"Okay, Ellie, drums! One, two, three, four."

What I would describe as the most adorable but tone-deaf performance of "You Are My Sunshine" begins, and I adore every second of it. Some sing, some play the xylophone, and some clap their hands or shake a tambourine. Giant smiles cover their faces, some missing front teeth, and this is probably the cutest image I have ever seen. Two young boys shake their bums at the front, bumping their hips to the beat together. In the back, I spot one teenage girl playing an electric piano. While they near the end of the song, I find myself inching closer to her. Once the final note rings, I clap enthusiastically, and some of the kids get up to bow.

"Great job!" I say, smiling so wide it hurts. Addy looks a lot like me, pride showing in her eyes.

"What about 'The Itsy Bitsy Spider' now?" Addy says, and after a couple of nods, she leads the way again. This time, she leans forward to help one of the kids get a better grip on the handle of the tambourine so the sound is better, then teases a kid not to be shy and to sing louder. Just like before, my attention drifts to the little girl who's playing the piano, her focus on the keyboard as she only uses her thumb and index fingers on both sides instead of using her whole hands. I hesitate for a moment, but when I see her struggle over another combination of notes, I kneel next to her stool and say, "May I?"

She looks at me cautiously, her black eyes wide, but as I slowly inch my hand toward hers, she offers me a single nod.

"Look at my fingers. See how my thumb crosses under my other fingers like a bridge?" I repeat the movement a couple of times while she watches attentively.

"Your turn?"

She hesitates again, but when I give her what I hope is an encouraging smile, she nods and does it.

"That's it! You got it," I exclaim, maybe a little too excited.

And for the first time, she smiles at me, and my whole heart melts.

I spend the rest of the hour alternating from kid to kid, helping some with more difficult techniques, adapting the instruments for others, all the while singing and clapping with the students who don't play an instrument.

"Great job, everyone!" Addy finally says after a dozen songs, applauding everyone. I join her, and eventually, the whole class does. Most of them are smiling and laughing, the simple act of playing music for an hour enough to bring them joy.

And that's when I realize I don't remember the last time I felt like this while playing. When did piano stop being fun? *This* is what playing music is supposed to feel like. Liberating. Exciting. Amusing. I went down the wrong path somewhere.

"Bye, guys!" I wave as the kids pass in front of me. When the piano girl gives me a shy lift of the hand, I feel like I've won a Grammy.

"So?" Addy asks me once the kids have all left the room.

"That was...amazing. Really. And *you're* amazing."

She gives me a shy smile, but I know she knows she's good at it. It's obvious.

"I was trained in special education. That's probably why."

"Well, whatever it is, please never stop." I look around the room again, so lived-in, the instruments all over the place, and I already miss the sense of satisfaction that's been filling me for the past hour. "I know summer's almost over, but do you think I could come back again before the end?"

"Of course!" she says, her curls bouncing around her face. "I'm not here all the time, but every day there's at least one music class being offered, so just come to the front whenever you feel like it."

"Thank you. I think I will."

"You were good at it too, you know," Addy tells me with a wink.

"Thanks again, for everything."

Even though we barely know each other, she leans forward to give me a quick hug, and I reciprocate before I walk away, feeling like a thousand bucks.

Who knew I could feel like this about music?

The whole walk back to my cabin, my grin stays in place, and there's nothing fake about it. I don't think anything could drag me down after that.

"Hey, Julia!" I say when I cross her path. I don't even think to tame my intensity with her.

And when she rolls her eyes without answering, my smile finally dims. It hurts every time she answers rudely at something I've said or tries to take Jesy away from me, but this? It's worse. Like I'm an annoyance in her life.

Usually, when we see each other, Jesy is there as a middleman, but now we're alone, and I'm not sure what it is, maybe the loss of the joy I'd been feeling seconds before, but something pushes me to say, "Have I done something to you?"

"Hm?" she responds with a blasé look, barely stopping in her steps.

"I'm just wondering if I've ever done something to you. You've hated me from day one, and I'd like to know why." Getting the words out sends cold sweat running down my back, but it's too late to take them back.

She looks at the sky, snickering. "Of course you'd want to know. How could anyone not love you, huh? So perfect."

I frown. "I never said that." In fact, it's one of the last things I'd ever say about myself. Doesn't this summer prove I make mistakes left and right?

"Maybe not, but you expect people to believe it."

Already regretting the confrontation, I say, "I don't understand."

"Look, it's nothing about you in particular. I just hate fake people."

That feels like a punch to the stomach. My mouth opens, but no word comes out.

As if seeing my confusion, Julia says, "Yeah, you are. I don't think you've been real one time this summer. No one can be this cheerful and smiling and 'fine,'" she says with finger quotes, "all the time."

While I know she's made a point, I say, "Jesy can."

Julia purses her lips. "Yeah, okay, maybe, but that's because Jesy's special. Nothing can piss her off. But I've seen you. I see your face when you say everything's perfect. It's bullshit."

I don't think anyone has ever spoken so bluntly to me before, and while I should probably be insulted, I'm not. At least not entirely. No matter how much I'd like to say it's false, she has a point. I *have* lied. I *have* made things appear better than they were. I *have* hidden my relationship trouble from people, including my good friend, to look like everything in my life was good.

"I know Jesy doesn't mind because she's too good a person to notice, but I don't like being lied to. My life sucks sometimes, which means yours must too," Julia says, arms crossed. We've stopped in the middle of the path separating two rows of cabins, and thankfully, no one else is here to see us.

I close my eyes. I feel like laughing when I realize the thought I just had proves her point.

"You know what?" I tell Julia, opening my eyes back up. "You're right."

She tucks her chin in surprise, but quickly recovers with, "I know I am."

"I don't like airing my dirty laundry in front of everyone, but I *should* be more honest, especially with people close to me." I lick my lips. "I'll try to do better."

She twists her mouth to the side, her brows furrowed in doubt. "That's it?"

"Yeah, that's it." I cross my arms. "I think I needed to hear that, actually." I flash back to my mother, who cannot even ask for help from her closest friends, pretending and pretending and pretending again. It was time I came to the conclusion that I'm no better.

After looking behind her shoulder, she scratches her bleached scalp and says, "Look, I know we're not close, but if I can offer you any advice, it'd be to be honest with Jesy. No one will be happier to be let into your *real* life than her."

I rub my lips, then nod once and say, "Thanks." It's time.

"Sure."

A moment passes before I say, "Does that mean we're okay now?"

"Not sure. I guess we'll see."

I lift one side of my lips. "I'll take that."

Julia shakes her head, but for the first time, I get a smile out of her. To me, that's like winning the lotto.

When she turns to leave, I continue on the path to the cabin, my step even more determined than before. There's someone I need to talk to.

CHAPTER 28

Emma

"Hey," I say with a soft knock on Jamie's booth door.

His head snaps up, eyes softening when they meet mine. I spot a tag on the back of his shirt, which he probably put on groggily this morning without realizing it was inside out. "Hey. Everything good?"

"Yeah." I step inside the cramped room. "Just coming to see if you'd eaten anything today." Pulling the sandwich out of my bag, I say, "Brought you this just in case."

By the half smile he gives me, I know I was right.

"Thanks." He grabs the sandwich and unwraps it, immediately taking a large bite. The hum he lets out tells me it must've been hours since he ate last. "I get wrapped up in this sometimes," he says, pointing not only at the piano but at the entire room. The showcase. NAMA. Everything.

"I know. It's okay." And really, it is. Me and the piano don't have to be mutually exclusive.

"It's good you came, though." Getting to his feet, he grabs the score sitting on the lectern and throws the sheets haphazardly in his bag. I cringe at the sight of the wrinkled and mixed papers but keep my mouth shut. "We're going."

"Going where?"

"I thought we could go to karaoke night again?" His gaze trails down to his watch. "Yeah, we still have time. If you want?"

I don't remember a time last year when he would've asked me that, even before I injured my hand and had to leave camp for my surgery. To be frank, I'd never have suggested it either. Everything I've reproached of Jamie, I did too, at least in some part, which makes me the worst hypocrite. We've changed, though. There's more to life than playing, and it's like we're both starting to fully realize it.

"I definitely want," I say, grinning.

Jamie finishes packing his things, then we leave the music building for the cafeteria, where the karaoke nights take place. Dusk is slowly settling over the camp, crickets chirping from the woods and birds cawing above us. A redhead is breakdancing on the grass beside the water, his portable speaker blasting foreign rock music, while a trio of girls is sitting on a picnic table, building gorgeous harmonies on top of a pop song that was playing nonstop on the radio last year, which means they're right on trend. The air is warm but not too humid, the perfect late summer night that makes you realize just how much you'll miss this in a few weeks. To the far right, a group of preteens is entering a cabin, giggling at something one of them said. Closing my eyes, I take a deep breath of the fresh air, so different from the one surrounding us in our daily lives. When I arrived in July, the freshness felt overwhelming, but now, I recognize what I used to love about it. Home away from home, a place so peaceful in its chaos.

"Will you miss this?" I ask, gravel crunching under my feet.

"Allegro?"

I nod.

"Yeah, I will," Jamie says, looking around. "It's been such a huge part of our lives. Made us the musicians we are today."

"Mm-hmm." While we've had lesson after lesson over the years at home, it's never been the same as learning in an environment that lives and breathes art.

His hand brushes mine as he says in a low voice, "And it's also where we rediscov—"

"Emma!"

Jamie and I both turn around to find Cole, the teacher I worked with at the beginning of the summer and who's been at Allegro on and off since, walking in our direction.

"Oh, hi." When he stops in front of us and looks at me expectantly, I say, "Uh, Cole, this is Jamie, my…friend. Jamie, this is Cole."

"Pleasure to meet you," Cole says as he takes Jamie's hand in a firm grasp and shakes it.

"Likewise," Jamie says, but from the air he's sporting and the tightness in his shoulders, I'd say he's thinking the complete opposite.

The shake lasts a second too long, both men staring intensely at the other. Finally, Cole turns to me, his blue eyes crinkled at the sides as he squints against the sun. "Just wanted to make sure we were still on for tomorrow."

"Oh, yes, of course." The rehearsal had completely slipped my mind.

"Great."

I offer him a tight smile as I wait for him to say something else.

"Okay, well, I'll leave you guys. See you, Emma." He dips his head in Jamie's direction, then turns and leaves toward the beach, going to meet a group of people there.

Jamie and I resume our walk toward the cafeteria, but the lightness from earlier is gone. A muscle ticks in his cheek, and his hands are buried deep inside his pockets, not a word coming out of his mouth. While the outdoor warmth was welcome before, now, it feels stuffy. I glance his way again, but his attention is stuck on his feet.

I hope he's not mad I called him my friend. I didn't know what word to use. It would've been strange to call him my boyfriend when I promised we wouldn't pretend any longer, and as long as things haven't been clarified between us, I don't know *what* we are. "Friend" seemed the safest option.

After a minute of silence, I put on my big girl panties and ask, "You okay?"

He hums in answer. Nothing else.

"Jamie."

His gaze flicks my way.

"I know when you're lying."

His jaw tightens before he says, "Fine. Who's he?"

"Who? Cole?"

He nods tightly.

"He's a teacher here. He replaced Dr. Podimow a few weeks ago, and I just crossed paths with him yesterday. He offered to give me an extra tutoring session tomorrow."

Jamie lifts his brows, waiting.

"What?" I ask.

"And? What else?"

"What do you mean?"

"Emma, come on. That guy wants you."

I pull back. "He's my teacher. That's it." A teacher I've spoken to about five times, if that.

"A teacher who was imagining you naked right in front of my fucking face." He huffs. "Trust me, he wants more than that."

"Well, I don't." Have I noticed Cole was a little intense with me? Sure. But I won't say no to any help I can get, and he's a great tutor. That's all there is to it.

The look he gives me is full of doubt.

"That's what's up? You're jealous?" I say.

His silence is my answer.

"Jamie, look at me."

He does. His ebony eyes framed by long lashes are on me, focused and intent. I have the entirety of his attention, just like a composition he's deciphering.

A side of my lips climbs up. "When will you get it?"

"Get what?"

"There's never been anyone else for me but you." I can't believe he hasn't wrapped his head around that yet. I've been head over heels in love for him for so long, I don't remember what it's like not to be. "If it wasn't you, it wasn't anyone."

He blinks. Blinks again.

Then, a sunrise of a smile lands on his lips, so beautiful it's almost blinding. I don't have time to prepare before his lips land on my cheeks, a chaste kiss that ends up sending shivers down my spine and an ache in my lower belly.

"Okay," he says, as if he didn't need anything more than that.

"Okay," I repeat.

When we resume our trek and his hand reaches for mine, I gladly take it.

* * *

We arrive at the small building just in time for the karaoke to start. Jesy is there with Julia, both seated at the front of the room, and without asking, Jamie heads there so we can sit with them.

"Oh my god, guys!" Jesy says with the happiest expression on her face before leaning over to hug me. "What are you doing here?"

"Enjoying ourselves," I say with a knowing smile. It feels so good for Jesy to finally know everything. Last night, when I told her what had happened to us this summer, including the part about traveling back in time, she didn't bat an eye. Never did she call me crazy or out of my mind. When I finished telling her the entire thing, she simply said, "Okay, so what's next?" I'd rarely felt that much affection for her.

"That's good," she says, eyeing Jamie in that not-at-all-subtle way of hers. She also told me yesterday that she would be Team Jamie until the day she dies and that we simply had to figure out how to work together again. I said I'd been coming to a similar realization myself, and I think tonight proves we're on the right track. Only full honesty between us, yet we're still there, even stronger.

"You going to sing?" she asks us.

"Never," I say at the same time as Jamie blurts, "Maybe."

Chin tucked in, I eyeball him.

"What? Can't deprive the whole camp of our golden voices."

That makes me laugh because if there's something we don't have, it's golden voices.

"In your dreams, Montpellier."

He grins, then puts a hand on my thigh. It's not a propositional gesture, but it makes me jump all the same, not from discomfort but from surprise.

"This okay?" he says, as if I can only say the word and he'll remove his hand.

"Yeah, it's okay." More than okay.

"Good."

The audience around us starts clapping and cheering as a black girl comes on stage and starts singing a rendition of a Beyoncé song that would make the singer proud. I haven't seen her before, but I hope she's in a singing program because it would be a waste if she wasn't.

"Better than the 'Lady Marmalade' ones," I whisper in Jamie's direction.

"They did give it their all, though. I respect that."

I snicker.

Once the performer finishes, the thunder of applause is deafening. Some guys lift one another on their shoulders to cheer even more wildly for her. By the time the girl comes off stage, I realize my neighbor to the left has disappeared, and when I look up, I find Jesy on stage, lowering the microphone so it stands in front of her face.

"What's she doing?" I ask, even though it's a stupid question because I can see what she's doing.

"Singing," Julia says simply, beaming. I've never seen this girl so happy as when she's looking at Jesy.

"I didn't know she sang," I say.

"Only at karaoke, but she does almost every time." Julia throws a look my way that is far less friendly. Maybe even shaming me. She has every right to. I should've known that about my friend and been there for her. I'll do better. I *am* doing better.

Instead of continuing to feel sorry for myself, I whoop a cheer for my friend and whistle, two fingers in my mouth.

"Jesus," Jamie says, jumping. "Who knew you had that in you."

I straighten my shoulders, smirking.

"I'm a box full of surprises."

"I can see that," he says, and I see there's something alight in his eyes at the thought. I like it too. Knowing that even after all these years, there are still things to discover and fall in love with.

Jesy's voice is low and raw as she starts singing a soft melody that soon turns into a metal song, and everyone in the room goes crazy, including me. My classical violinist friend is also able to sing heavy metal without a single ounce of awkwardness or shame, and I love it. I get to my feet, jumping with the others and whistling again, and when she's done, I sit down with my hair matted to my forehead and pride filling my chest.

"You were freaking amazing up there!" I shout at Jesy the moment she comes back to our seats. My voice is loud, and I must be hiding some people's views when I jump to hug her, but it's like this evening has taken some of my inhibitions away. I'm with friends, this is so much fun, and I'm *happy*.

"Told you you should've come more before."

"I promise I'll listen next time you tell me to do something."

The wicked smile she gives me makes me wary of what's to come, but whatever it is, I know I'll try it.

The room settles down as two white guys get to the stage to sing a love ballad. It's sweet and raw, and for a minute, I pretend Irène and Alessandro are standing there at the back of the room, feet shifting from left to right as they dance to someone singing about loving someone for a lifetime. In reality, I know she is still in bed—I went to see her again this morning, and she looked even worse than the last time—but it's nice to imagine.

Leaning back in my chair, I close my eyes to feel the music even better, and just as I start swaying, I freeze.

Because on my thigh, Jamie's fingers have started moving, and

I recognize what it is in a heartbeat: he's playing. It's soft, but it's there. And it's not even to the rhythm of the ballad that's filling the room. It's his showcase piece. I recognize it after a few runs of his fingers. I force my legs to remain immobile so as not to scare him away as one of my favorite sensations on earth comes back to me.

He plays and plays, even as the performance ends and another begins. Eventually, I get more relaxed, even at one point leaning forward to whisper in his ear, "I'd go harder here. It might make the decrescendo more powerful afterward."

He freezes for a second, but when he sees that I'm smiling, he nods, then continues playing.

It's one of the most magical things I've ever felt. Finding this again, after so long.

Once the performer—a brown-skinned man who sang a questionable rendition of "Mamma Mia"—finishes, he gets off the stage, but no one comes on afterward.

Someone touches my left shoulder before I hear Jesy's voice say, "Come on, Emma."

"What?"

"Your turn now!"

My jaw drops. "No. No, no, no."

Jamie nudges my shoulder, then says, "Come on. Time to go."

"What? What are you talking about?"

"We signed you up," Jesy says, and I don't know if that's what her wicked expression before was for, but I don't like it. At all.

"I'm not going up there. Everyone's looking."

"Come on," Jamie says, slowly getting up. I immediately miss the comfort of his hands on my leg. "You know Luke Bryan's songs better than anyone here."

"You want me to go up there to sing country music? In front of everyone? Are you out of your mind?"

"It'll be so much fun!" Jesy says, her hands in a praying position. "Pleasepleasepleasepleaseplease. For me."

I huff, but can't find any words. I can't go up there. It would be humiliating. I don't have a nice singing voice, and as Jamie has repeated on multiple occasions, country music is not what's most common for a classical musician to listen to.

But when I look again at Jesy, I find Julia's eyes on me, her lips pursed as if I'm currently proving her point.

Crap.

I *am* proving her point, aren't I?

"You don't have to do it if you don't want to," Julia says, which somehow makes me feel like she means the exact opposite.

"Yes, she does!" Jesy says, nudging her with her hand. "You'll love it, Em."

"I'll go with you if you want," Jamie says from in front of me. "Would you really pass on an opportunity for me to sing 'Country Girl' in front of an audience?"

I can't believe I'm even considering this. I also can't believe he's offering. Jamie willingly putting himself in the spotlight? It's almost impossible.

"Will you shake your hips like he does in concert if I say yes?"

"I have no idea what you're talking about, but if that's what it takes, I'll shake my hips for you, sweetheart."

I rub a hand over my forehead, groaning. This is bonkers. Absolutely bonkers. I can't imagine what my father would think if he saw me.

And that's the final straw that makes me get to my feet.

Jesy yells my name again and again as I walk to the stage. Without glancing at the audience, I grab a microphone, and after having gone to see the guy who's taking care of the music at the back of the room, Jamie jogs back to the stage, lifting himself from the side and jumping on instead of taking the stairs. It's one of the hottest things I've ever seen.

"This is a terrible idea. Why did you—"

The guitar riff begins, interrupting me. Jamie shakes his head and taps his ear as if can't hear me. Little heathen.

But it's too late now. I'm onstage, and it would be even more embarrassing to freeze and not sing in front of everyone, so when the first verse comes on, I close my eyes and leap.

The first lines come out stiff and low, people probably not hearing anything, but as the catchy song enters my chest and no one boos, I feel some confidence growing. Not a lot, but enough for me to open my eyes and smile when Jamie starts singing and sliding from left to right. He's getting all the lyrics wrong and doesn't seem to notice it, which makes my grin widen.

We get to the chorus, and now he's dancing full on, nothing like the time I went alone to see Luke Bryan in Boston, but I like it so much more. He's even air-playing the banjo in the back. I laugh out loud at the way he grooves to the sound of the drums and rough guitar. Jamie sings so off-key, I can't help but think he's doing it to make me sound better. He's the less horrible singer of the two of us, but now, I sound slightly better. Being up here must be a nightmare for him, yet he's giving it his all. For me.

I continue singing, even twirling a time or two for good measure, and when Jamie gets close to me and grinds against my hip like a dirty cowboy as he calls me his country girl, I feel my cheeks warm but still burst out laughing. I can't believe he's doing this in front of an audience, my shy love, and I can't believe I'm enjoying it. It's surreal. Amazing.

In what feels like both thirty seconds and two hours, the song comes to an end, and without thinking, I run to Jamie and give his lips a thick but quick kiss.

"Sorry," I whisper when I pull back, slightly horrified.

"Don't be."

Then he steps forward and grips my head and hip before making me fall backward and giving me such a theatrical kiss, it would be called cheesy, even in a movie. Behind us, the crowd goes wild, and I find myself smiling as I kiss Jamie even more passionately. His tongue breaches my lips, making me gasp before I collide mine with his. Sparks explode in my body, a choir starts to sing in my head, my legs feel like mush, and I've never wanted someone more.

We kiss for who knows how long, and that's when I realize one thing: there's nothing fake about it. I'm not kissing him for show or to try and convince anyone of anything. I'm kissing him for me. Because I love him.

I love this man so very much, I don't know how to keep it in. It doesn't matter that I've kept telling myself we might not be a perfect match and it might be healthier for us to part ways. My heart belongs to him. Just as I said before, it always has, and I fear it always will. It's scary to face the fact, but it is what it is. I love Jamie Montpellier, and I don't think I ever stopped. Maybe I fell out of love for a moment, but I've never *not* loved him. And now that I've fallen back, I'm terrified of what will happen next. My heart has healed, but it's fragile enough that it could break with the flick of one of his fingers, and I'm helpless to it. I am at his mercy.

But for now, I won't care about any of this, because I'm kissing the man I love, and we've just had the time of our lives, and I'm running on adrenaline, not even caring how some people must've cringed while watching us.

And when Jamie pulls back just an inch, we exchange a look full of meaning. In that starry gaze, I see maybe he truly meant it, when he said I was his happy place all along.

I grab him for one last kiss, my whole body lit up like a firework. When Jamie's lips leave mine and he swoops me back to my feet, I try to hide how big I'm smiling, but Jamie puts a hand on my cheek and says, "Don't. Show them how beautiful you are."

I swoon.

Grabbing my hand, he leans forward for a bow—also theatrical and wildly over-the-top—and I only hesitate a second before imitating him.

People can think whatever they want. I'm happy, and I'm starting to realize, that's all that really matters.

CHAPTER 29

Emma

"THERE HAS TO BE SOMETHING WE'RE MISSING," JESY says, head thrown back in desperation.

"I can't think of anything else," I say flatly. My electric keyboard is sitting on my thighs while I'm lounging in bed, doing reps of scales. That's where I'm at. Back to the basics. I can't even blame it on my injury because my right hand is slipping all over the notes too.

"It can't only be related to either Jamie or you because if it was, only one of you would've been sent back."

I stifle a groan. I should've told her everything before. Maybe with that reasoning, we would've avoided the whole "getting lost in the woods" debacle.

I run another A major scale, then another.

"There's only four days left before your showcase," she says before tilting her head. "Or ours, I guess. It's so weird to think about it."

"I know," I say. "We're out of time."

My hand slips, and a C flat comes out of nowhere. I turn my keyboard off. It's all I can do not to throw it against the wall, which is a type of anger I've never felt before. It's not me. I don't like it.

Five days ago, at karaoke, I felt hopeful, happy even, but the more time passes, the tighter my chest becomes. We're not only out of time, we're out of everything. Decisions. Solutions. Answers.

"This is stressful. What if you're stuck here forever?"

"Jes, I love you, but this is really not helping," I say, letting my whole body drop to the side onto the bed.

She winces. "Sorry."

After a few repetitions of flexing and relaxing my fingers, I notice they're shaking, as if I was fighting a fight-or-flight reaction. Is the piano really my enemy now? I bury my head deeper into my pillow. This isn't sustainable. Struggling a bit on my showcase is one thing, but being unable to play basic stuff is bad. And most importantly, it's making me miserable.

Ever since I attended the special music lesson with Addy and the kids, I've tried to find that kind of happiness in my rehearsals, but I haven't been able to. I returned twice afterward to see the kids, with different teachers each time. I wanted to see if it had been a fluke and I'd just fallen in love with those particular kids, but no. I had so much fun with the next batch of students, and then the next. And every time I came back to my booth to practice, that joy went away, as if sucked by a vacuum.

Which brings me back to my current predicament: this can't last in the long run.

"I'll keep thinking," Jesy says, now hunched over the vanity, where she'd opened a notebook. "There has to be something."

My lips curve up, but I fear it looks sad all the same. "Thank you." I should probably get back to it too instead of wallowing.

With a groan, I get up from my bed, and just then, a knock comes at the door. I get up like a slug, then drag my feet across the cabin.

"Hi," I say when I open it to find Alessandro standing on the stairs. Behind him, Jamie is standing, chewing on his bottom lip. "Is everything okay? Is it Irène?" My stomach drops as if the ground has let up under me. What date are we? I thought we still had a few days.

"She is good. More than good, actually," Alessandro says, flatly.

His words and expression don't fit. "Meaning?"

"She has a lot of energy today," he says. It should be good news, but by looking at him, you'd think he was just told it was the end. Maybe because it is.

"Oh," I say. I don't need him to continue. We both know what was coming: that it might be the last of her energetic days, and we should use it wisely. "I...I'm sorry."

He nods, lips pursed.

"I want to do something special for her," he says sternly. "And I would greatly appreciate your help."

Behind Alessandro, Jamie's shoulders straighten in a determined way. He must've gotten a similar kind of request and agreed.

"Of course. Whatever you need."

* * *

"Keep your eyes closed."

"I truly do not appreciate this," Irène says, her eyes covered by a bandana Jamie found in his suitcase as she walks slowly with her arms extended in front of her. I'm standing at her back with a grip on her shoulders to make sure she doesn't hit anything, but that also means I can't see if the bandana is still covering her eyes, and she can't cheat. Not today, when I promised.

"You're fine. We're almost there."

"I do not understand why I could not simply walk there," she grumbles.

"Have you never heard of a surprise?"

"I do not like surprises."

I grin. She's never lost who she was, even now, when we're so close to the end.

Don't you dare think about it. I won't survive today if I do. Not when I know what's coming. Alessandro wasn't joking when he said he wanted to do something special. Even if neither Jamie nor I have said anything about Irène's passing to him, it's like he knows it will be soon. Maybe it's an instinctual part of him that knows. Something we can't explain but which is present nonetheless. I have experienced stranger things.

In front of me, Irène breathes heavily, so I slow down the pace.

Even though she does look much, much better today, she is still sick, and her labored inhales remind me to take it easy.

"You still okay over there?" I ask with a squeeze of her shoulders.

"What happened to no fussing?"

"I'll fuss if I want to."

She groans, but despite not seeing her face, I can guess she's wearing an amused smile.

A smile I might not see much of after tonight.

God, how can I miss someone so much already when I barely knew her six weeks ago?

"In all seriousness, though," I say, sounding raspy, "I want to thank you for this summer. It was great, partly because of you."

Irène's steps come to a halt. "Oh, *chérie*, no need for thanks. It is my job to be here for you."

"You did more than a simple job, and we both know it." Advising me about my career and my relationship is not something that's in the task description of a camp owner, and I doubt she does it for everyone. I have no idea why she decided to do it for me, but she's helped more than she could ever know.

"You have your whole life in front of you. It might not seem like it now, but you are so young. A world of possibilities is out there. You just need to see them."

"I think I'm starting to," I croak. "So, again, thank you." My hands are trembling as I rub her paper-thin shoulders.

"It was a pleasure," she says. Thank god her eyes are covered. This feels like a goodbye, and I know she knows it too. She's too smart not to. If I had to truly face her, I would probably break down in tears, and that can't happen. I have a job to do.

"Okay," I say, clearing my throat. "Just a few more yards." I start walking again, forcing her to take small steps. As we cross a clearing of trees, I finally see it. Candlelight by the lake. There's also Jamie's silhouette, standing farther in the back of the scene with his hands behind his back, while in the middle of everything stands Alessandro.

It takes a minute before we're close enough to the setup Jamie helped arrange, but once it all comes into focus, I pinch my lips not to gasp. The large rectangle made of small candles, the beautiful button-down shirt and polished shoes Alessandro is wearing, the portable speaker Jamie has at his feet. It's almost midnight, which means most campers are already sleeping or hanging out with a drink in their cabins, and even if they weren't, this isn't a place we visit often. It's my go-to part of the lakeside, where people don't usually venture. We're all alone tonight.

A few steps away from Alessandro, I slip my gaze toward Jamie, who's watching me with bright eyes and a small smile that makes everything in me erupt. He looks so incredibly handsome, his profile stark against the moonlight.

Coming to a stop, I whisper, "We can remove this now."

Irène squints as I pull the bandana off, but when she finally realizes what this is, her face lights up and her eyes well. "Alessandro," she says with a perfect Italian accent.

Lips pressed tight, he takes a step forward. His hands are held solemnly at his sides, but even so, I see the way they are trembling. "*Amore mio.*"

As subtly as I can, I walk to the right to join Jamie and give these two their moment of privacy. Even so, we can hear most of what is said, but some is spoken in Italian, some in French, and only a small part in English. Probably what they don't mind us hearing. It's beautiful, how their love has no official language. It doesn't need any when it has its own.

They talk in hushed tones, hand in hand and forehead to forehead. The scene is so beautiful, it steals all my attention. After a moment, Jamie's hands land on my hips from behind. Without hesitation, I let myself fall back and lean against him, his clean scent wrapping me up. Neither one of us talks, but it's not needed. I'm pretty sure we both know what the other is thinking.

"We met by interpreting *Romeo and Juliet*. Do you remember?"

"I remember everything," Irène says.

"It is a tragic story, but to me, it will always be the best love story of all time, not because of the characters, but because it has led me to you."

I close my eyes. I can't cry now. Not when it's barely begun.

Alessandro looks back at us and nods at Jamie, who presses play on his phone. Instantly, music fills the lot, a piece by Tchaikovsky composed for a duet in the ballet.

"What would you say to recreating it today?" Alessandro asks Irène, his back bent and a leg straightened in front of him as he extends a hand.

"One last time?" she says.

Alessandro squeezes his eyes shut, his chest trembling from the sobs he's holding in.

"No, my darling," Irène says, pressing delicate, wrinkled hands on his cheeks. "No tears. I am ready."

I clench my teeth so hard it hurts.

"I am not," he whispers, the words sounding painful coming from his mouth.

She shushes him, brushing her fingers once again against his cheek. She leans forward to whisper something in his ears, then pulls back and says, "Let's dance, my love."

My cheeks are glistening, I know, but I keep quiet as I watch Irène's hands drift from his face, one going to his shoulder, the other grabbing his hand. Their shoulders straighten, their bodies getting ready to remember a dance they last performed in their thirties.

And once they start dancing, it becomes obvious how they earned their titles.

The movements are not as fluid as they likely were when they were young. There are no lifts, instead only positions done on the ground. The flexibility isn't the same. The grace isn't the same. But despite all of it, it is, and I know it will remain, the most ethereal performance I have ever seen. There is so much love in every single movement, so much trust, a smile here and a touch there. It doesn't matter that they are in their eighties and that their bodies are not what they used to be. They're the picture of young, passionate love.

Alessandro is smiling through his tears now, the back of his hand fluttering against Irène's neck as they spin, eye to eye, and god, this is too much. The knot in my throat grows and grows until I can't control it. There is so much confidence in their love, like they know nothing, not even death, could shake them. What they have is stronger than everything. I'm jealous of it. They hold no confusion. They know who they are and what their love means. Dancers. A pair. Lovers.

I must sniffle because a hand moves from my hip to my arm, rubbing it up and down. Leaning on my shoulder, Jamie kisses my neck, then says, "This could be us one day, playing one last duet together."

And the bubble bursts.

Because who are we kidding? This could never be us.

Irène and Alessandro have been tied together all their lives because of their dancing. It's how they met, and it shaped their lives, just like Jamie and I with the piano. The thing is, I *don't* have the piano anymore.

It's been weeks since I've been trying to put my finger on the one thing holding me from giving in to Jamie once again, but now that he's said the words, the gates open. I finally see what it is. *This.* The problem isn't simply that Jamie didn't love me enough before. It's also that he's in love with someone who isn't me anymore.

What brought Jamie and me together throughout our five years, and even before, when we were just friends, has always been our passion for our instrument. We wouldn't be who we are without our high school music booths, or our shared tightly packed practice schedules, or our trips to Allegro, or our dreams of playing professionally. And that's still who Jamie is. A pianist, who's in love with a pianist at her core. Except I can't be that girl anymore.

So how can I be the one for Jamie?

Tears flow more profusely as I pull myself away. I can't have his reassuring touch and his familiar smell against me when I know it will all have to end. I'm being hypocritical with him, just like I was with myself, and this can't go on any longer.

I try returning my attention to Irène and Alessandro, but the only thing it does is show me what we will never be able to have.

"What's wrong?" Jamie whispers, approaching me.

I can't remain here, with the sight of the perfect couple in front of us. It's like I've repressed this feeling all summer, and now that I've let it take form in my head, I know there's no pushing it back down.

Holding back another sob, I shake my head. We can't make a fuss here. This isn't our moment.

"Emma, you're scaring me. What's wrong?" Jamie says, his voice so gentle it makes me hurt even more.

"I'm sorry," I say. Then I leave.

CHAPTER 30

Jamie

I F SHE THOUGHT I WOULDN'T FOLLOW HER, SHE'S DEAD
wrong. I would follow this girl to the ends of the world if I had
to.

She was careful not to make any noise as she escaped the clearing, so I do the same, hoping we won't have bothered Irène and
Alessandro. At this point, it felt like breaching their privacy anyway,
so I don't feel bad for leaving. We did what we had to do, and now
they can enjoy their time alone to say their final goodbyes.

Emma left through the woods, so I do the same. It's dark out,
especially once we get farther away from the candlelight. Even when
I lose her from view, I keep running, my pulse skyrocketing, more
from the situation than the exercise. How did we get here? It all
seemed to be going so well. In the past few days, I'd been met with
the same stars that used to fill her eyes when we were younger. She
would speak to me like a lover. She'd cuddle, and even give my hands
or shoulders a kiss here and there. Even when Alessandro and Irène
started talking and dancing, she got closer to me, as if she needed to
lean on me, and I was glad for it. Ready. If she'd fallen back or had
needed a shoulder to cry on, I would've been there. I'll always be
there. But instead, I said something I thought was benign, and her
entire being changed. Her body became rigid, jaw tight and eyes
spilling tears again and again. I don't know what I did, but clearly
I once again put my foot in my mouth. Maybe she wasn't ready to
hear it. She might have needed more time.

Even then, I'm not letting this be it. I'll find her and do whatever
it takes to make this right. No way am I letting her go a second time.

The small wood that leads from the lake to the main campground finally thins, and eventually, I see a shape I would recognize anywhere, running. She's not going toward her cabin, but that's not surprising. If she's going through something, she won't want to have someone else around. Instead, she seems to be heading toward the music building. No one ever goes inside this late, but I know it's not locked. After a few occasions of bothering the security guard and asking him to open the door for me so I could practice a little more, the guy ended up giving me a key. He now leaves it unlocked, and I lock it once I'm done. I've been using it all summer so that I could spend more time with Emma during the day. She was right when she said I wasn't there enough for her. I was careless with our love in the past years, thinking that nothing would ever change, even if I didn't prioritize her, but I've learned now, and that's never happening again. Not after feeling what it was like to lose her.

Out of the forest, I walk the gravel path that leads to the music building, then follow Emma inside, not caring whether she wants time or not. She can't keep hiding stuff from me. We need to be crystal clear for once in our lives.

The clang of the door closing makes the both of us jump. The main room is drowned in darkness, the porch lanterns creating slivers of light through the windows. Emma's shadow is larger than life behind her.

"Please, I—" Emma starts, her back facing me.

"What's going on?" I take a few steps forward. Her shoulders jump with hiccups, yet she remains silent.

My arm reaches for her, but I pull it back before making contact. "Talk to me."

She only cries harder.

"Emma, you're scaring me. Please."

"We're..." she says in between sobs. "We're not going to make it."

My heart drops to the ground.

"What?" A wave of cold hits me, shifting my body to ice. This can't be the end. Not after all this. I force myself to keep my cool as I say, "Why?"

"Because I…" Her shoulders hunch as if she's trying to make herself smaller than she is. "I can't play anymore. Not like you."

I blink. What in the world is going on?

"So this is…what, jealousy?" My head shakes on its own, over and over again. It makes no sense. Emma wouldn't decide to end things over something so petty. She's always been supportive of me. I won't act as if I haven't noticed her playing hasn't been at its best recently, but I never would've thought she'd resent me for being successful. I rub at the burning feeling in my chest.

"No." A pause. "Well, yes, in a way." She's still facing away from me, but I can see the way she wipes under her eyes with the meat of her palms. "I'm not jealous because you're great. I'm jealous because you love it."

"I'm confused here," I say, heart in my throat.

She sighs, then sobs again.

"Can you please turn around?" I ask in a weak voice, needing some kind of reassurance, which I'll find in her eyes. We can get through anything, and if she looks at me, she'll see it.

Slowly, her feet shift so her body is angled my way, but she's still covering her eyes with her hands. "I don't like to play anymore, Jamie," she says on an exhale. "I hate it, really."

This makes me take a step back. I repeat what she's just said in my head, but it still makes no sense. She's been practicing almost as much as me throughout the year, and again this summer. She would've stopped if she hated it, no?

"When… I… Why didn't you tell me?" I end up saying, my thoughts a mess.

"I didn't realize it at first."

"But you knew things weren't going okay," I state.

She waits before nodding.

"Why? Why didn't you tell me?" I say, but as the words come out, I'm brought back to the time while camping when she said her

261

playing wasn't great, even before the accident. Was that what she meant? I thought she'd been struggling over one piece, not...*that*.

"You did tell me," I whisper, feeling like a dick for not questioning it more. I lean forward to touch her wrists. Her lids scrunch as I do, but she doesn't move away. "Just not all of it. Why?"

"I couldn't." Her ponytail swishes as she says, "I would've lost you, and I wasn't ready for that."

"Sweetheart, you're not making any sense right now." She's still crying, and the sight coupled with her alarming words makes panic rise in my body. Tilting her chin up with a knuckle, I finally meet her watery indigo eyes. "You're not losing me. You could never lose me."

She looks up, blinking fast. Tears are flowing down her cheeks, a faucet left on. I need to hold myself back in order not to wrap my arms around her and hold all the sadness inside, but I have a feeling it's not what she needs. It's as if all summer, we've been beating around a bush we had no idea even existed, and finally, it's out.

"You want to stop playing? Then stop," I say with a lift of my arms. If I'd known she was thinking about it, I never would've even talked about practice with her. I only thought her hand was bothering her, but clearly, the problems ran deeper.

"It's not that simple," she says with a sigh, eyes closed.

"Yes, it is. You can change your mind about things. It happens. It doesn't matter."

Her arms go flying around her as she takes a step back. "Of course, it matters!" Pointing at my chest she says, "Jamie, you fell in love with who I was at seventeen, and that was a pianist, first and foremost. It's what we bonded over. It's why we're together today. But I've lost it, and I'm not getting it back." She rubs her lips. "Don't you see?"

She truly believes this. It's written all over her face. The pain of not feeling adequate for me, when I never would've asked that of her, if only she'd talked to me.

In a calm voice, I take a careful step in her direction and say,

"It's not why we're together, Emma." Her eyes squeeze even tighter, so I repeat, "It isn't."

She's not hearing me. Her head is shaking as if she's having a different conversation inside her head. My words aren't registering to her. Like now that she's made up her mind about things, there's no way back.

I roll my lips behind my teeth as I inhale deeply, then say, "You know what the first real thing I noticed about you was?"

That seems to get her attention. She freezes, but she's listening, probably expecting an answer like how well she played Chopin at fourteen.

"It was how gentle you were with everyone."

I can picture it still. The days of staring at her every chance I had, forgetting about the tasks I needed to do. A kid who'd come in sight of his aurora, with the rest of the world blind to it.

"It didn't matter who you were talking to in class or during lunchtime. You always made them feel listened to and worthy of your time, and I wanted you to make me feel that way too. That's why I almost puked the first time you talked to me in my booth. It had nothing to do with the piano."

Her eyes glisten still, but I know I've got her now. She's watching me intensely, so beautiful I could die.

"And you know why I wanted more of you afterward? Because you weren't just gentle. You were magical. You made me, the loser new student, feel like a thousand bucks. I couldn't get enough of the way I felt when I was with you, and imagining being loved by you? That was a dream I never could've expected even if I'd wished for it all my life."

A shuddery breath comes out of her mouth as more tears fall from her eyes to the corner of her mouth, but this time, they seem to be of the happy kind, at least partly. Unable to resist, I lean forward and kiss the tears away from the side of her lips. When I pull back, she inhales sharply as if she doesn't want me to go away. I know that sound, because I know all of her. Or maybe I only knew most of her, but that's a thing of the past.

"It was never about the piano, sweetheart. You could decide to never play a single note in your life again and I wouldn't care. You know why?"

She swallows, once again answering with silence.

With a hand on her soft cheek, I say, "Because your music is great, but I much prefer the sound of your laughter."

She leans against my hand, and at this moment, I know there's still hope. We'll both do better, but we can't let go of this love. It's too precious. If she wants it, then I'm all in.

"I see you, Emma, and I love all of you."

Even through flutters of her lashes, I can see the serenity taking form in her.

In a small voice, she says, "You really think we can make it?"

"I *know* we will."

As I wipe under her eyes with both my thumbs, her face between my hands, another tear falls, warm on my skin. And then, I hear the most beautiful words I ever have.

"I love you so much."

I pull back in surprise, the knot in my throat so tight my voice sounds off as I say, "Yeah?"

She nods hard. "I couldn't stop even if I wanted to."

At that, I laugh out loud, and before she can move away, I scoop her up and kiss her so hard I'm afraid I've hurt her, but no, she's answering with the same fever.

"We'll figure it all out together," I say against her lips. "You'll see."

She smiles, her teeth a bright white against the dark hall of the music room, then she dives for another kiss.

And I'm in heaven.

Never breaking from our kiss, I walk toward a surface we can use, anything, careful not to trip and to repeat our dangerous stunt near the parking lot. Thank fuck the room is empty and no one comes in at night because I don't think I could pull myself away from her even if I tried.

Emma's nails dig through my scalp as I walk blindly, and finally, we hit something solid.

The grand piano in the middle of the room.

To hell with it. I let Emma sit on it, her legs on both sides of my hips. My lips trail a path from her mouth to her chin, and then to her neck, where I kiss and suck sharply in the way I know drives her crazy. The tightening of her thighs around me proves I got it right.

"We can't..." she pants. "God, we can't do this here." The way she throws her head back to give me easier access goes against every word she's saying.

"Don't worry. We're good."

Her absence of argument is a testament to the way she wants this.

I'm trying to keep calm, to go slow, but it's impossible. Her breaths are coming fast. Mine too.

"Fuck, I've missed you," I whisper against her skin as I kiss up her neck again, the smell of vanilla everywhere.

She moans, grinding softly against my dick, and I'm hard already. It reminds me of the night in our shared tent when we humped like teenagers and I couldn't get enough of her. It's crazy how taking a step back from a relationship can make you see all the things you've taken for granted.

Never again.

I kiss her once more, her tongue entering my mouth, tasting of the cherry cola she drank earlier and of my Emma. I undo her ponytail before my fingers dig through her hair, now wild just like mine, the dark strands all over the place. She's wearing a long, silky skirt with a tank top, the material so thin I can feel everything. Her perfect breasts pressed up against my chest. Her ass, squirming against the table. Her soft heat, waiting for me.

"Can I?" I say as I brush a knuckle against her panties.

She nods, panting.

I slide my hand inside, finding her wet already. I didn't think I could get harder, but somehow, I strain even more against my zipper, so much it's almost painful.

And when she presses her palm against me and rubs me up and down, I know I won't last long like this.

"Shh," I whisper, rubbing her clit in tight circles while pulling myself back. She's strung tight, and I don't think she'll need long either. Her lips are parted on a gasp, eyes half-mast, chest pushed out. It's the sexiest thing I've ever seen.

With my other hand, I push down her top and her bra so her breasts are exposed, then take one in my mouth, licking at the nipple while never taking pressure off her clit.

"God," she moans, still squirming on the piano. I don't remember the last time I've seen her so out of control, in need of this, of me. Hungry. It's not even like when we were teens, because now, we know what we're doing. There's no need to experiment anymore. I know just the way to touch her to make her come, and she does too.

"Jamie," she sighs, rocking faster against my hand.

"No," I say, stopping. "Not like this."

She looks worried for a second, as if I would leave her like that, wanting. When I drop to my knees and part her thighs, she relaxes.

"I need to taste you," I say, not even looking at her face anymore. I pull at her panties and bare her pussy to me, glistening and smelling like all of my daydreams. I pull her closer to the edge so she's hanging off the piano, her ankles on both sides of my head. "Can I?"

She's still leaning back on her elbows when she says, "Please."

So I do.

The first lap of my tongue is slow and rough, her moan echoing against the high ceilings. My hands grip tightly at her ass as I lick again and again, the taste making me feral. I'm tall enough for my mouth to be at the perfect height when kneeling, and when I look up and find her eyes closed and teeth biting her lower lip, I know we'll both remember this moment for the rest of our lives.

After sucking at her clit, I lap again, this time faster. Her breathing accelerates and her thighs start to shake around my face. I pull away for a moment, kissing her thighs, her belly, sucking her lips, anything to make it last longer.

"Jamie, I want you," she moans, gripping her calves behind my head.

"Uh-uh, sweetheart. Let's make you come like this first."

She doesn't argue, just like I knew she wouldn't.

I resume my licking and sucking, but this time, I add a finger inside her, so wet and warm. She gasps at the fullness. I grin. I love the way she lets herself go like this. She's giving me full control, which means more to me than she could imagine. That kind of trust is mine and mine alone.

Wetness is dripping down my chin as I pump and lick, making her moan. Her legs start to shake again. This won't be long now. Keeping the same pace with my tongue, I add a second finger, hitting at just the right spot.

And there she goes.

I continue pumping as she tightens against me again and again, her moans low and rough. Her orgasm lasts longer than usual, and I make sure to prolong it as much as I can. When she finally comes down, I pull away, her legs still shivering while she catches her breath.

"Jesus," she says, exhaling sharply.

Without giving her more respite, I get to my feet and grab her face in my hands before kissing her with all I have, her wetness between our lips.

This time, when her hands drifts to my cock, I don't stop her. After seeing her come apart like this, I need release. Her skirt is bunched around her hips as my hands come up, grazing her ribcage, then playing with her exposed nipples. Despite having just come, she's still grinding against me. We both need more.

"Unclasp my belt," I plead. I don't want to stop touching her, and she seems happy with that. Letting go of my cock, she removes my shirt, then my belt, and finally pushes my pants down. I'm only in my boxer briefs, my hard-on obvious.

"Can I do something about this?" she says, running her pink nails over my dick. I swallow roughly.

"Can *we* do something about it?" I ask, grinding against her wet center.

She licks her lips, and as she nods, she pushes my boxers down, freeing me. I step even closer, the front of my thighs touching the side of the piano as she wraps her legs behind my ass. We don't need condoms; neither one of us has ever slept with anyone else, and Emma's on the pill.

Nudging myself against her entrance, I say, "You sure?"

"Yeah, I really am." There's no doubt in her voice, only happiness and confidence.

I give her lips a peck, then pull back. Our breaths mix as I enter one inch, and against her lips, I say, "As you wish." Then I slam home.

We both gasp as I sheathe myself fully inside her, the warmth of her so good I need to hold on in place to make sure I don't come yet. With the way Emma is gripping my shoulders, her nails sharp enough to leave marks, I'd say it makes two of us.

"You okay?" I ask.

"Yeah. You?"

I answer by pulling back and sliding in once again. She makes the most delicious fucking sound as she leans her forehead on my shoulder. My arms form a tight band on her back. Every inch of our bodies is touching, no space between our chests, as if we can't bear distance any longer. I try to keep a slow pace, but it doesn't work. With the way she's moving against me, like she wants more and more and more, I can't stop. I'm sliding in and out, my pulse sky-high as I think about how good it feels to be here again. It might have been similar to when we were in the woods, but in a way, it's entirely different, because now we're open to each other. No more hiding. This is us.

Pulling back slightly, I give space to one of my hands so it can come to Emma's clit and start circling again. She cries out, then lets her head fall back to my shoulder, this time softly digging her teeth into my skin as she lets out another sinful moan.

Tension builds in my spine. I increase the pressure on her clit; I want her to fall with me this time. The room is silent apart from the sounds of our bodies meeting, and I don't think any music could top this.

I grind fast against her, and when I bury my face in her neck and whisper, "I love you so much," she comes apart, and I'm right there behind her. I spill inside her as she clamps around my cock, and for a second, I feel like I might pass out, head thrown back, eyes clamped shut. The world feels like it's shaking around us as we go through pure bliss together.

"God, I love you too," she groans once she's come down from her high. I'm still inside her, jerking with the last of my orgasm, but I still hold her even tighter.

Pressing a kiss to her damp forehead, I say, "Promise me something."

"Hm?" she says sleepily.

"Tell me we're always going to resolve our issues like this."

She erupts in laughter, and I wasn't kidding earlier. It truly is the most beautiful sound I could listen to.

CHAPTER 31

Emma

DAWN HAS RISEN BY THE TIME WE FINALLY DECIDE TO get back to our cabins, with the hope of catching a few hours of sleep before needing to get back to real life. Once we came down from our high of making love for the first time in what felt like a lifetime, we put on our clothes and made our way outside the music building to watch the stars and talk about everything and nothing, lying on our backs, surrounded by the forest and the song of the cicadas. And then we were kissing again, and we were naked again, and my world was trembling again.

I can't believe it happened. We've always been so conservative, and now here we are, having sex in public twice in one night. And even worse, I don't feel bad about it. I feel a surge of heat as I remember it, perhaps, but I wouldn't regret it. Ever.

"What are you thinking about?" Jamie asks as he grabs my hand, our arms swinging between our bodies as we walk away through the utopian lilac and marshmallow sunrise, dew tickling my sandal-clad feet.

"Oh, you know." I shrug. "Boring stuff."

"Yeah?" he asks, smirking, his glasses perched in his hair. "That why your cheeks are red?"

"They're not."

He grins; I'm caught.

"Sure thing," he says.

"You're giving yourself a big head with all that talk."

"I don't need to when you do it for me," he says, then kisses my cheek noisily. I laugh.

I don't think I've ever felt this euphoric in my life.

"Hey, what's that?" Jamie asks after a moment, tipping his chin toward something to our right, which is tacked on a tree. I don't remember seeing that on my way around the campground yesterday, but I also wasn't in the best state of mind.

"It looks like…" I squint to make sure my eyes aren't deceiving me, but when I realize what it actually is, my knees buckle.

"What?" He squeezes my hand. "Emma, What?"

"Jamie…" I jog toward the white paper fluttering with the morning wind, then pull it from the bark. "It's a showcase pamphlet." Blinking fast, I turn to him and shove it his way. "*Our* year's showcase." I remember seeing it online a few weeks before the end of our junior year. There was this particular symbol of a drum I'd thought looked weird. I'd recognize it anywhere.

"Impossible," he says, snatching the piece of paper to read it through. "How?"

"I don't know," I say with a hopeful smile, my eyes welling. "But look." I point toward the cabins in front of us, which I notice now are painted a darker color than they were a few hours ago. "That can't have happened overnight."

"Is this real?" Jamie says, looking all around us before landing back on me, his face drained of blood.

The last piece of confirmation we need happens when Jesy comes out of our shared cabin to our far left, which in and of itself seems strange since she never got up earlier than 9:00 a.m. all summer, but what's most striking is her hair. Long gone is the cropped bob, instead replaced by long black strands.

Clapping a hand to my mouth, I look up at Jamie and nod. "It's real," I say in a muffled voice.

Jamie's face takes time to transform, as if he needs time to wrap his head around the fact that we actually did it, but when it does, god, it's beautiful. A large smile curves his lips, teeth all in view, before he crouches, picks me up, and starts twirling us around.

"We're back!" he shouts. Somewhere, someone yells at us to

shut up, but I don't even care about being a peace breaker. This is too good a moment not to shout.

Above all, though, is the relief that being back isn't nearly the best thing that's happened overnight. If staying in the past had meant being with Jamie, happy and honest and in love, it wouldn't have been the end of the world, and *that* feeling is the most important thing.

"But wait," I tell Jamie. He slows his spins, then sets me down. "When did it happen? And why?"

He drags a hand through his already mussed hair, then says, "I can only come up with one good explanation."

"Which is?"

Looking me dead in the eye, Jamie says, "We had magic sex."

I shove his shoulder playfully. "I'm being serious!"

"Me too!" he says. "What else happened last night that could explain this?"

I shrug. "This is becoming a little too esoteric for me."

"Think about it," Jamie says, his hands on my shoulders. "We knew this thing was related to you and me. We knew it had something to do with something that went down last summer. We knew we had to change things."

"And what changed?"

"Us," he says, caressing my cheek so tenderly I feel like bursting. "We figured out how we went wrong. We were finally honest with each other. We worked to make our relationship work." Lips curling up, he tilts his head and says, "And then we had magic sex." He closes an eye as if thinking. "You think it's the first or second round that did it?"

I shake my head like I can't believe he's making jokes right now, but deep down, I know what he's saying has to have some kernel of truth. What else could it be? It's impossible it was a coincidence that we came back at the same time we worked things out.

"So, what, you think the universe wanted us to get back together?"

"First of all, we were never *not* together. We were figuring it out." He smiles. "And second of all, yeah, maybe that's it. Maybe it's a soulmate thing."

"So we're soulmates now?" I tease.

"Did you really doubt it?" he says, palms warm on my lower back.

My grin is an answer in itself. If he'd asked me weeks ago, I probably would have doubted it, but now? No, I don't.

"What if it's something that happens to all people who are supposed to be together but somehow stray away from each other?" he says.

"And you think no one in the history of the world would've talked about it?"

"Are *you* going to tell people about this?"

"Are you insane?" I say, which makes him laugh. "Although someone does know about it."

Both our heads turn in Jesy's direction. She's currently making her way to the cafeteria, her violin in her lap. "If we want to know what our current selves did this summer without sounding crazy," I say, "she's the one to ask."

Without a word, we trudge toward her.

"Hey guys," she says just before reaching the front door. "Seriously, Jamie, I can't believe you get up at this hour every day to practice."

"I do?" he asks. Maybe that's something he's changed. Maybe he spends more time with me during the evening and practices early in the morning instead.

"Yeah...?" Jesy says, eyeing us both. We must have weird looks on our faces because she says, "What is going on here?"

I only hesitate a second before saying, "Jes, do you remember if I mentioned something weird last year about, um..." Oh boy. What if time travel makes people forget about what we've told them once we get back to real time? She'll never—

"When you guys traveled back in time?" she asks, as if we're talking about our favorite perfume brand. Jamie and I exhale loudly.

"Yes," I say. "That."

"Yeah, of course."

All right, then.

Jamie and I spend the next ten minutes explaining everything that's happened to us this summer—or I guess, last year—and Jesy takes it like a champ, never blinking, even at the strangest parts. She's much better than I would be in her position.

Once we're done, the only thing she finds to say is, "Shit, that means I've been hanging out all summer with someone who is you but also isn't you."

"About that," Jamie says. "Can you give us a rundown of what happened this summer so we don't look too lost?"

"Please," I add.

"Sure," she says. "So basically, Jamie has been waking up at the ass-crack of dawn to practice, and then you two got breakfast together with me and Julia, and then you went and did your own thing, and then Jamie went for his second practice of the day while you hung out with me in the music room, and then—"

"Wait, wait, wait," I interrupt. "Jamie did all this practice, but what about me? The showcase is in two days."

Jesy laughs with her brows furrowed. "Emma, you're only playing for fun now."

I inhale sharply. "Really? But... How?"

"Since you decided you didn't want a career as a musician last year, you took a step back."

"I didn't do that last year," I say. Last year, I hurt my hand, and then—

"Yeah, you did," Jamie says slowly. "If I'm getting this right, the summer we just had is the new version of last year's summer, which means the first summer doesn't exist anymore."

"So, what? Does that mean all the past year is now different too?"

"I guess so," he says.

Turning back to Jesy, I ask, "Are Jamie and I still struggling?" His eyes widen, but at this point, there's no need for sugarcoating. Jesy knows everything, and that's probably the only question that really matters.

"Quite the opposite," she says, smiling. "I've never seen you guys so happy."

And as she says it, it's like a cogwheel is turned on. My head fills with glimpses of scenes, blurry and short, like snippets of a life I didn't live. Or perhaps a life I *did* live. Rainy Sunday mornings spent in bed, reading a book with my feet in Jamie's lap. Study sessions in the library with messy kisses between chapters. Date nights in the park on warm May nights, when the weather has just turned to a silky summer and the days are longer.

Memories.

I grin as Jamie's hand folds into mine. To him, I whisper, "So the current us were actually having a good time, huh?"

"Lucky motherfuckers," he grunts in a low voice, making me laugh.

Jesy waggles her brows at us, and I clear my throat. "Right, sorry."

"Told you you were good," she says, and she even has the audacity to wink.

More memories start emerging. I see it in Jamie's face too— the remembrance.

I feel too calm considering the weirdness and the gravity of the situation. I have lived an entire year twice, with double the amount of memories I should have. Or at least, I think I will have all those memories in double. Right now, I still only have flashes of the year that actually passed. My mind is full of the shitty year Jamie and I had, but the good year we had is in pieces. I get glimpses of fights with Jamie that were resolved quickly and clearly. I see all the extra care he gave me, and all the tension that evaporated from our relationship. It's almost too good to be true.

"Eight weeks in," Jamie says with a slow blink, "and I still haven't sprouted the intelligence to figure all this out."

"I love you anyway," I say. He squeezes my hand in return.

While I'm sad I might never recover every single memory of this timeline, if I had to choose which year to remember, I'm glad it's the one we actually lived, where we struggled and fought and made up. This way, I'll never forget how we came apart, and how we came back to us. We won't repeat our mistakes if we know what they were.

"Important question," Jamie says, interrupting my thoughts. "If I practiced in both timelines this summer, does it mean I have double the skills?"

"I don't think that's how it works," I say. "Or maybe it is, if current you built upon what you practiced last summer."

Jesy grins. "Guess we'll see at the showcase."

"Hope that guy didn't slack all summer," Jamie mutters.

"You really hold a grudge against him, huh?" I tell him.

Jamie shrugs. "Whatever. He's fine." He looks me up and down, making me feel like he's imagining me naked. "He doesn't have the real you, so I'd say he's kind of pathetic."

I laugh. "You're becoming cheesy, Montpellier."

"Guilty."

Jesy proceeds to give us a more detailed rundown of the past year, but my mind sticks to one thing. "Jes," I interrupt, "did I tell my parents about not doing the showcase?" I ask. If I decided to stop pursuing a career as a performer all these months ago, what happened between then and now? I rack my brain to find the information but come up empty.

She shakes her head. "You haven't seen them much this whole year because they extended their world tour and traveled a lot, so you decided to wait until they came here at the end of the summer to tell them. You still wanted time to think things through."

"All right," I say, more flashes of what she's just said coming in. "I think my decision's made anyway."

"You're not doing it?" Jamie asks, no judgment in his voice.

"I don't think so, no."

He nods, then kisses my hand, and it's all the proof that he meant what he said last night.

"Current me was a coward, though," I say. "She left me all the crappy stuff to do."

"They'll understand," he says.

Let's hope so.

"One last thing," I tell Jesy, who was turning her wheels toward the cafeteria.

"Yes?"

"Why was I able to come to camp this year if I'm not a real pianist anymore?"

"You *are* a real pianist. You just don't want to be *only* a pianist." She shrugs. "But Mr. Sancerre also approved it."

"Alessandro?"

"Didn't know you were on a first-name basis."

"It's a long story," I say. Then, after remembering that while we saw him yesterday, I have no idea what happened to him all year, I ask, "How is he doing?"

"Not sure. He hasn't been around much this summer. You know, after losing his wife and everything."

It feels like a knife to the chest. She's gone. Of course she is.

I wrap my arms around my middle, trying not to panic. I don't know why I didn't think about it first, but if we're back in the future, she can't be here too. It's over.

More memories come back. A ceremony by the lakeside, a dozen people dressed in black, mourning. A visit to her grave in the winter months, with snow falling like thick cotton balls over my hair.

Tears spring to my eyes. I'll never get to hear her call me her *chérie* again, or get chastised for fussing over her. She'll never counsel me again. Never show me what true love looks like. Yesterday *was* our goodbye.

A comforting hand lands on the small of my back, centering me. I breathe in and out. It's okay. I knew this would happen. It's not a surprise. It hurts, so much, but it's still not a surprise. And in a way, it makes me happy that this was the way we parted. That the last time I saw her, she was in her element, dancing with the love of her life. It's how she would've wanted me to remember her, I know. Full of life and joy.

"I'll expect you to tell me more about all this," Jesy says, bringing me out of my stupor. "Already rude enough that you haven't told me everything this summer."

"That wasn't the real me," I say, although I'm not sure exactly who it was. "But I'm back now."

"Really happy about it," she says before giving me one last smile and disappearing inside the cafeteria.

"It's so strange," I tell Jamie, letting myself fall to the ground with my legs crossed. He joins me there, all gangly limbs spread out on the emerald grass.

"Tell me about it."

"And poor Alessandro," I say. "A year without his love already. I can't imagine it."

Pressing a kiss to my head, Jamie says, "Hopefully, you won't have to for a long, long time."

* * *

Jamie is leaving a trail of kisses down my back as I read a book—finally, I've given myself time for it—which makes me squirm and giggle.

"Stop, you're tickling me."

"Why do you think I'm doing it?" he says before pressing another tongue-filled kiss along my spine. Shivers erupt on my skin while I continue laughing.

"If I donkey-kick you in the face, don't say you haven't been warned."

"Emma," he says solemnly, making me glance over my shoulder. "It would be an honor to be donkey-kicked in the face by you."

I roll my eyes. "You and your weird fetishes."

He snorts, then resumes his kissing.

I still can't believe he's hanging out with me in my room the day before the showcase. Sure, he practiced for four hours this morning, and I know he'll be going back after lunch, but still. Everything is so different, both from his side and mine. I tell him, now, when I'd like something to be done differently, and when he doubts himself, I reassure him the best I can. It's not perfect, but we're getting there, and that's more than I could've ever hoped for.

"Jamie!" I squeal when he bites softly into the skin on my hips, making me roll onto my back. "Stop this!" With the way I'm laughing, I don't sound convincing one bit.

"I'll think about it," he says. Just before he has time to torture me again, though, a knock comes at the door.

"Wasn't Jesy out to practice?" Jamie asks.

I nod.

We both get up with a frown, but when we see who's on the other side of the door, being bothered during our alone time is the last thing on our minds.

"Alessandro, what a lovely surprise," I say, hoping I don't sound too weird. After all, from what I know, he hasn't seen me for an entire year.

"Hello, you two," he says with a smile.

"Come in!" I say, running inside to make sure the place is in order. I hide a pile of clothes Jesy left on the ground under her bed, then throw a bunch of stuff Jamie had littered around onto the top bunk. With a hand, I invite Alessandro to have a seat at the vanity.

Even though I feel like it's only been days since we've seen each other, he's aged a lot. Dark circles underline his eyes, and his gait is less steady than it was.

"How are you doing?" Jamie asks once we've all found a place to sit.

"Good days and bad," Alessandro answers honestly. "It is hard to be here without her."

We both tip our chins in understanding, no word appropriate enough in response to this.

"Is this your first time since?" I ask tentatively.

"Almost." His nose twitches as he sniffs. "I missed Allegro, but it is not the same without her. It does not feel… How do you say it…" He rubs his lips with his fingers before saying, "*Whole.*"

There goes that knot in my throat again.

"But I needed to come see you today."

"Oh," I say. "Why?"

"Because she asked me to."

I look up, blinking fast. I still haven't taken the time to properly grieve for Irène, but now is not the time.

"When she knew her time was almost up, she told me to make sure to come see you before the showcase this year." I expect him to look at both Jamie and me, but his gaze stays on mine. "She wanted me to tell you that whatever decision you made, she knew it was the right one."

I bite firmly on my shaky lips. Even though I did make my choice, the past two days have been filled with moments of self-doubt, wondering if my decision will lead to regrets in the future. I still don't know what I want to do with my life, after all. I want to continue studying, but what exactly, I'm not sure. Maybe music, or maybe something completely different. But knowing Irène thought I would choose right brings me relief.

"She believed in you. I told you last year that she saw herself in you."

I give him a tight but true smile. "Now that I got to know her, I can say that's a real honor."

He doesn't ask what I mean by that, and I'm grateful.

Before I can stop it, a tear falls from my eye.

"Excuse me," I say, rushing toward the bathroom with my gaze down. Once the door is firmly closed behind me, I let myself exhale, a sob stuck in my throat. I need to get myself together. Mumbled voices come from the other side as I wipe my eyes and nose with toilet paper.

"I was right when we talked last year," Alessandro says, his voice muffled by the bathroom door. I press my ear closer to it.

"About what?" Jamie answers.

I hear sniffles, then a pause. My eyes swim again. He's so brave for coming here and telling us this. I can't imagine how much strength he must need to be holding himself up right now. Even though I don't remember the past year, I hope Jamie or myself contacted him to make sure he was doing okay.

"About the way I miss her," Alessandro says in a thick voice. "It truly did not matter that we had spent all these years together. The moment I knew she was gone, I would have given everything to get an extra minute with her."

I hear footsteps from the other side of the door before someone blows their nose. I blink fast. I need to be there for him right now, but I don't think I'd be any help. Not with the way I'm crying.

"Enjoy every second of it. Time flies when you are in love."

"Don't worry," Jamie says. "I'll never forget it."

I have such a surge of love for this man at this moment. I want what Irène and Alessandro had, or at least our version of it, and the confidence in his voice tells me he does too. It's such a profound feeling, to be seen so completely, and to still feel loved in your entirety.

Don't worry, Jamie. I'll never forget it either.

CHAPTER 32

Emma

"HOW ARE YOU FEELING?" I ask as I straighten Jamie's bow tie.

"Like I'm about to pass out."

"You're going to be amazing out there," I tell him before kissing his shaven jaw. My words don't seem to reassure him much. He's performing in the showcase in less than two hours, which means today is one of the most important days of his career, at least as of yet.

"And what if I'm not?"

"Then we'll figure it out. One step at a time, okay?"

He nods stiffly. Tension is emanating from his entire body, but at least he's still here with me and not lost in a world of his own. I don't know if the strange summer we just went through did something for his self-confidence or anxiety, but seeing him like this—so much better than he usually is before an important concert—makes my heart full.

He looks down at his watch, jaw tight.

"Time to go?" I ask.

"Yeah."

"Break a leg." Squeezing his hand, I add, "I'll be right there in the front row."

"Thank you." He exhales slowly through pursed lips, then turns to leave his cabin. However, before crossing the threshold, he turns and rushes to me, hugging me so tight I can't breathe. Then, without a word, he leaves.

I don't know why this has made me so giddy.

Smiling, I clean up some of the mess he made this morning

while getting ready, then head outside toward the concert hall. I'm wearing a flowy white dress with embroidered flowers, which I had packed for one of our free days at camp and definitely not for showcase day. If this summer hadn't happened, I would be in a stiff shirt and cigarette pants, running over bars in my head while stressing about how I would perform in front of everyone and how it would reflect on my parents. Instead, I am here to support my boyfriend who *wants* this and nothing else. It's such a change from what I was expecting eight weeks ago, and I wouldn't change it for the world.

A crowd has formed in front of the performance hall while guests are waiting to be let in. Today is officially the last day of camp, so most parents, siblings, and friends are here to see what their loved one has worked on throughout the summer. The fresh end-of-August wind contrasts the warm sun on my skin as I look at all the bright, happy faces everywhere. Jamie's family must be there somewhere—his parents never miss an opportunity to support their son. I know it's caused tension in his family, that he wanted to pursue music, but I'm proud of him for having stuck to his desires. That determination will make him the best one day, and I'm excited to see it happen, and be right by his side. Music will not be a sore point between us any longer. I make a vow of it.

"Emma?" a voice I've only heard through the phone for a long time calls from behind me.

My mother is standing there, wearing a fitted black suit with sharp Louboutins and large sunglasses over her eyes. She looks thinner than when I last saw her. While my life was technically different in the repeated past year, hers didn't change, so she still must've gone through a hard time in this timeline.

And yet, she's still my mother, with her straight posture and crimson-painted lips. A mother I was scared for a moment I wouldn't see again if I'd been stuck in the past at camp.

"Hi, Mom," I say as I go to hug her tightly, her lilac smell reminding me of mornings at the park and of Christmas mornings, when nothing could bother my parents from home.

She makes a sound of surprise, then chuckles. "What's this about?"

"I just missed you."

"Since when do you miss me?" she says, tapping my back like I'm a baby. It's been so long since we've properly hugged, she probably forgot how to.

"Always," I say with a shrug when I pull away. "It's hard for me when you leave for tour."

"Really?" She frowns. "You never said a word about this."

"I'm learning," I say.

She glances at her phone, a notch forming between her brows where a permanent wrinkle resides. "Isn't it time for you to go in?" She then notices what I'm wearing. "You're not even ready. You're not performing like this, are you?"

I shake my head, gulping. Now or never.

"I need to tell you guys something." Realization dawns on me as I look around her without recognizing a familiar face. "Where's Dad?"

"Right. He was busy working with this pianist he's discovered during one of our shows," she says, her jaw shifting. "Wishes you good luck, though."

"Oh," I say because nothing else comes out.

I try not to let it hurt me. It was supposed to be an important day for me, but he decided to prioritize something else instead.

It's okay. It doesn't matter anyway. One person less to confront. If he's not here, then he has no right to be mad about my decision. Plus, I want to focus on the good. My mother is here, even though I know she's been having a rough time, and that means everything.

"Mom," I start, my hands shaking. I knot them in front of me. "I'm not doing the showcase."

"What?" she says, laughing humorlessly. "What do you mean?"

"I mean I won't pursue NAMA any longer."

"Honey," she says, her smile disappearing. "Where is this coming from?"

"It's been in the back of my mind for a while," I say, not wanting to get into the semantics. "It's never been my goal to disappoint either one of you, but it wasn't..." God, I hate the way she's looking at me. My mind goes back to my conversation with Irène by the lake, when she said parents can only hope for one thing for their children. I clear my throat. "It wasn't making me happy anymore."

Mom blinks once, twice, and when I see her eyes filling with water, I feel my chest cave.

"Oh, Mom," I plead, though I'm not sure what for. Not to cry? Not to hate me?

Not to see her daughter as a failure?

"No, no," she says with a shake of her head as she takes a tissue out of her purse to tap under her eyes. "It's not what you think. I'm happy, really."

"You sure seem like it."

"I am." She finishes wiping her tears before she puts the tissue away and takes my hands in hers. "Emma, I didn't want this career for you."

"I'm sorry?"

"I didn't. Never did. I made my choices, and I have to live with them, but..." Her chest rises. "But it's impacted so much of my life in ways I hate and strained my relationship with your father, and I've seen you with Jamie. Your love is good. I don't want that for the two of you."

My jaw hangs open. I've beaten myself up so much for not being good enough when in truth, she never wanted this for me? She hasn't said my dad thinks the same, but honestly, I don't really care. I'm an adult. I would have gone through with this whether they agreed with it or not. Having my mother's approval is more than enough.

"Couldn't you have said something before?" I say with a wet laugh.

"I wanted whatever you thought was best for you, and I thought you loved playing."

"I love playing for fun," I say, finding it to be true.

"Then that's good enough for me."

Without thinking about it, I throw myself in her arms again, and this time, she doesn't hesitate before hugging me tightly against her.

"Thank you," I whisper against her perfectly brushed hair, which is similar to my own.

"I love you, Emma. I hope you know that."

"I love you too," I say. We should've talked about this so much sooner. She would've helped me, and I could've helped her in return. Before I lose my brave streak, I say, "And if Dad isn't making you happy, then maybe you should do something about it." I never thought I would one day say that to my mother, but here we are. I don't like that she doesn't like her life anymore, and if my father is partly responsible for that, then she should change things.

"It's a little more complicated than that," she says as she pulls away from me. "We love each other."

"I understand," I say, because I do. I never stopped loving Jamie, and having to break things off at the beginning of the summer in the hope it would make me feel better one day was excruciating, but in the end, I'm glad I did it. It led us exactly to where we needed to be. "Just think about being honest with him."

She smiles. Maybe she'll never consider it, but I've said my piece.

"Come on," I tell her as I see the crowd starting to move. "It's show time."

* * *

The artists this year are good. Really good.

The showcase goes by cohort and category, from dance to poetry, and then finally, to music. The theater and visual arts crowd will have a showcase later today, but what's important to me is happening right now.

Jesy has just finished performing a violin concerto that brought me to tears, and I've given her a standing ovation even though that's not what people usually do at these concerts. When I sit back down, my mother is looking at me, not with judgment, but instead with amusement.

"She's a good one," Mom says.

"Amazing." I don't think I could be prouder of my friend. She was fearless out there. Yesterday, she told me she still hadn't decided whether she will accept the offer to NAMA if it's given to her, but she's still given it her all, keeping her options open.

While I'm coming down from my high after Jesy's performance, the applause starts dimming, which means it's time for the next performance, and when I look at the program and see Jamie's name, my heart starts jackhammering in my chest. This is the moment he's been waiting for all his life.

A heartbeat later, Jamie appears on stage, all gangly limbs and messy hair, and I don't think I've ever loved him more than I do now. He's so unapologetically himself, and he will succeed, not despite it, but because of it. His gaze remains on the piano as he walks toward it, just like I expected it to. Before performing, he's always in his zone, not giving any attention to the crowd. He could be playing in front of one, ten, or a million people, and it wouldn't change a thing. It's always been him and his instrument against the world.

But when he looks up and his eyes land straight on me, a warm emotion fills my body. Maybe it's him, his instrument, *and me* against the world after all. He doesn't bother looking anywhere else. Once I've blown him a subtle kiss, he dips his chin, then returns his attention to the keyboard in front of him.

And when he starts to play, I know I worried for no reason.

He's magnificent. Humongous. This isn't just a man playing the piano. There's an entire universe hidden in the notes he's making. It's so much bigger than him. No one in the room can look away, I'm sure of it. I've seen captivating musicians before—I've spent my life surrounded by them. But this moment? It tops all the ones that came before. His body is close to the keyboard like always, the two of them forming a single unit. The piece he picked back in June is perfect for him, showcasing all the intricacy and nuance of his talent.

From where I sit so close to the stage, I can see the moment when he stops worrying about the score he knows by heart and instead lets himself feel the music completely, lids closing. The sight brings tears to my eyes. You could hear a hairpin drop in the room, as if people are holding their breath as they're watching. I know I am.

I don't know where the NAMA recruiters are located in the room, but I don't waste a second looking for them and their reactions. My attention remains fixed on Jamie until the last note rings.

A roar of cheers and applause rises through the auditorium. In an instant, I'm on my feet once again, and my mother is too, and soon, everyone in the room is standing, proving what I've known all along: he's a supernova.

No combination came out wrong. The parts of the concerto flowed from one to the next so smoothly, it was like it had been written for him. There's no doubt about it. He's getting in.

"This man is going to be big," my mother says.

"I know," I answer, the biggest smile on my face as I whistle once again.

After his second bow, Jamie disappears backstage, not even seeming to realize what just happened. How good he was. His face betrays nothing of what's going on inside.

Once everyone has sat down, the showcase continues, but my hands are still shaking from Jamie's performance. I have a hard time focusing on the following performances, no matter how good they are. The second the last performer leaves the stage, I jump up, giving my mother an apologetic look.

"Go," she says. "I'll be fine here."

"You sure?"

"Yes. I have some people I want to say hi to anyway." She shoos me away. "Go find him."

I hug her close and thank her one more time before running

to him. Without thinking twice, I climb backstage and pretend it's not against the rules for non-performers.

It doesn't take long for me to find him. It feels like no matter where he is in the room, my gaze always lands right on him, as if my body is attuned to his. There's also the fact that he's taller than everyone here.

Without wasting a second, I run his way, and even though he's standing with his back to me, I jump on him and wrap my legs around his hips.

"Jesus," he says, catching his balance. "You trying to kill me?"

"You were so good out there," I say, ignoring him and instead pressing a wet smooch on his neck. "So, so good."

Shifting me so I'm facing him, he says, "Thank you. It went well, I think."

"Well? That was freaking insane!"

He smiles shyly, and I kiss both his cheeks before saying, "I'm so proud of you."

"I'm proud of me too."

And somehow, that makes me even happier.

I drag my fingers through his hair, strands sticking up and curling in the wrong direction. It makes me smile. To the world, he's a prodigy, but to me, he's just Jamie, and that's so much better.

I let my feet fall to the floor but keep my arms wrapped around his neck, so Jamie is bent toward me. Tilting my head up, I say, "Once you go to NAMA and become a famous pianist and composer, you won't forget about me, will you?"

"Sweetheart," he says, tucking a strand of hair behind my ear, "all I've ever written are love songs about you."

He kisses me, soft and slow, not a single hurry in the world because really, there isn't. We have our entire lives in front of us.

Once he pulls back, I take a second to admire his face. His long nose and sharp cheekbones. His dark eyes and darker brows. The soft bow of his upper lip. He's so different from the boy I met at fourteen, and at the same time, he's exactly the same. The shy boy who loved the piano with his whole being and still found a place for me in his life. The same person I've loved for five years now. We've both made mistakes, and still, we're here.

Like Irène said, there's something so beautiful about knowing everything about someone, the good and the bad, and choosing to stay anyway. It's a kind of love that doesn't compare. I love Jamie. I know it, just as I know I was born on the nineteenth of January and that my favorite smell is that of coffee in the morning. It's in my blood, and at the end of the day, our trials and errors don't define our love. It's bigger than all of that.

Adjusting his glasses, I say, "Thank you, Jamie Montpellier, for giving me a piece of your heart at sixteen."

He strokes his thumb on my cheek. "You don't just have a piece of my heart. You own it all. Every crook and crevice. It's yours."

"That sounded both incredibly romantic and somewhat creepy."

He grins. "All me."

I laugh, hugging him again, and then we hear a chant of "Jamie!" coming our way. Behind him are his parents and his four siblings, who all came to support him today. I give them space as they congratulate him for his performance and tell him how proud they are of him. Even Jonah, his oldest brother, pats his back and tells him, "Good job." I know the two words must mean more to Jamie than he shows.

Behind the group, I spot Alessandro, who's standing in the shadows but still succeeds in making eye contact with Jamie, clapping his hands with a proud twinkle in his eyes. Jamie mouths a "thank you," to which Alessandro nods.

Once everyone has had their turn with him, Karen, Jamie's mom, puts her arm around his trunk and says, "You guys ready to go home?"

Eyes on me, Jamie grabs my hand. "Yeah. Let's go home."

EPILOGUE

10 years later
Emma

I CAN'T BELIEVE WE'RE STANDING HERE.

It shouldn't surprise me; Jamie's always been too talented for words. But this? Playing Carnegie Hall accompanied by a fifty-person orchestra only seven years after graduating from NAMA? It's surreal.

"Stop looking at me!" Colin whines to my left, his voice high-pitched. "Mommy, she keeps looking at me!" Beside him, Franny grins. She reminds me so much of her father sometimes, with her curly brown hair and teasing looks, it steals the breath right out of my chest.

"Guys, not the moment, okay?" I say softly, giving them both a stare down that is nowhere near as serious as I'd like. I'm such a sucker for those chubby faces. "This is a big person event."

"It's boring," Colin says, pouting, his small tuxedo too cute for words.

I roll my eyes with a smile. Of course, they wouldn't understand how big this moment is.

Being selected as the principal composer for the original soundtrack of one of the biggest romance movies of the decade barely five years out of school was already a huge win for Jamie's career. The night he received the call from his agent, we celebrated with a bottle of champagne I was saving for this occasion, and Franny and Colin, two years old at the time, cheered with us with crystal glasses of apple juice. There was music in the living room of our Greenwich townhouse, and dancing, and kisses, and so, so much love.

And the win didn't stop there. *An Ocean Apart* became an international success, some calling it "The *Titanic* of our generation," in part due to its ethereal orchestral score. It won award after award, and Jamie did too. His Grammy sits proudly on our fireplace mantel.

"When can we go home?" Franny asks, pulling at the sleeve of my black silk dress. "I'm hungry."

"After Daddy's done playing," I tell her with a hand smoothing down her hair.

For them, this might be a day-to-day thing, but Jamie and I realize how lucky we are. Leading an entire orchestra to play the live soundtrack from *An Ocean Apart* at his age is almost unheard of. I keep having to remind myself this will be my husband onstage. Even after attending all of his NAMA showcases and important performances over the years, seeing him play never gets old.

Someone taps on my shoulder, and I turn from my seat to find Leah, a bright student I've had for two semesters now.

"Oh, hi!" I say.

"Hey, Dr. St. Francis," she says with a shy smile.

"Emma, please." I get up, fully turning to her. "And what are you doing here?"

"I'm a fan. Of your husband, I mean." She points at the stage behind me.

It makes me smile. Jamie doesn't realize the impact he's had. To him, he's still just a guy who makes music and plays shows from time to time. He's shaken every time someone tells me they admire his work.

"That's not, um…" She blushes. "That's not why I picked your classes. I didn't mean to say—"

"Leah," I interrupt, chuckling. "You're good."

At school, most people know who my husband is, but that's never impacted my career. In fact, I got my job before he composed his first full score.

During our last year of undergrad, I questioned myself day after day about what I wanted to do with my life. In the end, when the only thing I was certain of was that I liked academia, I decided to apply for a master's in music theory at NYU. After getting in, I moved to New York with Jamie, and we never looked back. We both love the bustling of the city, the opportunities lying left and right, only looking to be found, and the intensity of everything. Living together after all these years, in a city that felt like ours from the moment we stepped foot in it, was a dream come true.

Once I was done with my master's, I stayed on for a PhD, tutoring while at it, and I realized then just how much I liked teaching. I might not have wanted to play the piano every single day, but I knew just about everything there was to know about music theory and history, and sharing that passion with others felt like putting the final piece of the puzzle into place. Once I received my offer for an assistant teaching position, I didn't hesitate before taking it.

"Mommy, can we get some popcorn?" Colin asks from my left, making Leah laugh.

Just then, I spot my mother at the end of the aisle, excusing herself to other attendees while trying to make her way to us.

"Why don't you ask Grandma?" I tell my kids as she arrives closer to us.

Mom rolls her eyes before she leans for a quick hug, whispering a quick "you owe me" in my ear.

I blow her a kiss, then turn to the kids and say, "Come on, Grandma will buy something for you at the gift shop."

They clap their chubby hands, then follow her, both holding on to one of her arms.

"They're really cute," Leah says, bringing my attention back to her.

"Thanks. They can be little monsters sometimes." And I wouldn't change them for the world.

For a while, I debated having kids. I didn't want my kids to feel the same kind of loneliness I did when I was a child, and I didn't know how to prevent it from happening. Jamie's the one who convinced me. "If we were able to travel through time and space, I think we can pretty much figure out anything," he'd said before pressing a kiss down my spine as we were lying in bed one night. That morning, he'd brought me back to Allegro to propose. I'd said yes in a heartbeat, but as the days went by, the concern of kids kept popping up in my head.

"But what if I'm bad?" I'd said, flopping to my back and looking at him with pleading eyes. Pleading for what, I'm not sure. Maybe for another kiss.

"Sweetheart, you're a natural with kids. I don't think you could be a bad mom even if you tried."

And after all these years, I'd say maybe he was right, at least a little.

We got married a few months later, once again at Allegro, the place that brought us back together. Alessandro officiated the ceremony, and the wedding was small. It was unconventional and sweet, not at all what my parents had described a wedding to be when I was a kid. There were no media, we ate a rhubarb-and-berry cake for dessert, we danced by the lakeside with candlelight illuminating our way, and it was absolute perfection.

Less than a year later, our babies were here, and I forgot why I'd ever doubted this life was the one we were meant to have.

Once again, I'm reminded of Irène. How she'd said the small flame we could keep ablaze was the best gift there was, and I couldn't agree more. There's nothing I loved more than coming home from work and seeing my husband there, feeding our kids as he practiced a piece on their onesie-clad bodies. The first time I saw it, it brought tears to my eyes. So much beauty in such mundane things.

"Okay, well, I just wanted to say hi," Leah says, bringing me out of my reverie.

"That's nice of you," I say, a hand on her shoulder. "Enjoy the show."

"Thanks."

"Hey, Leah?" I say once she's turned toward her seat. She looks back my way.

"I know Jamie would be really happy to help you with your playing if ever you wanted to."

Her mouth opens and closes like a fish out of water. "Oh. That's not why I came... I—"

"I know it's not, but I'm offering anyway." I wouldn't have said it if it wasn't the truth, but Jamie *would* be happy to do it. He always says it's an honor for him to be asked.

She grins like she's just won the lottery. "Okay. Thanks, Dr—Emma."

"You got it."

She leaves, and for the first time today, I'm alone. Well, as alone as can be in a roomful of people. I look around, admiring the theatrical room, with its red-velvet seats and majestic ceilings. People swarm the place—we're minutes away from show time—and the thrill in the air is palpable. This sensation of anticipation at hearing live music remains one of my favorites. It's something that brings all these people together, that makes them root for the same thing. There's nothing quite as powerful as music.

"Emma!" a voice calls to my right. I turn to find Molly coming my way, her red hair thrown haphazardly in a bun, trench coat clearly buttoned in a hurry.

"Hey!" I say with a wide smile before hugging her tightly. "I missed you. How are you?"

"Okay," she says. "Forgot how much traffic there is here. Barely made it."

"He'll be so happy to see you here."

"Everyone else said to wish him good luck, but I guess I'm too late, huh?"

I wince. "He knows."

Our families still live in Maine, which makes it difficult for them to attend all of Jamie's big events, but most of them try to make it to some, which I know means the world to Jamie, even when he doesn't show it. When he learned Molly would be here tonight, his stress level increased tenfold, as if one person meant so much more than the thousands of people who were already planning on attending.

The lights dim in the room, and people's voices lower as they take their seats. I look down at my watch. Five minutes.

Molly sits while I crane my neck to find the kids, finally spotting them rushing back to our seats with Mom, both holding a teddy bear wearing a Carnegie Hall T-shirt.

"Want to inherit two creatures for the duration of the show?" I say with a grin, but when I turn to Molly, I find her tense, away from here. I don't think she even heard me.

"Hey, what's wrong?" I ask her.

She shakes her head, but something's going on. Her skin is paler than usual, circles lining her eyes.

"You can tell me anything, you know."

She licks her lips, eyes flitting left and right before landing on me. "It's nothing. Just... something a little strange happened with me and Carina. That's all."

I notch a brow. "Weird how?"

"I don't... I don't think you'd believe me even if I told you."

I blink. Now my curiosity is definitely piqued.

"I swear, I will believe you. Trust me," I say. If I'm able to believe what happened to Jamie and me ten years ago wasn't a dream, then I can believe anything.

She hesitates for a moment before she leans forward and whispers in my ear what happened. My lips part with a gasp.

I can't believe it. Jamie might have been right after all.

When she pulls back, seeming on the verge of a nervous breakdown, I tap her hand resting between us and say, "It's all going to be fine."

Her jaw shifts. "What do you mean? You think I'm crazy?"

"Not one bit."

"Mommy, look what Grandma got us!" Colin says, making me look his way. One of his front teeth is missing, which has been making his sister jealous for days.

"Amazing!" I smile at them, then mouth a "thank you" to my mother. Finally, I turn to Molly and say, "One day, you and I will need to have a conversation about something *weird* that happened a few years back between your brother and me."

Molly stares at me for a long time before she gasps, her eyes round. She opens her mouth to say something, but just then, people start to clap loudly, and I join, grinning.

And then he's there. My sun.

It doesn't matter that I see him every single day, when I wake up and when I go to bed, when we do the dishes and when he plays something for me in his studio. He will always remain my favorite thing to look at.

He doesn't need to introduce himself. Just like he did ten years ago at the end-of-year showcase at Camp Allegro, Jamie walks straight to his piano, which stands in the middle of the room. It's unusual for the composer to play with the orchestra instead of leading, but it's the way he wanted it. Everyone cheers for all the musicians, but my heart is here only for one. And when Franny shouts, "Go, Daddy!" I know I'm not alone. Quickly, Jamie looks up, only for us, and he smiles his megawatt grin.

The room falls silent, and the moment Jamie's hands start moving on the keyboard, I'm entranced. I don't pay a single ounce of attention to anyone in the room. And sure, I listen to the orchestra as a whole, but my eyes remain on my husband. It doesn't matter whether he's an international star, a stellar student, or a teenage boy who's learning to find himself. He's still the same in each one of these scenarios, bent over his piano, pouring his heart into every note. I take each second in, my heart swelling with all the passion and emotion he gives us. Even the kids are fascinated, neither one of them uttering a sound. That's the kind of talent Jamie has.

The concert goes by in a blur, and by the time the last song ends, the one he recycled from the composition he once made about a blue-eyed girl and a messy boy, I'm in tears.

Just like that last day at Allegro, I'm on my feet before the last note has finished echoing through the room, clapping so loudly it makes Colin wince.

Standing up from their seats, the orchestra bows, and Jamie's the first to leave the stage. I know where he's going.

"Come on, kids," I tell them, grabbing their hands. Molly and Mom follow us as we wiggle through the crowd in search of the door leading us to the backstage area. Once we find it, I open it, and before I know it, my brown-haired, dark-eyed twins have let go of my hands.

"Daddy!" they shout, running their little legs toward Jamie, who laughs out loud before picking them both up and twirling them around, just like he did to me after his NAMA audition.

I cannot stop watching them, my face split into a grin. Sometimes it feels like the love I have for the three of them will overwhelm me. Like no person could hold that much emotion inside of them. I'll surely burst with it one day.

Jamie's glass frames have changed over the years, but even so, I notice the left arm of his current ones is wrapped in duct tape. It's like they're a magnet for destruction.

I walk toward him, then say, "Really?" as I tap the broken part.

He winces. "Sat on them while reading the news this morning."

I shake my head slowly, grinning. After pressing a kiss to the heads of Franny and Colin, he puts them down, then wraps his arms around me.

"You were wonderful," I tell him, pride filling my voice.

"Thank you, sweetheart." He has the audacity to appear shy before he adds, "You know what it means coming from you."

I hug him again, and this time, I whisper in his ear, "I need to tell you something about your sister."

He pulls back, brows furrowed.

"No, nothing bad. Something that happened between her and Carina." I give him a look, and after a moment, he gets it.

"No."

"Mm-hmm."

"So I was right?"

"Possibly," I say.

"Admit it. I was right."

"Can't do that without scientific proof."

He grins widely. "You know I'm right."

I shut him up with a peck on the lips.

Does the universe really send soulmates back in time when they try to split? I guess we'll never know.

Still smiling when we pull apart, we turn to face the rest of the world. Mom is playing with Franny, who pulled a My Little Pony out of god knows where, while Molly is listening to Colin tell a story about what happened at daycare last week, both of them wearing serious expressions. Beyond them, we can see the stage, with the stunning auditorium in the back, row after row of people chatting while exiting their rows.

"I knew you'd fill concert halls one day."

Humble as ever, he simply shrugs, his eyes on our babies. I know if I asked him right this second what he's the proudest of, his career wouldn't come first. Our family would be at the top of his list. Still, I know he realizes how big this is and is enjoying every second of it.

Taking my husband's hand in mine, I exhale and say, "We made it, didn't we?"

He looks down at me, so much love in his dark-brown eyes. "Yeah, sweetheart. We really did."

And then he leans down and kisses me properly, one out of millions we've shared, each as precious as the last.

Life with Jamie has been multiple things. Fulfilling. Challenging. Surprising. Loving. But if there's one word I had to use to describe it, only one comes to mind.

Magical.

ACKNOWLEDGEMENTS

Writing a book is never easy, but writing a book with a time travel element was a whole new challenge. Only a few chapters in, I realized I'd had a really dumb idea because I wasn't smart enough to pull it off, but thank god, I had a lot of people by my side who were able to save the day.

First of all, I want to thank Gabrielle, my childhood best friend who's been with me every step of the way and is always the very first person to read my books. I think you know how much I love you.

To Rebecca, who had to take a step back from this book because she was busy raising a tiny human, but who was still there every single day to answer my unhinged questions and freak-out texts. I couldn't survive this crazy industry without you.

I of course need to offer a thousand thank yous to Murphy and Ashley who created the absolute perfect cover for Emma and Jamie. You have more talent than I could ever dream of having and I'm so lucky to have you in my corner.

To Jackie. There are literally no words for how good of an editor you are. I could see it with previous books, but with this one? My god. Even *I* couldn't understand my two sets of timelines, yet you were able to keep track of everything and make sure this book wasn't a complete dumpster fire. I promise I won't ever play with time travel again, but if I do, you're the first person I'll call. Please never stop doing what you're doing, okay?

To my wonderful sisters-in-law. I'm so damn lucky to have such amazing women in my life. And to my brothers, I guess you're pretty cool too.

To my parents, who have given me endless love and support every single day of my life. You're the best.

To my in-laws, who really are a second set of parents. You're the best too.

To my med school friends who've either been with me from the beginning of this journey or who have joined along the way. I love you guys so much. Your sideline cheering makes me so happy and thankful.

To Louis, who makes all my little girl dreams come true with every day we spend together. Please forgive me if the time travel in this book doesn't respect every single law of physics. I promise no one will actually care except for you anyway. ♥

To all the bloggers, bookstagrammers, and booktokers who have shared my books on your platforms. I literally would be nowhere without you. These books have been read by more people than I could ever have dreamed of because of you, and I will never be able to thank you enough for it. I hope you'll have loved Jamie and Emma just as much as you did the previous couples.

And finally, to every single person who's read my books, thank you. Your support, your DMs, and your posts mean the world to me. You make all the hard work worth it. I started writing for myself, but I keep writing because of you.

ABOUT THE AUTHOR

N.S. Perkins lives the best of both worlds, being a resident physician by day and a romance author by night. When she's not writing, reading, or studying, you can probably find her trying new restaurants, dreaming about the next beach she'll be visiting, or creeping the cutest dogs in the parks near her house. She lives in Montreal with her partner.

Find her on:
Twitter: @nsperkinsauthor
Instagram: @nsperkinsauthor
TikTok: @nsperkinsauthor
Website: www.nsperkins.com

ALSO FROM THE AUTHOR

Made in the USA
Middletown, DE
20 June 2023